BINDING THE CUCKOO

DAUGHTERS OF DEFIANCE

BOOK ONE

GABRIELA HOUSTON

Changeling Books

Book design: Gabriela Houston

Editor: Michelle Lam

Changeling Books

Paperback ISBN: 978-1-0681866-0-8

Ebook ISBN: 978-1-0681866-1-5

❀ Formatted with Vellum

CONTENTS

CHAPTER 1

She sat very still, ignoring the flurry of activity around her. The eye of the storm was a deceptively peaceful place, as it turned out.

The servants around her tried not to disturb her. There was a strange solemnity to the proceedings. The stripping of the illusion. Like theatre workers taking away the set after the play was done. The painted trees and the facade of Juliet's balcony. The paper moon and the tin stars. Pulled away bit by bit, till you couldn't help but see it for what it was: makeshift scaffolding, where hope and imagination fill in the blanks.

Once she could have woven illusions herself and far more skilfully than any earthly theatre worker. But such memories were faint, faint like the red string around her wrist, turning paler with each heartbeat.

As the men pulled the paintings off the walls and carried the Chinese wooden screen out the door, she noticed, with some surprise, that she didn't regret the loss of the items themselves. It was what they had represented to her.

Each gift, each little bauble was to fill the set. But the play was over now and so the things she had been surrounded by had to be gone too. They would no doubt be repurposed for another place and actor.

"Miss Hare..."

Someone was talking to her, she realised. How strange. She had half-believed herself to be a part of the scenography.

"Miss Hare?" The repetition brought her back. She looked up into the ruddy face of one of the workers. He stood over her, nervous, worrying his lower lip. He had the kind of face that was pleasing to her kind, yet alarming to the humans. The teeth just a little too sharp, the eyes just a little too big. Tufts of hair growing on the tips of his ears. A thin red thread sparkled around his wrist. "It's just..."

She wondered why he stood on ceremony with her. Maybe she should have tried to enjoy it. Heavens knew it would likely be the last time anyone did. "Yes?" Maybe he carried new orders. Maybe it was all a terrible mistake. Perhaps she was to be safe after all.

The man pointed down. "It's just, I'm to take the rug."

The realisation dawned. She lifted her feet, so he could pull the rug out. Of course. It was an expensive one.

"I'm sorry, miss," he said, before he carried it outside. She bent her head in acknowledgement.

After a time, she couldn't say how long, she was finally left standing alone in the bare room. She was already told she'd have to leave by end of the week, which was three days away. Sam would have likely denied her even that little security, but the rent had been paid up till then. A small loss for him in the grand scheme of things. Somewhat less than a victory for her. She lay down on the bare wooden floor. From this perspective the room looked huge. Nothing as big as the halls she grew up in, with their shining domes and crystal pillars. Nothing like the home she'd been ripped out of. She shut her eyes tight, a tear rolling down the side of her face. Humans talk of the summoning as a peaceful process. Benign. Makes them feel better perhaps.

But humans were always like that, weren't they? Drunk on the power they discovered. That they could rip the very fabric of their reality and pull through creatures of stories, bind them to this world and themselves. After all, they argued, the fay, the *dushki*, the *haltijas*, whatever they were called, were not God's children. They were barely even real. Like make-believe. The kind of convenient make-believe that could sew your clothes, and clean your rooms and prepare your meals.

A sudden pain shot through Hare's wrist and up her arm. The final link to him was now broken. The string tying her to him glittered and changed colour. And then it was gone. She waited for a while, for another string to take its place. Mythics like her were expensive, she knew. The summoning was not a tidy process. You could not predict what kind of a mythic a summoning would produce and each still had to be paid for. Sam had paid a tidy sum for her to the academy. He would obviously try to recoup some of the cost, now that he was done with her. But as the moments passed, no new string took the last one's place. She lifted her hand against the light. Was she simply free?

The joy was short lived. She was stranded. She could never go back whence she came, even if she could still remember where "whence" was.

There was nothing left except for a pile of her clothes, removed from the more valuable chests and wardrobe. That and her notebooks, her charcoals, watercolours and inks. It suddenly became imperative that she touch them. She crawled towards the corner and ran her fingers across the fabric and the covers of the sketchbooks. She did so slowly, reverently, making herself notice the texture of the paper, the indentations where the pencil pressed too hard. Then she moved to the clothing, touched its stitching, observed the way the fabric pleated along the seams. Her fingers curled around the sleeve of a dress and she pulled the garment towards her, clutching it to her breast.

It was *hers*. Something she'd made herself and so the only

thing that truly belonged to her. There was a comfort in the possession.

A sharp knock on the door caught her attention.

She crouched like an animal and snuck along the wall. She was weak in this world. Very weak. She flexed her fingers. A pathetic little spark passed between them.

"Would you open the door, please?" A sharp voice came from the other side. A woman's voice. Unusual.

Hare pushed her hair out of her eyes and opened the door. A thin and rather gaunt-looking woman stood just outside. Hare wasn't good at assessing the age of humans, but she guessed this person was no longer young.

"You must be wondering," the woman said as she pushed her way into the room. "Why you are not bound." She pointed to Hare's wrist. "After all, you're not a brownie one can get for three dollars at a corner market. Here," the woman dug into her purse and gave Hare a folded piece of paper, "To show the transaction between myself and your last master."

"You bought me?" Hare looked into the woman's eyes. "Why then…"

"Why have I not bound you to me?" The woman pinched the sides of her purse with a white-knuckled grip. "Because I have a proposal for you. One that might benefit us both, but such an agreement has to be entered freely. Will you listen to my offer?"

A bargain. Hare knew of bargains. She remembered. They were always sharp-edged. Always.

She smiled.

To Baroness Winchfield
The Winchfield House, Mayfair, London

New York, March, 23rd 1899

Dearest Posy (I hope you will forgive the familiarity, but I shall forever see you as my favourite student and quite struggle to adjust to the changes the last five years must have inevitably brought out in you),

I was ever so glad to receive the news of your marriage to Baron Winchfield and of the birth of your two darling children, though I was not surprised; you were quite the best pupil we had at the Bonningham School for Young Ladies, in all the ways that mattered in any case. I never doubted that you'd go far in life, though, of course, England is rather farther than one would wish a friend to be.

I must admit, however, that there is something quite serendipitous about your current location. You see, a tragedy has struck my family, burdening me with a great responsibility. My dearest sister, Hortense, who had herself made a rather advantageous marriage, perished with her husband in a railway accident, leaving behind their only child.

My twenty-year-old niece, Edwina Walker, is the loveliest girl you could ever hope to meet, second in my heart only to yourself, dearest Posy. She possesses that charm that has already garnered her a number of admirers, but it had always been my sister's dearest wish to have Edwina married to an Englishman. After all, our own mother's family was related to a Viscount and my sister Hortense, who never had to toil like I did (not that teaching you was ever a chore!), but rather was used to the comforts her husband's wealth provided her, felt the loss of title and position greatly. As it was Hortense's plan to bring Edwina to London this coming season and as the girl's mourning period will be over by then, I am quite determined to honour her parents' wishes.

While Edwina is well enough provided for, arriving alone in a new city, the trouble of finding rental properties, as well as procuring servants all feel like an insurmountable difficulty for an old maid such as myself.

Which brings me to the request I am shameless enough to make of you: namely that you would not mind a visit from your old school mistress and her niece and that you could lend your excellent judgement in guiding us to secure a good future for the poor orphan.

Yours affectionately in friendship,

Anne Bonningham

* * *

From: Baroness Winchfield
The Winchfield House, Mayfair, London
April, 20th, 1899

To: Anne Bonningham, Bonningham School for Young Ladies, New York

My dearest Miss Bonningham,

As thrilled as I was to receive your correspondence, I was deeply saddened by the news enclosed therein. I hadn't remembered you mentioning your family, but because Hortense was your sister, I am quick to imagine her to have been the kindest, wittiest of creatures. Such a terrible loss and with such a heavy burden placed on you in the midst of your grief!

Of course, I would not consider myself worthy of the title of your friend if I refused my help in your hour of need. And if your niece possesses a fraction of your intelligence and practicality, we shall see her engaged within a month or two! I am quite determined to see to it myself. What practice it will be for when my own dear children are grown!

I entreat you to make the journey at the earliest opportunity and I await your arrival with the anticipation of the very great pleasure your presence will bring me.

Your ever-grateful pupil and friend,

Posy

CHAPTER 2

"You haven't exaggerated, Miss Bonningham!" Lady Winchfield tapped the side of her teacup with her index finger as she regarded Hare, who was obediently standing in front of both the Baroness and Miss Bonningham. "Turn around for me, Miss Edwina, there's a dear!"

Hare did as instructed, gritting her teeth as she did so.

Her *domovoy* regarded her with an air of amused contempt from his space on the chaise longue. Miss Bonningham had insisted on getting a Eastern European cat-shaped spirit, as the exoticism of it was to further cement the illusion of her fashionable existence. In reality it was not particularly expensive, as the Eastern mythics were considered as somewhat less sophisticated than their Western counterparts, though useful for scrub work. Still, owning an imported *domovoy,* who, as far as the humans were concerned, served no practical purpose, was somewhat elevating. While one could, in theory, summon any kind of mythic from anywhere, scientists have found that the type of the creatures summoned corresponded to the location of the summoning. Hare sometimes wondered what she herself was. By the time she'd been broken in enough to speak on the subject, she had hardly any true memories left. Merely the suppositions of those who first bound her. Now this poor creature did not take to her, of course. He considered her a traitor and rightly so. *Domovoys* served for love and for a crust. The little string that shone around his paw was a betrayal.

"Smile, child, don't forget to smile!" Miss Bonningham tapped the floor with her cane. Hare obeyed. She thought if she smiled any wider the top of her head might fall off.

"Well now that's charming!" Lady Winchfield winked at her friend. "Your Edwina is quite the jewel. I think an introduction at court might not be out of the realm of possibility, even."

"You jest!" Miss Bonningham, clearly delighted at the idea, put a hand to her mouth.

"I never joke when marriage is concerned. Of course, we will need to prepare. Is that padding?" She reached out and for one horrifying moment Hare wondered if the Baroness truly planned on feeling up her bottom. She was rescued by Miss Bonningham, who exclaimed "Of course not!" with such a school-teachery air of authority that Lady Winchfield immediately withdrew her hand.

Hare breathed easier, though she suspected Miss Bonningham's intervention was not so much aimed at sparing her ward's feelings, as an expression of irritation at having the quality of her wares questioned.

"Well, I must say you are quite fortunate in your figure," Lady Winchfield said. "Skinny girls are no longer in fashion. After all, with all the skin-and-bones mythics running around, it makes one once again appreciate a properly robust figure. Once my modiste is done with you, men will be lining up for a chance to talk to you."

"Modiste?" Hare raised her eyebrows at Miss Bonningham. "But I've a case of dresses we brought from New York..."

"Hardly suitable!" Lady Winchfield wrinkled her nose, stuffing another cucumber sandwich in her mouth. "Though being foreign might bring just the pinch of exotic spice to set you apart from the other girls in the ballroom, there are certain occasions where only a seamstress we can trust will do. I have just the right one in mind for you. A *bwbachod*." She raised her hand. "And I know what you're going to say. A Welsh mythic does not sound... Well... Very *Beau Monde*. But for all that her origins are modest, she's the most talented seamstress in all of London. Some of her little magics remained in her after the binding. Quaint, is it not? Pity it's so rare. In this case it's proven beneficial at least. She can turn plain cotton into silk, they say." She laughed. "Of course, it doesn't *quite* endear her to the silk merchants. But as long as her owner keeps a guard or two, we can rest assured their wares are not burnt down with the shop."

Hare felt queasy at the casual mention of the threat to the poor mythic's safety, but she smiled sweetly, aware of Miss Bonningham's eagle-eyed stare.

AFTER TEA, Lady Winchfield finally allowed Hare and Miss Bonningham to escape to their rooms. Rooms, plural, which is why Hare groaned inwardly as Miss Bonningham followed her into her small bedroom.

"My Posy is one of a kind." Miss Bonningham rubbed her hands together, casting a critical glance over the furnishings. "I knew she could be depended on."

"And where will you find the money for a modiste she can trust, Anne?" Hare asked. She sat down in front of the small dresser and began pulling her gloves off. "Ouch!" she squealed as Miss Bonningham gave her a sharp rap on a calf with her cane.

"Do *not* call me that!" the older woman said.

"We're alone..."

"Not even when we're alone! Not even here, perhaps *especially* not here." Miss Bonningham stood over Hare, her eyes narrowing. Hare always thought the older woman looked a bit like an old bird, especially when she was in ill humour. Miss Bonningham's face, though fine-boned, was severe to an excess and adding to that, her somewhat old-fashioned hairstyle, with the hair all mercilessly pulled up into a tight little bun, she had not an ounce of softness to her. Right now, as if reading Hare's thoughts, she leaned forward, bringing her sharp nose to just about an inch away from the girl's face. "We have one shot at this, *Edwina*, one. There will be no repeat seasons for you, no slow-burn romance. We are each other's one chance at a better life."

"I understand," Hare whispered.

"I understand, *Aunt*."

Hare jutted out her chin. "I understand, Aunt."

The *domovoy* stretched just in the corner of Hare's vision and made a noise that sounded very much like laughter.

"Now," Miss Bonningham said, pacing about the room. "Make sure you curb those rebellious glances of yours. Don't think I didn't notice. Every word out of your mouth is another word that might betray you. Some lapses might be chalked up to you being foreign. Might even add a certain charm to the image. But be a bit *too* foreign, a bit *too* strange and they might start noticing other things. The shape of your eyes, the way you move. Your weak little glamours will only take you so far. Luckily for you, they see what they want to see. But make no mistake. You're a betrayal of all they believe in. A summoned pet with opinions, with a mind of her own." She sniffed. "Though perhaps the very fact that you seem to have a brain is what protects you from recognition. To see you for what you are, they'd have to admit that the summoned are more than soulless toys and they would never willingly do that. I know those people. The old money people." She let out a mocking laugh. "Even when they no longer have the money. Perhaps especially then. But…" She walked towards the *domovoy* and gave him an absent-minded pet on the head. "…a little goes a long way when it comes to having opinions. You cannot be more outspoken than they let their own women be."

"Then what am I to say when they ask?" Hare said before she could stop herself. "Ask for my opinions that is."

Miss Bonningham spun around and looked for any sign of mockery in Hare's face. Not noting one, she relaxed somewhat, or at least made the closest approximation to relaxed that she was capable of. "You will say whatever they *wish* to hear. You have experience with that, do you not?"

Hare looked down. "Yes."

The older woman gently pushed Hare's forehead up with the tip of her finger. "When I found you, you had already learnt how to become whatever others wanted you to be. That was a hard lesson, was it not? At the academy?"

Hare looked down. When she was first summoned, ripped from her world, she couldn't understand what was asked of her. To sit still, for hours, while the studying artists inspected her every feature, every curve, every exotic, foreign inch of her.

"Being an art model had taught you to be what they expect. Just think of this as a particularly long sitting."

"A life-long one," Hare said.

"Yes." Miss Bonningham nodded. "But this time round you will be sitting in luxury, with only one man's hands on the goods. You know what sort of life awaited you when we met. And now you're our ticket to a better life, Hare. If you trust me and do *exactly* as I direct. My pretty cuckoo bird."

AFTER MISS BONNINGHAM LEFT HER, Hare stared at the closed door. She was patient. She had to be. She had spent most of the ten years since her summoning carefully cultivating patience. Smiling politely at the crass jokes and the wandering hands. Then the long hours staying perfectly still, as the men surrounding her painted her body. She listened to the drawing masters at the academy discuss her body as a collection of parts. The proportions that were to be captured by a brush or a piece of charcoal. The curve, the muscle tone, the way the skin stretched or rolled on her stomach. She listened and had taught herself to ignore the way it felt to be an object in another's gaze.

She'd rebelled at first, of course. They all did. But the binding held fast, robbing her of her powers even more than the gravity of this world did. And soon, after her memories of her earlier life began to fade, she found a small pocket of freedom, things she could do on her own, with the scraps of paper left by the wasteful students. Small pieces of charcoal, little dabs of paint.

It made her feel a small measure of safety. For a mind that can express itself is a mind that cannot be altogether destroyed.

But what felt safe and what *was* safe were two very different propositions. Because she'd never felt as safe as she did with Sam. He told her he *saw* her. He made promises to free her. To release her so she could choose him of her own free will. But he said it was complicated. That to find someone to release a mythic without then binding them to a new owner was near impossible to arrange. But that he'd never treat her as property. And she believed him, she was protected. Until she wasn't. Until his words and promises turned out to be just that. And it turned out that the unbinding was neither complicated nor impossible. That it could be done when it suited the humans' desire.

Hare understood now that in this world, at least, *feeling* free didn't make you so. But money did. And position. And she'd make sure to have both.

CHAPTER 3

Ernest Thompson refused to look up from his newspaper. He could feel the eyes of Duke of Brandon, his best friend and a semi-professional "tryer" of things, practically boring a hole in the paper, which was all the more reason to not pay him any mind.

"You can't pretend to ignore me forever," Brandon finally broke the silence.

"No, but I can *actually* ignore you indefinitely." Ernest reached for his coffee without lowering the paper and took a sip, a small smile curving his lips. He'd come for lunch alone because that is what he had done every Friday since, at twenty two, he first arrived at the Atheneum club with the first paycheck he'd earned himself as a newly-minted solicitor. Becoming a member made him feel so terribly sophisticated back then. Of course, in the five years since, the shine had worn off somewhat, but the habit remained. Yet the club's restaurant was a good place to meet prospective clients. He couldn't just rely on his Eton friendships for the introductions after all.

"Ignoring your friends is terrible manners, you know!" Ernest could sense Brandon was starting to sulk. “And you haven’t even heard me out!”

Ernest rolled his eyes.

“I assure you that, should you hear me out, you will soon acknowledge that this idea will change both our lives!”

“I will not join the Royal Geologist Society with you, Brandon.” Ernest turned the page. “Primarily because I do not care for rocks.”

“I’m sure you’re just saying this to annoy me!” Brandon, encouraged by Ernest breaking the silence, reached over and pulled the newspaper down. “Because you know for a fact I have quit that society barely a month ago.”

“Having first paid their fees up till Christmas.” Ernest frowned and straightened up the paper. Not that he cared for the soap advertisement he had been pretending to be so engrossed in. But his friend would surely be irritated by the gesture and that was amusement all in itself.

“That was hardly my fault!” Brandon threw himself back in the chair. “Turns out all they do there is discuss rocks and how they suppose those same rocks came to be and the shapes of rocks and good grief, it was enough to turn a man’s brain to pebbles!”

“And what, precisely, did you expect of a geological society?” Ernest raised one eyebrow.

Brandon waved him away. “I freely accept that one was a flop, I grant you that much. But this time it’s different!”

“Is it different enough for you to pester a different friend about it?” Ernest drummed his fingers on the edge of his seat, abandoning all pretence of reading. “You realise that unlike you I actually have to earn a living?”

“A dreary point, hardly worth mentioning in polite society.” Brandon sniffed.

“And yet I mention it. I do not have the time or the means to waste, I’m sad to say.”

Brandon brought a hand to his heart. "You wound me!"

"And yet you live."

"I'm like a cat, you know. Nine lives and all that. Ah, it's here." Brandon rubbed his hands together as the waiter brought his luncheon. "Like I said, nine lives and each one requires its own occupation and purpose." He tucked into his food with gusto. Ernest sometimes wondered how much energy Brandon could expend merely consuming the food.

"Nine you say?" Ernest smoothed down and folded his paper. "By my count you're on occupation fifteen and that is just since we left school. You will be a whole clowder of cats by the end of the decade." Brandon gave him a wounded look, never once stopping the chewing. Ernest took the opportunity to enjoy his meal while he had the chance, and they both ate in silence for a while. Brandon attempted to resume the conversation a couple of times, each time silenced by Ernest, who strongly indicated he had no desire to see the half-chewed food fall from his friend's mouth.

Once he could tell Brandon's patience was at an end, Ernest finally put his fork down. "Fine. What is this newly discovered passion you must share with the world?"

"Painting!" Brandon flashed his brightest smile. "I have been taking classes at the Royal Academy!"

"The Royal Academy?" Ernest signalled to the waiter to bring his bill. "I thought they required a significant level of proficiency before even accepting new students."

"The bursar is a cousin," Brandon said. He tucked into his food with gusto.

"Of course."

Brandon lifted his eyebrows. "You're really quite a terrible snob, Thompson, you realise that."

"Am I?" Ernest settled his part of the bill, not deigning to look at his friend. "How exactly?"

"You look down upon those of us who are born with some small perks that make one's life run smoother."

"Small indeed. Fortune, title and connections. However *do* you manage?"

"Aha!" Brandon stabbed his fork into his cutlet with a ferocity. "But what you fail to realise is the terrible ennui that is the result of those advantages. You have no idea how lucky you are, my friend!"

"In what way?"

"You *have* to make your own way in the world. You get to make your fortune. Whereas look at me, all I have is the, admittedly significant, fortune I was born with. No matter how much I increase it, it's never truly *mine*. I'm merely a custodian for the next generation and I never get the recognition for having a good business sense. Yet the world being what it is, regardless of my efforts, most would agree that the future belongs to the young, the bold and the ambitious like you and yours, my American friend—"

Ernest winced.

"—while I can merely watch from the sidelines."

"Like the champagne-sipping horse owner, while the jockey struggles across the finish line on a horse he could never afford." Ernest stood up and tucked the still-unread newspaper into his pocket.

"Indeed!" Brandon smacked his hand on the table. "And who wouldn't wish to be the jockey! The one who gets the glory?"

"I think I'd rather get paid," Ernest said. "Glory fades. People respect money."

"They don't respect it, my friend, they covet it."

"For someone like me," he patted Brandon on the back in a half-hearted goodbye, "It might seem like a welcome change to have something deemed worthy of coveting."

CHAPTER 4

Hare was exhausted. She had spent her morning trailing after Miss Bonningham and the Baroness, who, truth be told, barely noticed her existence, so enthralled she was with the company of her old school mistress. Beyond, that is, getting Hare measured for a small number of dresses, which Miss Bonningham paid for with a pained expression. It was, Hare knew, not a gift, but a loan.

And so now, as her "aunt" and their host chatted away, Hare allowed herself to trail somewhat farther behind them than was strictly speaking proper, thinking on the strange circumstance that brought her two companions together. Miss Bonningham and Lady Winchfield, while dissimilar at first glance, seemed to understand each other instinctively. Hare was almost jealous, before she remembered Anne was in fact deceiving her younger friend. But seeing the two of them like this, in such easy conversation, made her feel somewhat lonely.

She passed a boy selling little pies. As she walked by him, she could feel, through the sheer fabric of her sleeves, the warmth his wares still gave out. Her mouth watered at the smell of the crust and she wished she could just buy one and spend the day wondering the streets. But it was not to be and if she didn't hurry, she'd have to put up with one of Miss Bonningham's black moods. As she glanced above the pies, however, she noticed their seller. He had a fox-like little face, which made Hare pause. A halfling, maybe? One not summoned but born of this world? His red lashes shaded large green eyes. His wrist was bare. It wasn't common to see unbound mythics in New York, but perhaps it was different here. The boy looked up into her eyes, then turned to her wrist. A look of recognition passed between them. "Have a pie, miss," he said, picking up one pastry.

"I haven't the money," she said. She knew he wouldn't betray her. None of them would, not even the *domovoy* she was forced to keep herself. None of the mythics held any loyalty to the humans they served. And the humans knew not the ways or the charms to compel such loyalty.

"For you, miss." The boy kept his arm outstretched. "From you, I don't ask for money."

Nothing was free in this or any other world.

"What do you ask then?" She smiled. A little game. She liked the little games.

"A kiss." He tapped his cheek.

She leaned down and gave his cheek a little peck.

"Be careful, miss," he whispered when their faces were close. "Make your step heavier, miss. You tread too lightly." He beamed at her then. "May you get what you hope for from them."

She nodded and took the pie, waving a goodbye to the small well-wisher.

Her two companions had already crossed the road and were barely a stone's throw from the restaurant Lady Winchfield was determined to show them off in.

Hare stuffed the pie in her mouth with one hand and, lifting the hem of her skirt, she picked up the pace.

The next moment was a blur. Hare heard an angry scream.

Immediately after, someone's arm grabbed her by the waist and half-lifted her up, roughly pulling her off the road.

"You got to be careful, miss." The words sounded strangled, oddly formed by the beak-like mouth of the mythic who pulled her out of the way of the coming carriage, which passed her close enough so that she felt the rush of air against her face.

"Thank you," she managed, before looking at her saviour. The mythic was poorly dressed, his dirty brown clothes sitting strangely over his feather-covered body.

"It's no problem, miss…" His extremely wide-set eyes narrowed as he turned his head to the side to see her better. "…I don't know your kind. Are you an import?" Hare winced at the word and became suddenly aware the bird mythic still had an arm around her. There was something odd about him. Damaged. Scarred. Confused enough to betray her. "No thread…" The mythic let out something akin to a laugh. "Like me." He lifted his wrist, which, conspicuously, had no thread around it either. "But you have pretty clothes. I have no pretty clothes. Pretty feathers, but can't show them." There was nothing but curiosity in the mythic's voice, but Hare glanced around, scared someone might have heard him. Before she could answer, somebody brutally pulled back the bird creature, who squawked loudly in surprise.

"What do you think you're doing?!" A human faced her saviour, anger written all over his face. "How dare you touch her!"

The bird mythic cowered. A small group of men, poorly dressed, gathered up within moments. The man who'd pulled him away was squaring up to the confused creature. "It's not enough that freaks like you are taking our jobs, you now think to put your 'ands on a fine lady like 'er?" The edges of his coat were frayed and the man's face looked red from anger and drinking both. A small crowd was gathering, their rage palpable.

Hare's breath caught in her throat. This was going to go badly. She'd seen these kind of men before, in New York. Angry at the mythics for taking their jobs. As if any of them had the slightest choice in the matter.

"This is all a misunderstand—" Before she managed to finish the sentence she was roughly pulled aside by one of the men, who all started rounding up on the poor bird mythic, closing his way of escape.

"Please, sirs, I didn't mean—" the bird mythic looked at Hare pleadingly, before the ringleader of the humans punched him in the face.

Hare screamed and started hitting the man on the back, before she was pulled off him.

Suddenly, another man burst in between her and the men and started barking out threats. He grabbed the man who was about to kick the cowering mythic and pushed him hard enough to make him lose his balance.

"There now, that's enough." The man glowered at the mythic's attackers. "I can hear the police whistles and I don't think you want to be here when they arrive, do you?"

The men hesitated, but Hare could see the anger they felt was not yet spent. There was a longing there for violence and the bird mythic was meant to satisfy that need. "I will tell the police you have attacked me and the mythic," she said, hoping her voice carried. She stepped between the mythic and the men. "Leave now and you might avoid arrest."

A small crowd was gathering to gawk and the curious glances seemed to sap the angry men's confidence much more than her words could have.

The ringleader spat on the ground. "Mythic lovers," he said, before leaving.

"Are you alright?" Hare bent over the injured mythic.

"Yes, miss." The bird creature lied, for she could see the already swelling skin under his eye where the punch landed. "Thank you, miss." He glanced at the man who had helped them.

"And thank you, Sir. It would have gone badly for me if it weren't for you."

Something like shame crossed the dark-haired man's face. He fished in his pocket and brought out a coin and a piece of paper, which he placed in the mythic's hand. "Here, for your trouble. Take my card, I might know someone needing workers."

"Workers like me?" The bird mythic turned the card around in his hand. When the dark-haired man nodded, the mythic seemed to brighten and thanked them both before going away.

Something in the poor creature's demeanour infuriated Hare. To see him bow and scrape for a small kindness. "And that makes it all alright, I suppose?" she said, turning back towards the stranger.

"I beg your pardon?"

"He saved me, was abused for the privilege and now he's rewarded..." she glanced towards where the mythic was already rounding the corner. "...with the promise of what I can only assume is hard labour."

"It's more than many get these days." The man's dark eyes went perfectly round as he stared at her. "In any case, you're welcome."

"Welcome?" She sucked in a breath.

The man stared at her as if she'd gone silly. "For saving you?"

"I had it under control." Hare smoothed the sleeve of her dress and jutted her chin out. He might have had a point, dammit, but she wasn't going to admit that. Not when he clearly seemed intent on patronising her. An idea flashed in her head and the words were out before she could stop them. "I accept your apology."

"My apology?" The man froze in mid-movement, as he had bent down to pick up his hat which fell on the road.

"I see you have the habit of repeating people's words. It's really very odd, you know." She righted her hat, which had loosened and was threatening to slide off her head. "And, like I said, I accept your apology. You clearly thought I was at risk, but you now understand that I was, in fact, in no kind of danger. And so I accept your apology as it seems to me to have been an honest mistake."

"I didn't apologise."

"Well, you ought to have." Hare gave him a level stare.

"Don't get me wrong, miss." The man cocked his head to the side. "It's not that I don't have *regrets*. For example, I regret enquiring after the safety of an ungrateful American harridan, when I could have just continued with my day, which I now intend to go back to."

Hare folded her arms. "Far be it from me to stop you."

"Good day to you, then." The man was already walking, but she could just about make out the words he muttered under his breath, *"And good riddance."*

Hare took a breath to compose herself, but even that moment of peace was denied her, as she heard Miss Bonningham call to her from across the road.

DINING WAS PRACTICALLY a sport in the Winchfield's household. The rich and the fashionable had long followed the Prince of Wales' example in both the style and the sumptuousness of their eating habits. At least that's what Baron Winchfield, freshly returned from his country estates, was more than happy to tell Hare. The Baron had turned out to be a rather unremarkable man, bred to perfection for a life of indulgent indolence and not much else. His conversation was limited to food and clothing and he took a great interest in both those topics, just as he took no interest in almost anything else.

"Now, our Prince Albert, that is a man who knows how to live!" Winchfield dabbed at his forehead with an already crumpled handkerchief, as he signalled to the footman to bring in the next dish. The ninth by Hare's count.

Hare smiled and muttered something that she hoped could pass for interest.

"Did you know, I ordered a morning suit from the exact same tailor our future king uses, only to find a week later he had switched to another one!" Winchfield shook his head.

"Does it matter terribly?" Hare asked, as politeness seemed to require it. Seeing the Baron's shocked expression she added quickly, "If the suit is what was asked for, I mean?"

"Ah, you see, dearest, as the girl's only recently arrived, you shouldn't wonder at her ignorance." Baroness Winchfield interjected, placing her hand on her husband's hand.

"I don't remember you not grasping such simple things when we were courting." Winchfield looked at his wife, affection temporarily softening his expression. "But I suppose I can't expect all of your countrywomen to have your excellent judgement." Hare thought it was remarkable how such two thoroughly appalling people managed to find each other.

"Bertie, I would remind you of your duties as a host," the Dowager Lady Winchfield piped in from the other side of the table. She seemed to dote on her son and rarely missed a single word of his tedious conversation. "The girl is staying with us for the first time and it is our responsibility to introduce her into polite society. We can hardly do so while leaving her ignorant of the *ways of the world*." The last was said with a great reverence. The dowager loved to explain the way her world operated to all who'd listen. Of course, the way her world worked was quite, *quite* different to how everyone else's did. That seemed not to deter her, however.

"You're right, Mummy, as always. And yes, Miss Walker, to answer your question, it matters very greatly." Winchfield sniffed. His face reddened. "How you're seen is everything in this country of ours. A man dressed by the same tailor who dresses the future king is a man to be reckoned with. Not so a man dressed by his *old* tailor."

"But do we know why the Prince rejected his services?" Lady Winchfield leaned forward, the two blonde curls on either side of her face bouncing as she did so.

"Ah and as always, it falls to my Posy to ask the pertinent question!" He turned again to his wife, his eyes misting over. "I'd heard a rumour he was using… brass buttons."

Lady Winchfield gasped, her hands flying to her mouth. The Dowager opened her fan with a quick sharp movement and began fanning herself as if she'd suddenly been transported to the tropics. Miss Bonningham and Hare stared at each other blankly.

"That sounds…" Miss Bonningham coughed, struggling for an appropriate remark. "…unfortunate."

"It is a *scandal*!" Lord Winchfield slapped his knee. "The colouring alone should have been abandoned in the 1880s, where it belonged. It's like he hadn't even *heard* of silver web-work." He sniffed. "What's even the point of summoning mythics if you're not going to learn from their excellent tailoring?"

"Indeed." Miss Bonningham nodded. Hare lifted her glass to her lips to hide a smile. Her "aunt"was trying so hard to take this seriously, a vein popped up on her forehead from the effort. "Now, dear Posy," she turned to the Baroness. "I understand your brother might soon be visiting?"

"Oh, I didn't realise you have a brother, Lady Winchfield." Hare grasped at the conversational straw.

"Oh yes, he visits often." Lady Winchfield was clearly eager to end the conversation.

"He's a solicitor." The Dowager shot her daughter-in-law a critical look and Lady Winchfield seemed to shrink into herself.

"Now, Mummy, he's a perfectly decent sort of fellow, though he could pay more attention to his clothing." The Baron came to his wife's defence. "His profession is a respectable one at that. This is a new age. We don't sneer at business men anymore."

"You see, Miss Edwina." Lady Winchfield leaned over the

table and dropped her voice. "My parents secured a first rate education for my brother...."

"As well as a first-rate dowry for you, my dear!" Lord Winchfield laughed at his own joke.

"I don't think they have done so badly by yourself, where schooling is concerned," Miss Bonningham said with a benevolent expression. "Your education has been most carefully considered."

Lady Winchfield, realising her mistake, squeezed Miss Bonningham's hand. "Of course! I didn't mean to suggest anything else. Your school will forever be etched in my memory as the most edifying place." She nodded to Hare. "You cannot imagine, in your youth, how much our experience of girlhood defines us. It was a merry time for me. Merry and carefree. And your aunt was a most beloved teacher, guiding me into my future life. How fortunate you are to have her as your mentor."

"I thank for it each day," Hare said, taking a sip of her drink.

"As you should!" Lord Winchfield said, clearly loath to be left out of the conversation. "Miss Bonningham well understood the requirements for a woman of my Posy's standing. When others would poison her mind with useless knowledge, Posy learnt something which will last her a lifetime!" He brought his wife's knuckles to his lips.

"And what is that?" Hare couldn't help herself. Miss Bonningham stared daggers at her.

"Why, my dear," Winchfield looked at her in surprise, "*style*."

"Indeed, some finishing schools these days," the Dowager piped in, pushing her small spectacles back up her nose, "some of them positively *finish* the young girl's marital prospects." She paused, looking around the room, to see if her joke landed. Hare smiled politely. "In any case," the old woman continued, clearly disappointed at the luke-warm reception of her humorous remark. "We are grateful that the Baroness' parents had the foresight to send her to your establishment, dear Miss Bonningham."

Miss Bonningham blushed and brought a hand to her heart. "I'm honoured by your words."

"Now, Miss Edwina," Baroness Winchfield turned to her, "what would you say *your* accomplishments were?"

"My... accomplishments?" Hare looked blankly. *I once could spin silver thread from the air, freeze and shatter a man's lungs with a kiss and dance-call flowers up from the ground.*

"She draws," Miss Bonningham said. "Rather prettily, I must say."

"That is a skill..." Lady Winchfield didn't appear enthused. "Drawing is not exactly a social activity, however. Do you play an instrument?"

"Not at all, I'm afraid."

"Dance?"

Beautifully enough to make your heart break.

"My aunt taught me."

"She's tolerable," Miss Bonningham said, picking up her wine glass.

"We must make sure you practice." The Dowager shook her head. "Do you sing at least?"

Hare glanced at her "aunt", but finding no help there, she answered weakly. "Not particularly well." That was a truth at least.

"But," the Baron leaned forward, heedless of his elbows dipping in the sauce he'd splashed around his plate, "Do you know *geography*," he put the emphasis on the word, "and a-rith-me-tic?"

Hare cleared her throat. Her heart dropped. "Not in the least."

"Now, that's a relief!" the man laughed. "We might find you a husband yet!"

HAVING ESTABLISHED Hare's suitability for matchmaking, the entire party proceeded to ignore her. After the meal, which took no fewer than three hours to finish, she skulked off into her room, where she found somebody had drawn her a bath. On the side lay a piece of carved pink soap. She picked it up reverently, cradling it in the palm of her hand. She took a sniff. It smelled of roses. How extravagant it was, to have a coloured soap. A *perfumed* soap. She chuckled to herself. How easy it was to impress her these days.

Hare undressed quickly and stepped into the warm water. She sighed as she felt her muscles relax.

How well you're doing. She felt the voice rather than heard it. She turned towards the *domovoy* and splashed some water at him.

"I know, cat." She knew it annoyed him to be called that. "What do you want?"

Many things. He growled and began to clean his paw. *Some bread and a scratch behind the ears. Oh and a return home.*

"You know I can't give you that." Hare let her hand float. She wondered how much time and fuel it took to warm such a vast amount of water. A smile, the first real smile of the day stretched her lips. It was all worth it. Dealing with those people, enduring their inspections. Even to marry one such as them. She steeled herself, as an unwelcome image of the Baron popped into her head. To marry one like him was a shocking, a horrifying prospect. And yet. It appeared she was ready to go through with it, if only to be able to relax into the heated water, to feel clean and warm and full of food. She wasn't sure how she felt about that. She glanced at the *domovoy*. He was beautiful, truly. The long, shining fur of silver, the golden eyes. Something like guilt squeezed her heart. "I wish I could, truly. I wish I could send us all back."

He sighed and walked close to the bathtub, allowing her to stroke his luxurious fur.

But you could *free me. And that is the next best thing.*

She thought about it. "When I succeed."

And not before?

"I can't. You know I can't."

I know you choose what you can and can't do.

"Choice is very much an illusion in this world they pulled us into, I think."

'Only one man's hands on the goods.' Anne's words came back. They were unkind words, perhaps. But there was truth in them and Hare preferred truth to kind lies.

She splashed water in her face, then used her fingertips to drag the droplets down her skin. How many times was she forced to laugh off men's hands tracing the contours of her body as she worked. Their leering gaze, their grasping fingers. But as she was, she didn't have to. She thought of the dark-haired man who'd saved the bird mythic from the mob earlier. She knew he didn't deserve her anger, but it had been so satisfying to express her displeasure, with no consequences to be feared. This status, this image of who she was, gave her the right to choose who touched her. And that was worth the whole trick.

CHAPTER 5

Ernest was possibly the last to notice Miss Walker as she entered the ballroom, flanked by Baroness Winchfield and an unfamiliar, pinched-looking woman. His eyes passed over the newcomer, already barely visible through a throng of men. He picked a tall flute of champagne from a footman. It must have been a Finnish mythic. Very tall, with more joints in his many fingers than Ernest could count. The creature's malevolent eyes watched him with feigned disinterest.

"Look, Ernest! A brand-new lure in a pretty frock, guarded by a maternal Cerberus." Brandon pulled on Ernest's sleeve as he narrowed his eyes towards the newcomers. Brandon was rather short-sighted but refused to wear spectacles, which he claimed made him look like a "tradesman's clerk". "I imagine a lure *this* shiny needs protection when you're around," Ernest said. "Anyway, we both know she's not here to catch the eye of a lowly solicitor, so I will just enjoy the champagne over here."

"Where's your curiosity, man? Come, let's not be the last to get a closer look." His companion patted his shoulder and charged ahead, never doubting he'd be followed. Ernest sighed and downed his drink. If he was to be forced to spend the evening watching his friend flirt, he would be damned if he were to do it sober.

* * *

HARE COULD FEEL everyone's eyes on her as she was ushered into the ballroom. They were tardy, intentionally so of course, as what else could have secured her such undivided attention of every single man in the room. Hare plastered an appropriately serene expression on her face, lifting her eyebrows ever so slightly. It reportedly gave her the appearance of one of the "Gibson Girls", those pretty models of feminine grace invented by the artist, Charles Dana Gibson. Hare thought it funny how the tastes of one man, an American at that, had so successfully influenced the fashions of *Le Beau Monde,* even as far as England. Which was just as well for her, she knew. Her hair was the fashionable chestnut, her eyebrows and lashes dark and she had learnt to assume the languid expression considered to be so very fetching.

"To your left. That's the second son of Duke of Chichester. The family's poor as church mice, reportedly looking for an American heiress," Anne whispered urgently in her ear. "Make sure to avoid him. We don't want him telling all of his friends at the club about how he rejected *you* as a candidate because of your lack of dowry."

Hare looked in the opposite direction and tilted her head up. "You're right, Aunt, the chandelier is quite lovely," she said out loud. "It reminds me of the one at the Carnegie Hall, do you remember?"

"Don't overdo it," was the reply, though Hare noticed a hint of a smile on the old school mistress' face. The woman had a sense of humour, though she was currently as tense as a piano string. Hare wanted so badly to roll her eyes. After all, wasn't this what her "aunt" had schooled her so carefully in? Hinting at the knowledge she did not possess and feigning interest in everything but the actual object of their visit to London?

"That one wearing a coloured cravat to your right." The Baroness, excited to be once more on the prowl, albeit in a different role, tapped her fan on Hare's shoulder. "Owns three cotton factories in the North of England. As rich as Cresus, though untitled." She paused, then added. "Keep him in mind and keep him sweet if nothing better comes up."

Hare shivered. Three cotton factories. She wondered how many mythics had been bound to his service. She'd heard rumours of the working conditions in such places, where the white fibres in the air made the halls look like it was always snowing. The cotton would float between the machines, slowly making its way into the workers' lungs. But they were mythic lungs, so nobody worried too much about it.

But Hare knew her duty here. And so she lifted her eyes to the man in question, who, in spite of the early hour, was already watching her with eyes hazed by liquor.

"He inherited his factories from his father and they are run entirely by his mother and younger brother," the Baroness added.

"Dear Lady Winchfield, would you introduce me to your companions?"

Hare glanced back and widened her eyes, ever so slightly, as if surprised to see a man standing there, pretending not to see the increasingly disorderly queue of the men behind him, all hoping to make the same request.

"Of course, Mr Stirling, this is my old friend, Miss Anne Bonningham—" The man gave Miss Bonningham a smile, friendly enough so they could all pretend he cared two figs about her. "—and her niece, Miss Edwina Walker, who came to visit us all the way from America."

"America, eh?" The man smoothed his moustache with the back of his hand. "I haven't been myself, of course, but I've heard *interesting* things." He raised his eyebrows and, just in case Hare could miss his meaning, added, "Such lively and charming women it seems to birth, that I'm in half a mind to sail over there tomorrow, except," He reached for her—thankfully gloved—hand and lifted it to his lips, "except so many of you seem to be coming over *here* instead. And seeing you, I said to myself: 'Joseph Stirling, you won't forgive yourself if you miss the opportunity to make this charming creature's acquaintance.' And so here I am, at your service."

"You're too kind." Hare forced herself to smile. Thankfully the man was only a "Mister" and so unlikely to be seen as a first round prospect for her. The small mercies. The man's moustache had left a damp spot on her gloves where he kissed her and it took a great deal of self-control to not wipe her hand on her voluminous skirts.

In any case, her hand was already picked up by another man, who'd conveniently elbowed Mr Stirling out of the way. This one seemed less repulsive, but Hare was under strict instruction to not show any particular interest until signalled to by Miss Bonningham. He introduced himself in an accent so heavy, she couldn't quite make it out. The man must have been wealthy, for Lady Winchfield gave Hare a little wink, before she pressed her fingers into the younger woman's arm. *Good grief, if they were to make her marry the man, what would their life even look like?* She supposed she'd eventually end up more able to understand him, though that seemed a risky strategy for picking out a life mate.

"And this, dear Miss Walker, is Duke of Brandon." Lady Winchfield nodded to Miss Bonningham in satisfaction and Hare felt both her arms squeezed in unison by the two women, as they bodily turned her around.

She took a deep breath and looked towards the man standing to the left of Lady Winchfield.

Her heart sank. Standing before her was the very man she'd abused for the crime of helping her and the bird mythic who'd saved her.

His face was carefully blank and she allowed herself to hope he didn't recognise her. Remembering where she was, Hare beamed her brightest smile at him and held out her hand. "How do you do?"

The man raised one eyebrow at her and his lips twisted in a strange expression, even as he took her hand. "How do you do? Pleased to make your acquaintance." He squeezed her fingertips and leaned down. "*Again*." The last word was whispered, meant for Hare's ears alone and she could feel the red creeping up her cheeks.

"Oh for goodness' sake, Ernest, are you really going to misrepresent yourself?" Lady Winchfield smacked the man on the shoulder, with an air of exasperation.

Another one pushed in front. He gave a curt bow. "*I'm* Duke of Brandon, Miss Edwina. This sad impostor," he nodded towards the clearly amused man still holding onto Hare's hand, "is my friend, Mr Thompson."

"Mr Thompson?" Hare repeated the words, inexplicably disappointed.

The man nodded. "I'm afraid so." He flashed a smile at her. "I hope you will forgive me for not putting things right immediately. A lowly solicitor seldom gets the treatment a Duke does. I merely wanted to soak in the experience."

Hare smiled in spite of herself, even as she tried to extricate her fingers from his grasp. "I assure you, I bear no grudges."

"No, I didn't think you would," he said. And there it was again, that look in his eyes that made a mockery of her, without as much as him uttering an untoward word.

"That's quite enough, brother," Lady Winchfield said, staring daggers. "Can you release my charge from your grip, please?"

Hare realised he was still holding her hand and she pulled it away, as if scolded. "Mr Thompson is your brother?" The two looked nothing alike, the Baroness plump and fair and her brother lean and tan, with black hair and eyes.

"Yes and my cross to bear as well!" The Baroness examined her brother. "You could at least have the decency to pomade your hair! If Lord Winchfield sees you, he'll have a conniption fit."

Ernest brushed his curly hair out of his face with a sheepish grin. "I did do so! My hair won't stay put!"

"I think you're boring the young lady with the hair talk, Thompson," the actual Duke of Brandon said, after clearing his throat. It seemed he was unused to being ignored.

Hare made sure to turn towards him. "It's quite a joke Mr Thompson played on me." She looked down. "I'm pleased to make your acquaintance." She looked up at the Duke, remembering him to be one of the top prospects on Miss Bonningham's list. She gave him a quick look. It could have been worse, she knew. He was tall and trim and not unattractive, even if his very pale skin and very pale hair made him look like all pigment had been drained from him by a particularly greedy paint-maker. But she could tell Miss Bonningham beside her was making her calculations in an altogether different manner. The Duke was still young and good looking. A rich, attractive aristocrat would most likely be aware of his worth on the marriage mart, making Hare's job that much harder.

"Now that my friend has skipped the queue for introductions, seems only right I do so with a dance. If her guardian would allow me." The Duke turned to Miss Bonningham who seemed to have actually gone rigid with excitement.

Hare didn't reply, since nobody really expected her to. She took the proffered hand and joined the other couples on the dance floor as the musicians began to play the waltz.

But while she twirled around the ballroom she couldn't help but feel a pair of dark eyes following her. A feeling she didn't find unpleasant at all.

CHAPTER 6

"You could at least have danced with her!" Brandon pulled at his bow tie once he and Ernest sat in the coach which was to take them to Brandon's London residence at number 6 Grosvenor Road. "Heaven knows everyone else did!"

"We both know she wasn't there to dance with the likes of me." Ernest shrugged. He too had loosened his tie the moment the footman closed the coach's door behind them. "I would have merely taken up a precious spot on her dancing card, one which could have been taken up by a more appealing prospect."

"True enough." Brandon laughed.

"And how kind of you to agree so quickly." Ernest leaned back with folded arms.

"Oh please, you must have seen the poor girl's aunt. She practically squealed at the sight of anyone known to have a fortune, which, I grant you, is a rare enough thing to witness in London these days. A horrid, vulgar sort of woman." Brandon pushed the curtain with one finger and glanced out. "Still, the niece is worth having to deal with her unpleasant relations, especially as there are so few of them."

"Oh?" Ernest kept his eyes half-closed. Showing interest would only serve to make his friend withhold the information, all the better to tease him with.

"An orphan."

"How peculiar that the aunt would bring the girl across the ocean then."

"Nothing peculiar about it," Brandon said. "You know how those American matrons are. Living vicariously through the younger generation. If the niece marries well, the old bat will be living off her for the rest of her life."

"Seems to me there are plenty of rich men on the other side of the ocean. Distinctly more so these days." Ernest waved away a cigar offered by his friend.

"Ah, but the title, my friend. The old blood." Brandon winked at him. "How that stirs the romantic in the most dried-up crone."

"Yes, well, I wouldn't know anything about that."

"Then you must live vicariously through others!" Brandon blew smoke out the window. "And isn't it just lucky that you have me around to give you a glimpse of the high life?"

"Of course. I live for it." Ernest said flatly, making his friend burst out with laughter. "But what was your opinion of Miss Walker herself?"

"Pretty," Brandon said. "Very pretty."

"That much could have been ascertained by anyone with eyes, myself included. But what else?"

"Not sure there's a lot of 'else' to it, my friend."

But as Ernest walked to his bedroom that night, he thought of the dark blue eyes which for a moment sparkled with interest when they turned to his face and of how entirely unpleasant it was when they turned to another.

CHAPTER 7

The blue salon in the Winchfield house was filled with flowers. The bouquets began arriving early in the morning the day after the ball. Roses were passé and so a great array of exotic blooms, arranged extravagantly, were now all releasing their pollen till the air was thick with their scent. Which is why Hare, sneezing and with streaming eyes, but with one of the nicer boxes of chocolates (sent by one of the more sensible suitors) under her arm, trudged towards the green sitting room, where the Winchfield children were allowed to spend a few carefully structured hours each day. The green room was the least showy of the day rooms in the house and with the most lived-in furniture, which is why it was that the two small children of Lady and Lord Winchfield were not seen as out of place there. The new generation of the Baron's family were a boy, Stephen, four and his younger sister Francine, three years old and full of sass.

"Edwina!" Stephen threw his arms in the air and charged at Hare, nearly knocking her off her feet.

"Master Stephen!" The nurse groaned. "It's *Miss* Edwina. We spoke about this." The servant gave Hare an apologetic look. A small shiver ran down Hare's spine. The nurse was a *nickert*. Her double-pupilled green eyes regarded Hare for a moment, before returning back to the children. The look of longing in there was like hunger. It took a special kind of self-assurance to buy a child-stealing mythic to look after your children. But then, Hare thought, seeing how carefully the nurse watched the children's every move, there could be none more attentive. While the *nickert*, like all mythics, could see through Hare's thinly woven glamour, she showed no interest, so focussed she was on her charges.

"I don't mind in the least." Hare laughed. "And how are you spending your morning, Stephen?"

"Playing with you," the young boy said, confidence oozing out of every word. "And your cat. Where is your cat?"

"We like your cat," Francine added. "He's fluffy."

Stephen eyed the box in Hare's hand. "Are those *chocolates*?"

"I'm not sure." Hare pretended to inspect the box and wrinkled her nose. She sat on the low and well-worn sofa and winked at the children's nurse conspiratorially. "I rather suspect those are dried beetles."

"No!" Francine trotted up to Hare and stood on her tip toes.

"Are you funning us?" Stephen narrowed his eyes. He turned to his nurse. "Nurse Nic, is she funning us?"

The nurse covered a smile with a cough. "I'm sure I wouldn't know." She stroked Stephen's head with one long finger.

"I want to see!" Francine reached towards the box.

"Oh no, we have to be careful!" Hare held the box out of the girl's reach. "Some might still be alive!" She raised her eyebrows. "And *poisonous*!"

"In that case I best intervene then," a voice came from the doorway. "I wouldn't want my sister's guest running any unnecessary risks. It would reflect badly upon the family to have the police come round."

* * *

ERNEST STIFLED a laugh at the surprise on Miss Walker's face. He walked up to her and with a bow said, "May I?" gesturing towards the box.

The corner of the woman's lips quirked, as she held out the chocolates, pulling the lid open.

"Hmm..." He scratched his head. "They all look exceedingly suspicious. But if one is to test them, one best start with the little one." He picked up a small, round truffle and inspected it against the light. "What do you suppose this one is called?" he asked.

Miss Walker, glancing at the children, assumed a serious expression. "That, I believe, is a dung beetle."

"A *dung* beetle?" Stephen whooped with delight and his sister jumped excitedly.

"Horrible, yet, I believe, safe." Ernest nodded gravely and popped the chocolate into his mouth.

"How do you feel?" Miss Walker turned her head to the side, resting her cheek on her index finger.

"Oh I feel just... just..." Ernest suddenly straightened his back and clutched his throat. "It... was... not... a dung beetle!" He threw up his arm dramatically and collapsed to the floor to the delighted squeals of his niece and nephew, who, far from concerned, proceeded to climb on top of him.

Seeing as his pretence wasn't getting the expected result, Ernest raised his head and looked to Miss Walker. "Aren't you going to help me?"

"I don't think so." She popped a praline in her mouth and leaned back into the sofa.

"I've been warned about women like you!" He heaved and rose up, a child under each arm.

"Women like me?" She sniffed another chocolate suspiciously. Her nose creased, giving her the look of some small animal. "Whatever do you mean, Mr Thompson? For it doesn't sound like a compliment." She assumed a perfectly haughty expression, though he could see she was fighting a losing battle against her lips, which kept threatening a smile. She bit into the truffle and Ernest found himself temporarily hypnotised by the sight.

"Yes, what *do* you mean, Uncle Ernest?" Stephen's voice came from somewhere under Ernest's armpit. "If you're mean to Miss Walker, I will tell mummy!"

"Oh will you?" Ernest started spinning, still holding Francine and Stephen, who both squealed in delight, until he finally put them down.

"That's enough now. I need a breath. And sustenance" he said, sitting heavily next to Miss Walker, glancing hopefully at her chocolates. But perhaps he sat too closely as he felt her stiffen next to him. "I'm sorry." Too late, he noticed his faux pas. He moved as if to stand up. "I'll sit over there."

"No," she said quickly. "It's your sister's home. You shouldn't move on my account."

That, more than anything else, made him stand up. "I wouldn't dream of imposing." He moved to the chair opposite. It was narrow, with unfashionably ornate back engravings which dug into his ribs. He smiled politely. The ease of the prior moment was lost in an instant. Ernest brushed his hair out of his face. He was too informal with her, he chided himself. It was quite clear she was not in London to flirt with young solicitors and she must have thought him terribly presumptuous. A sense of humiliation hit him like a memory. He'd been too familiar and he knew it. He could feel her eyes on him. She must have thought him ridiculous really. Not proper at all. Yet why was she so informal with him if she disliked it so? But then she was an American after all. Different rules applied. To her, not to him, naturally. It wasn't the kind of influence he needed in his life. What if any of his friends saw him. Perhaps the servants would gossip. He glanced towards the children's nurse, who was quietly mending some clothing in the corner. They'd all just see two foreigners in London. No, he best stay away from this pretty young woman. She was not interested in his company, that much was clear.

* * *

HARE WATCHED as the different emotions ran across Mr Thompson's face. She marvelled at the strangeness of his reaction. He needn't have gone and sat in that ridiculous little chair in the corner. She more than suspected the chair was there for decoration only, as there was little chance of it being comfortable, with those excessive carvings. The man wasn't looking at her, which was a little rude in fact. His eyebrows were knitted together and his dark eyes seemed to grow darker still. *Was he angry with her?* That seemed unlikely. She felt after all those years since her summoning she'd become an expert at reading human expressions. Perhaps he thought she was being missish and so decided he didn't want to be seen as making improper advances. She's heard of men living in fear of being trapped into marriage by a dishonest accusation. She set her lips into a line and looked away. He couldn't possibly have thought that was the case, could he? Like she would set her cap after a man like that. So maybe she was flirting. Just a little bit. It was hardly flirting, really, what with the children and their slightly unnerving nurse just there.

Hare looked at him again, catching his eye. She straightened her back and jutted her chin out. If he thought to see her cower, he was very much mistaken. She had nothing to be ashamed of here and really, he was being quite a boor. Perhaps he thought his looks were likely to turn a girl's head over a couple of innocuous comments and chocolates. Well, the joke was on him. She'd seen more beauty in her past life than he could imagine, even if she could barely recall the specifics. She was quite immune. She cleared her throat. "Your friend, Duke of Brandon, told me he will be going to the Summer Exhibition at the Royal Academy," she said. "I am myself looking forward to it, as the Lord and Lady Winchfield have tickets secured."

"I expect they would, even if they are unlikely to use them." Ernest said, shifting once more as the chair dug into his back. He noticed Hare's surprised expression and added, "My sister and her husband are not very much interested in the arts. Their patronage is expected, yet they miss it yearly with the flimsiest of excuses. In any case, I wouldn't expect much art conversation once there. It's quite the social affair, the paintings being a pretext."

"To some people, perhaps." Hare put her nose high in the air. "I'm told the Duke is an avid lover of the arts and he's offered to accompany me to the exhibit."

"Has he now?" Ernest raised his eyebrows in mockery. "How fortuitous."

* * *

ERNEST WASN'T sure why the revelation that Brandon had extended an invitation to Miss Walker had irked him so much. But he knew he was being rude and was not sure how to fix it. They sat in an uncomfortable silence, until Francine brought a sheet of paper and a pencil and plonked them in Miss Walker's lap.

"What would you have me do, Francine?" the woman was clearly relieved to turn her attention towards the child.

"Draw me!" the girl demanded and struck a pose, fingers laced under her chin.

The woman picked up a book from the side table next to the sofa and slid it underneath the sheet of paper. "Very well, Francine. But you have to stay still."

"First me!" Stephen stepped in front of his sister, who scowled at him. Ernest saw Miss Walker struggle to put on a stern expression as she looked at the boy.

"Alright, alright, *also* me..." The boy was chastened and Ernest almost burst out laughing, his mood lifting again.

"There is many a schoolmaster who could take lessons from you, Miss Walker."

"How so?" she asked, without looking at him. Her eyes were focussed on the children, as her hand glided across the paper. Her movements were practiced and economical. Ernest found himself oddly hypnotised looking at her long fingers.

"Stopping a disturbance with barely a look, without as much as raising your voice. It's a skill."

"A skill your schoolmasters didn't possess I take it?" She glanced at him from beneath her long lashes before returning her attention towards the children.

"No. No, they didn't." Ernest found himself suddenly uncomfortable.

"I see." A few moments passed, until Miss Walker took one last look at the drawing and, satisfied, presented it to the children, who immediately started fighting over it.

"Now uncle!" Stephen said, fetching another sheet of paper.

"Come now, Stephen, you know I can't draw," Ernest said with a smile.

"We *know*!" Francine rolled her eyes.

"Miss Francine, young ladies don't roll their eyes," the nurse said automatically from the corner of the room.

"Edwina does!" Francine said, folding her arms. "I *saw* her!"

"Traitor," Miss Walker muttered under her breath, exchanging an amused look with Ernest.

"Indeed. Very quick to point out my lack of talent, as well." Ernest rubbed his chin.

"You did so yourself a moment ago." the woman quirked her eyebrow at him.

"I *hoped* my niece and nephew would disagree to spare my feelings."

"No. Fibbing is bad. The nurse says so." Stephen came up to

Miss Walker and put more paper in her lap. Miss Walker snorted at the four-year-old's callous honesty. "Edwina will draw uncle now."

Miss Walker reddened, suddenly embarrassed. Ernest knew he should probably alleviate her discomfort. But as he looked at her blushing face, he found he, well, didn't really want to just yet.

"Well, Miss Walker, as the young Master Stephen's wish is our command, I think we best comply."

She narrowed her eyes at him. With a grin he spread his arms over the back of his chair. "How should I pose to the best advantage?"

Francine walked up to him and looked pensive for a moment, an index finger to her lip. After a moment's thought, she pulled a bow off her head and placed it on Ernest's lap. "This is pretty. Put on your head."

"Well, Mr Thompson, their wish *is* your command, I hear." Miss Walker smoothed her skirt, looking altogether too delighted.

Glowering, Ernest put the damned bow on his head. It was some sort of divine punishment, he reckoned. What did he think would happen, after all? That, forced to look closely at him, the beautiful Miss Walker would notice how dashingly handsome he was and would turn her attentions to him and away from the very rich, irritatingly eligible Duke? Fat chance.

* * *

Hare straightened her back and let the pencil tip hover just above the paper.

"Start drawing!" Francine screeched, climbing onto the sofa next to her.

"I'm trying!" Hare cringed. There was nothing to it, really. She had to look up eventually. She took a breath. It wasn't different to drawing a still life, after all. Like she heard an art professor say once, it was all geometric shapes stacked together. *See the form, not the man.* She glanced up and wished for a different maxim, because his "form" was very much the issue here. He appeared entirely relaxed, his arms thrown casually backwards, his broad chest stretching the fabric of his high-cut waistcoat. Hare swallowed and forced herself to begin sketching. Once she'd started, she would fall into the familiar rhythm of it and forget about his eyes, which remained fixed on her face. Quite scandalously, really.

"You don't need to look at me so intently, Mr Thompson," she said, somewhat irked. "I'm the one drawing you, after all."

"Does it bother you?" he asked. "Me watching you?"

"Not at all." By god, he looked smug right now. "I merely meant, as long as you don't move too much, you can look anywhere you like."

"And so I am."

Hare was grateful for the high collar of her shirt which was now performing a Herculean task of hiding the somewhat blotchy rush of blood to her chest and neck. Did she use to blush in the before times? She couldn't remember. The gravity of this world seemed to pull her down, fixing her to her mould in ways she wasn't comfortable with.

She focussed on her drawing, outlining his shoulders and the curve of his crossed legs. Once the outline was there, she turned to the details. The straight line of his jaw and the way his hair curled above his forehead.

"You didn't draw his lips!" Francine bounced next to Hare. "You forgot!"

The man cleared his throat, doubtless to cover up a chuckle. He assumed a theatrically concerned expression. "Why, Miss Walker, does the shape of my lips displease you?"

She pretended to consider what he said and tapped the end of her pencil on her chin. "Only the words pouring out of them." She smiled to soften the retort.

"Ah, so their shape *pleases* you then?"

Was the man flirting with her? He must have been. Hare might not have been English, but even she knew the shape of a man's lips was not a topic for polite conversation. But good heavens, now she was thinking about his lips. They were, in fact, rather nice lips. Which she didn't want to think about at all.

"I haven't given them any consideration," she lied. From the amused expression on his face she knew he realised she was lying. It was all very irritating.

"But you're looking at them and so I thought, as an artist, you might have formed an opinion."

She tightened her lips, ignoring his question. She had to get a hold of herself. He was the Duke's friend. If Duke Brandon thought Hare might be interested in Mr Thompson, he would doubtless bow out. And Hare couldn't afford to give any excuse for the man to bow out. Therefore, she couldn't flirt with Mr Thompson. It would be stupid to do so. She had a plan and it was a good plan. It didn't involve a handsome, dark-eyed solicitor. *He wasn't even that handsome. He was, in fact, somewhat funny looking. He had...* She looked up at him, looking for a ridiculable feature. She didn't find one. "Has long lashes" didn't quite cut it as a put-down. Which the man richly deserved. And she rather liked his lashes.

She liked a lot about him, as it turned out.

With a determined look on her face, she drew the folds of Francine's bow, by far the most intricately sketched-out part of the drawing and she presented it to Francine with a flourish.

"I want to see! I asked first!" Stephen climbed next to his sister.

The model stood up and sauntered over. "May I?" His niece placed the paper in his hand. He studied it for a moment.

"You're a very accomplished artist, Miss Walker," he said, a note of surprise in his voice irritating Hare.

"You weren't expecting me to be so?" She gave the pencil back to Stephen, who took it back to the art materials' box on the table by the nurse.

"Not exactly," he admitted.

She looked up at him sharply.

"While fashionable young women often have drawing instructors as a part of their education, this..." He paused as he considered the drawing. "... This looks somewhat more polished than I've ever seen from a mere amateur."

"Do you know what 'amateur' means, Mr Thompson?" Hare pulled on the cuff of her shirt. When he shook his head, she said, "It means 'a lover of'. I'm rather proud to be a lover of the arts. After all, that is the full extent of what a woman is allowed to be, isn't it?"

He cocked his head to the side. "And if you were given the opportunity to, would you wish for more?"

She chewed on her lip, thinking how annoyed Miss Bonningham would be with her. This was not the image Hare was meant to project. Yet this man irritated information out of her, more effectively than a detective ever could.

"I..." She stood up abruptly. "I just remembered I must get ready for lunch. We're expecting callers in the afternoon."

"Of course," he said with a voice as dry as wood chippings. "All the flowers and chocolates didn't materialise out of thin air, after all. Their senders will inevitably descend upon the house imminently."

"Just so." She nodded and walked out of the room. Mr Thompson was quite dangerous to be around and so she wouldn't be. She'd make sure to stay out of his way as long as possible. Somehow the thought, valiantly formed though it was, did nothing to lift her mood.

CHAPTER 8

Surprises were seldom a pleasant thing in Hare's estimation. She thought they were, generally speaking, like biting into a cupcake and tasting broccoli. And so she was less than pleased to find Mr Thompson in the pink breakfast room of the Winchfield house in the morning two days after the ball.

That morning she'd come down later than usual. The previous afternoon was filled with visits from a great number of her dance partners from the night before and she went up to bed after dinner with a pounding headache. It would have been stressful enough without Miss Bonningham's watchful presence, as Hare's partner in the scheme had all the suitors carefully catalogued according to the levels of personal wealth and social standing, as well as the likelihood of them actually marrying a woman who was neither English nor an heiress. "A great deal of time wasters, come to flirt and stare at your bosom, but not willing to pay the price of admission!" she had said when it was just the two of them. Now, as Hare entered the room, Miss Bonningham looked keen to ascertain where Mr Thompson's friend, the Duke, was to be positioned on the time-waster's list.

"I understand Duke Brandon must have a great deal of responsibilities to do with his estate," she said in a tone which could only be described as "simpering". "I thought his observations were so clever, we'd all enjoy his visit, should he find himself with a free afternoon."

"Indeed," Mr Thompson said, placing cold meats on his plate with a pair of silver tongs. "And which of his observations did you find particularly clever?" He looked up at Miss Bonningham. "Just so I can pass on the compliment."

Miss Bonningham became flustered, worrying the edge of her shawl. "I mean, in general, I found—"

"Lord Brandon seems to enjoy art and has entertained us greatly with his thoughts on the Impressionist Movement and its significance." Hare walked behind Miss Bonningham and kissed the air beside the older woman's cheek; a pre-agreed show of affection. "Good Morning, Aunt. I trust you slept well?"

"How could I not, after such a pleasant day yesterday!" Miss Bonningham said in a chirpy voice, which didn't fool Hare for one moment. The bar had been set and Hare better keep up the level of interest she'd elicited at the ball.

"I've noticed you have a great interest in painting, Miss Walker." Mr Thompson tapped the side of his teacup with his finger, his head cocked to the side.

"Are you of an opinion women ought not to have an interest in such things?"

"I don't believe I ever said such a thing."

Hare sat down and smiled at the footman, who poured her a cup of tea. "Thank you." The servant blushed and didn't seem to know what to do with himself at the attention.

"That'll be all, Thomas." Mr Thompson nodded to the man and waited for him to leave the room. Then he turned back to Hare. "You shouldn't thank the servants for doing their jobs."

"Whyever not?"

"It's not… done…" Mr Thompson stuttered, as if looking for a plausible explanation. He found one and grasped at it. "It marks you as a foreigner."

"I *am* a foreigner here," she noted with a smile hidden behind the teacup.

"If you wish to fit in, you need to adapt," he said.

"I couldn't have said it better myself." Miss Bonningham shot Hare an annoyed look. "It is imperative my niece is accepted into the society here. You should pay attention to Mr Thompson's advice, dear. As an American himself, he knows what he's saying!"

"I'd much rather have a coffee in the morning," Hare said, setting the cup back down. "Yet I drink the tea instead. Isn't that concession enough?"

"A great sacrifice indeed!" Mr Thompson laughed. He had a rather pleasant laugh, she thought.

"But I notice, Mr Thompson, your own adjustments are rather significant," she said. "Your accent…"

"Yes, well." He seemed flustered. She wondered why. "I've been here a long while. Eton, you know."

"The school?"

"Of course he means the school, girl, what a silly question," Miss Bonningham said, disliking being ignored. "You were very fortunate to have your parents send you there!"

"Yes, though at eight I found it hard to appreciate it." He reached for another sandwich from the platter.

"You were sent across the ocean at eight?" Hare looked at Mr Thompson with renewed interest.

"Yes, to the Preparatory School. My parents thought it best I adjust early."

"You must have missed them terribly." How strange they had that in common. Being ripped out of their home, transported to a whole new world.

He looked up at her for a moment without answering.

"Do you visit?"

"I haven't been back since. And then my sister came here after she met Bertie, which meant I wasn't completely bereft of family anymore" he replied. Then, after a pause, as if he felt the need to explain himself, "I do correspond with my parents, of course."

"Correspond indeed!" The Baroness said, coming in through the door. "If we got two letters a year from you, we were lucky!"

"Good morning, Posy," he said without looking up.

"And how is Brandon?" she asked. She sat down next to her brother and cast a critical eye over the breakfast foods on the table. "He was being so tiresome at the ball. I take it he has a new hobby." The Baroness picked on a strawberry. "Well, this too shall pass, as they say. If he hadn't been so obliging to Edwina, I was in half a mind to kick his shin."

Mr Thompson lifted his eyebrow at Hare, who chortled, then covered it up with a fake cough seeing Miss Bonningham's expression. The old schoolmistress looked ready to faint.

"Miss Walker was just telling me how much she enjoyed Brandon's opinions," Ernest said to his sister. His eyes didn't leave Hare's face, which irritated her. It felt very much like a test, one she didn't intend to fail. "She found them edifying, I believe."

Lady Winchfield's hand paused halfway up to her mouth. "She *did*?"

"I don't think I used that word, Mr Thompson." Hare's mouth quirked. "I believe I said your friend's opinions were interesting. He certainly speaks on the subject with great passion."

"If with little knowledge, yes."

"Ernest!" Posy looked horrified. "That is absolutely not what Miss Walker meant!"

"Certainly not!" Miss Bonningham added. "Your friend's conversation left nothing to be desired and we hope you will pass on that Miss Walker would happily enjoy a great deal more of it!"

"Aunt!" Hare was horrified. Anne's desperation, while understandable to her, would doubtless appear vulgar to Lady Winchfield.

"I will be certain to let Brandon know of your sentiments, Miss Walker." Mr Thompson leaned back and added, "I'm certain there's a lot more *interesting* things for you two to discuss."

The man was mocking her. Hare tightened her fingers around a napkin, dearly wishing it was Mr Thompson's neck. "I wouldn't dream of presuming that the enjoyment might be mutual. I'm not accustomed to imposing on others, as I quite simply don't have the need to do so."

"Edwina, hold your tongue." Miss Bonningham was getting redder by the minute.

"Not at all, Miss Bonningham." Mr Thompson put a hand on his chest and bowed his head. "I'm afraid I was being rather rude. Of course, Brandon shouldn't assume Miss Walker will be available for conversation, no matter how long he might wait to seek it out."

"But she will be, of course!" Miss Bonningham glared at Hare, daring her to disagree.

"You're too kind." Mr Thompson nodded, disgust written plainly on his face. He stood up and leant over, planting a peck on the top of Lady Winchfield's head. "I will be going now, Posy."

"But you have only just arrived!" she objected. "You haven't even spoken with Bertie yet."

"Small mercies." Hare could swear she heard Mr Thompson mutter under his breath, before he said, loudly this time, "I must go back to the office. I have work to do, you know."

"But will I see you for lunch?"

For a brief moment Mr Thompson raised his eyes to Hare, before looking away. "I don't think so. I will eat at the club. It's closer."

"And you remember we're hosting a dinner tonight?" Posy grabbed her brother's sleeve, thus effectively stopping him from leaving, lest he was willing to wrestle with her in front of her guests.

"I'm busy, Posy." He groaned.

“So are we all,” she said. The Baroness seemed to have a grip of steel, Hare noted. “But if you don’t come, Brandon won’t come and then he’ll miss out on the opportunity to bore us all into an early grave. We can’t be having that, can we?”

“I’m not Brandon’s nursemaid, you realise.”

“Then should we turn our minds to the matter of *your* matrimonial plans or the lack thereof?” Lady Winchfield smiled sweetly at her brother. It was the first time Hare noticed a similarity between the siblings. Though the Baroness had a milk-and-blood complexion, with blue eyes and blond hair, so unlike in colouring to her dark eyed and dark-haired brother, there was the same kind of determination in her gaze and an expression about her mouth, which instantly marked them as relatives.

Now, as Lady Winchfield turned her hawkish gaze on her brother, Hare noticed with pleasure how much he squirmed under it.

“I will come,” he said with a sigh.

“But of course you will! *And* to Lady Leicester’s ball as well, naturally.” His sister let go of his sleeve with a grin once he grunted an acquiescence. “Now, don’t forget to pomade your hair this time. Bertie will be here and he’s still talking about the scandal of your loose cravat from the picnic last year.”

Mr Thompson groaned. He turned and gave a curt bow to Hare and Miss Bonningham. “I will take my leave now, before my dance card gets filled.”

“We look forward to seeing you tonight,” Miss Bonningham said. Hare made an unintelligible grunt. He could divine whatever he wanted from that.

CHAPTER 9

The dinner was spectacular. No other descriptor seemed to fit. Dish after dish after sumptuous dish was carried out and placed in front of the expectant guests. No fewer than twenty-five people arrived in the afternoon, warmly welcomed by the Winchfields. The Baroness wore a gold-thread gown, which trailed behind her as she walked. The fabric seemed to change colours as she moved through the room, no doubt a small magic performed by her Welsh modiste. Hare wondered how much it cost the seamstress, to strain to the limits of her power every day. She must have been tremendously powerful before her summoning.

The Baron's impeccable black tailcoat sat over the fashionable striped trousers and his white waistcoat had the bottom button already undone, doubtless in anticipation of the meal. He seemed in an exceedingly good mood, making snide comments to his mother and wife about any guests whose appearance failed to meet his high standards. There weren't many of those, however. His wife wouldn't have allowed it.

Hare watched it all with interest and couldn't help but make comparisons in her head. Though her memories of her previous life were blurry, there were certain things she remembered. The food in her old home had so much more flavour, the colours were brighter. The music softer and more nuanced. She searched the faces of the bound serving folk for similar signs of recognition. They all avoided her gaze. She was thankful for it. It was a boon. The servants here were taught to be invisible. Should any pay any particular attention to her, it would draw dangerous glances from the humans. Her hand flitted to her hair. She'd dulled its colour, ever so slightly, removing the sheen that might have been too obvious in the light of the candles. Her ears were as round and smooth as any girls' in here.

As the guests began to arrive, Hare assumed the languid, serene expression Miss Bonningham had insisted on and smiled politely at each new introduction. There were quite a few gentlemen who'd arrived with a sister or mother, conspicuously unattached, yet politely keeping up the balance between the sexes.

"There's been a fair bit of clamouring for invitations, I'll have you know!" Miss Bonningham crowed this morning, as she helped oversee Hare's preparations. "Now you make sure you don't discourage any of them in case the Duke doesn't pan out."

And now, in her pale blue dress, too low-cut and too tight for comfort, Hare fluttered her eyelashes and smiled at the weak jokes, as her hand was lifted in greeting again and again.

"This, Miss Walker, is my good friend, Viscount Thomas Culross." Lord Winchfield ushered a stocky, moustachioed man of about forty to the front of the line. "He'd been keen to secure an introduction."

"I'm enchanted, Bertie, simply enchanted." the man's moustache twitched. He took Hare's hand and raised her knuckles to his lips. She fought down revulsion, as his thumb gently stroked her fingers, the gesture hidden by his face. She tried to extricate herself, gently pulling her hand away, but she realised he was holding her firm. She smiled, as was expected of her.

"I'd been unfortunate in arriving too late at the ball some nights ago. I was quite put out at finding your dance card already full."

"I'm... sorry to hear that..." Hare said through her teeth. The man was still not letting go of her.

"Now, I'm rather put out myself, Tom, truth be told," The Baron said, smacking the Viscount on the back. "I'd have thought Posy would have the sense to secure you a dance or two!" He wagged a finger at his wife, who stood a few paces away. Lady Winchfield took in the scene with a pinched expression, which told Hare the omission was intentional. She found herself unexpectedly warming to Lady Winchfield. "Anyway," the Baron droned on, "A better companion you won't find, Miss Walker. Posy almost sat poor Tom at the far end of the table, but I have your back, I made sure he'd be sat right next to you!" He leaned forward with a confidential air. "He is a smart man for horses and hounds, my friend here. Make sure you ask him about his hounds."

"Miss Walker can talk of whatever she likes, Bertie. A girl as pretty as that could discuss ship building and make herself no less enchanting," the Viscount said, already pulling Hare by her hand. "If you'll let me escort you to your seat, Miss Walker."

"Lord Culross." A voice came behind them. "A surprise to see you here."

* * *

ERNEST WATCHED Miss Walker's face as she looked at Brandon over her shoulder. There was a look of pleasure on her face, though it was hard to say if she was more happy to see Brandon, or to have a reprieve from Culross' company. Watching the white-knuckled grip the Viscount had on her hand, Ernest had figured on the latter.

"Miss Walker had promised me a seat by her side tonight."

Brandon smiled broadly. "We've a great deal to discuss, you see, as since our last meeting I'd promised to do some more research on the fine points of art history, which I'm now keen to consult her on. I'm sure you won't mind."

"Well, I—" Culross grew as red as a beetroot, his chest puffing up with indignation.

"Miss Walker, I'm glad to see you so well this evening." Ernest offered her his arm, effectively forcing Culross to let go of her. "As the hostess' brother I feel it my duty to escort you to the table." She laced her hand through his arm, Brandon stepping in between her and Culross, cutting off the access.

"Thank you," she whispered, once they were out of earshot.

"Don't mention it," Brandon said. "As payment you can entertain me with your conversation."

"If you can get a word in edgewise, that is," Ernest said.

"I'll rally," she said, laughing. She had a nice laugh.

"I was in two minds if we should rescue you, I admit," he said.

"Is that so?" Brandon pretended to be offended. "I had no doubt in *my* mind. I wouldn't leave a dog I liked in that man's company."

"Oh, I'm given to understand he likes dogs," Miss Walker said. "And horses. But as I'm neither, I'm rather glad to have made an escape."

"But you see," Ernest said, rather unwilling to concede the point, "Miss Walker is not the type who likes to be rescued." She reddened at the words.

"I think it best to not be in a position where a rescue is necessary," she said. They had come into the dining room, which was already filling up with people. "But I am not so picky as to object to it." She shot Ernest a warning look.

"Very wise," Brandon said. He shooed away the footman so he could pull out a chair for Miss Walker, then sat down next to her. "Ernest, where do you think you are going?"

Ernest, who was about to take his usual seat closest to the door, looked back. "To my seat?"

"And leave Miss Walker's left flank open to attack from the Vicious Viscount? I think not!" Brandon put a hand to his heart. "I'm surprised at you, man! Rally the defences!"

"The 'Vicious Viscount?'" Hare snorted. "Somewhat melodramatic, don't you think, Your Grace?"

"You shouldn't call him that," Ernest said, before he could stop himself. Miss Walker turned back towards him and narrowed her eyes, ever so slightly. "I mean..." He could sense her annoyance, sensed he deserved it and yet the words tumbled out all the same. "It's the lower classes who address a Duke in this manner. You're not familiar with the conventions, but it marks you as being in a lower station. You should call him 'Duke'..." He trailed off, flustered at her stare. Her blue eyes had a dark line outlining the iris, a mark he'd noted even as her gaze seemed to cool, her eyebrows raised high. She wouldn't tell him how rude and patronising he was, he realised and that made it more biting, somehow. It was as if he'd marked himself as below her notice. And she knew it too, knew how much worse it was to be ignored by her.

"I think we could avoid the difficulty altogether, if you'd agree to call me by my Christian name," Brandon said, clearing his throat. "I think I'd much prefer that, truth be told." Ernest sucked in a breath. He saw Miss Walker's eyes rest on him for a moment and he struggled to compose his face. Why should it bother him, after all?

Miss Walker turned towards Brandon, effectively turning her back on Ernest. "I think that's a rather lovely, if a not entirely proper, idea." She cocked her head to the side and a wisp of her dark hair escaped from the bun on her head, coiling along the column of her neck, drawing Ernest's eyes lower, to where the line of the evening gown hugged the body, just across the shoulder blades. A sudden desire to pick up that strand, to feel its silky texture between his fingers intruded on his thoughts. He pushed the compulsion down, his back tensing, as if everyone around could read his thoughts. As if *she* might know them.

Brandon lifted Miss Walker's hand, a mischievous smile stretching his lips. "I'm sure there'd be no impropriety. My friend's rather awkward suggestion has merit, after all."

"Really?" Miss Walker cast a dismissive glance over her shoulder. "How so?"

"We English do put excessive stock by titles." Brandon was staring into Miss Walker's face, his own irritatingly close to hers. "Should you be kind enough to call me Ben, but I were to continue addressing you as Miss Walker, surely it would mark me as what I am…"

"Which is?" She chuckled.

"Your faithful servant, of course." Brandon planted a kiss on her knuckles.

Ernest turned towards his plate. The first course had been served, which he'd been too preoccupied to touch and now the footman was about to replace it with the soup course. But Ernest preferred to pay attention to his plate, rather than to Brandon's flirtation with Miss Walker. Except it was impossible to ignore her. She was sitting too close. Warmth emanated from her skin, her bare shoulders. Her elbow rested on the table. It was so close to Ernest's hand. He imagined moving his hand a little to the right. Two inches, that'd be enough. He could then pretend it was an accident, that he didn't intend to touch her at all. Plausible deniability. He tightened the grip on his spoon. It was ridiculous, he was being ridiculous.

"Thompson?" Brandon's voice managed to pierce through the fog of Ernest's thoughts and he realised with a start that his friend had addressed him a few times, leaning so far back in his chair he looked like he was about to fall over.

"I'm sorry, was lost in thought."

"Glad we found you, then." Brandon laughed. "I was about to ask if you're looking forward to this evening's entertainment."

"What is it, do you know?" Miss Walker asked. Asked Brandon, that is, pointedly so, even though it was Ernest who was the hostess' brother.

"It's a seance, or a Tarot reading, something of this kind," Brandon said. "Very fashionable these days. Thompson will know more."

"A seance?" Miss Walker turned her face back to Ernest, her curiosity overpowering her earlier irritation. "Who is going to perform it?"

"Perform is right." Ernest shrugged. "My sister hired someone's mythic who lays a claim to supernatural powers."

Miss Walker stiffened visibly. "And you're sceptical, of course," she said. Her impossibly blue eyes focussed on him with an expression of... disdain? "In spite of all the wonders hum—people get to witness all the time? The marvels of the other worlds we access?"

She was goading him, but he couldn't resist. "Why 'of course'?"

"I simply don't see you thinking of the metaphysical as occupying the same high perch as yourself." Miss Walker lifted a glass of Madeira to her lips.

As the glass touched her skin, the red of the wine cast a shadow on her bottom lip, turning it dark cherry for just a moment. He swallowed hard.

"I don't see myself as occupying any sort of perch in the first place. I'm not a chicken." He said, trying to use a carefree tone. He sounded childlike to his own ears, like a boy whingeing to be seen. "And I don't pretend to be above anyone much."

"Then how do you explain your penchant for talking *down* quite as much as you do?"

Brandon, ever uncomfortable at being left out of conversation, even one as tense as this one, cleared his throat. "I'm sure the unfortunate impression my friend has managed to make on you, Miss Edwina, will haunt him in the coming days more than any ghost we're likely to encounter tonight."

"That is certainly something to be grateful for, *Ben*." The playful emphasis she put on the word nearly made Ernest choke on the soup. Of course, Brandon delighted in it and prattled on, flirting outrageously with Miss Walker. Of course he was delighted. Why wouldn't he be. Ernest would be delighted in his place.

Miss Walker and Brandon chatted on as if Ernest wasn't there, as course after course appreared on the table. The fish and the roast and the game and by the seventh course Ernest felt like his bow tie might strangle him. He would fall face first, dead, suffocated among the grapes and the steaming meat and nobody would even notice.

* * *

HARE WAS UNCOMFORTABLY aware of Mr Thompson's presence to her left. The man was eating sullenly, like it was he who'd been aggrieved. He wasn't important, she reminded herself. The important thing was to continue her conversation with the Duke —Ben—she reminded herself, who was delightful and charming. Miss Bonningham kept casting approving glances in Hare's direction all evening. If Anne didn't feel the need to intervene, then it meant Hare was doing well. And in the end, she did manage to enjoy this. Not the husband hunting, perhaps, but this conversation. It was light, breezy, unhindered by any difficult emotions. It was just so pleasant. Ben Brandon was *pleasant*. It sparked a memory of something, deep in the recesses of Hare's mind. She glanced at the servants here and there. The mythics, all chosen for their roles based on how agreeable and human-like their appearance was. Most were common folk, mostly Finnish, she thought. There was one among them with skin shining like amber and hair curled and black. *A* djin*? It couldn't be!* But, she supposed, the humans knew as much as they were told. And a *djin* would not tell a truth where a lie would serve just as well. They likely thought he was some common fairy, completely unaware of the power that rested in his hands. The *djin* could feel her eyes on him and met her gaze for one moment, before again fixing his eyes on the wall, a small smile dancing on his lips. Hare noticed the thread on his wrist. It was faint, thin, fraying. She forced herself to look away from it. Humans couldn't see the binds they put on their slaves. She must not give herself away. Ben made a joke and she laughed, half with him, half at how unaware they all were. How great a power the *djin* must have had in his world… That now he had enough of it left to slowly chip away at his chains. She was glad of it.

The conversation between her and the Duke flowed easily. *Too* easily, perhaps. She barely had to pay attention. It was all fluff, a sugar-puff of an exchange. Such as she enjoyed before… She shook her head, to shake out the thought. It was important to focus on the now and *him*. Hare liked the man, in spite of all expectation to the contrary. If only he had better taste in friends. Now Mr Thompson dug into the food behind her with a sort of grim determination, like he would punish the meal for his own lack of grace. She wished he would just go, else she would have preferred him to be unpleasant and condescending *all* the time. Rather than the incessant see-sawing between this intelligent, interesting person and the one who seemed to judge her every move. It was unsettling. Made her want to be in his company and strangle him, all at the same time.

The food itself was lovely, of course, but so absurdly plentiful that Hare felt guilty for not being able to finish it all. Which, of course, was rather the point. The waste, the excess, were intentional. The food wasn't there just for the guests' enjoyment, it was there to show off the hosts' status and wealth. She understood that and yet hated it as well. It was hard to remove herself from the girl she was just a few months ago. After Samuel had left her, plunged her back into the despair he'd promised to raise her from forever. She thought herself so clever, so savvy then. She had already lost everything, she thought, when she was taken from her home. Even her memories of the other world slowly became clouded till they disappeared, pushed out by this place, this Earth. So jealous a world it could not countenance a stranger's memory. She was suspicious of Sam when he first approached her. But he had the sense to woo her before he bought her. Giving her the illusion of choice. And so for all her experience it was easy in the end. For him to convince her he loved her, that he'd care for her, marry her maybe. Convince her she was safe.

Well, she knew better now. Feeling safe was not the same as being safe.

"I think we're being called for the entertainment part of the evening," Mr Thompson interrupted her thoughts. She looked up, startled and met his eyes. He had a curious look on his face, his eyes fixed on hers, like he was analysing her for a drawing.

"Miss Walker!" A voice carried across the table. "Would you indulge me—"

"Shall we go?" Brandon had already secured a place by Hare, threading her hand through the crook of his elbow. "We shouldn't miss the fun."

"Yes," she said, pretending not to hear Viscount Culross' increasingly urgent tone, as he jostled the other guests to try and approach her. It was extremely chivalrous of Brandon to escort her away to safety, but Hare didn't fool herself he did it out of any special affection for her. Not yet, anyway. Maybe not ever. But she suspected Ben was the kind of man who valued entertainment above affection in any case. And that his interest was not easy to keep for long, so she needed to secure him before it inevitably shifted away from her.

She beamed at him. "Are you much of a student of the metaphysical, then?"

"I used to be, a while back." He shrugged.

"That was two interests before the geological society," Mr Thompson added. She noticed that, in spite of her snubbing him throughout dinner, he still had the decency to block Culross' view of her. "I seem to remember you were very intent on speaking with your French great grandmother."

"There's another 'great' in there." Ben raised his chin with a playfully haughty expression. He turned to Hare and lowered his tone to a conspiratorial whisper. "My great-great-grandmother was a girl during the French revolution. The family story goes, she knew where her family had buried their jewels. But…" He shook his head. "Since she was the only one of her family to survive, after marrying and moving to England she had developed a terrible fear of ever returning to her homeland. She would never in her lifetime disclose the location of the treasure, lest some of her descendants would be tempted to go back to retrieve it."

"How horrible!" Hare raised her hand to her lips.

"Oh, she was fine in the end," Ben shrugged. "She was rather happy with her English husband, my family claims, even if she did think him rather uncouth."

"In any case, it's not like you actually needed the jewels," Mr Thompson interrupted.

"Ah, but the adventure!" Ben laughed. "Where is your sense of adventure, man!"

"I have plenty of it." Mr Thompson paused by the door to the drawing room, gesturing for Hare to pass through first. "I just don't need to prove it by travelling abroad to dig around for a treasure which had been either invented or long since uncovered by the locals."

"Do you see what I have to contend with?" Brandon lifted his eyes up to the ceiling and shook his head.

"An abominable lack of curiosity!" Hare laughed. She cast a glance at Mr Thompson, who stiffened at her words. *What did he have to be upset about?*

But her attention was quickly diverted, for the blue drawing room of the Winchfield House had been transformed for the evening. The curtains were drawn, so that no orange glow from the street lamps could filter through. A large number of candles was strategically placed about the room, surrounded by red and purple flower arrangements. Ivy was hanging off the chandelier and the smell of incense filled the air.

"It's like a fairy grove…" someone whispered.

Hare winced at the words. She looked around, forgetting for the moment who she was with and why she was there. It was pretty, very pretty even. A strange approximation of how humans imagined the lands they'd kidnap their servants from but which they themselves could never visit. Eerie music came from beyond the room, a single flute's notes adding to the atmosphere. She smiled, recognising the tune as one she'd heard in the before time.

The small hairs on the back of her neck stood up and she became aware of someone's intense gaze. She turned around and saw Mr Thompson, who, instead of looking around the room like the others, was staring at her, a smile on his face.

"What?" she asked. She coloured, realising too late how rude it must have sounded.

He leaned forward so that she'd be the only one to hear him. "It's the first time I've got to see you like this."

"Like what?"

"Like you're not thinking of people watching you."

She tightened her left fist till her nails dug into the soft flesh of her palm. The discomfort, even through the gauzy fabric of the gloves, helped her focus, to shutter her expression. "I'm not sure I get your meaning, Mr Thompson." She forced herself to meet his eyes, which in the low lighting seemed almost black. His lashes were long and dark, almost like a woman's. She became annoyed at herself for noticing that. For noticing him at all, or anything about him. So she lifted up her chin and said, "People are *always* looking at me." Then she turned away from him and towards Brandon, to make it even clearer how irrelevant the solicitor's words were. "Ben, what do you think is going to happen now?" She was aware Mr Thompson was staring at her still, but she would not look at him again. He clearly took pleasure in making her feel self-conscious, like she was a silly girl waiting for his guidance and advice.

"What I *hoped* might happen is my great-great-grannie might finally make an appearance," Brandon said, winking at her. Winking was progress, Miss Bonningham would enjoy hearing of it. "But what is *likely* to happen," he continued, "Is a session of tarot reading in polite company. Which, considering *my* companion." He brought his elbow a little closer to his body, effectively giving her forearm a squeeze, "Is probably the more pleasant option on balance."

"More pleasant than the prospect of a treasure?"

"Ah, but it's not just about the treasure, it's who your partner is in the search of it!"

* * *

ERNEST COULDN'T BELIEVE BRANDON. The man was ridiculous. He might as well announce his engagement there and then. A few more whispers and the vicar might just as well be booked in. Brandon leaned towards Miss Walker to say something, bringing his face so close to her ear, that the air from his breath moved the wisps of the hair curling above her neck. Ernest held his own breath, feeling like his stomach was gripped in a cold vice. He clasped his hands behind his back, feeling like he didn't trust himself to not push his friend away.

Before he could ruminate on the unwelcome thought, a

hooded figure entered the room, followed by Posy, who could barely contain her excitement at the theatrics. She looked at Ernest, who rolled his eyes. Walking past him she jabbed a finger into his stomach, so sly that nobody noticed. She liked a show, his sister.

And now the hooded figure sat in a large velvet chair by the window, her arms straight up and the hands gripping the edges of the armrest. A murmur rolled through the room, as the guests stared with an excited anticipation.

"Welcome, honoured guests!" The figure said after a moment. She lifted her hands to raise her hood in a practiced motion, exposing her face to the dance of candlelight and shifting shadows. Her skin was polished wood, her hair willow twigs covered in long soft leaves. A *nymph,* he supposed, brought from the Mediterranean at a great expense. He wasn't very familiar with this type of a mythic. Miss Walker stiffened when she saw the fortune teller. He noticed, though he couldn't imagine why. "It is my pleasure to bring to you the secrets of the other world, but beware!" the fortune teller raised one finger. "For the secrets, once revealed, can never again be hidden. And though I can glean the future, it is not within my power to change it." Ernest winced as the woman looked around the room with a satisfied smile. Her lips were stained a very unnatural red tint and she had lines of black kohl around her eyes, making her look hawkish in the dim room. He had the uneasy feeling the creature was laughing at them. And could he blame her really? What wonders was she pulled away from, to now spend her days and nights on such cheap theatrics? All for the amusement of her captors. He couldn't begrudge her a small private mockery.

"My name is Otithéleis and it be my pleasure to meet with you this evening. I will require a volunteer to begin. Any soul here brave enough to look into the unblinking eyes of fate?"

Ernest shifted his gaze from the performer and once again he found himself looking at Miss Walker. The young woman had clearly put in the effort to appear relaxed, but there was a bend to the neck and a tension to her shoulders that showed her to be on edge. She turned her head slightly towards him, till he was in the periphery of her vision. But she wouldn't look at him directly. And he suddenly wanted her to. The desire to be noticed rose up like a wave and before he could think it through, he found himself saying, "Madame Otithéleis, I believe Miss Walker would enjoy a reading!"

Miss Walker spun around and stared at him, the surprise ripping off the mask of indifference. He grinned at her. It might have been childish, but having her annoyed at him seemed suddenly so much more preferable to being ignored.

"Very well. Approach, Miss Walker." Otithéleis exaggerated way of pronouncing the woman's name made Ernest snort. He covered it up with a fake cough, which wouldn't have convinced anyone, much less Miss Walker, who stared daggers at him. But resistance was futile, for Otithéleis reached a hand towards Miss Walker with a flourish, the bracelets on her arm jingling as she did so. "I will require your hand."

Miss Walker approached the palm reader as if the *nymph* was a foam-mouthed squirrel. She sat in the chair next to Otithéleis and slowly pulled on each finger of her right glove, pulling it off her forearm in one smooth movement. Ernest watched in fascination and felt the urge to remove every other man from the room, so that none of them could watch her, as she stretched out her bare arm and placed her hand in the other woman's palm.

The palm reader leaned forward and ran her thumb across her palm. "Yes, very nice," Otithéleis drawled. "I see great sadness in your past, Miss Walker."

"Her parents died not long ago." Posy's urgent whispers carried across the room. Ernest wondered if his sister was aware that whispers were technically supposed to be quieter than shouting. But something like a shadow passed the young woman's face. Her eyelashes fluttered. Ernest's lips tightened to a line. If Posy had given the performer this information, then he would have a word with her. Surely she must have known how uncomfortable it would be for Miss Walker to hear.

"A great sadness. A great disappointment as well." The *nymph's* shrewd eyes were upon Miss Walker's face, trying to decipher the small hints of emotion written there. The wood creature patted Miss Walker's palm, the gesture uncomfortably intimate. "I see you travelled far to escape it."

Miss Walker's eyes shot up, a strange expression crossing her face.

"But the future, Miss Walker, the future is bright!" Otithéleis smiled broadly. "You will make a model fiancée for a very, very lucky man!"

Something in Miss Walker's eyes shifted and she withdrew her hand, a little too stiffly. "Thank you, Madam Otithéleis, that's... thank you." She stood up and turned to the guests. "I think that's enough fortune telling for me, I prefer to end on a good note." She smiled, a little too broadly. The other guests started jostling to get to Otithéleis, each eager to hear a pleasant little lie about their own futures and none of them seemed to notice how Miss Walker moved, with a strange awkwardness, away from the fortune-teller's velvet chair. Too late, Ernest noticed the candle, sitting precariously on the side table, as Miss Walker backed into it.

As the flames licked the perfumed silk of the artificial flowers on her waist, Ernest was already in motion, taking off his jacket. Before anyone else even had the chance to notice, before Miss Walker herself voiced the fear which had widened her eyes, he pulled her away from the candle, smothered the fire with his jacket, wrapping it in one swift movement around her.

She looked up at him. She wasn't scared, he noticed with surprise. She wasn't scared at all, but he was. He suddenly realised he still had his hand about her waist, his singed jacket now trailing on the floor. He peeled his fingers away.

"You seem determined to keep saving me, it seems." She found her voice first. She made sure to add an edge to it.

Was she mocking him? A wave of irritation flowed through him. But it was stilled by her hand, which found the edge of his sleeve. "Thank you," she whispered. Her hand felt warm on his wrist. He could feel her fingertips through the fabric of his shirt.

"It seems my brother is the hero of the evening!" Posy's voice broke the spell. Someone started clapping. Like it was a roadside show. Just another part of his sister's dinner entertainment.

He ground his teeth and, reluctantly, looked away from Miss Walker. "It's always a pleasure, Posy!" Ernest grinned, the very image of a debonair hero. He bowed with a flourish to the sound of the guests cheering. Not because he enjoyed the attention, but because it would distract the Baron's guests from Miss Walker and the strange intimacy of how he touched her, of how he looked at her.

"Seeing as I'm now less than appropriately dressed, I fear I must remove myself from the gathering." He pointed to his ruined jacket and moved towards the exit.

"Oh no, you don't!" Posy was quicker.

So close.

His sister was unstoppable. "You are staying here tonight. Bertie will have an old jacket to fit you."

The realisation dawned on him. He was going to be trapped here. Posy never met a ridiculous scheme she didn't like, and he had delivered himself right into her hands. "I think I should really…"

"Nonsense." Posy waved away his complaint. "You're not going anywhere in this state, not after your heroics. We must make sure you are well! What kind of a sister would allow her brother to go off alone after he nearly burned to death, saving her guest no less!" Miss Walker looked at Ernest over his sister's shoulder, catching his eye. He reddened at how ridiculous his sister was making him out to be.

"I'm absolutely fine—"

"I think you're right, Lady Winchfield," Miss Walker piped in with a smile.

Traitor.

The damned woman continued, the picture of innocent concern, "I've heard smoke inhalation is quite, quite dangerous." She was clearly enjoying this. An impish grin stretched her lips.

"Smoke inhalation?!"

Posy nudged her husband, who finally found his voice under the haze of the drink he'd consumed. "Indeed, dear chap, you *must* stay!" Winchfield patted his stomach, as he liked to do for comfort. "Mr Tallow, find my brother-in-law something to wear, don't just stand there, man!" he called out to his butler, who, until called upon, had seemed to melt into his surroundings.

"If you please, Sir." The butler held the door open for Ernest.

"I'm not sure I please at all," he grumbled, going through.

The servant said nothing, though a strange twinkle lit up his eyes, before his face once more became passive.

Ernest sighed, even as he heard his sister behind him, "And, of course, dear Brandon, you will drop by in the morning? To check up on your friend?"

CHAPTER 10

She couldn't sleep.

The clock down the hall ticked as loud as the church bells and, combined with the creaking of the old house, Hare felt like she might as well attempt to sleep in the middle of a village fair. She'd tossed and turned for two hours since everyone went to bed. She knew it was two hours because the damned clock announced it. How could anyone sleep through that?

She sat up in her bed, pushing her hair out of her face. It'd been braided for the night, as usual, of course. But she never slept still and so her hair would slip out and fall around her face within moments of laying down. It had always been so. Hare wondered briefly how some women were capable of just going to sleep and waking up in the same position. Or else falling asleep with loose hair and not wake up with it caught in their armpits and mouth. Of course, the point was moot, at least at the present moment, because there was little chance of her actually sleeping.

The clock's ticking was a funny thing. She hadn't even noticed it the first few nights at the Winchfield house. But once noticed, it was impossible to ignore. *Much like one other thing.* She pushed the thought down. She let her feet slide to the floor.

She might not have been able to fix the thoughts nagging at her ever since the events of the evening. But she *could* do something about that clock!

She shivered. The air was cold beyond her covers. She didn't have a shawl with her, a shawl being unessential for the purpose of her visit to London. Nobody would see her in a shawl and so it'd be a waste of money for Anne to provide her with one. A corner of Hare's lips twitched, as her hand slid along her nightgown's fine, *thin* fabric. That was considered important, on the off chance an entrapment turned out to be the more practical choice in the husband-hunting. But not a shawl. Shawls were for comfort.

Miss Bonningham had actually forbidden Hare from bringing her own. Not fine enough, evidently.

Luckily, the blanket from off the bed would serve the purpose. She wrapped it around her shoulders, enjoying the way the solid woollen fabric was the promise of imminent warmth, even if she didn't feel it just yet.

Where are you heading, my deceptive mistress? The *domovoy* stretched and yawned at the edge of her bed.

"Be more respectful, cat." She smiled in the darkness.

Did I offend you? The creature purred and jumped off the bed. *You can always set me free, so I trouble you no more.*

"In time, cat, in time." She stroked the *domovoy's* back.

She briefly considered lighting an oil lamp, then decided against it. The whole house was asleep, so she didn't need to keep up the pretence of poor night vision. And a glow from the lamp might creep under the doors she would pass. She looked around her room, bathed in the moonlight streaming through the window. It was a small, but beautiful chamber. Perhaps she might have one just like it for her own, one day soon. She walked towards the door.

She listened for a moment. No sound of footsteps carried

across the hall. Only the damned clock, tick-tocking the night away.

She turned the handle, the metal chilling her fingers.

Hurts, does it? The *domovoy* chuckled, as it wove its way around her legs. *You hide it well, but I feel it as you do.*

"No," she lied. The touch of iron would always bother her, but it no longer had the power to truly hurt her. A poor exchange for her magic and memories, but this world was full of poor bargains, and of fools who'd take them. Slowly, she opened the door. It didn't creak, though she'd half-expected it to. That was what happened in the stories, wasn't it? The heroine betrayed by an unoiled hinge. But then, she reminded herself, she was no heroine, but rather the villainess of her own story. There was no shame at the thought. It was rather enjoyable, the power it gave her; the sense of control.

Hare tiptoed down the dark hall, passing a number of doors, the *domovoy* trailing behind her. It was a strange comfort to have him with her. She would have to speak to Miss Bonningham about releasing him. *Domovoys* bound themselves to those they sought to protect. To bind them against their will was somehow a double betrayal.

Mr Thompson was sleeping in one of those rooms.

It was an unwelcome thought. She thought of how quickly he was at her side, smothering the flames before she'd even noticed them herself. He smelled like cloves, wasn't it ridiculous that she'd noticed. She didn't want to notice him, or his smell, or how dark his eyes were. He'd helped her, much like any man in a similar position would have. She refused to feel indebted to him. He did the decent thing, because what was the alternative? Let her light up like a torch and burn the house down with her?

Besides, the man seemed determined to make the most inappropriate comments, telling her how to speak, how to address people. Everyone knew her as an American, so what did it matter that she didn't do things the English way?

So why should she care the rude man was sleeping in one of those rooms, under the warm covers.

The small hairs on Hare's neck stood up. She was cold, that's all. Thinking of warm beds and warm covers made her wish for her own. It made sense, of course, in the way the Baroness' ridiculously transparent schemes usually did, to keep Mr Thompson in the house. Now Ben would come in the morning, giving Hare the opportunity to better ensnare him. She winced at the word, crossing her mind unbidden. Brandon was rather a lovely man really, if somewhat on the silly side. He deserved somebody who would want him for himself. But few ever got what they deserved, wasn't it the way of things? And if she had to trick and bring disappointment to one decent man in order to secure her safety, then so be it.

She was pulled out of her thoughts by the towering shape of her clock in the drawing room at the end of the hall. The door had been left open, perhaps by a servant who'd not yet learnt that carelessness was not tolerated by those rich enough to bind them. But that was beside the point, really. At least Hare would benefit. After all, asking for two sets of well-oiled hinges in one night would have been greedy.

She stepped into the room and froze.

For there, kneeling by the clock's open underbelly, was Mr Thompson, his head inside the machine itself.

He hadn't noticed her. If she was quick and quiet, perhaps he wouldn't. But she found herself frozen into place, staring at his back. He wore only his shirt and breeches and must have been cold, for she saw goosebumps on his forearm. His very nicely muscled forearm. She swallowed. If she was noticing the man's forearms, it was certainly a sign for her to leave.

Her bare foot slipped backward over the carpeted floor, as soundless a step as only the folk could make. But then the dratted *domovoy* pushed ahead of her and purred. Mr Thompson snapped his head towards her and attempted to stand at the same time, banging his head hard on the clock. He folded down like a pen knife, falling onto the floor.

Hare rushed towards him, pausing just as he sat up at her feet, groaning. Groaning was a good sign. Groaning meant he was alive and awake.

"Miss Walker?" He rubbed his head, staring up at her. "I'm afraid you have me at a disadvantage." He reached towards her and she realised he expected her help in standing up. A natural gesture, really. It would have been rude to refuse.

She braced her feet and helped pull him up.

"What are you doing here?" he asked, focussing on her face. She noticed his eyes watered from the blow.

"I—" she stopped and pointed. "Same as you, I expect." They both looked at the huge ungainly clock, now gratefully silent.

"That clock belonged to the late Baron, I hear." Mr Thompson looked up at it.

"Is he 'late' because of its infernal ticking, I wonder," Hare said.

"Did you just make a joke, Miss Walker?"

She reddened.

"You *did*." He laughed.

"It wasn't *that* funny." She shrugged and looked away from him.

"No, it certainly wasn't."

She snapped her eyes towards him.

"It was a terrible joke." He grinned. "I liked it."

Hare bristled. "You must have hit your head harder than I thought."

"Perhaps." He raised his hand to his head and winced.

"You should put ice on it."

"It's fine."

She shook her head. "It is most certainly *not* fine. Come, I'm sure a kitchen in a house such as this has a sizeable ice box." She turned towards the exit and started walking. As she was about to cross the door into the dark hall she paused. "Where is the kitchen?"

He chuckled. "It's fine, I can find it myself." Suddenly his face fell and he leaned against the wall.

"Nausea?"

"Not at all," he said through gritted teeth. "Now, go along to bed."

"You expect me to just leave you here, concussed?"

"I expect you to know what's good for you." Mr Thompson's face turned an interesting colour in the candle light. He waved towards her. "And I expect you to know that being found in your night gown while conversing with a man is decidedly not good for you or your *prospects*."

Was she mistaken or did he put an undue emphasis on the last word? Hare's fingers tightened around the blanket. He was right, of course.

"Do you intend to take advantage of your sister's guest?" She turned her head to the side.

He looked stricken. "Of course not!"

"Well, then I can't very well leave you alone to possibly pass out on the floor, can I?" She smiled and held the door, gesturing for him to lead the way, but not before shutting the door in *domovoy's* smirking face. That seemed to affect him not a bit and the creature was soon padding next to her. *You do realise I'm a house spirit, right?* Its thoughts rang in her head. *What exactly did you think a shut door was going to do?*

"Let you know your company is undesired?" Hare whispered.

The cat spirit just gave her a contemptuous glance. *You forget, Mistress, you have bound me to you. I can but follow.*

Right. The damned thing was laughing at her and she couldn't blame him, not really.

* * *

Ernest's head was pounding. He shouldn't have allowed her to remain in his company, not like this. His sister would have his head if she found out about it. But something about Miss Walker made him think she was unlikely to be swayed once she'd made a decision. And, truth be told, he wasn't entirely certain she wasn't right here. He probably shouldn't be left alone. Though ,if he were to drop dead from a bleed on the brain, then it would be a doubtful comfort to know there'd been witnesses. Death from a collision with a clock would be a dumb way to go. They walked slow, she shuffling behind him, the large blanket wrapped around her shoulders. It must have been cumbersome, for every now and again she'd stop and readjust, careful to remain covered. Ernest found himself wishing her hand would slip, just a bit, once more exposing the curve of her shoulder. He reddened at the thought, suddenly grateful for the half-dark. She glanced at him, as if reading his thoughts.

They descended the long staircase to the kitchens in silence. The narrow passage was only used by the servants and so lacked the carpeting and the decoration of the floors above. But it felt reasonably warm, strangely so, perhaps still holding the heat from all the cooked dishes of the prior evening. Which was just as well, as he realised her feet were bare. She curled her toes unconsciously once she stood on the tile flooring of the Winchfield kitchen.

"There must be an ice box somewhere," she said, looking around, her brows furrowed. "Aha!" She practically hopped and rushed towards a big cabinet at the edge of the kitchen.

"How can you possibly tell?" he asked. It looked just like a cupboard to him.

She rolled her eyes and opened the lower compartment, where sat three melting ice blocks. She moved as if she'd try to pick one up with her bare hands, causing the blanket to slip off her shoulders. Ernest caught a glimpse of the wide neckline, framed by a simple wide frill. Miss Walker glanced at him, probably to reassure herself he didn't notice and he pretended to be very interested in his shoes. The cat spirit that always hung around her made a noise in the back of its throat and Ernest couldn't help but feel it was laughing at them. It made him uneasy. As far as he was concerned any ordinary cat would have been more desirable than this foreign thing, a malevolent intelligence gleaming in its golden eyes.

"Can you take one block and put it on the floor?"

He was happy to have a task, for he really couldn't be expected to make conversation when she was just there, her collarbones showing above the blanket. He wasn't sure he understood himself. What did it matter if he saw her collarbones. After all, her dress last evening had been far more revealing. But in here, alone with her, there was something dangerously tempting about the small glimpses, the image they hinted at.

He placed his candle on top of the ice box and lifted one of the blocks from the open drawer, placing it on the tiles. It occurred to him how ridiculous the situation was. That he was simultaneously the patient here, apparently unwell enough he required her presence and the one lifting the heavy ice blocks. And by the way she reddened, he'd bet the same thought must have occurred to her. And yet they both upheld the fiction of this being somehow necessary. Because without the fiction, the reality was they were both standing scandalously undressed, scandalously alone in the darkness.

"I need something to shave the ice off." Miss Walker breathed on her fingers to warm them up. He noticed, from his crouching position, how she unconsciously rubbed one foot on top of the other, trying to warm her toes. The woman grabbed a rolling pin sitting on the worktop and suddenly whacked the ice block, chipping a bit off.

Ernest brought a hand to his face, instinctively protecting his eyes from any chippings which might have gone flying in his direction. He raised his eyebrows at her. “Is blinding me part of the therapeutic process?”

“It could be...” she mumbled under her breath.

“You know, well-brought-up English ladies do not mumble threats,” he said, placing the ice back in the box’s drawer, while she wrapped the chippings in a cloth.

“I’m not English and neither am I a lady,” she said, passing him the cloth with ice. Seeing how he seemed unlikely to drop dead, he thought it was redundant, but he obediently placed the pack to his head, as it was, after all, the only viable excuse he had for continuing this conversation.

“But you want to be,” he stated the obvious. Her eyes shot up to meet his, a shrewd expression crossing her face, so quick he almost missed it. “You want to be one of them: English and a lady both.”

“It seems you are rather focussed on the former. Why?” she turned her head and leaned back against the wooden worktop. He couldn’t explain why it bothered him that she didn’t contradict him.

“Because I know what it takes to survive among the people here. And I know what it takes to thrive.” He tensed his shoulders. “And I know the difference between the two.” Nobody could have been more surprised than him at the honesty of his answer.

She regarded him for a moment, her face betraying nothing.

“Do you thrive then?” she asked, simply. “Among these people? In their world?”

He almost told her the truth. But the truth was unpleasant to voice, so he settled for half of it: “They accept me. I’m more than the ‘funny foreigner’, because I know how to blend in, till they forget I wasn’t born here, that my family doesn’t own land somewhere in Surrey or Hampshire.”

"And you think it's because you mask your accent? Because you have memorised the forms of address and all the rest of it?" She walked up to a chair and sat down, lifting her feet so she could place them inside the blanket trailing around her ankles. "Not because your sister married a title?"

"I've been here a long time, remember?"

"I admit I don't." She brushed one finger across her lips and looked to the side. She was lying. But why would she bother to, about such a small thing. It irked him, she was trying too hard to convince him of her indifference.

"There's some truth to what you say," he admitted. "Titles matter a great deal here, though not as much as they used to. But a title of, say, a Duke, still carries weight."

She snapped her head, suddenly alert.

"But you know, Brandon isn't *just* a Duke." Ernest scratched the back of his neck. "He's a decent man. A friend. And he deserves to be seen as more than his title."

"And he is," she replied, her tone guarded. "You'd have to be blind to not see that."

"Do you like him?" Ernest asked. "I mean, really like him?"

She watched him for a moment. "As much as I can after a mere two meetings. He's funny and clever and I feel comfortable and safe around him, which is saying a lot." She shrugged. "Pretending money and title don't matter would be ridiculous. But I feel he'd be likeable even without the two."

It wasn't the answer he'd hoped for. If she'd professed herself madly in love, Ernest would have felt confident in seeing her as a simple title-chasing chancer. Her honesty made him uncomfortable. He realised with a start that he didn't like her feeling too comfortable around Brandon. As she swung one foot under the chair, he thought he didn't much care for her feeling too comfortable around any other man.

"Why were you so startled by what the *nymph* said?" he asked suddenly.

She leaned on the table, her fingers working at the fraying edge of her blanket. "I wasn't."

"You backed up into a lit candle."

"There were too many candles."

He chuckled, backing off for a moment. "Yes, that is true enough."

"In any case, it's late and you seem well enough. I think it best I go back to bed before we risk being found." She stood up and tucked her hair behind her ear.

He held his breath. He had pushed too much and the spell was broken. She was going to leave. He searched for something to say. It was suddenly imperative that she stay. "So, you're fond of art?" *Fond of art?* He could have kicked himself. As if mirroring his thoughts, she raised her eyebrows, a mocking smile twisting her lips. Even the cat spirit at her feet opened one eye and regarded him with cool judgement.

"You want to discuss art in the middle of the night? In your sister's kitchen?"

He would have been happy to discuss the growing patterns of moss and lichen if it would keep her in the room with him for a few more minutes.

"I just want to know more about you." He reddened. "In case it comes up. You know, when I speak with Brandon." *God, how he loathed himself.*

"I am *indeed* fond of art, then." She was laughing now, though she tried to hide it. It lit up her eyes. She must have thought him a fool.

"You're very knowledgeable about it." He stared at his shoes. "I heard you speak, you know. You must have had a very clever governess."

"I attended classes…" she trailed off and suddenly reddened. "I'd better get back now. I should probably get some sleep." She turned towards the door.

He had upset her. Taking a step towards her, he thought of a way he could apologise. He wasn't sure what he ought to apologise for, but he supposed it didn't matter. She looked upset and flustered and as there wasn't anyone else around to blame, he was happy to accept it to be his fault. She stood so close to him now.

She looked up at him, her eyes widened. They reflected the light strangely and he found himself staring. Ernest forgot the words he meant to say and just watched her. If he reached towards her, he was close enough to touch her now. It would have felt so good to touch her, which was why he wouldn't, of course. He put his hand inside his pocket to avoid the temptation.

The moment of silence stretched between them, where he searched for the right words and found nothing. Which was probably for the best, considering his powers of conversation seemed somewhat reduced that evening. His mouth went dry at the sight of her, the dark hair wild about her head, her body hidden by the coarse blanket, her hands gripping the edges of it to her. Her mouth opened and he couldn't tear his eyes away from her lips. She smelled like roses. He wondered what she would taste like.

He hesitated and moved his hand up, slowly, giving her the chance to move away. She watched him like a small animal, alert.

His knuckled brushed against her jawline, just a feather-light touch.

* * *

His hand touched her skin, leaving a hot trail. There was no question as to what she should have done. But her feet, she found, were planted quite firmly on the floor.

She leaned into his hand, knowing she'd regret it. There was a danger there and she couldn't pretend she didn't know exactly what kind. Hare focussed on his face, his unbearably handsome face. Had she noticed his lips before, dark and full like a woman's? What business did a man have having lips like that? She made an effort to meet his gaze. A slight crinkling in the corners of his eyes told her he noticed her staring. She felt a flush rising up her skin and was suddenly grateful for the itchy blanket, which she pulled up higher to hide her neck, which in a moment would become red and blotchy.

He took half a step towards her.

"Mr Thompson..." she said, not certain if it was an invitation or a warning. She supposed she could plausibly deny either.

"Do you think you could...?" He swallowed and raked his fingers through his hair, as he seemed to consider his next words. "My name is Ernest."

"I'm not sure..." The words came out as a rasp, so she cleared her throat. She was just thirsty, is all, she should have some water. She swayed gently and tilted her face up, telling herself it was only to see him better. Certainly, it wasn't so that their faces would be closer. So that his lips would be closer. *What the hell was she doing.*

"No, I don't suppose it is proper." He leaned forward. Something changed in his expression. "But I would like you to call me that anyway." There was an urgency in his voice. A doubt and something else Hare couldn't decipher.

"Ernest?"

The word was barely out before his lips were on hers. She leaned into him. A low growl rose in his throat which sent a shiver down her spine.

His hand moved up her neck and sank into her hair, pulling her closer. He felt so warm and so safe and... He wasn't safe at all. He was the opposite of safe. He threatened to destroy everything. She was an idiot. Not again. Never again.

Hare jumped away, as if scalded. The cold air rushed between them and she felt it like a lash across her exposed neck. She stared at him for a heartbeat, marking the confusion in his heavy-lidded eyes, the way his chest rose with a held breath, his lips. For a second she almost went back to him, to feel him against her again.

"Edwina..." he spoke the name and the spell was broken. Because it wasn't real and neither was any of *this*. She turned on her heel and ran, leaving him alone in the kitchen.

CHAPTER 11

Hare paused for a moment on her way up to listen for his footsteps. He was still there, downstairs, probably still leaning against the wooden worktop. Perhaps he was giving her space to return to her room. An unwelcome image of him standing there in nothing but his shirtsleeves and britches popped up in her head. With an irritated grunt, she pushed a lock of hair out of her eyes.

It was too close.

It was too close and she would be damned if she let herself repeat her old mistakes. Squeezing her hand tight till her nails dug into her palm, she continued the walk towards her room, desperately aware of how the skin on her jaw tingled, like an itch you can't scratch. If she could stop thinking of his hand on her face, then she could pretend it never happened.

She entered her room, just as cold and empty as she left it. Sliding into the once-more-cold sheets made her suck in a breath.

Hare pulled the blanket under the sheets and closed her eyes, cocooned in its scratchy fabric. A noise kept ringing in her ears, but she couldn't blame the clock this time. She held her fingers to her chest and tried to steady her breath, waiting for the mad rhythm of her heart to once more find its regular pace.

She shouldn't have let him touch her. A touch was a claim of sorts, with this kind of man, wasn't it? A kiss even more so. She squeezed her eyes shut. He didn't know her. He didn't want *her*. He'd have recoiled if he knew what she was. Or, if not, he would have thought her a plaything. Something to claim and discard. But she was *protected* now. Shrouded in the kind of propriety he had to respect. He wouldn't repeat the kiss. He probably already felt regret at his actions.

A wave of sudden disappointment at the thought hit her in the chest. It was easy to pretend it was relief.

The morning came at long last. It found Hare wide awake, staring at the ceiling. A servant girl knocked on the door and brought in a jug of steaming water. She curtsied, waiting patiently as Hare washed herself, before helping her to put on her undergarments. The girl was a plain sort of *pixie*, with her greenish face and needle-sharp teeth. Her hair was kept tight under a snow-white cap. This propriety of the English amused Hare. The *pixie* likely knew no clothes but the spring spider webs before she was bound. She walked stiffly in the many layers of starched respectability forced upon her. Like the others, the *pixie* could see Hare for what she was, yet pretended otherwise.

Like a large living doll, Hare stepped into the chemise, the pantaloons, the corset, corset-cover and finally the petticoat: a layer after layer of enhancements and decorations. So much effort went into beautifying all that was unseen. Hare sighed, feeling lucky Miss Bonningham didn't insist on the bust and derriere padding at least.

"Is everything alright, miss?" the *pixie* servant took a half step back. "Did I tie it too tight?" Something in Hare's chest squeezed at how this *pixie* had been trained to listen to every sound her employers made, to anticipate their wishes and to readily accept the blame, should it be unfairly aimed at her.

"It's nothing," she smiled, trying to reassure the girl. "They call you Bess, is it?" They both knew that wasn't the *pixie*'s real name, or even the name she'd been called by before.

The girl coloured. "They call all of us 'Bess', miss.."

Hare narrowed her eyes. "Do they now.."

"You can call me Bess, if you prefer, miss." The girl spoke quickly, ready to appease.

"Where are you from?" Hare said, carefully.

"Blackpool, miss."

"That's not what I meant."

The two looked at each other.

"The Ivy pathside. One of the lower courts," the *pixie* said. "I remember. It was lush and the wild roses bloomed all winter long." She stared at Hare for a long moment. "You know it?"

Hare shook her head. The *pixie*'s face dropped.

"How long since you've been summoned?" Hare asked.

"Long enough so that my wings grew dry and brittle." She pointed to the folded and covered bundle on her back. "I will never fly again."

"You don't know that," Hare said, her voice cracking.

"The string is tight, miss," *pixie* said, pointing to her wrist. "I cannot pass like you do and I have no glamours to change my face. I will not get away. But we are all watching you."

"You are?" Hare didn't know what to say. Of course they did. Some with jealousy, maybe, some with hope.

The servant called 'Bess' smiled. "Take them for all you can, miss."

"I intend to." Hare wondered if it was true. Anger and intent were not the same.

"'Tis a good trick, miss. A very good trick." Bess nodded with appreciation. "I used to be tricksy in the time before. I'd bargain your eye for a cup of milk, I could. But I forgot most of my tricks here."

"I see." Hare's lips tightened to a line. "What did they call you? Before?"

The *pixie* smiled, her needle teeth gleaming white. "Anou, miss."

"Thank you, Anou. I will remember."

"Even when I don't anymore?" A challenge in the question. A boon asked. Hare nodded and the *pixie* left her alone once more. This was a reminder. Nothing was truly yours if someone could just take it away. And Hare was determined not to let anyone take anything of hers again. Mr Thompson would best learn that too.

AFTER THE MAID LEFT, Hare looked for the string, ever hovering around the air. She tugged on it.

You called? The *domovoy* appeared, as he usually did, suddenly, as if the walls and doors were less of a barrier than the air he breathed. There was annoyance in his voice. Hare couldn't blame him. She remembered what it felt like. The tug of the binding.

"Do you remember what your life was like, Maletki?" She looked into the amber eyes. "Before?" She used the *domovoy's* name. His kind didn't guard their names as others did, but she made sure to say it with respect nonetheless.

The *domovoy* regarded her cautiously. *Some. Less each day.*

"I wonder if it's a small mercy," she said thoughtfully. "If we can't go back, at least we might forget what was lost."

The *domovoy* jumped up onto the dresser next to her, his silver fur flowing as he did so. *What do you want of me?* There was tension in the thought.

"Give me your paw," she said.

The cat spirit eyed her suspiciously. *I'm not a rabbit. My foot will bring you no luck.* In spite of the derision in his voice, he obeyed, lifting one paw for her to touch.

"Don't be stupid, cat." She focussed on the string. "I've never done this before, you understand. "

Nothing happened.

Maletki was watching her, hopeful.

Try again.

"Maybe I should say something?" She wasn't sure how the bindings worked. "Maybe 'Be free!'" They waited a moment. Nothing happened.

"Wait!" Why hadn't she thought of it before. She looked in the drawer of her dresser till she found what she was looking for.

She put the papers in the fireplace and put a match to it.

She watched them burn then turned around. "Maletki?"

The *domovoy* was gone, the binding broken.

Thank you. She heard the voice in her head. It sounded like a purr.

Hare smiled. That was one wrong righted at least.

CHAPTER 12

Ernest came down for the breakfast early. He had an appointment that afternoon and would have to leave soon, if he was to make it to the office. But he listlessly picked at his food, half-listening to the Dowager Baroness, his eyes firmly on the door.

"And there he is, the candle-hero!" Brandon came through the door, tossing his coat to the footman, before sitting down at the table. "How are you feeling this morning?" He raised his eyebrows. "I've been told I absolutely *must* enquire after your health, you see!" He bowed his head at the Dowager. "Lady Winchfield."

"And you can see as well as I that he is very well indeed." The old Lady Winchfield tapped her tea cup with her index finger. A footman approached in a flash and poured the woman more tea. "You might show the same solicitude towards your elders, you know. Duke or no, some rudimentary manners ought to remain." She waved her hand in the air. "But nobody cares for an old woman. It's the way of the world, I suppose."

"*I* care for you, Mummy," the Baron announced cheerfully, as he came in through the door, his wife on his arm.

"Ah, but you're one in a million, Bertie!" the Dowager said, though she was clearly pleased. "Now, but where are Miss Bonningham with her charge?" She turned towards Ernest and leaned towards him. "Now Anne is a *delight*. How a charming woman like her has lived to be six-and-fifty without a man snapping her up—" she snapped her fingers to demonstrate. "—that really speaks ill of your sex."

Ernest made a non-committal noise, since an answer was not exactly required. He'd himself failed to see the charm which Miss Walker's aunt was described to have such an abundance of.

Brandon caught his eye and wiggled his eyebrows conspiratorially. Ernest looked away, ashamed, his thoughts taking him back to last night. It was a mistake. In the moment, he thought she welcomed his kiss, but he was clearly wrong. He would have to apologise, of course. She must have thought him the worst kind of man. His best friend was courting her, rather openly so. And she welcomed it. A blind man could see she welcomed it and here Ernest was, almost ruining it for her. For Ben. But perhaps they could pretend it hadn't happened. A midnight kiss is easily denied. He hadn't compromised her. *But he wanted to*. Ernest batted the thought away.

"Where *is* Miss Walker—" Brandon looked at Miss Dowager "—and her lovely aunt?"

"Miss Bonningham is laid out with a headache this morning," Posy answered him. Ernest imagined it had something to do with the amount of wine imbibed by the old schoolmistress the night before. "I imagine Miss Walker will be down momentarily."

Brandon lit up at the words, making Ernest feel like the worst friend on Earth.

"Do you have any plans this morning?" Posy directed that at Brandon, as she swirled her spoon in the teacup. She always ladled the drink with more sugar than it could possibly absorb, to then energetically swish the spoon in an act of unwarranted optimism. "Only the weather's been so pleasant—" Ernest looked doubtfully at the window, beyond which the heavy dark underbelly of the clouds was just about visible. "—that we were planning on a walk in Hyde Park."

"Posy, I'm sure the Duke has better things to do than go on silly walks with a group of gossiping women," the Baron said, crumbs falling out of his full mouth. "I was about to suggest he join me at the club."

"The club in the morning?" the Dowager piped in. "Surely not! You can go in the afternoon! After you escort your mother and wife to the park. You wouldn't let us go alone. Who knows what might happen." She leaned in towards Ernest. "It's the way of the world, you know, though the young seldom think of such things."

"Very well, Mummy." The crestfallen Winchfield nodded like a sulking child. He glanced at Brandon. "Perhaps you'd consider coming with us then?"

"You mean, to accompany 'a group of gossiping women'?" Posy said archly, putting one dainty morsel in her mouth.

"I didn't mean it like *that,* Posy." Winchfield leaned towards his wife, who would no doubt make him pay for his mistake later. "You're just the sort of woman any man would count himself lucky being around."

"And don't you forget it." Lady Winchfield allowed herself a small smile and patted her husband on his hand.

"Well, I'd be delighted to come for the walk," Brandon said, winking at Ernest. "Being the indolent sort, really, I find myself with oodles of time."

"I hardly think you indolent." Everyone at the table looked towards the door. "Not with all the interests you're pursuing."

Ernest's jaw went slack. Miss Walker walked into the breakfast room wearing a blue morning skirt and a white blouse. The latter, buttoned up to the chin and draped down in small pleating, followed the contours of her body in a way which, while covering every inch of her skin above the wrists, was very efficient at suggesting the shape of the curves beneath. A little black bow at the neck made Ernest think of a parcel of biscuits, tied with a string. Simple and yet tempting beyond measure.

Miss Walker smiled brightly at Brandon, who stood up and pulled out a chair next to himself. She ignored Ernest completely and sat down next to the Duke, who immediately proceeded to monopolise her attention.

"I'm very glad to hear you'll be joining us this morning, Ben." Miss Walker's hand hovered dangerously close to Brandon's, as she fiddled with the silverware.

"If I'd known this had been planned I would have brought my sister." Brandon leaned towards her. "She's been dying to meet you."

"Yes, dear Anastacia is always welcome here," Posy piped in. "How come we didn't get to meet her at the ball? She's well, I hope!"

"Ah, yes!" Brandon smiled. "She is very well. She's been visiting a relative in the country. A productive visit, I'm told, for she's bringing with her a fiancé, I hear."

"A fiancé!" The dowager Baroness looked up. "Well that's a surprise!"

"It was rather a shock for me as well, believe me, Lady Winchfield." Ben smiled fondly. "And he's Miss Walker's compatriot as well!"

"Indeed?" Posy looked to Miss Walker. "What's the name? Perhaps they might be acquainted?"

Miss Walker opened her mouth as if she was ready to say something, but Brandon cut her off. "I'm afraid I can't tell you!" Brandon laughed. "Anastacia sent me a quick message. I will supposedly 'love him when I meet him' and she did go at length about how handsome and dashing and elegant he was. But such trifling details as his actual name were not included." He turned to his right. "Miss Walker, this must seem extremely strange, but once you meet my sister, you will understand."

"I'm very much looking forward to meeting her. I'm sure we

will become good friends." Miss Walker looked warmly at Brandon. It was frankly quite sickening, Ernest thought.

"I'm sorry I can't join you all this morning," he said, unasked. "I've work to attend to."

Her eyelashes fluttered, but otherwise she gave no sign she even heard him. Ernest tightened his lips into a line. It was like last night didn't happen. Perhaps she wanted him to pretend it didn't happen. He wasn't sure he had it in him, though, even though moments earlier this had been his plan as well.

It fell to Brandon to acknowledge his friend. "You'll be missed, Thompson." Which was possibly the worst thing for him to say, as from the way he looked at the prettily blushing Miss Walker, it was clear that he would barely notice Ernest's absence.

"I've never been to Hyde Park." Miss Walker pulled a little piece of the crust off the roll on her plate. "I hear it's quite beautiful this time of year." She placed the morsel in her mouth, her sharp white teeth flashing for a moment. Ernest forced himself to look down at his plate.

"I'm glad to see you looking so… refreshed this morning, Miss Walker," he said. She couldn't very well ignore *that,* could she? She would surely at least look at him.

And she did, a polite, insincere smile stretching her lips. So unlike the girl from last night. "A quaint way of putting it, Mr Thompson. I'm not quite sure how to take it. I look 'refreshed' as opposed to my usual dishevelled and crumpled state, I presume?"

"That's a daft thing to suggest, Ernest!" the Baron, who seemed to wake up to the conversation, looked up, mortified. "As if any guest under our roof would be anything but perfectly turned out!"

"I didn't mean…" Ernest looked to his sister for help, which was not forthcoming. Posy seemed to enjoy herself immensely.

"What *did* you mean, Mr Thompson?" Miss Walker narrowed her eyes.

"I think we best not match wits with Miss Walker, Thompson!" Brandon laughed. "I for one am impressed by anyone who can make my solicitor friend here run out of words!"

"Is your assumption that Miss Edwina's goal is to impress you?" Posy teased the Duke.

"Goal? No. I wouldn't dare presume." Brandon inclined his head towards Miss Walker in a way that implied exactly that.

The room was suddenly unbearably hot. Ernest put down his fork and stood up. "I really must be going now, Posy. I thank you for your and Bertie's hospitality, but I mustn't be late."

His sister seemed startled. "Already? I thought you said your first meeting was at noon?"

"Yes, but I've things to do before then." He hesitated, feeling everyone's eyes on him. *Everyone's but hers*. "Urgent things," he added lamely.

"We mustn't keep Mr Thompson from his important work, Lady Winchfield." Miss Walker looked to Posy. "I imagine a walk in the park must seem quite a silly waste of time for one with such a busy schedule."

"I don't believe I ever said that." Irritation rose in his chest. She wasn't even looking at him. *Why wouldn't she look at him?* "I wish I could join you, but, like I said, I have work."

"I'll still see you for lunch, Thompson?" Brandon called out as Ernest was collecting his coat from the footman.

Ernest could think of nothing he fancied less than eating a lunch to the accompaniment of Brandon waxing lyrical about Miss Walker, but he grinned and confirmed the appointment, as if the whole breakfast hadn't been the most irritating meal he'd taken in recent memory.

CHAPTER 13

Hyde Park was extremely busy, in spite of the rather underwhelming weather. Hare and Brandon walked together, sandwiched between the Baron, his wife and the old Lady Winchfield walking arm in arm with Anne. Miss Bonningham, who roused herself after hearing The Dowager Baroness had requested her company, was deep in conversation with the older lady, though every now and again Hare felt Anne's steely gaze drill into her back.

The many servants, whose sheer numbers allowed the upper classes to conduct their lives in luxury and comfort, took the smaller paths, or else trailed behind their employers, carrying refreshments, or pushing prams. Most servants were human, of course. But then many were not. Always apart from their human counterparts, the mythics performed the mundane tasks with a fleetness and grace no human could match. The threads that bound them, invisible to their masters' eyes, crisscrossed in the air. So many. Hare's fingers passed through them as the group walked on. Many of the mythics noticed her, yet none would betray her with either word or action.

Hare reminded herself, as she half-listened to her companions, to notice her kind. To never stop noticing them. What mattered her small deceptions in the face of this crime? Of so many ripped from their homes, bound to servitude and loneliness.

She forced herself to pay attention to the man beside her. There was no question, of course, what the real purpose of the walk was. It was not to admire the leafy path running alongside the pond, or even to enjoy the wholesomeness of the exercise. It was to be *seen*. And seen they were. Hare smiled at so many members of London's high society that her cheeks ached. In her "career" as an art model, Hare was used to having eyes on her. But this, this was entirely different. Brandon seemed entirely oblivious to it. Perhaps he was used to the attention. She imagined it came with the title and the position. It felt strange, still, to think of him as simply "Ben", not Duke, or Brandon. *Or a mark.* The unwelcome thought came. She steeled herself against him. The trick, after all, was not as substantial as all that. He knew she was not an heiress, like so many gilded American debutantes flooding London. If he'd offered to marry her—and that was a substantial if—then he offered on the basis of her looks and how pleasant she was. And the former was a fact, uninfluenced by the money in her purse and the latter… It's not like she intended to suddenly make herself *unpleasant*. She could make it work, if he'd let her.

She was *determined* to make it work. She thought back to the morning and the shame she had felt at Mr Thompson's abrupt departure. It was imperative that she put him in his place and his place was to be far from her. If only he could be simply *friendly*. Was it really so hard? She could be friendly, if he stopped looking at her like that. Like he would peel the layers of her skin till he saw all she was and what she wanted to be. And then last night he touched her. She could have been his friend if he hadn't touched her. But now she needed distance, she needed space between them.

Her fingertips rose to her lips. She had to run last night. She was scared of what she might have done if she didn't.

"—and this morning I got the telegram; he's coming to London!" Brandon's voice pulled her out of her thoughts

"Who is?" she asked, immediately blushing as he looked at her, amused. "My apologies," she added, too quickly. "I was lost in thought."

"Apologies not accepted," he said, leaning close towards her ear. "Until you tell me what it was you were thinking about that engrossed you so much more than my conversation."

She stammered. She couldn't very well tell him she was thinking about another man's lips. And how they felt on hers.

Brandon smiled. "I do like the look of that blush, though. Perhaps I'd like the thoughts that caused it too." *Thank heavens for male confidence.*

"Perhaps you would," she said, a hint of flirtation in her voice. "But thoughts are private, are they not?"

That drew a delighted laugh from him. "I wish you'd allow me a peek, at least."

"Such access has to be earned, you realise." She hated the falseness of her words, the drawing him in, the promise in them. The invitation.

"And what would you have of me?" he asked, a drawl of his voice familiar and unwelcome. *Necessary*. Wasn't this what she was supposed to be doing?

"I haven't quite decided," she said. "I'll know it when I see it."

"What if I see what *I* want?" There was a tension in him.

She looked up, meeting his sparkling blue eyes. "Then you need only reach for it."

"Miss Walker!" A flock of sparrows rose up at the shrill call, as Lord Culross spotted them from the path parallel to Serpentine and practically ran across the lawn to greet them, hopping over some family's picnic basket.

Noting the horror in Hare's eyes, Brandon leaned towards her and whispered, "Don't worry, you're safe with me."

But are you safe with me? She gave a curt nod to show she heard him, her lips tight.

"Culross! What a surprise to see you here!" Winchfield shook the man's hand. "I thought the walk was shaping up to be a dull affair indeed and here you are to rescue us with some conversation!"

"Bertie!" Lady Winchfield smacked her husband's arm, thus bringing him to his senses.

"No offense, of course!" Winchfield said.

"It is not *such* a surprise, to find me here" Culross said, pulling a handkerchief from his overcoat's pocket. He wiped his forehead, breathing heavily. "I came calling this morning, to enquire after Miss Walker after yesterday's debacle." He nodded to Hare and walked up, trying to crowd out Brandon. "The butler told me where you were and as I had a morning free, I thought you wouldn't mind me joining you for a stroll." He took Hare's hand and bowed over it. She tried to calculate if she could lean any farther back, without actually stepping away or losing her balance.

"You're too kind," she said. "As you can see, I'm quite well." The damned man wasn't letting go of her hand, lingering longer than was strictly speaking proper.

"Culross." Brandon reached his hand out in a greeting, forcing the other man to release her. She warmed inside. He was a good man, Brandon, too good for her trap really.

"Brandon." Culross' eyes barely shot up to the Duke's face, before they once more settled on Hare. The viscount's eyelids were low on his eyes, as he let his gaze linger on her face and neck, allowing himself a quick glance lower still. She felt like she needed a bath.

"Lord Culross." Miss Bonningham approached with Dowager Winchfield. "What a pleasure to see you again."

Hare shuddered, as she recalled her aunt's admonitions from last night. After the party was over, Anne had come to Hare's bedroom, to advise her not to reject any good prospects prematurely. "After all, if the Duke slips through your fingers, a Viscount will do!" she'd told her. What a horrifying idea.

But help came from a surprising quarter, as Winchfield's mother piped in, "Perhaps you'd care to walk with me and Miss Bonningham, Lord Culross? As you see, Miss Bonningham and myself are short on male escorts."

"I rather thought…" Culross looked less than pleased at the suggestion, eyeing Brandon in an openly hostile way.

"Come now, we're blocking the path." The older woman let impatience seep into her voice and, just like that, Hare was saved.

As they continued their walk by the pond, Hare found her voice once more. "You've been very kind."

"Have I?" Ben looked at her curiously. "I rather think I was protecting my own interests."

She coloured. "I think running interference on my behalf is hardly in your own interest."

"No?" Brandon's brow furrowed. He dug in his pocket and pulled out what seemed to be an invisible piece of paper. He mimed reading, his lips moving silently. "I've just consulted my interest sheet and pleasing you appears to have made the list." She chuckled as he turned towards her. "Am I not making a good job of it?"

"Pleasing is a skill," she said with a teasing smile. "Like all skills, it can always be improved upon."

"Then I shall take your instruction in this matter." He pressed his arm closer to his side. Doubtless, in part at least, to irritate Lord Culross, whose eyes Hare felt on her back still. "As we say, in for a penny, in for a pound?"

"I think you're going to be a quick study."

CHAPTER 14

Ernest's morning had been going rather terribly. He had half a dozen contracts piled up on his desk and the distinct lack of ability to focus on any of them. Guardianships, trusts, wills, contesting wills. All the intricacies of human relationships carefully codified and written down in neat black scroll. He loved his work, usually. Simplifying the complex and clarifying the unspoken. It gave him a sense of calm and purpose, which was not easily found in the other aspects of his life. In those documents, whole lives unravelled in front of him. The secrets of births, the loves abandoned, the obligations shirked or fulfilled: all made clear to him.

But there was no clarity to be found there now. Not where it mattered.

He arrived angry at his office, tucked into the corner of Hay's Mews. Over the course of the morning his anger had gradually shifted and transformed into something entirely different (he didn't quite want to admit to himself what). And so he attempted to work through the irritation, the disappointment and the anxiety that somehow *he* was the one who'd messed up. Failed in his obligations as a friend, a brother. And with what? A touch, as brief as a brush of a butterfly's wing. But even in that, he'd crossed the line, he knew that now. She made it clear to him at breakfast. Last night he disrespected her and she was right to be angry. He should have felt remorse. Shame even. After all, she was clearly courted by Brandon. His friend, Ernest reminded himself for the hundredth time. She had clearly showed her preference and Ernest had no choice but to respect that.

And yet, last night there was a moment. Her lips slightly parted, her pupils widened as she looked at him. Like she would have welcomed more, like she was waiting for more. The thought sent a shiver through his body as he remembered the small intake of breath as he touched her cheek. He could have sworn… But it was his imagination. It must have been.

"Mr Thompson, your friend is here to see you." The office clerk peeked behind the half-opened door. Ernest groaned. Brandon. The last person he wanted to see that day.

And yet, see him he must, for lack of a decent excuse.

He pulled on his morning coat and sighed, tightening his cravat. His brother-in-law would have a conniption fit if he heard of Ernest being in town with a loosened cravat. Presumably, Bertie would find Ernest's suffocation preferable.

Ernest met Brandon pacing outside the door, his straw hat still on. He was in a terribly good mood, meaning the walk in the park with Miss Walker was a success, which did nothing to lift Ernest's spirits. He didn't want to think of Brandon having a good time with Miss Walker.

"I've work to do, you know." He grumbled, but followed the grinning Duke nonetheless. "I have an appointment in less than two hours."

"Your appointment is in four hours." Brandon gave him a side-eye. "Mr Woods assured me we have plenty of time."

"Mr Woods talks too much." Ernest narrowed his eyes.

"Which begs the question, of course, why you'd seek to cut our lunch short." Brandon brought the handle of his umbrella to his chin, looking up in a mock-thoughtful gaze. "A more insecure man might even feel hurt."

"If I tell you when my appointments are, you always make me late for them. If I tell you my appointment is in two hours, it will be three before you release me."

"Nonsense. It's barely a ten minute ride to the Atheneum in any case. We can eat there and you'll be back in plenty of time for your meeting." Brandon raised his umbrella at a passing hack.

Ernest groaned.

Brandon turned towards him. "You cannot mean you would abandon me at such a crucial turning point in my life?"

They climbed inside the hack and the driver clicked his tongue at the horses.

"Well," Brandon drummed his fingers on the side of the hack, "aren't you going to ask me about the momentous decision to which I refer?"

"You've spent your morning with Miss Walker," Ernest said, trying to sound bored. He looked at the people in the street as the hack rolled by. "Therefore I assume it has something to do with Miss Walker." He didn't trust himself to look at Brandon.

"It does." Brandon sat back in the chair, his umbrella held between his legs, his hands folded.

"Am I to congratulate you?" Ernest asked, ignoring the heavy feeling in his chest.

"Not yet! Oh, I don't mean you, man!" Brandon said the latter to the hack driver, who almost let the horses pull them past the club. He turned to Ernest. "But I think she's amenable."

"Of course she is. You're a Duke and miraculously not an impoverished one. You have most of your teeth and all of your hair. A rare breed," Ernest said, jumping out of the hack, as Brandon paid the man. "And she not an heiress. She couldn't do better and she knows it."

"I like that she's not an heiress."

They entered the club and handed their coats to the servant, before climbing up the carpeted stairs to the coffee room. Ernest usually enjoyed the club, with its white columns and mock-Greek statues. It was a club for men of substance, as it styled itself. And Ernest was rarely as gratified as when his membership was approved. It was a silly conceit, really, but it gave him a strange sense of safety, this place. Its library was magnificent and there was always an interesting conversation to be had within its walls.

"You *like* that she's not an heiress." Ernest rolled his eyes. "Your family would roll in their graves."

"Since they would be rolling in their marble mausoleums, I rather think that the lack of Miss Walker's funds would not concern them overmuch." Brandon shook his head. "I'm somewhat of a realist, Ernest."

"I've three unused society memberships that say otherwise."

"In *this* matter, I'm a realist then." Brandon grinned, smacking his friend on the back. "I've money. I'm uniquely positioned among my peers to choose for myself, to please only myself. Others are not as fortunate and I cannot blame them, but I don't have to settle, you see. The laws of probability say a woman might have good looks, intelligence, or money. Two out of three is a rare breed. Three out of three? Almost an impossibility. And since I've my own fortune, I don't have to settle for less than a partner pleasing in other ways."

"You find Miss Walker pleasing?" Ernest asked.

"Don't you?" Brandon's eyebrows shot up in surprise.

"No, of course I do." He thought of Miss Walker's dark hair, falling in messy waves over her shoulders, of a freckle he noticed over one shoulder blade. "She is beautiful. And clever."

"But?" Brandon nodded to a servant, who led them to their usual table by the window. "I feel like there's a 'but' in there."

"While I admire your lack of mercenary motivations, are you certain Miss Walker is free of them as well?"

"What?" Ben laughed then, throwing his head back.

"Do you not suppose her and her aunt's interest in you might also have to do with your money?"

"But of course it does!"

Ernest looked at him uncomprehendingly.

"I'm not an idiot, Thompson. Of course my money has something to do with it." Brandon leaned back and watched Ernest, one hand propping his chin. "So what?"

"You don't mind?"

"Why would I mind? Do you think she doesn't know the qualities that make her so attractive to the male half of Beau Monde?" Brandon smiled. "She's beautiful and though she has a brain in her head, she knows it's not the part men notice first. And if she's to be selected for her looks, why should she not be free to make her own conditions in return?"

"That's very forgiving of you." Ernest accepted the menu and pretended to inspect it.

"Of course, I hope my money isn't the *only* reason she considers me a serious prospect."

"Don't forget your title, the aunt seems very keen on the title."

"And that. I could do without the aunt, to be honest." Brandon made a face over his champagne glass. "But I have one or two unfortunate relatives myself, so who am I to criticise."

Ernest leaned back in the chair. Trying to compose himself. He knew what his friend wanted him to say. It would be natural to ask it and somewhat suspicious not to. But he found he couldn't find the words.

The moment stretched between them.

"Well, aren't you going to ask me?" Brandon cocked his head to the side.

There wasn't a way out of it. "You will marry her?" The words tasted like dust on Ernest's tongue. He took a sip of water to cover for the emotions he worried would show on his face.

"Well, I will *ask* her to marry me first."

"You will marry her. She won't say no." He saw Brandon

brighten at the words and for the first time since he'd known him, Ernest felt jealous. He never was envious of Brandon's looks and position and title. Of his family, who loved and kept him close. But this was different. Ernest hated the truth in his own words. Because of course Miss Walker would accept. And then he would spend a lifetime watching her, happy with his friend. Loving his friend. Touching his friend.

All the small intimacies of marriage, the small looks, the fleeting touch on the arm, all of those Ernest would be forced to witness.

"I'm very happy for you, Ben," he said, even as he felt as if a knife's edge had cut a deep ridge in his chest.

CHAPTER 15

"—And remember not to talk too loud." Miss Bonningham's voice droned on, one admonition after another. "And take your glove off before picking up a biscuit, Lady Winchfield noticed you forgot to yesterday."

Hare listened carefully, wondering whether she'd have the space in her head to remember to breathe, or else if all the additional tasks had the power to override the lower body functions. But she saw there was a new sense of urgency in Miss Bonningham that morning. A sense of foreboding which filled the older woman with a new sense of determination.

"Is there something amiss?" Hare lowered her voice.

The other woman's eyes shot towards the maid, standing in the corner of the room. "You can leave us now," she said. "We shall call for you if you're needed." They both waited in silence till the doors closed behind the young girl.

"You've received a letter," Hare said. Miss Bonningham's eyes shot up in suspicion.

"What do you know of my letters?"

"Only that you got it and that it seemed to fill you with the kind of nervous energy which is bound to get noticed." Hare scratched at the scalp where it itched from hair being pulled up too tight.

"Don't do that." Anne smacked Hare's hand down. "It's ill-bred. Do you want people to think you've fleas?"

"What are you not telling me, Anne?" Hare's voice was low, barely loud enough to be heard. The older woman, usually composed and imperious, flashed a glance at her, one glance which softened Hare's heart.

"My remaining funds back in New York..." the woman's voice broke. Hare waited patiently. "They're frozen or gone, every last cent."

"What's happened?"

"They call it 'irregularities'." Miss Bonningham pulled a letter from the pocket in her bodice and gave it to Hare, who passed her fingers along the broken wax seal and the name at the bottom of the letter. "They're asking for an explanation, as you see. Since I have not made an appearance on the appointed date, whatever I still owned has been liquidated. But," Miss Bonningham seemed to kind of fold into herself, shame and fear written plain on her face, "I don't believe for a second the people involved will just leave the matter like this. Not even with the ocean between us."

"What have you done?" Hare gasped.

"There is no way back for us, Hare, that's all you need to know." Miss Bonningham shook her head and blinked a few times, like she'd try to stop the tears welling up in her eyes. "The school's been in a bad way for a long while. I was squeezed out, on one side by the finer establishment for those honouring the older ways and on the other by colleges opening their doors for the blue stockings. A small school like mine has no place in this bright new world."

"You stole money." A sick feeling went over Hare and she leaned against the wall, fearing her legs would give out.

"I had to make sure the wages of the staff were paid!" Anne shot her an angry look. "Don't look down on me for the rest of what I had to do!" She pushed up her spectacles and Hare noticed the woman used the movement to surreptitiously wipe an errant tear from the corner of her eye, before folding her hands in her lap. The teardrop darkened the tip of the index finger of the woman's glove and they both sat in silence for a moment, watching that dark spot. "I had discretionary access to funds, through the solicitors working for the girls' families. A few forged signatures and you'd be surprised how easy it was to obtain more, especially when impropriety was hinted at. Women are never suspected in such cases. They think us too feeble minded to even notice they're being fleeced."

"Except they *did* notice." Hare raised the letter. "And now you've put us both in an impossible situation!"

"The situation you were in was already 'impossible', as I seem to recall." Miss Bonningham looked at her archly. "You were lucky that I knew enough of New York's high society to catch wind of the gossip regarding your paramour, as well as his actions towards you, or I never would have even known where to find you."

"And I'm grateful that you did," Hare whispered. "And for letting me free… I owe you." She tensed. "You know my kind doesn't say such things lightly." Anne noticed the emotion in her voice and awkwardly patted Hare's hand. Hare was grateful for the gesture.

"It suited us both, girl. You don't owe me for that. I might be a little too direct with you sometimes and for that I am sorry. I suppose…" She sighed. "I suppose there's a comfort in having another soul know all you've done and still be able to rely on them. I'm just grateful that the scoundrel who abandoned you was quite so popular. He did business with every wealthy family in town and so his comings and goings were well known and discussed." She snickered. "The interest rates the man was offering on his investments were so preposterously high, he was proclaimed a genius at every step and so he was welcome everywhere. In any case. The fact remains, we are in trouble, Hare and I don't know how to get us out of it, unless we succeed in snaring the Duke or a man very much like him."

"Perhaps the matter isn't so urgent?" Hare said. "After all, what can the American police do here?"

"The New York police might have no jurisdiction here." Miss Bonningham sat straighter, if that was even possible. "But secrets like this have a habit of coming out. This is our one shot, Hare. Should we fail, there will be no second chances. I have worked my entire life. And I have nothing to show for it. If I'd continued as I was, I would have been lucky to secure the position of a governess or a piano tutor in my old age. And you..."

Hare knew the words were coming, but they hurt anyway.

"You, girl, might be free. But freedom means nothing with no money and no prospects of obtaining it. Your kind are kept as a sign of prestige and status, as well as for the specialist skills you might possess. But you aren't trusted. Who would hire an unbound mythic? You can't go back to your home and you're not welcome in respectable circles. You know the paths open to you lead to one thing and one thing only." Miss Bonningham reached a hand and briefly squeezed the tips of Hare's fingertips, before withdrawing the hand once more. "And I don't want it for you, anymore than I want what's coming for me, should I ever step foot in America again. But that means we cannot get romantic or sentimental about what we're about to do. You must secure a match. And soon. The Duke is handsome and pleasant and he might yet offer for you. But he has dozens of beautiful women, much richer than yourself, buzzing around him. And so we need security."

"What kind of security?"

"At this point the society's already noticed the Duke's interest in you. That might work in our favour, for a gentleman would not allow a *well born* girl's reputation to suffer because of him. But this—" she pointed at the letter in Hare's hands, "—could be a very big problem for us. Few people knew where we travelled. If we've been tracked to the Winchfield house, then the whole thing could unravel before we're safe under your husband's protection." She pinched the bridge of her nose, pushing up her spectacles. "Therefore we have to make sure that if one prospect falls through, another is lined up."

Hare knew what Miss Bonningham was talking about. "No." She shook her head.

"Lord Culross is rich and smitten with you." Miss Bonningham reached over and with her index finger turned Hare's face towards her.

"No." Hare curled her fingers in her lap, bunching up the fabric of her skirts.

"I've looked into him. He was by all accounts a decent husband to his first wife." She hesitated. "As good as would be expected at least." She brushed off an invisible speck of dust off Hare's shoulder. "There's no reason to think he would be otherwise to you. But you mustn't continue discouraging him the way you have. A man, even one as ridiculous as him, perhaps especially one such as him, will only accept so much rebuffing. You must play the game so if one option doesn't work out, you have another waiting."

Hare took a deep breath, but before she could reply the older woman shook her head.

"The comfort of the last couple of weeks is an illusion, Hare. Such as your kind can spin. It will not last much longer. You might have convinced yourself that you have options now. But you don't. Not really, not yet."

"I know that. Don't you think I know that?" Hare stood up and walked to the fireplace, letting her hands trace across the white, subtly-veined marble. "I know what I've committed to. But surely, if I appear to encourage the odious man, then that will raise questions about my devotion to Ben."

"'Ben', is it?"

Hare coloured. "He suggested it."

"That's promising, I'll admit." Miss Bonningham got up from the sofa and stood next to Hare. "But we are both staking our futures on this. We need you to marry a man whose position and title can shield us both. Because if the truth comes out, you can't fool yourself that *Ben*—" she let her voice hang on the word. "—that Ben's feelings for you can outlast the fallout. But an aristocrat would deny to the death the truth rather than admit he'd been duped. Because he knows his social standing can weather it, since all the sycophants will pretend alongside him." She put her hands on Edwina's shoulders. "You must remain clear-headed about it, Hare. We can't afford for you to develop feelings for the man." She paused for a moment, watching the younger woman's face. "Have you…?"

"No!" Hare looked away. "Of course not."

"Good." Miss Bonningham seemed reassured. "Make sure you don't. It would only complicate the issue and hurt you needlessly once he learns to hate you."

"Maybe he won't." She couldn't stop herself. "After all, it would still be me."

"Still you?" Miss Bonningham laughed then. "You've been playing this game for a while now, Hare. You know better than most, that it's not really you they see. This kind of man, he might fancy himself in love with a beautiful, graceful, well-born woman, but it's the last of those attributes that make you a potential wife, rather than just a bed-warmer. The rest of it doesn't matter. Not to any man. Certainly not to a powerful one. Believe me." She tucked an errant curl behind Hare's ear. "It's been my life's work to know what they want. To deliver it to them." She smiled and ran her fingers along the plume in Hare's hair. "Just like I'm delivering you, my pretty changeling."

CHAPTER 16

Lady Leicester's ball was very grand indeed. The hostess, an ageing paragon of good society, seemed made for this new era of opulence and extravagance. Her youth had been spent in the kind of primness and restraint which characterised Queen Victoria's influence on society and Lady Leicester seemed determined to make up for it now, especially as a well-considered marriage of her son had brought in the much-needed improvement to her financial situation.

The decorations were predictably lavish. A fortune in flowers spilled down the bannisters and draped over every horizontal surface. On arrival and after the necessary introductions, Hare was offered a tall champagne flute. It was a rather useful accessory, she thought, as she leaned the top of the cool glass against her lips, wrinkling her nose as the bubbles rose up. It gave her hands something to do and allowed her a moment to scan the crowd, just as everyone there turned their eyes to her.

"Courage, Edwina, dear" Lady Winchfield whispered, taking her arm. The woman was a head shorter, so that all Hare saw when she glanced to the side, was the Baroness' blonde hair, piled up high like a cake. "They will all love you." A strange feeling of warmth spread through Hare's chest. There was no doubt that, for the most part, Lady Winchfield was a rather ridiculous woman. But here she was like a battering ram, spearing through the highest echelons of the English society, forcing them to pay attention. Hare never had such a protector before and it made her warm towards the woman.

"May I?" A young man, whose name had passed by Hare's ears without registering, bowed low, reaching towards her. With a small push from Miss Bonningham, who plucked the champagne flute right out of her hand, Hare found herself led out towards the centre of the dance floor for the first quadrille. She wore a new gown, deep blue with a silver trim, with a skirt made for swishing, the multitude of petticoats whispering as she walked. The dress was tight in the waist and low cut over her breasts, half a breath from vulgarity and yet still staying in the propriety lane. Hare's partner was pleasant-looking and light on his feet and she allowed herself to enjoy the moment, as the couples around them swirled in perfect time. That was the magic of dancing, to forget everything but the movement and the rhythm. To be able to clear their heads of all but the moment they were in. Humans had no true magic at their disposal. And yet, this came pretty close. Hare needed to clear her head. Everyone was watching her. She knew what they expected. So she smiled serenely, like a young and innocent girl might. To give hope, without overpromising and to keep the distance while encouraging.

Once the dance ended, her partner escorted her back to the Winchfields, but not before extracting the promise of another dance later in the evening.

"Very well done, Hare," Miss Bonningham whispered into her ear. "That was exactly the display you needed." And indeed, there were at least half a dozen men now weaving their way across the room, attempting to catch her eye.

"So this is the delightful creature my brother cannot stop talking about?" A pretty blonde, dressed in a rather daring yellow dress, approached the party. The woman was so strikingly tall, that it was only a moment later that Hare noticed Brandon himself trailing behind, an apologetic smile on his lips.

"Miss Walker, if you'll allow me to introduce you to my—" He was promptly waved away by the blonde at his side.

"I'm Anastacia, his sister. It's 'Lady' Anastacia, really, but only to those I dislike, so don't you dare use that title with me," she prattled away, taking Hare's arm, as if they were the oldest of friends.

"Stacia, would you let me finish for once—"

"So Ben was talking so much about you that I just *had* to come to London earlier." The woman's blue eyes were as pale as her brother's, but her expression was quite different, probing almost. Hare stiffened slightly. The last thing she needed was perceptive relatives looking into her too closely. Lady Anastacia continued, "I'm sure we will become great friends, Miss Walker… May I call you 'Edwina'?" She turned her head to the side, looking rather like a curious bird. "After all, I hear you've been calling my brother by his Christian name, which I do think wise. His title definitely goes to his head."

Hare laughed, in spite of herself.

"Stacia, you will exhaust Miss Walker, before the ball has even began in earnest."

Hare's head popped up at the last word and she immediately blushed. Of course Brandon wasn't referencing Mr Thompson's name, what a ridiculous notion. And she shouldn't be thinking of Ernest either. She *earnestly* thought that.

Lady Anastacia observed the blush and misinterpreted, as quick minds sometimes do. "My brother thinks no ball has truly started till *he* has graced the dance floor." She playfully tapped her fan on her brother's shoulder. "*But* if he only cared to look around the room, he'd know that Edwina's conquest of London is already fully underway. But never mind all that," she said. "For I insist we take a turn around the room, just the two of us." She grabbed Hare by the elbow and began walking the outer perimeter of the room. Though 'walking' might have been a somewhat tame way to put it. Hare soon realised that Lady Anastacia only ever marched. Hare had to practically jog to keep up with her.

"I understand your parents have passed, rather tragically," Anastacia said. "I'm very sorry. It must have been an awful shock. And then to be moved to another country altogether and exposed to this." She sniffed contemptuously, "this *meat market* must be unbearable."

Hare was stunned. It was her understanding that it was generally impolite to reference someone's dead family members quite so directly. But perhaps the sisters of Dukes didn't have to follow quite the same set of rules. "It *was* a shock." She thought for a moment, choosing her words carefully. If she stumbled, she was certain Brandon's sister would sniff out any inconsistencies. "I was worried about coming to London, of course, but I was met with so much kindness here."

"Such a well-bred answer." Brandon's sister laughed, attracting the attention of several revellers, clearly hungry for gossip. Luckily, the two women walked far too fast to allow anyone to join them. "I understand my brother has been especially welcoming."

Hare met Anastacia's eyes. "I've grown to consider him a friend, that's true."

"Oh please." The tall woman rolled her eyes. "Like we don't both know my brother is considering you as a wifely prospect. Just as you and your aunt are considering the wider implications of you becoming a Duchess. That's why I came to London, you know."

"I suspected as much," Hare said weakly. The harridan was clearly going to investigate her. To shrink away would be to arouse suspicion, so she had no choice but to put her poker face on. And she had a dreadful poker face.

"Now, don't get despondent." Lady Anastacia waved her hand in the air, as if she could simply dissipate any worries her words might naturally elicit with a mere gesture. "My brother is not a complete booby and I'm inclined to like you. I simply would wish to know you better."

"And I look forward to getting to know you too, La— Anastacia. I understand you're recently engaged?"

"Ah yes, a foolish thing for a woman to do, I know." Anastacia shook her head. "I'm sorely disappointed with myself, to tell you the truth and had half a mind to reject the man outright."

"Why?"

"Any woman who has no qualms about signing herself off into the power of another human being ought to have her head examined." Anastacia made a face. "Yet he wore me down, truth be told. He holds to the same principles at least and promises to use his considerable resources in advancing the cause…" the woman paused and gave Hare a questioning look. "The *causes* I'm interested in. In any case, as we get to know each other better, I'm hoping I can interest you in some of them as well. After all, if we're to become sisters, we should join forces."

"He sounds like an unusual man."

"He does. And handsome as the very devil, as well. I just hope the latter isn't influencing my decision overmuch. I do dislike being misled." Anastacia turned her attention back to Hare. "But let's talk more of you. I understand you've a great interest in the arts and are an accomplished artist yourself."

"I'm afraid your brother is too hasty to ascribe to me accomplishments before they're earned." The room felt suddenly quite hot. "I do love drawing though."

"You must show me some of your art soon," the woman said. "And to my fiancé. He's rather a connoisseur himself."

"Of course. I find I'm thirsty," Hare said, suddenly eager to extricate herself. "I will go to the refreshments room."

"Of course, I'm sorry." Anastacia's eyes widened. "I've been dragging you around the room and you in this beautiful, but—forgive me for noticing—clearly uncomfortable gown."

"I'll be back in a moment." Hare smiled reassuringly and rushed towards the corridor.

After enquiring a footman for directions, Hare walked through a columned corridor. It was too early in the ball for many to be seeking the same direction and so she breathed a little easier. She looked around. The stone floor tiles were black and white, like an enormous chessboard. On a whim she hopped from one to another, feeling like an oversized pawn figure. Leicester's London house was at least twice as large as the Winchfield's and richly appointed, with enormous paintings in gilded frames hanging on every wall. The dowry of the future Earl of Leicester's wife had paid for the necessary repairs, as Lady Winchfield told Hare on the way. Baroness' words were more than mere gossip, of course. They were a reminder, that Hare competed against a clutch of rubber barons' daughters, all flocking to the British capital to secure themselves titled husbands. Hare had to be twice as cunning to succeed without a dowry.

She sighed. It had been clear from the start the whole situation would be hard, but she hadn't prepared herself for the strain of it. Best case scenario, she was going to trick a decent man she rather liked into marrying her, endangering his reputation. The letter Miss Bonningham had shown her helped to underscore the point.

"I must say, I'm rather delighted to find you here, Miss Walker."

Hare groaned inwardly and turned to find Lord Culross' smug face staring at her.

"I'm looking for the refreshments room, Lord Culross." She bowed her head. "Would you be so kind as to point me towards it?"

"Point?" The man feigned shock. "Dear Miss Walker, I would

consider myself no kind of a gentleman if I didn't escort you there myself!" He offered her his arm, leaving her no polite way to extricate herself.

Once she placed her hand on his arm, he brought his elbow close to his body, effectively trapping her.

"I must say, it's such a rare opportunity for us to be able to converse properly, what with those pups always monopolising your attentions."

Hare attempted a smile and made a non-committal noise, as the Viscount practically dragged her along the corridor. "Lord Culross, are you quite sure this is the right way?" she asked. The hall they found themselves in was quite dark, which made it unlikely it was the intended route for the revellers.

"I'm certain it is, do not fret." The man smiled, showing a few gaps in his teeth. "I'm here to protect you from any dangers!" He let out a self-satisfied chuckle, raising the small hairs on the back of Hare's neck.

"I find myself no longer thirsty," she said. "Let's go back to the ballroom." When he ignored her, Hare added. "My aunt will be looking for me."

"Your aunt will understand." He smiled then and she saw a familiar look in his eyes.

She tried to pull her hand out of his grip. "My Lord, I need to get back now."

"Such formality." he pulled her towards a closed door in one of the alcoves. "Just call me Thomas."

"Lord Culross, this is highly inappropriate!" She tried to escape, but he pushed her against the door. The horror of her situation fully dawned on her and she struggled against him.

His breath stank of whiskey and cigars as he leaned over her, breathing heavy. He had her trapped against the door, placing his hands on either side of her head. "Don't worry, Edwina." She winced at him using her name. "I'll even marry you after."

A fury tensed her shoulders and with a swift motion, Hare

kneed Culross between the legs. As the shock twisted the man's features, she brought her foot down onto his instep.

The man howled and bent in half, but she was still trapped between his arms.

"You bitch!" he managed.

"Careful, *Thomas*," she said. "Bitches bite." And with that Hare brought her head forward, her forehead connecting with his nose. He fell backwards, releasing her for a moment. She knew he'd come back at her though and she wouldn't be able to surprise him again. Hare looked around frantically and suddenly realised the cold sensation on her hand was the doorknob of the door she was still leaning against. She twisted it and snuck into the dark room, just as Culross, blood streaming down his face, got up, a murderous look in his eyes. She whispered a silent thanks as the door had a key still in the lock. She turned it with a trembling hand, just as her attacker slammed into the door from the other side.

"And what will you do now, Edwina?"

"I suppose you simply leaving and me returning to the party is out of the question?" she said, looking around the room.

A nasty chuckle made her flesh crawl. "I find I have very little to do, Miss Walker. I might just as well wait for you here."

Oh yes, such a 'decent husband' he would make. Hare's nostrils flared remembering Miss Bonningham's characterisation of the man. She wondered where Anne was getting her information, because she might need a better source.

She walked towards the wallpapered wall, tracing her fingers along it. Rich houses like this one often had hidden servant doors. But, apparently, not this one. Just her luck. She walked up to the window. She pushed it up and poked her head out.

The house was on a slope, meaning that though she was only on the first floor, it was at least a five-yard drop to the ground. With rose bushes growing directly below. She groaned.

"Have you realised yet that you have no way out of there,

love?" Culross asked from beyond the door. "I might forget you attacking me, *if* you apologise, of course. If you apologise *very nicely*."

She felt bile rise in her throat. After she'd been brought to this world, she had to learn quickly how to fight off unwanted advances. But here, she thought she was protected by the status of her hosts. But clearly that protection only lasted till nightfall. Such a thin armour it turned out to be.

There was nothing to it then. She had to be her own hero.

Hare swung her leg out of the window. If she swung her lower half she might just about reach the drain pipe with her feet. She hiked up the multitude of her petticoats to allow her to move her legs freely. She slid onto her stomach, both legs out, the bunched up skirts around her torso making it hard to see. The pipe was only about a yard to her right. She could do it. *One, two...* Her foot hit the lead pipe. At least she had a feel for where it was now. *Again.* Hare swung her legs from left to right, till she managed to hook her foot against the pipe.

* * *

ERNEST WAS late to the party. If he thought Posy would forgive him, he'd skip it altogether. He could think of nothing less fun than watching Brandon dance the evening away with Miss Edwina. But Posy would have his head if he skipped this event. The event of the season, apparently. Funny how every other night was the 'event of the season', according to his sister. At least he could eat something here. His stomach rumbled. He was too busy to go out for lunch that day. And it was all for the best really, as the club was now buzzing with the gossip of Brandon's seemingly inevitable match. Ernest winced. Gossip was certainly not limited to the society mamas, but was practiced in its cruder, crasser form by the so-called "gentle" men, who alternately bemoaned Miss Walker's lack of fortune, which made those paragons of male virtue discount her as a matrimonial prospect; then complained about her station, too high to take her as a mistress. Brandon was universally envied, of course, though Miss Edwina's finer qualities were rarely the object of envy. The previous afternoon Ernest left the club in something of a huff, knowing if he did not, he was likely to punch one of the leering faces.

And that would have been a bit of a scandal in itself. Some might consider his intervention a show of solidarity towards his friend. Some would assume he was himself after the girl, which would raise a lot of other, more uncomfortable, questions. There would also be those who'd shrug and suddenly remember Ernest's American pedigree, making mental notes to downgrade him in their estimation.

Absolutely not one of those men would think anything about their own behaviour was deserving of any kind of repercussions.

So he just left.

He sighed, striding through the long-walled garden. The hack dropped him off at the gates and he needed a walk to brace himself before he was to face the combined horror of witnessing the intricate mixture of thinly veiled lust meeting tragically ignorant naïveté, motherly predators and dandied-up fortune hunters. All moving to the soothing rhythm of Austrian waltz.

A noise made him look up. There were no lamps or lanterns on that side of the house and the building looked dark and somewhat imposing in the moonlight. Only a patch of white seemed to hang off one of the windows. Ernest squinted. Did somebody hang out a sheet? Whichever servant was guilty would likely have to face Lady Leicester's wrath. Then the sheet moved. In spite of there being no wind.

Ernest's eyes widened as the realisation hit him. The billowy white fabric was actually a woman's pantaloons and their clearly deranged owner was trying to hook her foot against the lead gutter pipe close to the window.

The woman was going to fall down and break her neck. Ernest broke into a sprint.

But before he got to her, the ridiculous creature had swung her legs high enough so she could grab the gutter with her slippered feet.

"Stop it!!" he called out. "You'll fall!"

The woman didn't reply, but she momentarily stopped moving. It likely had occurred to her, at the same time it occurred to Ernest, that she was hanging above a strange man, the underwear closely hugging her derriere fully on display.

"Go away!" The woman's muffled cry came from above him. With her head still on the room-side of the parapet, she couldn't get a look at him, but she wiggled, making an attempt to push her skirts back down over her legs.

"Don't!" If she fell now because of trying to preserve her modesty, then it would be, philosophically speaking, his fault. He considered her position, scanning the wall for anything that might help her.

"You already have the pipe! Try to hold onto it with your legs and slowly slide down over the windowsill! There's a narrow ledge by the window, which you can move your hands along to get close enough to grab the pipe!"

There was a pause, long enough for Ernest to consider repeating the instructions, but then the woman began moving her body down. She slid her hand, fingers splayed out, trying to feel for the ledge.

"Lower!"

She obeyed, sliding further down. And then he saw her. He stared for a moment in complete disbelief, as Edwina's dark hair and the unmistakable line of her neck came into full view. Fear dried up his throat, so that he wasn't sure he could manage more than a croak. He walked up right beneath her. The rational part of his brain argued that she was high enough that if she fell she'd likely break his neck as well as her own.

And yet he couldn't help standing there like an idiot, arms outstretched.

"Am I close?" she called out, as her hand continued searching for the ledge.

"Almost! Just a little to the right!" His legs felt weak as he watched her fingers finally close over the ledge.

With the victory in sight, she slid further alongside, till she could begin shuffling along the ledge to bring her body in line with the gutter.

With a small victorious whoop she slowly slid down the pipe, seemingly oblivious to how it creaked under her weight.

As she came close enough, Ernest grabbed her by the waist and lowered her down. She turned to him with a somewhat outraged expression, but her face fell when she met his furious gaze.

"Ernest! What are *you* doing here?" She suddenly looked self-conscious, smoothing down her skirts.

"It's rather too late for modesty, isn't it?"

She shot him a furious look, which in turn irritated him further.

"What were you thinking—" he started, but then, hearing voices nearby, grabbed Hare by the wrist and pulled her towards the closest hedge.

"Let me go!" She squealed, but was quickly silenced, with Ernest's hand over her mouth.

"Will you stop that?" he whispered, but he himself had to stifle a gasp as she bit his hand.

"Now you let go of me or I'll scream!" Hare said, as imperious as a queen, as if she hadn't just shimmied down the side of a building like some burglar.

"Oh, go ahead then!" He threw his arms up in the air. "Be my guest, if you want to have to explain your unchaperoned visit to the gardens well known for romantic trysts. But do me a favour. At the very least wait for me to remove myself from your presence so I'm not caught up in whatever nonsense this was."

"Oh." The infuriating woman had at least the decency to look embarrassed. "All things considered, perhaps I've overreacted."

"You think?" If that was her attempt at an apology then he was honestly not interested.

She frowned. "I expect you're owed an explanation."

He clenched and unclenched his fingers, inspecting the bite marks her teeth left on his palm.

"Well." She cleared her throat, looking at his hand.

Oh she noticed, did she? He winced, perhaps over-dramatically. The truth is the bite wasn't too bad. She didn't need to know that, of course.

"I'm sorry," she managed. When he remained silent, she added, "I was startled, that's all. And if you knew the evening I've had, you'd be more understanding, you know."

"I'd love to understand, as a matter of fact." He narrowed his eyes. "I'd like to know, for instance, why you were risking your life up on that window."

She narrowed her lips and took a small step back, till the back of her skirts were leaning against the hedge. Unconsciously, he followed her, till she was so close he could smell the rose soap on her skin.

"I'm not your enemy, Edwina," he said quietly. "I'm sorry, if you can't bear to see me as a friend, but at least know that. I didn't tell Brandon about our kiss."

"You mean about how *you* kissed *me?*" she said immediately, but her heart wasn't in the barb.

"Very well. I didn't tell him that. Perhaps I should have. But I didn't anyway."

"Should I be thanking you for it?" One of her hands was worrying the leaves off the hedge, absent-mindedly pulling them off and shredding them.

"No, I suppose not." *Gods and he would kiss her again, if she let him. He'd do so much more if he thought she wished it too.* "But you can tell me what happened today."

She looked to the side, the moonlight reflecting in her shiny dark hair. There was a piece of moss, or something very much like it, on her forehead, threatening to lean on her long lashes at any moment. His fingers itched to brush it away. But he knew if he moved, she might not confide in him. And something in him craved her confidence far more than anything else.

"Lord Culross," she said.

An anger like nothing he'd ever known before rose in his chest. "Did he touch you?"

"He tried." She snorted. "He thought to make me an un-refusable offer. I kicked him and managed to lock myself in an empty room. The only way was through the window or through him. I picked the former."

"That pig!" Ernest ran his hand across his mouth. He'd kill that fat hog. Suddenly he looked up. "You say you kicked him?"

"He wasn't expecting it," she said, jutting out her chin. She looked into Ernest's eyes, as if daring him to comment. "'Surprise is a weapon you have at your disposal in the world which expects nothing of you. But it's a weapon you can only use once.' My mother used to say that." A small smile curved her lips. "I remember her lessons."

"Your mother must have been an exceptional woman," Ernest said. He took a step back. The mention of Hare's dead mother had a sobering effect. "You must miss her terribly."

She wrapped her arms around herself. A sudden breeze lifted up a strand of hair coiling around her neck. "It was a long time ago," she said wistfully.

"I admire your self-possession." He smiled, sadly. How brave she was trying to be. "But a year is still a short time to mourn somebody who was clearly so beloved.

"A year..." She turned sharply to him and her expression changed, hardening.

Ernest felt suddenly ashamed. Here she was, a vulnerable orphan in his sister's care and they'd put her in the path of danger, introducing her to the likes of Culross. And here *he* was, thinking only of himself. While she was so clearly shaken and upset, he was thinking… If she could read his thoughts she would have thought him the lowest sort of man, as low as Culross. Lower, perhaps, for he had the arrogance to consider himself above such baseness. "I will speak to my sister. She'll make sure Culross will have no opportunity to accost you again." He paused, fearing his voice might betray his emotions. "He deserves a more severe punishment than a lack of invitations to my sister's luncheons, but it is the best we can do without exposing you to gossip."

"I wish you wouldn't," she said suddenly.

"What?"

She didn't look mad, but then her words made little sense. "I don't want to have the news of this reach the Duke." A thoughtful look crossed her face. "Or anyone else. It'd be dreadfully embarrassing. They'd be liable to think I had encouraged his… attentions. People are quick to judge."

"If my sister is not told, you must know you're likely to come across Culross at more social gatherings."

She looked thoughtful. *Not shaken. Not scared.*

"I can manage him. Don't worry, I'm not scared of the likes of him." She raised her chin.

Ernest stood quietly, watching her. With her back straight and her head held high, she looked like a painting. Not of a simpering maiden in a fashion catalogue, but of an Amazon, contemptuous of her enemies and certain of victory. A smile stretched his lips, before another, a far less pleasant thought occurred to him. Of course she didn't want anything to jeopardise her blooming romance with Brandon. "You can't think Brandon would blame you?"

He could tell that irritated her by how her chest rose and fell rapidly at his words. But she held her temper. A somewhat remarkable achievement, considering how quick to anger she'd proven herself to be before.

"How can I know what he would and wouldn't blame me for?" She took a step towards Ernest, switching roles. Now he was the retreating one, the one made uncomfortable by the intensity of her gaze. "I know men don't like scandal. Or even a *hint* of scandal. If a man accosted me in a dark corridor, then the question asked is always 'what was she doing in the dark corridor', isn't that so?"

"Still, if you're serious about Brandon, shouldn't you at least trust in him a little?"

"Trust?" She laughed at that. Then the laughter died in her throat, in an instant and she placed her palm on Ernest's cheek. "I'm not sure I trust anyone very much these days, Mr Thompson. Much less myself." And, quick as a flash, she lifted her mouth to his and kissed him, soft and fleeting. Just as he lifted his arms to pull her to him, she evaded his grasp. She took a couple steps back, a strange expression on her face, before lifting up her skirts and running off into the night.

CHAPTER 17

As Miss Bonningham left in the morning to accompany the Dowager Baroness on her walk, Hare was left to her own devices. She slept in, after the London fashion, which helped her to somewhat recover after the ball.

Hare picked at her breakfast, which was brought to her on a tray. An indulgence due in large part to the Baron's own splitting headache, she imagined. She'd seen enough drinking to know when a man crossed the line from merely inebriated to "won't be able to get up in the morning" and Baron Winchfield had a couple more drinks after that point. Not that he was alone in the excess. The London high society rather indulged in too much of everything, it seemed. And though they couldn't match the resources of the American rubber barons, they certainly carried on with a sort of brazen disregard of their own rules. Because as long as the line (a practically transparent one as far as Hare was concerned, but very much present and visible to the English), remained uncrossed, then the veneer of lineage and respectability was used to hide all kinds of goings-on in plain sight. Hare had counted at least four mistresses at the ball. The beautiful women were so swaddled in riches they were untouchable, though the more respectable women took great pains to ignore them. There were also the infidelities, with the not-so-subtle signals sent across the room, by the fluttering lashes and gently folded and unfolded ostrich-feathered fans. Hare saw them all.

Once dressed, she walked down the long staircase, hurrying past the unforgiving stares of the Winchfield ancestors. They were pigment and oil, linen canvas and varnish. She could see the paint-strokes, could tell how the fashions of the time influenced each painter. Yet the sum of those individual parts managed to put a fear in her. She felt as if the ghosts of the old Barons and their progeny would reach out from their framed prisons and grab her, the imposter.

She felt guilty about the ball night. After she left Ernest in the garden, she managed to sneak back into the ballroom. She danced with Brandon and chatted with his sister and was vivacious enough to satisfy even Miss Bonningham. Gratefully, Lord Culross, with a tenacity worthy of a better cause, had clearly expected to wait her out where he had still imagined her locked in a room and so he'd not made an appearance for the rest of the ball. But plastering a smile on her face talking to Brandon filled Hare with a deep distaste for herself and her position. She had kissed Ernest. There could be no doubt this time that it was her doing. All the while she actively pursued his best friend. It put them both in a position where they were dishonest towards a clearly decent man. But there was no way she could see of extricating herself. She couldn't just leave now. She had no money, nowhere to go. The position she held was as fragile as sugar-floss and, thanks to Miss Bonningham appropriating the school's funds, just as sticky.

A soft cough startled Hare out of her reverie. She looked up, her fingers pulling on the frilled edge of her blue blouse. A footman, a tall and lanky mythic of a kind she didn't recognise, looked at her sheepishly. "Lady Winchfield and her guest are in the morning room, miss."

"I see." She looked at the man, who backed up against the wall, as if he meant to melt into the wallpaper. This deference embarrassed her more than she could say. It felt different to the acceptance of London's Beau Monde and made her feel ashamed. They were her own kind, yet she was held so high above them. She marked the string of binding around his wrist. The skin there was chafed and red, like he'd tried to gnaw it off. "Thank you," she whispered. "You mustn't try to pull it off," she said on an impulse, pointing at the string. "You will only hurt yourself."

"It hurts that I keep it on," he said, his expression suddenly guarded. "Maybe one day someone can help me shake it off. I would be forever indebted to such as this."

She nodded. She understood this. The desperation. Yet what could she do? She thought of Brandon's family. How many mythics did they keep? Would they all look to her with hope? Yet she could do nothing without exposing herself. She was committing herself to this deception. For life, if she truly married Brandon. She would become who she pretended to be. Or she could go back to being nothing, having nothing. A nothing with dreams was still nothing. A nothing with ambitions was a pitiful object of ridicule. Her eyes stung. She sniffed. It took her a while to see it, but now she knew. And she had to be strong.

An unwelcome image of Ernest popped into her head. His lips, slightly parted, as he looked at her, surprised in the garden. A kiss was just a kiss. He would put it down to the confusion of the moment and so would she. He'd say nothing. After all, Ben was his best friend, wasn't he? And she'd say nothing, because… What was there to say, truly? She couldn't marry Ernest, even if he asked her. Which he hadn't done. And even if he *did* ask her, then she couldn't become his wife. For a wife of a solicitor *had* to be respectable after all. Any hint of the truth would have the world turn against him. Now, a Duke's position could weather any scandal. Perhaps render him even more interesting to his peers. She could see Brandon, how easily he would be able to turn her true identity into an exciting adventure. Or some mystery. A mythic Duchess might have been unpalatable, but a *part* mythic? They could invent her watered-down heritage. A hint of a scandal was just exotic really.

But Hare's identity was not all she had to contend with. There was Miss Bonningham to think of, after all. And the small matter of the missing money.

Lady Winchfield's laughter came from the morning room. Hare paused for a moment and straightened her blouse before going in.

Lady Anastacia was looking extremely comfortable in Lady Winchfield's sitting room. She was feeding pieces of a strawberry tart to the Baron's poodle Iris, who lay her head in the lap of this unexpected benefactress.

"Edwina! Just who I was waiting for!" she exclaimed, the moment Hare walked in. Lady Anastacia clapped her hands over a small plate to get rid of all the crumbs before putting her gloves back on. "I'm so grateful, Posy, that you're willing to part with Edwina for a day." She beamed at Lady Winchfield, who smiled weakly. She looked like she was getting a headache.

To her credit, Lady Winchfield tried to preserve some sense of decorum. "Miss Edwina, Lady Anastacia was hoping to—"

"Ah yes, Posy, she heard me well enough, I'm sure." Anastacia winked at Hare. "Come, put your coat on, we're going on a walk, you and I." The woman stood up and patted the dog's head in a cursory goodbye.

"We are?" Hare tried and failed to put on a stern expression. Even though the blonde was somewhat unorthodox and her invitation had sounded more like a kidnapping, Lady Anastacia was very difficult to dislike. Even though, Hare reminded herself, she was somewhat of a threat to her plans. "I'm afraid my aunt might be expecting me to wait for her and could take it amiss if I left without her."

"Oh, hardly." Lady Winchfield laughed at that. "My dear

husband's mother is positively *besotted* with Miss Bonningham. I doubt your aunt will be released before dinner. If ever." She rolled her eyes. "My mother-in-law likes few people. But she's been dropping hints about needing a companion in her old age. Miss Bonningham was mentioned more than once."

"*Really?*" Hare coughed and added, in a slightly less shocked voice, "I didn't quite realise they'd gotten so close."

Anastacia burst out laughing. "That takes care of that excuse then! Let's go!" She walked up and took Hare's arm, half-dragging her out of the room.

"I have a surprise for you," she said, her voice low as they were walking towards the door.

Hare couldn't begin to imagine what it could be.

LADY ANASTACIA CALLED for a carriage as soon as they were out of the door. It took them down the small alleys, beyond the Winchfield's neighbourhood and into a part of London Hare didn't recognise.

The houses were less palatial here, but still quite beautiful. White fronts with half columns made her think of a painting she saw once depicting a half-naked model stylised to be Venus. She wasn't sure what made the woman in the painting particularly godlike, except for her naked body of course. But that alone seldom inspired lasting respect, in Hare's experience. Put a person in lush surroundings and a whore becomes the goddess of love. Put a goddess in the scullery and all she becomes is a pair of useful hands, making your life comfortable.

Hare glanced at her companion, who was being unusually quiet. The woman was wearing away at the tips of her left glove, as she looked out the window.

"Where are we going?" Hare asked finally. Truly, Anastacia couldn't expect to just take her wherever and not provide any answers. Hare might not have been brought up among the rich folk of England, but surely this must have been outside of what was permissible?

"My brother told me how much you love art." Anastacia beamed at Hare. "So I have a surprise for you." Hare's companion had a long, angular kind of face, so unlike fashions of the time, but so full of expression it was hard to see it as anything other than agreeable. Hare couldn't help but smile.

"My entire stay in London has been one enormous surprise to me, La— Anastacia," she corrected herself as the other woman began to frown. She had told Hare she reserved her title for those she disliked, after all. "I admit getting used to the rules here hasn't been all that easy. *So* I hope you won't misunderstand me when I say, surprises fill me with more anxiety than pleasure these days."

"Oh of course!" Anastacia smacked her forehead. "I'm sorry, I hadn't thought of that at all!" She looked genuinely contrite. "But I assure you, Melody is the last person to judge you on forgetting some arbitrary rule or other."

"Melody?"

"Oh, to be sure, I gave the game away." Anastacia looked annoyed with herself, her lips tightening into a line. She looked so much like a petulant child, Hare couldn't help but laugh.

"Hardly. Remember, not being from London myself, I have never heard of Lady Melody. Who is she?"

"Ah, she's not a lady." Anastacia perked up. "But you'll soon find out on your own who she is! Because we have arrived."

Hare stepped out of the carriage, jumping over a puddle in the street. The sun was shining and she instantly began to sweat under her cape. She brought her hand up to her hair as Anastacia led her up the few steps. Hare looked around and noticed at least three men in the vicinity, all trying to look inconspicuous, while not taking their eyes off them.

"Anastacia!" She pulled on the sleeve of her companion.

"What?" Anastacia turned around and let out a small chuckle

at Hare's furious signals. "Ah, them. Hello, Rob!" She waved at one of the men. This particular one had a nasty-looking scar running down his cheek and over a white, unseeing eye. He grinned and raised his hand in a greeting. Anastacia leaned towards Hare and whispered "Security. You'll understand in a moment."

A butler, rather jovial-looking for the position, swung the door open before Anastacia even had the chance to knock on it. Hare tried to cover up her surprise, as the butler was a *hobgoblin*, unusual for such a high position in the household. But more surprising still, was the fact there was no thread of binding around his wrist.

"Lady Anastacia." The *hobgoblin* smiled broadly. "Mrs Addison is waiting for you. She's already asked three times if there's been any sign of you." He glanced at Hare and a strange look passed over his eyes. Hare shrunk into herself.

"I'm precisely on time, Hoggis, as always" Lady Anastacia allowed him to take her coat and signalled to Hare to part with her cape. "Now where's my friend hiding?"

"Mrs Addison is awaiting you in the drawing room," the butler said and led the way. He turned towards Anastacia and whispered, "There's that *pixie* from Albany, freed after his summoner died intestate. He brought over another *puck* musician to join the group and Mrs Addison was somewhat put out you weren't here, so she told him to come back tomorrow. She couldn't quite make her mind up without your expertise."

"My expertise!" Anastacia snorted. "My mother's connections, more like. If the musician was bad, she'd have sent the poor soul away already. What instrument is it this time then? A tin whistle? A gong?" She turned to Hare and rolled her eyes. "Last time it was a trumpet player. You know how excited the Beau Monde families are about employing a trumpet player these days?" Before Hare had the chance to respond, Anastacia answered herself, this time looking pointedly at Hoggis, "*Not* very excited. I wore my shoes out before I found him that job in a gambli—" She glanced at Hare. "At the club."

Interesting.

Hoggis coughed. "It's a fiddle player, Lady Anastacia." He pulled open a door to a brightly-lit parlour. The room was richly furnished, yet airy, with three large windows letting in plenty of light.

"And surely, finding a place for a talented fiddle player will be a doddle for you, my dear." A handsome *nymph* said from a velvet-covered chaise longue. The water kind, her hair and eyes were blue. She wore her hair up, after the modern fashion, with expensive-looking-pins decorating it. Edwina took a sharp intake of breath. To see a mythic so swaddled in wealth wasn't just surprising. It was unheard of. Especially one so obviously and unashamedly not human. The woman called Mrs Addison didn't even bother dyeing her hair a more common colour. Her voice was deep and raspy and when her eyes rested on Hare there was a long silence.

All was lost. This unbound mythic was going to betray her now. The *nymph* was a friend of Anastacia's. She was never going to just allow Hare to marry Brandon.

The *nymph* was peeling an orange, clearly the source of the pleasant scent. She calmly regarded her guests and smiled at Hare and brought a piece of the orange peel up to her nose and gave it a small sniff. "And who is this, Stacia?"

"This is the friend I told you about," Anastacia said, practically throwing herself into a wing-backed armchair. "Hoggis, be a dear and get us some tea. The flowery kind, if you would." She turned back to Mrs Addison. "Melody, this is Edwina. Edwina, this is Melody."

Hare, unsure of what was expected, gave a small curtsey. "It is a pleasure to meet you, Mrs Addison."

"Oh please!" The woman laughed and gestured towards a small sofa next to her chaise longue. "We don't stand on ceremony here. I insist you call me Melody. It's a ridiculous name, to be sure, but I certainly prefer it to 'Mrs Addison'." She made a face. "Anyway," A look passed between them, "we're among friends."

"Your house is very beautiful."

"Yes, it is." Melody propped up her chin with two fingers. "And yes, I'm a mythic. I feel we should get the obvious out of the way first, don't you think?" There was a challenge in that. Hare did not rise to it.

Instead of replying, Hare looked around the room. The paintings on the walls were unusual, in that they were quite unlike what one was likely to find in the houses of the London rich. There were no dark, looming portraits, or pastoral landscapes. The many paintings displayed on the walls were an explosion of colour and movement. "You are a fan of the Impressionists, Mrs — Melody?"

Mrs Addison raised her eyebrows. "You recognise the style?" She turned to Anastacia. "I didn't think an American would know them."

Hare stiffened. "It's been more than two decades since the style became popular. My mother would sometimes take me, whenever the exhibitions opened." She lowered her eyes. A small lie.

"Of course. I apologise for being so flippant. I didn't mean to imply anything untoward. The fashions, in everything, don't always travel fast across the continents." Melody held out a hand. "Orange?"

Hare shook her head.

"So, Miss Edwina, Anastacia wrote me all about the charm which made her brother so besotted with you and I admit, the tales were not exaggerated."

"You're very kind... But I wouldn't say the Duke is exactly *besotted* with me." She had to tread carefully. " We have become good friends, though."

"The kind of friends who everyone expects to announce their engagement any day, yes, I've heard of that too." Mrs Addison took a bite of the orange and a drop of juice trickled down her chin. "Don't worry, we're all friends here."

Are we? Hare wondered what the woman's game was. Why hasn't she betrayed her yet for what she was? *A fraud.* She pushed the thought out of her mind. It was important to remember, she was not safe. These two women were tigers circling around her.

"She doesn't trust us yet, Melody." Anastacia chuckled. They all fell silent as Hoggis returned with a tray.

Once he left, the *nymph* poured her guests tea. "She'd be a fool to trust us before she got our measure, Stacia. And you don't want a fool for a sister, I know that much."

"Speak for yourself, Melody." Anastacia stuck her nose up in the air. "I'm *extremely* trustworthy."

"What you are is *unusual*, my friend." Melody passed a cup of steaming tea to Hare. "And sensible young women don't trust unusual people. I understand you're something of an artist yourself, Edwina?"

Hare winced at the familiarity. But she was curious, in spite of her better judgement. "I draw and paint," she said finally. "A little. A normal amount." She blushed at the intense gaze of her hostess. She strove to salvage what was left of her composure. "I've always been interested in art. I was very happy to hear the Duke shares that interest."

"Oh, he will for about another month or two." Anastacia waved away Hare's attempt at polite conversation. "He rarely pursues a new interest for more than half a year and it's been at least four months now."

"But to the point, Edwina," Mrs Addison cut off her friend. "As you might have surmised, we dabble in a bit of art patronage here at 5 Carlisle Place."

Hare exhaled. "I see. But I'm... You see, I'm not in a position to offer anyone patronage..." She had exactly two shillings in her purse and that was the last of her resources. She almost laughed at the idea she could join these rich idle women in their charity work. But then, they had to continue believing her to be at least comfortable. Even if Anastacia's brother didn't intend to marry for money, then he would certainly not marry for the lack of it intentionally.

"Oh, of course not." Mrs Addison drummed her fingers on the arm rest of her chaise longue. "We're not looking to dip our fingers in your pockets, my dear. We do, however, hope to engage your services, using your not inconsiderable sway among the Beau Monde, as well as your artistic expertise, to find work for those who so sadly are yet to secure their employment."

Hare glanced at Anastacia, who was watching her, her chin propped up on fanned out fingers, like she was estimating the value of a mare. Brandon's sister, quite understandably, wanted to assess her brother's possible marital partner. Which had to mean Brandon intended to propose soon. Miss Bonningham would be thrilled. Hare wondered what kind of a sister-in-law Lady Anastacia might be hoping for.

"You don't know what my artistic expertise is," she said flatly. "Beyond me recognising the style of the painting on your walls." She hesitated. "I hope you don't consider me rude. I'm just not sure how much I can help. After all, Anastacia is the sister of a Duke and you are…" She wasn't entirely sure *what* she was. "… comfortably established."

"Not that well-established." Mrs Addison smiled. "And we both know why."

"Mrs Addison doesn't move in quite the same circles as Lady Winchfield." Anastacia explained, popping another biscuit into her mouth.

"I'm a bit of a disgrace, my dear," Mrs Addison said, leaning her temple on the steepled fingers of her right hand. "Aside from my very presence among the higher echelons of society being in itself considered inappropriate, I'm afraid I'm seen as somewhat of a radical and while my husband stubbornly refuses to acknowledge my failings and send me off to the asylum as has been suggested more than once, the Beau Monde is not as generous. They can't touch me, so they ostracise me instead."

"A radical?" Hare hesitated. If Miss Bonningham found out she'd been visiting a social outcast, she'd be furious. The last thing Hare needed was drawing negative attention to herself. But then Anastacia seemed to be close to Mrs Addison. So the disgrace couldn't have been all that bad. And Hare *liked* Melody. She was odd in an interesting way. And she dealt with artists. And she thought Hare could *help*.

Anastacia rolled her eyes. "You're scaring her, Melody." She turned to Hare. "By a radical, she means she's not merely content with not being bound and she seeks to emancipate other mythics."

"As well as provide more practical help to those who find themselves free yet without an occupation." Melody continued. "*Our* kind tends to be quite well suited to the artistic pursuits, as you might know." A little smile danced on her lips. Hare cringed. Surely Anastacia would realise now? But no, Brandon's sister, for all her astuteness, was just as prone to seeing only what she expected as the rest of her kind.

"I hesitated to bring you here, to tell you the truth." Melody sipped on her tea and regarded Hare cooly. "I felt it premature of Anastacia, to assume you would be amenable to our proposal. Yet, now we've met, I am inclined to think she was correct. So the question is, are you going to help with our endeavours here?"

"In whatever way I can, of course." Hare replied without thinking. This could be something hers. Something that *belonged* to her. "I can't promise radical acts, but neither am I afraid of them." Hare laughed. The two women joined her. And that laughter, the real laughter between women in on a secret, seemed a bit of a radical act in and of itself.

A polite cough at the door alerted them to Hoggis' presence. "Mr Thompson is here to see you, Mrs Addison."

"Oh yes, let him in" Mrs Addison said, wiping the orange juice off her hands with a napkin. "I've been expecting him."

"Mr Thompson?" Hare half stood up from her seat.

Anastacia, misunderstanding her companion's discomfort, laughed. "I thought you weren't afraid of radical acts, Edwina? Don't worry." She leaned forward and patted her hand. "Ernest is well used to our shenanigans. Only last month he recommended a talented pianist of… shall we say… rather alarming countenance and less than respectable past… to one of his clients and now the young lady is gainfully employed as a tutor in a country house in Gloustershire."

"But… Wouldn't her employers be angry? Should her past be discovered?" *As if I had the moral high ground when it comes to deception.*

"They would."

The voice made Hare snap her head around. Ernest had walked into the room, looking perfectly pristine and unmoved to find her there. *Damn him, why is he so calm.* The memory from the ball flooded back and she could feel the hotness of the blush making its way inexorably up her neck. She lifted her teacup and stuffed a biscuit in her mouth, just to have something to do with her hands.

"But then, we all know the rich have their secrets too." He was staring right at her, like he expected a response. He had a searching look in those dark eyes of his and she'd be damned if she gave him any answers. "Why should we deny the lower classes the right to privacy we so eagerly grant those above them?" She was so busy trying to avoid giving away her discomfort that his words took a moment to register.

But when they did a small sad smile turned up one corner of Hare's mouth. "I suppose we're all comfortable with people's secrets, only as far as they don't affect us directly."

"You speak very enigmatically." Anastacia leaned forward so fast is made Hare jump, spilling a bit of her tea into the saucer. "What secrets do you have then?"

"You're prying, Stacia." Melody's statement was so matter-of-fact, as if she had to repeat it multiple times anytime she was around her friend. Which she probably had to. She nodded to Hare and an understanding passed between them. A kind of promise, though Hare wasn't yet sure what the price of it would be. *Nymphs* were always hard to read in her experience.

"And whose life would I be more entitled to pry into than my brother's future wife, tell me?" Anastacia threw her arms up in the air, gratefully distracted for a moment.

"Am I to understand..." Hare looked at Ernest who seemed suddenly choked up and not at all like the ridiculously calm and collected man who'd entered the room a moment ago. "Am I to understand then, Miss Edwina, that I'm to congratulate you?"

"Oh no!" She laughed. *Except why was she so happy to be able to deny it? Deny the success of her plans?* "There's no engagement. And frankly, Anastacia," she turned to Brandon's sister. "I would be grateful if you didn't announce events which have not taken place, as far as I'm concerned. I would be very sad if your brother thought I was trying to pressure him into something by spreading false stories." *Except if she thought it would work, she would. After all, wasn't that the reason she was here, with these women? With this man...* She straightened up. So he was here. It couldn't be helped. It's not like she'd sought him out, after all.

"I'm sorry, dear." Anastacia scooched up closer. "It's just that after I have satisfied myself that you're precisely the sort of sister-in-law I would have hoped for, I pretty much accepted your engagement as a done thing."

"You do have a tendency to put yourself in the centre of business which doesn't concern you, Stacia." Melody sighed and shook her head.

Anastacia bristled. "That's what we're all doing here, isn't it?"

"That's true enough." Mrs Addison turned to Ernest and patted a cushion next to her. "Now, dear Ernest, I've called you here in the hopes you could assist Miss Walker. She's promised us her help, you see." She beamed at Hare. "I know she'll be a great asset to our little operation."

"I'm sure Miss Edwina is an asset in anything she puts her mind to." Ernest seemed to have somewhat composed himself, except for his hands, which he laced with a sort of white-knuckle-intensity.

CHAPTER 18

"Is it to your liking?"

The question broke Hare out of her reverie. She considered her answer carefully before replying. "Very much so. I think it's striking." She regarded the large drawing where a twisted, somewhat angular figure of a woman drowned among the flood of geometric shapes, hypnotic in their unpredictability. "Unusual. Who's the artist?"

Mrs Brown, the gallery owner and a portly, commanding woman in her mid-forties nodded with approval. "A German chap, a *rübezahl* if I remember correctly. You wouldn't have heard of him." She nodded fiercely. "But everyone will and soon, mark my words."

Hare couldn't help but be impressed. Mrs Brown set up the Brown Gallery four years prior with the money she'd inherited from her dead husband and had tripled it since, if Anastacia was to be believed. She not only acted as a go-between for the artists and potential patrons (for a fee, naturally), but also made it be known she could procure art to suit any taste and pocket. She judiciously didn't limit her clientele to the increasingly impoverished aristocracy, but sought out links to the Americas' rubber barons, rich merchants and even the more upmarket bordello owners. Once she took an artist under her wing, Melody told Hare, she made sure they didn't starve.

"Do you have commissions for him lined up already then?" Hare turned her head to the side.

"Miss Walker, who do you take me for?" Mrs Brown scoffed. "I'm not in the business on sitting on talent such as this. Artists are a delicate kind of creature, liable to starve in the hedges unless they have someone to take them in hand and champion their work." She nodded towards the drawing. "When dear Mrs Addison presented me with this one, he had not a single sock without holes in it."

"He told you that?" Anastacia, who was hovering in the corner, looked up with interest.

"Oh please, you don't think I would buy a hound without checking out its mother's kennel? I simply—"

"You wouldn't be buying a hound in any case. They make you sneeze." Anastacia said, casually browsing through a sketchbook sitting on Mrs Brown's desk.

"They certainly do not!" Mrs Brown straightened herself up. "Sneezing isn't genteel."

"I'm not sure gentility is a part of it. Everyone sneezes."

"Well, *I* do not! Anyway," Mrs Brown patted her black widow's cap.,"how I was saying, of course I took it upon myself to inspect the man's lodgings. I can't be presenting my clientele with an unreliable prospect. And you can tell a lot from the way a man lives."

"You mean, beyond the state of his socks?" Anastacia closed the covers of the sketchbook with a decisive movement. The woman did everything decisively, Hare thought with a smile. Anastacia was certainly growing on her.

"I'm not nosy, you know." The gallery owner shook her shoulders as if she would shake off the accusation. "I just want to ensure I'm not dealing with an opium smoker, or a gin devil. You can't be too careful these days. As for the rest of it—" she waved her hand. "—I don't ask my artists about their morals, or their... origins, same as I wouldn't ask my patrons."

"That's an unusual stance," Hare said carefully.

"A pragmatic one. But now that the pleasantries are done with and I've established Miss Walker can at least tell charcoal from turpentine, what can I do for you?"

"For *us*?" Anastacia walked up to Mrs Brown and put her arm around the older woman's shoulders. "Dearest Mrs Brown, are you offering us a percentage of the sales we help you make?"

"Don't be impertinent, child." Mrs Brown grumbled, but the affection between the two women was obvious.

"Lady Anastacia and myself, we have an artist in mind for you," Hare said. She tried to keep her voice level, but she could barely contain her excitement. "She's a young woman from Brighton, a *sprite* I'm given to understand, newly unbound. Specialises in ink drawings, ideal for reproduction in books and newspapers."

"I already have a few of those." Mrs Brown inserted one finger under the edge of the cap and scratched at her scalp thoughtfully. "What sets this one apart? Aside from her being a female mythic, which can only bring my commission down. Can't charge as much for her work, no matter how good she is."

Hare's heart sank. Anastacia huffed, however. "Mrs Brown, like you'd accept anything less than what you know your artists' work is worth."

"That's because this mother hen picks her chickies carefully in the first place, my dear." The woman looked to Hare. "So where did you find this diamond of talent you seek to pawn off on me?"

"She works as a cloakroom girl at the Ritz," Hare said. "She'd recognised Anastacia and approached us there."

"The word spreads." Mrs Brown pinched the bridge of her nose. "As long as all the hopefuls don't interrupt *my* lunch I suppose. So where is this woman's work?"

Hare was prepared. She opened a large satchel and pulled out a thick roll of papers, tied with a piece of brown string.

"Brown paper, brown string, I'm wondering if I'm unpacking a parcel of biscuits or a stale fish," the gallery owner muttered under her breath, as she took the drawings over towards her desk.

The ringing of a bell over the front door made them all turn towards the entrance. Mrs Brown instantly straightened herself, her face beaming a welcoming smile. But a heartbeat later her face fell. "Oh, it's only you."

"What a welcome!" Ernest laughed and shook the drizzle off his coat, before coming in. The hair not covered by his hat was damp and curled up tighter over his forehead. Hare held her breath. While most people's skin turned blotchy and red when the weather changed, his face was gleaming with the droplets of water reflecting the light in the shop. He turned to them and fixed his eyes on Hare. "Miss Walker, I'm sorry I'm late. Anastacia sent me a message when I was in the middle of a client meeting."

"Well, since you haven't the decency to be *my* client, you'll forgive me if I pay you no more attention for now." Mrs Brown turned away towards her desk and begun unrolling the drawings Hare brought her.

"Mrs Brown gets meaner the more she likes someone," Ernest said, tipping his hat.

"I didn't know you were coming today," Hare said.

"Does that displease you?"

"At least Ernest makes himself useful." Anastacia hurrumphed, not appreciating being left out of the conversation. "An Earl he represents has a mind to fund a new society paper. A great new source of income to the artists in my care."

"The artists in *my* care, I think you mean, young lady," Mrs Brown said without turning around. She reached out one hand and inspected the business card Ernest placed in it. "I'll make sure to give this gentleman a call."

"He's expecting it." Ernest smiled.

Mrs Brown pocketed the card and laid a drawing in front of her and tapped it with a finger. "This one would do well for the new catalogue services. The ready-made clothes' makers try to make up for the inferior fit with an excess of publicity." She shrugged "And who am I to complain."

"You never complain, Mrs Brown." Ernest winked at Anastacia. Hare set her lips in a line. She wasn't quite sure why she didn't like this show of familiarity between Mr Thompson and Anastacia. But she did, in fact, loathe it.

Ernest must have noticed a change in her mood, for he walked closer to her, as if pulled by an invisible string. "If you like these drawings, Mrs Brown, you should see Miss Walkers' work." He smiled broadly. He was too close. Hare could feel the warmth of him and smell the rain on his skin. Not skin. His *coat.* She had been noticing the smell of the rain on his coat. It wouldn't do to think of his skin. Even if it did smell nice. His nostrils flared slightly as he regarded her. "I've seen Miss Edwina's work. She's fast, but precise and, though I'm not an expert, her work shows far more skill than the society expects of accomplished young ladies"

Hare took a sharp breath, even as Mrs Brown turned to her with a renewed interest. "Do you dabble, Miss Walker?"

"Dabble is right," Hare said, hesitantly, painfully aware that everyone's eyes were now on her. "I haven't been able to do more than sketch since arriving in London."

"You work in paints or ink?" Mrs Brown turned her head to the side, rolling back the drawings on her table.

"Both."

"*I* will hold onto these, thank you." Mrs Brown held the rolled-up drawings away as Anastacia moved closer to retrieve them. "I can't promise anything, but send the girl my way. We might get her out of that cloakroom if she's a good worker. Anyway—" She turned her sharp eyes back to Hare. "Bring your work around sometime. We shall see if your talent warrants Mr Thompson's compliments, or if he was too busy looking at your pretty face to notice the fault in your draftsmanship."

"Oh, I don't think Edwina will have much cause to look for employment, Mrs Brown," Anastacia said with a laugh. She looked at Hare knowingly. "I don't think it's a secret, so I hope you don't mind me saying, dear, but she's likely to make the kind of match which would secure her more comfort than a lifetime of painting ever could." She leaned closer towards the gallery owner. "You know my own brother is a great admirer of hers."

"Perhaps." Mrs Brown looked Hare up and down and then let her eyes fall briefly on Ernest. "None of us know the future, chickies. So the offer is open, Miss Walker. Bring me what you think best. In your own time."

Something in the woman's tone made a shiver run down Hare's back. Did Melody say something?

"Thank you, Mrs Brown, perhaps I will." Hare looked down towards her feet. She couldn't, could she? But the possibility… What she would have given for such a possibility back in New York. Opportunities seem to come most often to those who don't need them, she supposed. Still… She looked at Ernest. If she had such an opportunity earlier, then she wouldn't have made the journey with Anne, she wouldn't have joined her scheme and… she wouldn't have met Ernest. And for a moment, she was rather glad things turned out the way they did.

* * *

BREATH CAUGHT in his throat at her smile. She beamed at him, for a split moment, before whatever thoughts running through her mind clouded her expression. Before he realised it, he'd taken a step towards her, drawn towards that smile, then grieving its loss when her expression changed. He wanted to see her smile like that again. He wanted to be the reason she smiled like that. And he wanted to dispel whatever worry chased that smile away again.

"As I've introduced you to Miss Walker, I think I need to be on my way." Anastacia straightened the cuff of her shirt. "Always a pleasure, Mrs Brown. Ernest?" She turned to him. "I'm terribly sorry, but would you mind escorting Edwina back to your sister's? I'm afraid I'm late for an appointment."

"Oh, there's no need,"Miss Walker said, blushing quite prettily. "I'm sure Mr Thompson has a great many things to do in attending to his practice. And I'm perfectly capable of finding my own way back."

"As it happens I don't have a lot to do till later today," Ernest lied, knowing full well his desk had a pile of papers on it high enough to drown a man, should it collapse. "And walking alone through London streets is not something generally advised to young women."

"Ah, yes," she said flatly, her expression blank. "Young women *must* be watched at all times.

"That's not what I—"

"Very well, Mr Thompson." She looked at him, her chin lifted high. "I suppose you better escort me then. We wouldn't want people thinking I was anything but a well-brought-up young woman."

Certainly an exasperating one.

"It was a pleasure, Mrs Brown. I will be in touch," she said, as regally as a queen, to Mrs Brown's clear amusement.

He opened the door and waited for Anastacia and Edwina to go through.

"Good luck," the gallery owner said to him, before he left.

"What do you mean?"

But instead of responding the woman just waved him away with a laugh.

"So what is this meeting you're rushing off to?" Edwina was asking Anastacia, who suddenly became very interested in her gloves. The drizzle had gratefully stopped and the sun was once more poking out from behind the clouds.

"Oh nothing much, just a group of like-minded friends."

"Like-minded about *what* exactly, Stacia?" Ernest asked. "Please tell me it's nothing like the last time..."

Anastacia didn't look at him. He groaned. "I thought you were done with all that. I know *Brandon* thinks you're done with all that."

"And he needs know nothing more," she said. She leaned towards the clearly confused Miss Walker and squeezed her hand. "Don't worry about it, dear. I will fill you in at some point."

"Don't you dare!" Ernest said, which earned him withering looks from both women.

"It appears the list of what well-brought-up young women in London ought not to do now extends to talking, so I think it best you go to your appointment now, Anastacia, before Mr Thompson decides to add other prohibitions."

"Yes, I think it best," Anastacia said with a chuckle. She shot Ernest a look that clearly showed she enjoyed his discomfort and thought he deserved every last bit of it.

"Fine." He threw his arms in the air. "Just try to avoid sedition if at all possible. For me?"

Anastacia winked. "For you, I will keep my seditious activities to a minimum."

Ernest turned to his remaining companion and offered her his arm, which she first regarded as if it was a coiled snake, before finally placing her hand in the crook of its elbow. She then proceeded to practically drag him behind, as if he was a child with a governess. A wall of anger rose between them again.

When they turned the corner, he stopped dead in his tracks. She half-tripped, her hand held tight against his body.

"What did I do *now*, exactly?" He said through gritted teeth. A passer-by gave them a curious look and Ernest lowered his voice.

"It seems I can't do anything right by you, Miss Edwina. Even an offer to escort you home is an insult, it appears."

Her jaw fell open and she had the decency to look embarrassed. "You didn't do anything wrong," she muttered.

"What was that?"

"I said, you didn't do anything wrong. In fact…" she looked up at him. "In fact it was… quite lovely, what you said to Mrs Brown. I…" She looked away. "It's the nicest thing anyone has done for me in a long time…"

"Then why are you annoyed with me? Enough to pull me through the street like a toy on a string?"

"I don't know." She looked at him again. *God, she was beautiful.* Her eyes shone like a cat's. Funny how he'd never noticed before. "I don't know why I get annoyed with you." She sighed, her chest rising and falling like the sea. He imagined a million other things that might make her sigh.

"Do you dislike me so much then?" he asked in barely more than a whisper.

She looked up at him, surprised. "Dislike you?" She laughed mirthlessly and tugged on his arm, gently this time. "No, I don't dislike you." They set to walking again, slowly, like they had the whole day to just wander around London. Ernest fervently wished he could make it so. A whole day, just walking, with her on his arm. Just one day. She was quiet, but Ernest had a feeling she was thinking through her next words and he didn't want to intrude on her thoughts. When she finally spoke, there was hesitation in her voice. "I think it's because I feel comfortable around you."

"I make you comfortable enough to irritate you?" He raised his eyebrows. "Do you dislike comfort that much, Miss Edwina?"

She laughed at that. A sweet sound, which he wanted to revel in.

"Comfortable enough to allow me to release the irritation which builds up in me every day." She chewed her lower lip and glanced up at him, immediately looking away when she saw he was looking at her. "Though I grant you, it's not exactly fair to you."

"I think I understand," he said. "There is a lot we must conceal and a lot we can't show. I'm... glad. That you don't need to pretend with me. I wish I could stop pretending sometimes too."

"I can believe that." She smiled gently and gave his arm a small squeeze. "I think you might be one of the most tightly wound-up people I've ever met."

"I'm not sure I like that description of me."

"Do you deny it?" There was a challenge in her voice. Like she was testing him.

"No." He thought for a moment. "Though I still don't like it. But then again—" He glanced at her. "I suppose we like what others truly think of us about as often as we learn their true opinions. Which isn't very often at all, really."

"Especially not here, I suppose." She sighed. "It's like everyone is playing a part in some play and I wasn't given the script."

He let out a barking laugh. "I think that describes it pretty accurately."

A loud rumbling came from the vicinity of Miss Edwina's stomach. He snorted. "Are you hungry?" he asked.

"What gave you that idea?" She looked away.

"Well, perhaps I was mistaken. Perhaps a thunder storm is coming." He made a show of looking up at the clouds.

"Perhaps." She pressed her lips tight together. He could tell she was trying to stop herself from laughing.

"I hope you don't mind then, that I get myself something?" He said. "I believe there is a pie vendor just a couple of minutes away.

"Oh?" She kept her face impassive, though he saw the edge of her lip quirk upwards. "While it is a bit of an imposition, I'm sure Lady Winchfield would be very disappointed with me if I allowed her brother to starve."

"Yes, Posy has a strict no-starvation rule for her relatives and guests alike." He nodded sagely. They turned into a small road. They could smell the pies long before they could see them. Miss Walker's stomach growled again. She shot him a warning look and he suppressed a chuckle.

"So those pies…" she said, as the vendor came into view.

"The best pork pies this side of the river.."

"Ah…"

"But you're not hungry, of course," he said lightly, as they arrived at the vendor's stall.

She jutted her chin out. "It wouldn't be proper to let you eat alone."

"I'm not familiar with that particular rule." He turned his head to the side.

"Oh, I'm positive," she said. Her eyes widened at the sight of the steaming food. "It'd be dreadfully rude of me not to have a pork pie right now."

"I thought you were perfectly happy not adhering to all the local rules of etiquette though."

"I never said that."

"I believe you said something about being a foreigner and not wanting to pretend otherwise, if memory serves."

"Your memory doesn't serve. But this good woman might. Serve two pork pies, that is." Miss Walker beamed at the vendor while holding up two fingers.

Ernest watched as his companion nibbled on the flaky crust. A few crumbs stuck to her chin and, on an impulse, Ernest wiped them off with his thumb. She stepped back, looking at him with a wide-eyed expression.

"Sorry," he said. He offended her. She'd turn to him in anger again.

But the pie had clearly put her in a good mood, for she waved his concern away. "It's alright. I'm a messy eater when hungry."

"Oh, so you *are* hungry then?" He couldn't stop himself.

She raised an eyebrow. “For these pies I am. What witchcraft is this?” She raised her eyes to the skies dramatically. “This must be the best pie I’ve ever had!”

“Well, don’t tell my brother-in-law that. He’d fire the cook on the spot.” Ernest took a bite out of his own pie. Which was rather excellent. He swallowed and then lowered his voice. “...But I agree.”

She giggled and put her finger to her lips. “It can be our secret.” The words no sooner left her mouth than she realised what other meaning could be ascribed to them. She looked around. “The pie I mean.”

“I know what you meant.” They ate the rest of their food in silence.

“Thank you,” she said. “For the pie.”

He inclined his head.

“I really enjoyed it,” she added. He glanced at her. There was a different kind of earnestness about her. Like she wanted to tell him something, but what it was he couldn’t guess. “It’s so nice to just enjoy a pie in the street with a friend.”

He nodded. “You find life among the Beau Monde constricting?” He understood.

“It’s not that,” she said quickly, too quickly to fool either of them.

“It does get easier you know,” he said.

“Does it?” He could feel her eyes on him, but he didn’t turn his head to face her. After a moment she continued. “You came as a child. What was it like?”

“It was...” *Cold. Lonely.* “....difficult. At first. But I adjusted.”

“You were very young. Children can adapt to almost anything. The rest of us just have to pretend.”

“And what are you pretending?”

She tripped and he pulled her up. For a moment, her other hand rested on his forearm, the small finger of her gloved hand resting just above his wrist. She recovered and pulled the hand away. He felt the loss of it and wished she would bring it back.

"I'm not saying I'm *pretending* anything exactly. " She turned away. "It's just that... The things I see. They fill me with anger and I can't express it. Because nobody does."

"Well, that's not exactly true." He smiled. "Anastacia expresses a great deal of anger and outrage and displeasure, at any number of things."

"I like Anastacia. Still, a woman in her position is free to express a great deal more than others."

"Seems to me you have no issue expressing yourself." He looked up at the sky. The heavier clouds started rolling in again. Seemed the drizzle was only a prelude. "Especially when it comes to expressing your anger towards me."

"How should I explain it..." She lifted her other hand in exasperation. "It's like this: would you be escorting me back to your sister's house right now if I was a serving maid in her employ?" She paused. "Or a mythic?"

He opened his mouth and shut it again. "I beg your pardon?"

"If it's somehow inappropriate and unsafe for me to walk the streets alone, then surely it'd be doubly so for the maid?"

"Is it a hypothetical maid?" He tried to follow her thoughts.

"It's a point I'm trying to make!" She huffed. "It's either safe for a woman to be walking through London or it isn't. So it's either reasonably safe and the escort is to emphasise how I'm just a delicate debutante, or it isn't safe. If it isn't safe, then surely the maids and mythics should have escorts too? Unless their safety is not seen as important. So which one is it?"

"The... former?" Ernest became aware of the passer-by's curious glances, as Miss Walker spoke animately. "I suppose it is *reasonably* safe. Anastacia, for instance, walks alone all the time. Nobody would dare suggest otherwise, truth be told. But you're a foreigner and a guest in my sister's house," *a woman I want to spend more time with,* " and so it's just... what's done here."

She thought for a moment. "Nobody learns their names, did you know?" She looked up at Ernest. "The servants' names. Their employers call them 'Bess', or 'James', but that's not their names."

"I admit I didn't notice that."

"No, I don't suppose you would." She laughed a mirthless laugh. "And yet so much is made over how the people of Beau Monde address each other. If it's "Lord" or "Sir" or..."

"...or "Duke," he added and immediately wished he hadn't. He found he didn't particularly care to bring up Brandon at this time. If she never thought of Brandon again, in fact, he'd be quite happy.

"Yes. Duke. You corrected me at the dinner that time, do you remember?"

"I did. I expect you thought it was quite presumptuous of me."

"It was." She laughed. "But I think I know why you did it."

"And why was that?"

She tucked a stray lock behind her ear. She was looking down and the brim of her hat obscured his view of her face so he couldn't guess what she was thinking. "You survived here, because you learned how things work among such people. I think you wanted to help." She moved her chin up, not quite enough for him to see her face. As if she was thinking to look at him and then changing her mind again. "It was awkwardly done, but your intentions were good."

"They were." He rubbed his chin. "When you make a mistake... You know, they won't tell you outright. But they *will* notice. And you will be judged."

"You're speaking from experience."

"Miss Edwina..." He closed his eyes for a moment. For a while they walked without speaking. He found he wanted to fill that silence. "I was just a young boy. Brought up in relative isolation. And then shipped off across the ocean the moment it was possible. Nobody taught me how to behave here. My accent, my looks, my ways, were all scrutinised and judged from the moment I set one foot on the English soil."

She looked up at him then.

"Your looks?"

And for a moment, he thought he would tell her. When she looked at him like this, he thought he could. He opened his mouth—

"Ernest! Miss Edwina!" A familiar voice interrupted them. Posy, accompanied by her husband, practically bounded towards them. "What a chance to come across you like this! Where did you go?" She narrowed her eyes at him, ever so slightly. He kept his expression blank.

"Miss Anastacia had another matter to attend to and charged me with escorting Miss Edwina back to your house."

"Did she indeed? We can take Miss Edwina back ourselves, seeing as we're on our way back now anyway. Will you stop by for tea?"

"I—"

She waved her hand in the air. "Well, but what am I thinking. Of course you can't. You are so busy these days."

"Actually I—"

"Never mind that, of course you must be going, don't worry, I shan't take offence this time. The Duke is coming later to call on Miss Edwina in any case." Was it his imagination or did her voice go up an octave? "And I know how you like to accuse me of taking you away from your important duties."

Knowing when he was defeated, he released Miss Edwina's hand and turned to her to say goodbye. But he paused as he saw her looking from him to his sister and back again, her eyes focussed. *She can see...* For a moment he thought she knew... But then she just turned back to him and smiled, reaching out to shake his hand.

He bowed and left, ignoring Posy's suspicious glance. And as he walked back towards his office, he wondered if the look he saw for a moment in Miss Edwina's eyes was understanding, pity, or both.

CHAPTER 19

Hare tied a ribbon around her neck. It was dark blue and set off her eyes rather nicely. She put it on because she wanted to, of course and not because she knew that Mr Thompson was coming for lunch. Whether or not he was going to be visiting that day was really immaterial.

She tugged on the cuff of her sleeve. This day dress was likely the plainest of all her clothes. And the fact that she had picked it showed clearly that she wasn't out to impress any solicitors that afternoon. She looked in the mirror. It wasn't the most elaborate of outfits, but, she realised, it *was* her favourite. The printed blue fabric was soft to the touch and the fit was comfortable. And that's how she felt whenever she was around Ernest. *Comfortable.*

She stood and shook out all the wrinkles in her skirts. She frowned at a tiny stain by the hem of her sleeve. She focussed and let her hand hover over it for a moment. When she lifted her hand again the stain was gone. How strange that even such tiny glamours were difficult these days. She looked in the mirror, letting the magic fall for just a moment. The differences weren't so stark. She wouldn't have been able to adjust them if they were.

Her real eyes were a little bigger, the hair shinier, the chin a touch more pointy. She wondered for a moment, what Mr Thompson would have thought at seeing her like this. Would he recoil? His involvement with Anastacia and Melody didn't give her any illusion he'd care for her as she truly was. Rich humans liked their charity, but within strictly defined limits.

She blinked and Miss Edwina Walker once more took the place of Hare. She stomped down the stairs, landing her feet heavily. She was telling herself that each step was increasing her determination. To focus on the man she was *supposed* to be focussed on. *Ten, eleven...* There were thirteen steps from the first floor to the half landing. Her hand glided along the smooth polished wood of the bannister, as it curled and swirled beneath her fingers. She wondered if the wood had been merely carved, or if it bent to the carpenter's will through other means. Bend or be cut down. Not much of a choice, really.

She reached the dining room and braced herself before coming in. From the inside came the animated voice of Lord Winchfield. At first she thought he must have found the cut of someone's coat disagreeable, as there were few things capable of whipping him up into such a frenzy, but as a footman opened the door, a familiar name made her freeze into a spot.

"—nobody will even acknowledge Culross at the club anymore! A shame, a real shame!"

The Dowager Lady Winchfield noticed Hare hanging by the half-open door and waved at her impatiently. "You're letting in a draft, child, oh do come in."

"Ah, Miss Walker!" Lord Winchfield threw his hands in the air, one of them still holding onto a fork. "But this affects you too, dear."

"Whatever's the matter?" Hare looked around the table. Ernest was the only one seemingly calm. He mumbled a welcome as he focussed on his breakfast.

"It's a scandal." Posy shook her head. "Lord Culross has been exposed!"

Hare's heart sank and she stared at Ernest. Surely he didn't betray her confidence?

"Exposed how?"

"It seems the man has built himself a veritable house of cards and it is now falling all around him," Miss Bonningham said.

"Aptly put, dearest Anne." The Dowager patted Anne on the hand. "It's the way of the world that men such as that can run only so far and no farther."

Lord Winchfield, loath to stay out of the conversation for too long, gestured to Hare to sit down. "You see, he has debts, but then many do and nobody holds it against them. Except he tried to swindle his late wife's family. And there's more! Though I should perhaps not pollute your young ears with such talk..." He looked embarrassed and patted his chest.

"Children!" Posy almost shouted. She clearly had no regard for anyone's delicate feelings. "Illegitimate ones! With a vicar's wife on one of his properties!"

"The man kept silent, for his living situation rather depended on Tom's good will." Lord Winchfield shook his head. "But now, all of a sudden, the vicar decided to sue."

"And he has a very good case, we're told." Posy added.

"And there's more! More lawsuits! Coming from every side, surrounding him like locusts. The man is finished, I tell you all, finished!" Lord Winchfield was clearly overcome with emotion and stuck the fork in his sausage with a flourish.

"All at once?" Hare looked at Ernest. He was very intent on whatever was on his plate, but he could feel her eyes on him. She could tell by how his ears reddened. She smiled and sat next to him. "That seems... coincidental. Wouldn't you say so, Mr Thompson?"

He cleared his throat. "I suppose a man can only hide his true nature for so long before it catches up with him."

He finally looked up at her. And she knew. She nodded a thanks only he could understand. It passed like a secret between them.

CHAPTER 20

"You've been avoiding me."

"Of course not!" said Ernest, who, most emphatically, had been avoiding Brandon. The feelings he seemed to have developed for Edwina were only eclipsed by the crushing guilt he felt whenever he looked at or even thought of his best friend.

He picked at the pork chop. It was overdone but he'd be damned if he was going to complain. Chewy meat was better than he deserved.

Even this lunch happened only because Brandon practically ambushed Ernest on the way back from the office and wouldn't take no for an answer.

"I know what you've been up to."

A rivulet of cold sweat ran down Ernest's back. He dared to meet his friend's gaze.

"Brandon, I—"

"No use denying it, your sister told me all about it."

So Posy knew as well? Did Edwina tell her they kissed? Twice? Of course, she would have. That's what women do, right? They actually talk. Ernest's hands dropped to his knees and he balled them into fists. "I'm sorry, Brandon. I don't expect you'll—"

"—I was very touched, actually—"

Ernest's jaw hung open. "What?"

Brandon looked at him strangely. "You and Anastacia trying so hard to make Edwina feel welcome. I heard how you two have been taking her around town, meeting art people, gallery owners." He smiled. "It's so thoughtful, especially since you know an interest in the arts is something she and I share..."

"You've been interested in art for the whole of four months or so by now, right," Ernest said automatically.

Brandon furrowed his eyebrows and then he laughed. He leant forward and patted Ernest on the shoulder. "You can send the jibes my way all you want." He leaned back in his chair. "I still thank you for looking out for my future bride like this."

Ernest dropped the fork half-way towards his mouth. It clattered on the plate, spattering the gravy on his shirt. He swore and started dabbing at the shirt with the napkin.

"Are you quite alright?"

"Yes, I'm..." Ernest paused. He looked up and finally met Ben's eyes. "Are things all decided between you then?" *She didn't say anything. But then... Why would she? She owed him nothing.*

"Not explicitly, no." Ben looked at Ernest over a glass of sparkling water. "But it's heavily implied by now. I plan to propose after my birthday dinner at my house, a month from now." He smiled. "It'll be a small gathering and I plan to celebrate with those closest to me."

"I'm honoured to be included." Ernest swallowed. And he *was* honoured. This was his closest friend; a brother couldn't be closer. And here he was, coveting the one woman Brandon ever got serious about. Ernest crumpled the napkin in his fist. "I know you'll be very happy."

"You know what?" Brandon beamed as he ran his fingers through his pale hair. "Somehow I have always expected to be."

CHAPTER 21

Hare watched him for a while, enjoying this sense that for once she was free to observe without herself being seen. Ernest was waiting for her by the Eros fountain, leaning casually against the pale grey stone. She followed the line of his vision, at the crush of men and women moving through Piccadilly.

When she first saw him standing there, she almost called out. She had so much to tell him. She'd spent the morning with Melody and Anastacia, to all eyes a trio of wealthy, overpampered and underemployed ladies traipsing around Mayfair. They paid fashionably short, yet clandestinely fruitful visits to a great number of bored ladies, all eager to spend their money as soon as a promise of outshining their neighbours was dangled in front of them. In the previous couple weeks Hare had gathered a fair number of artists under her wing, all seeking employment. And in a single morning, she had managed to secure no fewer than five family portrait commissions. At a time when photography was gaining in popularity, that was certainly no mean feat.

Hare smiled at how skilfully Melody had helped steer the conversation when Lady Hillstrop raised that point.

"But, Lady Hillstrop," Melody said, leaning back in her languid manner. "Indeed photography is so popular these days that *anybody* can save up for one. Such an equaliser it is. If the French had only waited a little for such as this, then the whole bloody business last century could have been avoided." She tapped her chin thoughtfully. "Though I never before thought you were such a revolutionary, as to seek the same for every class. *Fraternite* and *Egalite* indeed." Anastacia was by now working hard to suppress a chuckle at Lady Hillstrop's suddenly stony expression.

"Dear Mrs Addison, I must protest…"

"Oh please, Lady Hillstrop, I admire this, truly." Melody waved away the other women's words. "There is no better way to lead than by example, that's true. Though I don't mind telling you, I'm just happy for this artist's sake that Lady Binchfield is a tad more old-fashioned."

"What does that woman have to do with it?" Lady Hillstrop looked like she was about to fall down from her chair.

Hare, catching Melody's eye, leaned forward and lowered her voice in a conspiratorial manner. "Lady Binchfield has practically *begged* us to introduce her to the artist, Anna Green. She's known to capture not just the likeness of her subjects, but that certain something—" Hare clenched her fingers in the air, then opened her hand, as if it contained fairy dust. Lady Hillstrop was captivated. "—that only the *old* families can recognise." She whispered, "*True* elegance."

"Indeed…" Lady Hillstrop was staring with her mouth hanging open, as Melody went in for the kill.

"We did say that as you outrank her, we should give you the opportunity to employ this artist first, of course. But," Melody shook her head, "I now see that I have insulted you. Photography is the future, of course. I'm sure you can enquire with your housekeeper about securing a very decent sort of *technician* for that. She might already have a name for you. After all, isn't it the fashion these days for the staff to commemorate events with having a picture taken?"

"You misunderstood me, Mrs Addison," Lady Hillstrop interrupted. "I never said I preferred a photograph to a painting. After all, it is a kind of duty for families such as mine to uphold certain standards. If you arrange a meeting with this Miss Green, I'm sure we can come to an understanding." She narrowed her lips to a line. "Lady Binchfield will simply have to wait."

Later, after the trio had left Lady Binchfields' house, having extracted a similar commitment through similar means, Hare felt more elated than she had in… well, perhaps ever. Was this what it was like? To have the freedom, the connections? What she would have given even two months before to have someone like Melody championing her. But now she could *be* the champion and that tasted like a different kind of sweet on the tongue.

Now Ernest, still leaning against the fountain, closed his eyes for a moment, as the clouds moved, letting the sunlight warm his face. Hare watched him a moment longer. In the light his skin glowed and his hair shone blue-black, as if someone had dipped it in ink.

She walked up to him, quietly. "Mr Thompson?" He opened his eyes lazily, as if half-asleep. She brushed her hands over her skirt, all of a sudden self-conscious under his gaze. She bristled. She never felt self-conscious, before she met him. Not when men stared at her, not even when they painted her body. She had often felt annoyed, aggrieved and cautious. Never self-conscious. So what business did he have staring at her in this analytical way.

She cleared her throat. "Anastacia and Melody had business elsewhere. So it's just me today. Shall we make a move? Mrs Brown is waiting."

That seemed to shake him out of his stupor. He stood up straight and bowed his head. "They left you alone?"

"But I'm not alone, am I?" She turned her head. A small smile stretched her lips. She wasn't sure why it should please her so much, but the sight of him being discomfited had washed away her own feelings of disquiet.

"I suppose not," he said, staring at his feet.

"Do I have something on my face?" she asked.

"I beg your pardon?" He looked up at her then. And when his eyes met hers, her legs threatened to go soft under her. Which was irritating. Just as the man himself was: wholly irritating.

She was in control, she reminded herself. And so, with the most casual tone she could muster, she said, "I ask, because you seem more comfortable inspecting your shoes than looking at me. And as we have an appointment to attend together, it wouldn't do if that was the response my face elicited."

"No," he said. *He was annoyed now, good.* "No, you haven't anything on your face. It just surprised me that Anastacia would feel comfortable to just leave you walking through London alone. Or with just me for company. It doesn't feel quite right."

"I never knew," Hare said, false shock on her face.

"Never knew what?"

Hare turned her face this way and that, as if she was a spy, about to divulge national secrets and, palm to her mouth, she whispered. "That you're so worried about your virtue."

"My *what*?" He looked like he was either ready to fall dead of mortal embarrassment or to throttle her.

"Please rest assured, I have no indecent designs upon you." She nodded. *That was not entirely true, but she would not dwell on it.* "You're quite safe with me."

"Am I?" He took a step forward. She almost retreated, *almost.* But that wouldn't do, of course. So she just stared, her face impassive, at his suddenly changed expression. "I felt like my virtue was decidedly threatened not so long ago."

"I'm not sure what you mean." She knew exactly what he

meant, of course and she couldn't help her eyes flitting briefly towards his lips.

"Perhaps I was mistaken then." He said, his voice lowered. "Perhaps it was another young woman who kissed me in Lady Leicester's gardens."

"She sounds quite shameless," she said, swallowing. "I can't imagine why you'd entertain such company." He was too close now and she didn't feel quite as in control as she did a moment before. Still, it's not like she was actually *flirting* with him, was it? She was making conversation. Not the most polite of conversations, perhaps, but it was just talking.

"I thought so too," he whispered. "But then I thought perhaps she wasn't shameless enough."

"Oh?" Those knees of hers definitely needed to find their backbone, in spite of the anatomical difficulties. They were getting all jelly-like on her.

"Perhaps if she could forget about shame and propriety, she could actually go for what she wants. Or *who* she wants."

"And you think yourself an expert on the wants of the young lady in question?" She tried to add an edge to her words. But she found irritation quite difficult to summon for some reason.

"Not at all." He shook his head. "In fact, I'm not sure the lady herself is an expert on the subject." He offered her his arm. It felt like a challenge. She stared at it for a moment, then with a sort of casual grace laced her hand through it.

"And how could you possibly divine that?" It was definitely a warm day. But if she were to fan herself with her hand he might misinterpret the gesture.

"She behaves like she wants one thing, but then when she lets her guard down her actions contradict her," he said, as they crossed the road towards the Leicester Square. "Perhaps she lets herself be persuaded by others to go after one kind of life, when another might suit her better."

"And you think you're the best judge of that?" she asked, more sharply than she meant to.

He was silent for a moment. "No," he said finally. "But I wish you were. Postponing judgements is in nobody's best interest as a rule."

"Ever the lawyer."

"That's what I am," he said, quietly. "I'm not a Duke, or an Earl, or a rubber baron. I'm a foreigner in this place, making a living. That's all." She tensed as she felt his searching gaze on her face. "I'm just one option, is all."

WHEN HARE CAME BACK to Winchfield house, she felt as if somebody had singed her feet and fried her brain. The meeting at Mrs Brown's gallery was productive, though the woman was so sharp, Hare felt like she was walking on eggshells the entire time. Yet the most exciting thing of all, were the eight words Mrs Brown whispered to her when Ernest's back was turned. "I've reviewed your drawings. Call on me later." Surely this was the most exciting phrase ever uttered in the English language? On either side of the ocean? She paused as she was taking off her hat at the entrance, pulling out the long pin keeping it in place. What was she going to do about it, though? The reality of her situation settled around her shoulders like a lead weight. "I'm just one option," Ernest had told her. As if it were that simple. Which, from his point of view, it really was. She was a woman in a position to make any choice she wanted. From his perspective, her will was all that mattered. How nice would it be to inhabit that role truly. To choose what she wanted. To pursue what she wanted. To have the option to rely on her talents rather than her looks.

"What are you planning on doing with that pin exactly?"

Hare looked up to see Miss Bonningham standing in the

shadow of the doorway. Her eyes were sharp and the lines between her eyebrows were deepened.

"Oh, nothing, aunt." Hare tried for a lighthearted tone, which did nothing to change the older woman's expression.

"Thank you." Miss Bonningham nodded to the butler, who made a hasty exit with Hare's hat. Once they were alone, the woman turned to Hare with all the suppressed rage of a life-long teacher. "Follow me," she said through gritted teeth. "Oh and please don't try to stash that folder you're holding anywhere on the way."

Hare's heart sank. She followed into the library and waited silently as Miss Bonningham closed the heavy oak door.

The older woman reached out and waited for Hare to pass her the folder. She then took it to the chair by the fireplace and sat down, as if she was getting ready to review her pupil's spelling test. She took a deep breath, steeling herself and opened it.

"What have you been doing with this?" she asked quietly, lifting one of Hare's drawings by the edges, with an expression of such utter disgust she might have as well been picking up a dead mouse. A mocking smile quirked the woman's lips. "You should have told me if you were showing off your accomplishments to potential suitors. I'm not entirely sure walking around with a portfolio is *quite* the way to do it."

"Anne, I—"

"Don't bother." Miss Bonningham closed the folder with a loud smack. "Don't bother lying to me. It's not in the best interest of either of us for you to lie to me." She met Hare's eyes. "You *do* realise that, don't you?"

Hare sighed and sat in the chair opposite to Miss Bonningham. "Yes. Yes, I suppose I know that."

"There's no 'suppose' about it, Hare." Anne passed the folder back to Hare, who couldn't hide her surprise. "What?" The older woman chuckled. "Did you think the evil ogre that I am, I was going to keep them? Burn them in an act of dramatic oppression?"

"It crossed my mind."

"Of course." Miss Bonningham looked so tired all of a sudden. Tired and… sad. "The evil old spinster set on destroying the beautiful maiden's future. That's how the stories tend to go? Straight from Mrs Henry Wood's novels, I should say. I didn't take you for the fanciful type, Hare."

"If I were not fanciful, I would never have gotten myself in the position I was in when you found me." Hare exhaled. "I suppose I ought to try to be less so."

"Indeed." Miss Bonningham scooted over to the edge of her cushioned chair and squeezed Hare's hand. "I was suspicious of your frequent excursions, yet, since they were with Lady Anastacia, I thought they were in the best interest of our cause. The Duke does dote on his sister and securing her good opinion is likely one of the most important factors to consider. But imagine my surprise looking out of the window and seeing you with Posy's brother instead."

"He just walked me home after meeting us all earlier."

"I'm not an idiot, Hare." Miss Bonningham withdrew her hand. "I saw how he looked at you. How he looks at you every time he comes around here. He is dangerous for you. And most dangerously of all, he is the Duke's best friend. How are you planning on securing Brandon if Mr Thompson is so obviously pursuing you too?"

"I don't think he's pursuing me…"

"Then you're as blind as a mole." Miss Bonningham rubbed her temple. A lock of greying hair escaped from her lace cap, which she'd taken to wearing on advice from the Dowager Winchfield. "Mr Thompson cannot give us safety. He can barely take care of himself. His wife and children will never enjoy great comfort. And he would certainly be in no position to look after his wife's ageing 'aunt'. And while you might consider cutting me out of the deal…"

"I didn't—" Hare started, but Miss Bonningham raised her hand to stop her.

"Don't bother. I wouldn't blame you if you did." She put one hand in the other and rubbed her palm. "You think I haven't thought through all the contingencies? But the truth is, we're much too entangled at this point."

"You shouldn't be worried." Hare stiffened. "You know enough of me to destroy any chance I have of having a decent position on either side of the ocean."

"Is that what you think?" Miss Bonningham raised an eyebrow. "That I would destroy you? What would be the point of that?"

"Well," Hare sputtered.

"I don't need to blackmail you into honouring our agreement, even if I were so inclined. Even apart from the fact that I'm your only anchor in the respectable society, the only connection that believably can vouch for you. Even if we put all that aside. You're still forgetting about the money."

"The money *you* stole."

"The additional funds I have withdrawn, yes. To allow *both* of us to come here. To allow us *both* to have this chance."

A moment of silence passed before either stirred again.

"We are both embroiled in this. We both benefitted from the money."

"I've thought on this," Hare said. "It might be theft, but across the ocean, what judge could convict us?"

"You forget *how* I got the money, Hare." Miss Bonningham rested her temple on her fist and waited for her point to sink in.

"Forgery…" Hare hung her head.

"And while nobody would extradite us over a few hundred dollars, forgery is as serious a matter here as in is in America. And it will be only a matter of time before that is discovered."

Anne nodded. "I don't say it lightly, Hare, but Mr Thompson can't protect you. The Duke can. For him, the money I took is nothing compared to his reputation. He'd pay them off and we'd be quite safe."

"He'd hate me for it." Hare closed her eyes.

"Likely. But many spouses grow to hate each other. And if that becomes the case with you, you'd still have the white cotton sheets to dry your tears with and a number of properties to retire to in order to avoid him. And, perhaps even more importantly, judging by your expression, it wouldn't actually *destroy* the man."

"It might. It might crush him when he finds out about me."

"So dramatic." Miss Bonningham waved her hand. "It would sting his pride, but such men recover." She gave Hare a shrewd look. "While Mr Thompson would certainly *not* recover."

Hare looked at the folder in her hands.

"I can see how he looks at you. How you look at him. End it now."

Hare stayed quiet.

"You still have ambition, Hare. I see it in your eyes. You think you can... what? Become a famed artist and escape the past with a lover? How did putting faith in men work out for you before?"

The barb stung. Hare closed her eyes. "It was different. Mr Thompson is nothing like that. He would... He would not treat me like this."

"And wasn't that exactly what you thought before?" Miss Bonningham raised one eyebrow. "Such a great judge of men you have turned out to be. But I grant you, Mr Thompson likely would marry you... As he sees you now. " Hare looked up. "But would he *choose* you if he knew you were a mythic? And more than that. Another man's discarded mistress. A woman who was bound to bare her body in front of dozens of men at the academy. You think Mr Thompson would choose a partner such as that?"

Hare shook her head.

"Of course not. The man might be enamoured with you, Hare, but much like the Duke, he is enamoured with the carefully curated version of you we have created. He is not a fool. He would not risk his reputation to marry a mythic or a fallen woman. And he would not be able to protect us if he did." She stood up and started walking towards the door. She paused when passing Hare and put her hand briefly on Hare's shoulder. "Marrying him would destroy him. There is no other way to look at it."

CHAPTER 22

The Summer Exhibition at the Royal Academy of Arts was a beautifully organised affair. Hare rested her hand on the marble balustrade as she took a deep breath, surveying everything before her. The cream of London society attended, all dressed in their finest clothes, most being clearly more interested in comparing their outfits than the paintings displayed proudly on the walls.

"What are you waiting for, Edwina, the Duke is waiting," Miss Bonningham said. She turned to the Dowager Baroness. "Lady Winchfield, it seems we with our older legs can still find more energy than the young these days." She laughed as the older woman holding on to her elbow nodded gravely.

"How right you are, dear Anne." She tapped the steel tip of her cane on the marble floor. "Still, youth never think there is cause to hurry. They think they have all the time and then some to spare. Still, it's the way of the world and they find out the truth eventually. But you," she leaned conspiratorially towards Miss Bonningham, "are still surely too young for the comparison to be too stark. I told my dear Bertie just the other day, I told him: 'Our dear Miss Bonningham has the energy about her of a young filly, so that it is a pleasure to watch her bustle about.'"

"My dear Lady Winchfield, you flatter me as always." Miss Bonningham smiled and squeezed the old woman's elbow. "How fortunate I am to have found such a friend in you." She paused and glanced towards Hare. "Are you coming? The Duke can't have gone too far."

Hare nodded and followed. Each room was filled with grand paintings. Women in fine gowns trimmed with lace and gentlemen in their striped trousers and carefully tailored jackets, all those bastions of propriety, gazed upon the paintings of women dressed in nothing but wisps of muslin, their breasts' softness captured by the brush, their wet pink lips parted in smiles. Some of the paintings were of mythics, of course. Kidnapped creatures of legend, like her, reduced to the role of a professional muse.

Hare couldn't help but smile herself, imagining how those gathered would react to see those same models here in the flesh. If any of the women, human or otherwise, who had modelled for those fine artists dared to show themselves, how quickly would they be ushered out, not to offend the eyes of the respectable people. But here those women were just oil and pigment, their flesh stretched like the canvas that captured them. Safely contained.

Hare knew those who were *in* the paintings were not the important ones. It was all about the painters, who watched their models mercilessly, directing how to place an arm, how to turn the hip. The ones who measured with a cold calculating look and then squeezed them inside the frames. Not *them* truly, of course, not those women in their entirety. The painters always picked what they saw, after all, what they deemed important and discarded the rest without a second thought.

She wondered how the good people of London would react to see the paintings *she* herself had modelled for. Would they even recognise her? Or would they reject the evidence of their eyes. After all, a person couldn't be tricked by a painting. And a model, in their eyes was nothing more than a painting in waiting. An inanimate object.

"Miss Edwina..." A familiar voice broke her train of thought. She looked around. Ernest was standing there, a look of admiration on his face. That wasn't so surprising. Hare knew she looked beautiful. Beauty was, after all, what she had been selected for. She wore a pale pink gown with sheer purple overlay, buttoned right up to her chin. Miss Bonningham had herself overseen her hair styling, so that small curled strands would artfully escape and frame her neck. Admiring looks from men? Those she was used to. They brought her no pleasure.

But there was something else there in Ernest's dark eyes, which warmed something in her chest. He smiled at her, a deep dimple appearing in his cheek.

How curious she didn't think him very handsome when she first saw him. He was beautiful. The sun filtering through the window fell on his skin. It practically glowed. She suddenly reddened, wondering if he could guess her thoughts.

"Mr Thompson!" Miss Bonningham shoved herself between the two of them. "Have you seen the Duke? He was meant to be back after he went to look for his sister and her fiancé and we are quite lost now."

"I see." All warmth escaped from Ernest's eyes. "I'll try to do my best to assist you till he can be found again."

"Oh, very well." Miss Bonningham huffed. Hare bit her lip at Anne's rudeness.

On an impulse, she reached and took Ernest's elbow. He tensed for just a moment, making her think she had made a mistake, but then he beamed at her. "Shall we go then?"

As they moved through the crowd, Miss Bonningham and the Dowager trailing behind them, Hare looked for something to say, something to distract her from the warmth of his arm, which she felt through the fabric of his jacket sleeve. "I'm afraid your sister couldn't come with us today. She came down with a headache this morning, as has Lord Winchfield."

Ernest laughed. "Posy has as much interest in art as she does in the engineering of a steam engine." He winked at Hare. "Which is to say none at all. She would like to be *seen* as someone invested in the arts, which is why she promises everyone she will come to the Summer Exhibition every year, only to find a feeble excuse at the last minute." He ran his finger inside the high collar of his shirt, which must have been starched to oblivion, the way it barely bent at the pressure.

"Those collars look very uncomfortable," she said. "It looks like it's digging into your neck somewhat."

"And just how closely have you been watching my neck, Miss Edwina?" he replied. He blanched at her expression. "I'm sorry, that was inappropriate."

"Was it?" She gave him a side-eye. "I didn't hear anything."

"You're very gracious," he said with a chuckle.

"And what are you two laughing about?"

Hare looked up and saw Brandon watching her strangely. She let go of Ernest's arm as if it was a hot iron. "We were just commiserating with Lady Winchfield, who sadly couldn't join us today."

"Yes, *such* a shame," the Duke said flatly, his pale eyes not leaving her face.

Must he stare so?

"You leave Edwina alone at your peril, Ben, so don't sulk if another takes her arm," a familiar voice said from behind him. "Now move aside, please." Anastacia practically shoved her brother and grinned at Hare. "Edwina! I couldn't wait to see you today. Sam's finally arrived in London last night. Let me introduce you two. Miss Edwina Walker, this is my fiancé, Mr Samuel Willingham, but you just go ahead and call him 'Sam' for my sake.

He knows how I hate all the formality between friends and I fully expect you to be the best of friends and—"

As Anastacia prattled on, Hare felt all the blood drain from her face. In front of her stood Sam, just how she remembered him.

"Stacia..." he practically croaked, as if a frog had gotten stuck in his throat. "Me and H— Miss Walker, we've met before."

No, Hare thought. He wasn't *exactly* how she remembered him. He was more... ordinary-looking somehow. He still had the same brown hair, same brown eyes, the same narrow-bridged nose. But she was certain if she'd dug into her memories, of those few feverish months they had spent together, that this man standing in front of her would have been nothing like the man she once imagined him to be.

Even more so as a small sly smile stretched his lips now, giving him a predatory look.

Anastacia noticed nothing, but instead clapped her hands in delight. "Well, of course! After all, you're both from New York! What a small world this is after all!" She leaned into her fiancé, "I hope you were friends already then, because let me tell you right now, you will be quite the dearest friends from now on. I will expect nothing else once Ben and Edwina are..." She suddenly looked flustered as her brother glared at her.

"How do you do, *Miss Edwina*," Willingham said with a smirk, as he lifted Hare's hand to his lips. "I'm glad to see you looking so well. After all, the last time we met, you were rather upset."

"Why was Miss Walker upset?" Ernest asked.

"It was..." Hare said, watching Willingham. *Would he betray her?* But he could have done so straight away. What was he waiting for? "It was after my parents had died. It was... a hard time."

"Indeed." Willingham nodded gravely and perhaps only Hare could have noticed the note of mockery in his voice. "Such a loss that you suffered. One could say you really lost everything in that moment." His lips brushed against her fingertips. She fought against the revulsion which swept through her.

"What a strange thing to say, Sam." Anastacia smacked him on the shoulder with her fan. She smiled apologetically at Hare. "He's prone to philosophical turns of phrase it seems."

"Not a quality I'd ever noticed in myself, I have to admit." Willingham smiled at his fiancée fondly. "But I'm sure you're correct in this, as you are in all things."

"Sage words." Brandon nodded. "Also exactly what my sister expects from you."

"Don't you start now." Anastacia laughed.

She looked so happy. Hare forced a smile to her lips. That Anastacia, that fierce, clever woman would fall for a man such as… But then, Hare had once prided herself on being nobody's fool. And yet…

"It is always such a pleasure to come across old friends," Miss Bonningham said beside her. They locked eyes. "Mr Willingham, I'm afraid I haven't had the pleasure…"

"Oh yes, of course…" Hare took a step to the side. "Mr Willingham, this is my aunt, Miss Bonningham."

"Is she now?" *He looked so damn amused!* "I'm very happy to meet you, Miss Bonningham."

"Miss Bonningham was my sister's, Lady Winchfield's, school mistress," Ernest said. Hare chanced a look. He seemed serious, more than she'd ever seen him be before, as he cast a calculating look over Willlingham.

"I beg you excuse me," Hare said. "I will meet you in the Vestibule in a few moments."

"Should I go with—" Miss Bonningham started.

"No, please don't interrupt your enjoyment of the exhibition on my behalf. I will be only gone for a moment."

She turned around on her heel and walked off.

She was walking as if in a daze. *He was here*. What would he do? With a word, he could destroy all her plans and yet he just stood there, smiling. He must have been told by Anastacia that Ben and Hare were on the verge of an engagement. *And Willingham was not the sort of man to allow her to succeed.*

"Miss Walker—!"

Anne recognised him immediately. She looked like she was about to faint.

"Miss Walker—!"

Perhaps he didn't want to expose his own actions in front of Anastacia—

"Edwina!"

The voice finally broke her out of her thoughts. She spun around to see Ernest, looking at her with a mixture of concern and confusion.

"I've been calling your name," he said, his voice lowered. "Didn't you hear?"

Except you weren't calling me by my *name, were you?* But she couldn't exactly say that, could she.

"I was lost in thought. All this excitement is making me absent-minded." She laughed softly, covering her mouth with the tips of her fingers. It made her look flirtatious and drew attention to her lips. It also usually worked as a distraction. But his expression didn't change.

"Excitement, is it?" he turned his head to the side. A man walked past and gave them a curious look. Ernest moved forward and grabbed Hare's hand, which he laced through his arm.

"What are you doing?" Hare tried to pull her hand out, but Ernest held it in a vice-like grip.

"I'm taking you somewhere where we can talk without drawing attention."

"What do we have to talk about?" She tried the haughty expression, which did nothing but draw an amused look from him.

"A lot, as a matter of fact." They walked down the stairs and away from the crowds. He looked around and then beelined for a curtained-off alcove. "But let's start with how exactly you know Anastacia's fiancé."

"We moved in the same circles," she said. "I barely knew him. *Where* is it exactly you're taking me?"

Instead of answering, he just pushed her behind the curtain, as he spun around, checking there were no onlookers. "Get in," he said, before he followed her.

The small alcove was clearly used for storage and contained a couple of buckets stacked with still-wet rags hanging off the side, as well as a ladder and a couple crates. It was dark, the heavy curtain blocking out most of the light.

Hare mustered all the outrage she could manage. "I don't know what you think you're doing, but—"

"You ran away from him," he said. He was so close to her now she could smell him.

Her nostrils flared in annoyance.

"I don't 'run' from men."

"No, I suppose you don't strike me as the type. You're more likely to climb out of the window." He chuckled. "Let's say, then… a strategic retreat?"

She smiled, in spite of herself.

"That's better." He hesitated, then pinched her chin between his thumb and forefinger, tilting her face upwards. "If you can laugh, then perhaps it is not as bad as all that."

The scant light filtered through the heavy drapes, reflected off their rich red fabric, colouring his face with a warm tint, making it look like a flame was licking his skin. She raised her hand and touched his cheek with the tip of her finger. He swallowed and leaned into her hand.

"And why are you so interested in my troubles? Real or imagined—" she added quickly, "—my troubles are my own."

"What do you know of Mr Willingham?" He no doubt hoped to sound confident, but his voice caught in his throat and his eyes became unfocussed. His hand was still on Hare's face. She felt the warmth of his fingertips just below her lips.

"Careful, Mr Thompson," she whispered. "You're beginning to sound jealous."

"Do you—?" He inched towards her, so the length of his body pressed against her. Hare placed her hand on his chest. She meant to push him away. And any moment now, she would. And if she breathed in his scent, for a heartbeat or two, what harm could it do? She would push him away then. He wet his lips, before speaking again. "Do you want me to be jealous?"

"No," she said it quickly, too quickly. "Maybe." She bit her lip. "Jealousy implies possession. I don't think I want to be seen in that light." *Never again,* she almost added.

He lowered his face towards her.

She curled her fingers on his chest, her nails catching on the fabric of his jacket. A small piece of black thread stuck out from under a button. She stared at that piece and inched her fingers towards it. It suddenly became imperative that she inspect that little errant thread. And if she had to bring her face closer to his chest to see it properly, then what of it? She pinched the end of the thread and twisted it round the iron button, careful not to touch the metal.

"And how do you want me to see you?"

She looked up at his face sharply, but before she had the presence of mind to respond, she heard a familiar voice coming from behind the drapes.

Ernest's arm stole around her waist and pulled her farther from the curtain.

A sense of sudden panic filled Hare's chest. The Duke and his sister were right there, a couple feet away, their words muffled. She leaned against Ernest. She couldn't help it really, there was no space for her to move. He must have decided the same, for his hand never moved from her waist. She turned her head and his shoulder warmed her neck. She wasn't *technically* resting her head on his shoulder. And he definitely wasn't smelling her hair. Her hair was here and his face was right there and the poor man couldn't help it if his nose ended up right next to her head. All easily denied, all easily sidestepped. She wasn't removing her hand from where it rested on his chest, but that's because where else could she put it really.

"You smell like roses," he whispered in her ear.

Alright so that *was not as easily denied.* But then it was an observation. Observations were perfectly fine and perfectly reasonable. Observations were necessary to a perceptive mind. Like she couldn't help but notice that he smelled like cloves. That didn't mean anything. Still, she felt it necessary to explain. "It's the soap."

"There's the soap and then there's you."

What did that even mean? She breathed in to let him know such comments were entirely unnecessary and unwelcome, but then the breath was wasted on a gasp, as his hand moved upwards and pressed her closer against his chest.

"Do you want me to move away?" he whispered. His breath tickled her neck, the small hairs standing on end.

"I think..." She would say yes, but first she'd feel him for a moment longer, the warmth of him, the scent of him. A moment to collect her thoughts, that's what she needed. She closed her eyes. She couldn't do this. "Did you consider for a moment, what would happen if we were found like this?"

"I suppose I'd have to marry you."

She looked up at him. He was smiling at her, shyly, like he wanted to— *No.*

"I think we should go." She took a step back.

"Edwina..." He let go, but a hurt look stole over his face. "If it's about Willingham... I don't know what happened between you, but I don't care."

She snorted.

"Whatever happened, it's in the past. Why should I care about it."

"Few people are in a position to disregard the past," she said. "And I'm sorry to say, I don't think you're one of them."

"But Brandon is, I suppose?" His tone changed. She looked up and felt instant regret as a new kind of coldness entered his eyes. "Of course."

"Ernest—"

"We better go. I'll check if anyone is looking. You go first."

"I think you misunderstand my words…"

"I think not." He flashed her an angry look. "You have made your meaning abundantly clear. It's safe. You can go."

Hare raised her hand as if to touch his arm and then put it down again. What was the point of it, when she couldn't explain things to him, not really.

She joined the party with as much cheerfulness as she could muster, when stared at by Willingham. She purposefully stood as far away from the man as she could and took the Duke's arm.

"Did you not meet Mr Thompson?" Willingham seemed unwilling to let it rest. "He went to make sure you wouldn't get lost on the way back. It is a huge gallery, after all."

"As you can see he's not with me and I somehow managed to find my way back on my own." She didn't dare look in the man's direction. "Perhaps it is him who is lost." She raised her eyebrows in a mocking expression. "Do you consider women in general so feeble minded they are liable to get lost between three rooms?"

"Yes, what was it you meant exactly, Sam?" Anastacia playfully smacked her fiancé on the shoulder with her fan.

He must hate that. An unwelcome thought popped into Hare's mind. Willingham was never one to put up with a scolding, even in jest. Yet his face remained fixed in a pleasant expression and the look in his eyes was tender when he looked at Anastacia. Perhaps he had changed. Was it possible he could have changed?

"Miss Walker, I'm glad to see you've rejoined the rest of the company." Ernest's voice made her spin around. She could feel herself blushing and hated her body betraying her like that.

"I understand you went to look for me."

"I did. Seems it was a fool's errand," he said without a smile.

"Shall we continue with the exhibition?" Miss Bonningham asked.

"As usual, dear Anne is talking sense, when the rest of us chatter about who knows what." Lady Winchfield knocked the ground with her cane once to emphasise her point. "Miss Bonningham, lead the way. I would know your opinion on the nude over there since everyone keeps talking about it." The old lady pointed to the far corner of the room. "It'd be quite scandalous, of course, if it were not great art. But then I suppose the scandal melts away if the art is agreed to be great." The woman smiled fondly at Miss Bonningham. "It's the way of the world, you know."

* * *

As the rest of the group followed the Dowager and Miss Bonningham, Ernest kept his eyes fixed on Edwina. He saw the blush which spread up her back , visible like a shadow on the sheer white fabric of her shirt. She walked in front of him, holding onto Brandon's arm. Ernest stared at that arm as if he could make it wither away with a look alone.

But what was the point. Edwina made it clear that Brandon's position in life mattered to her more than whatever attraction she might have felt for Ernest. He couldn't fault her for it. Brandon had the money, Ernest did not. Brandon had the title of a Duke and the only reason Ernest was even allowed in the same room half the time was their friendship. That and Posy's husband. And Brandon was *settled* into this world. Ernest rarely allowed himself to feel jealousy of this aspect of his friend's life. But he felt it now. Was that what she meant when she said he wasn't in the position to disregard the past? She knew Ernest had been sent off as a child, to travel with strangers across the ocean. The fees his parents paid for his studies fulfilled their obligations towards him, as far as his father was concerned. And so he was left drifting. He adapted, he found a way to fit in. But it was, after all, learnt. Brandon knew who he was and he had as his birthright the ability to feel at ease in this world.

Ernest's wife would not enjoy the kind of life the wife of a Duke would. Would not command the same respect. An American beauty garnered interest as a debutante, but would become just another foreigner once married to him. Edwina would have to be foolish to disregard all of that.

And the fact that her feeling this way was in some way connected to Willingham made Ernest boil over with resentment. He glanced over ahead, where the rich boy was whispering something into Anastacia's ear. What happened between him and Edwina, exactly? He saw the man shoot her furtive looks here and there, even though she seemed determined to never acknowledge him or even look in his direction. Did he jilt her? Hurt her? Ernest found his hand balling into a fist at the thought. He thought about the ball and how Edwina forbid him from exposing Culross' behaviour. She made it clear then that Ernest did not have her permission to act as her protector. And the same was made clear to him now. Edwina wanted him to pretend he noticed nothing. It was infuriating.

They arrived at the painting the Dowager was so keen to see. Ernest looked up. It was supposed to represent some Greek goddess. Though the subject seemed only relevant in as far as it gave the artist the free license to dress her in nothing but some sheer ribbons, floating as if lifted by a, frankly improbable, gust of wind, so that they could fall artfully over the curve of her breasts.

"It's the newest Shewrey," Brandon announced. "His star has been rising steadily over the last few years."

"It is quite a stunning painting," Willingham said. "Wouldn't you agree, Miss Walker?"

"I suppose," she said it without meeting Willingham's eyes.

"You only suppose?" Brandon exclaimed, a hand to his chest. "Yet he is the darling of the Royal Academy."

"I suppose the subject itself might offend Miss Walker," Willingham once more piped in. There was a sharp edge to his tone when he added, "A young maiden who'd lived her life as innocently as Miss Walker, would naturally find this rather shocking."

"Hardly." There was a distinctly cold note to her voice, Ernest was pleased to note. Willingham's comment wasn't just odd. There was something else there, something he meant as a message. "It is just..." Edwina took a step towards the painting, tilting her head to the side. "The consistency of light is lacking."

"Perhaps for dramatic effect?" Brandon said with obvious interest.

"No, I don't think so." She shook her head slightly. "Look to this corner, here." She pointed to the right top corner. "There is a window here, where the natural light is meant to flood in. Yet that side of the goddess' body is drenched in shadow."

"So it is!" Brandon's jaw dropped. "Ernest, come look at this. I feel quite embarrassed I haven't noticed it myself."

"Understandable. When accompanying such a beautiful woman," Willingham said with a smirk. "Miss Walker far outshines *this* painting's model, after all."

"Now as compliments go, that's an odd one," Brandon said seriously. Ernest wondered if his friend too took offence at the man's words. But then Brandon smiled in his usual way and made a broad gesture towards the room. "I would challenge you to find a single painting in this room that would not be improved for having Miss Walker as its subject."

"I'm sure that *this* room possesses no painting that approaches Miss Walker's loveliness." Willingham gave a small bow. Something about his inflection made Ernest's heckles rise. What exactly was this man on about. Even Anastacia seemed somewhat uncomfortable and that woman could pull off wearing a pinecone hat in the Queen's ballroom.

"You're too kind," Edwina said. She looked like she was about to be sick. The feeling of resentment Ernest felt a moment before melted away.

"Miss Edwina, there was a particular painting I was hoping to get your opinion on, if you would." The words were out before he could stop himself.

"*Which* painting exactly, Thompson?" Brandon eyed him curiously. "I didn't see any of them particularly grab your interest.

"Oh, the one over there." Ernest waved vaguely towards another room.

"Shall we all make our way there?" Miss Bonningham asked. Ernest felt like strangling her.

"Oh no need. You've all seen it already," he said quickly. "Miss Edwina?" He offered her his arm, which she took, first glancing at Brandon. *As if asking permission.* He gritted his teeth.

As they turned to walk off, Brandon took a half step towards him and bent down towards Ernest's ear. "Ought I feel jealous, old friend?"

Ernest exhaled. Then he looked in Brandon's eyes. "You'd be a fool not to." A thread of understanding passed between the two men and Ernest felt as if the room had turned a few degrees colder all of a sudden.

* * *

"WHAT DO you think you're doing exactly?" Hare asked as Ernest practically dragged her off.

"Here, look at this painting and pretend to consider it." Ernest pulled her up in front of a particularly hideous pastoral scene, which had the benefit of having no onlookers close to it.

"I've considered it, it's awful." Hare grimaced.

"Will you tell me what it is Willingham kept alluding to?"

Hare looked up at him. "Nothing."

"Nothing, is it?" Ernest made a gesture towards the painting, as if he was enquiring about some aspect of the composition. "Your aunt looked ready to give up the ghost and you turned as white as a sheet. It's lucky for you Anastacia temporarily turned into a simpering fool next to that man, or she would have been the one to drag you off."

"It's..." Hare considered her next words carefully. A partial truth made for a better lie. "I know him to be a wholly unpleasant man."

A flash of anger passed through Ernest's features. "Unpleasant how?"

"As unpleasant as a young entitled man can be towards the young women of his acquaintance."

"I see." He remained quiet for a moment. "And what, if his fault is so universal, does he hold against you personally?"

She tightened her lips.

"Edwina..."

She ignored his use of that name. She wouldn't look at him. She had to think. She couldn't tell him, he couldn't...

He did nothing, that's what she was going to say. Instead, "He made promises he didn't keep," was what came out of her mouth. Her gloved hand immediately flew to her lips and she looked up at Ernest. His eyes darkened and there was an expression there which frightened her.

"Please, please don't say anything." She grabbed the edge of his jacket.

"Keep looking at the painting. You know they're all staring at us," he said. His hand brushed against hers, as he turned his body away and, so briefly she thought she might have imagined it, he squeezed her fingertips, before lifting his hand to make a vague gesture around the part of the painting, which the painter had decorated with—Hare squinted—possibly sheep.

"I won't say anything if you don't want me to," he said finally. "But please consider, Anastacia isn't just a sister of Brandon's. She's a friend of yours as well as mine. And she deserves better."

"I know she does," she whispered. She hadn't considered that till this point, so caught up was she in her own fear. But the only thing stopping the man now from denouncing her was his own reputation. If she took that away, there would be nothing left to prevent him from exposing her.

"But you're afraid of what Brandon might think," he said. After a moment, he added. "You should give him more credit. He's not the kind of person who'd throw over a girl because of a past flirtation."

Past flirtation... The silence stretched between them. She glanced at him. She wondered how much it must have cost him now to defend Brandon to her in this way. And as for her, she must have seemed like the worst kind of a coward in his eyes. And, she realised with a start, it hurt. She didn't want Ernest to think badly of her. Even if this… thing between them could go no further, she was somehow hoping they could remain—well, not friends maybe—but friendly. But here she could see his thoughts, as clear as if they'd been written out on his forehead. He thought her shallow, selfish. Disloyal. She could feel the tears threaten to rise in her eyes and she fought back against them.

But what did he really know about her? About the choices she had to make. She wouldn't be shamed for surviving.

"It's not what—"

"I think we ought to go back." He didn't even look at her. She swallowed. What would be the point of trying to defend herself. In the end it would all be the same.

They made their way back to the group. She didn't look back at him. She couldn't, not if she were to stand a chance at keeping her eyes dry.

"What was your assessment?" Brandon asked her.

"Assessment?"

"Of that painting Ernest was so eager to have you see, of course."

"Oh, yes," she said absent-mindedly. "Lovely."

"*Lovely?*" Anastacia laughed. "We can't be talking about the same piece! Ben?" She turned to her brother. "Is that the one by the son of the Royal Academy's president?"

"Lower your voice, Stacia." Brandon put his finger to his lips, but amusement twinkled in his eyes. "I'm not supposed to be telling people that."

"Oh, pish-posh." Anastacia shrugged.

Realising her error, Hare reddened like a lobster. "I didn't want to be unkind," she said, finally.

"Lying isn't kindness, dear Edwina." Anastacia gave her a meaningful look then sighed. "I rather expect the poor soul who committed that atrocity had rather too many people praising him, till he finally believed in his own genius."

Hare laughed. "I suppose, when you look at it like that, yes. It was rather bad."

"You were talking a long time just to arrive at that conclusion," Willingham said, looking at Hare.

"On the contrary, Miss Walker has helped me understand, with surgical precision, all of the painting's many faults. Now," Ernest turned to the rest of the party, "I admit to being quite hungry. Not being as artistically inclined as many of you, staring at paint makes me think of lunch more than of the spark of divine favour."

"Now here's a sensible man." The Dowager Lady Winchfield chuckled. "And an excellent idea it is. My old legs can't take much more of this standing around. Not even." She patted the hand of Miss Bonningham, "with dear Anne holding me up. So shall we return back to the Winchfield house?"

"I have a better idea!" Willingham said. Hare imagined how he'd look with a hairpin stuck in his throat. She rather liked the image. How could she have ever considered that man handsome.

She must have had an aneurysm. "Trocadero is practically a stone-throw away from the gallery. I haven't been before, but it is said to be quite elegant."

"Since Lady Winchfield has already told us she's tired, I'm not sure it would be kind to drag her to a restaurant for a meal likely inferior to what is usually served at her own home." Ernest went as stiff as a board, but Hare saw the glance he sent her way. He had his hands clasped behind his back and she saw how he kept clenching and unclenching his fist. She felt a surge of warmth swell up in her chest, followed by a crushing sense of shame. Because here he was, trying to protect her. Again. Even though by now he must have considered her the very worst of women.

"Oh no, I won't have you curtail your fun on my account, young man." Lady Winchfield shook the tip of her cane in front of Ernest's face. "Youth needs its entertainment, while age requires rest. It's the way of the world, you know. I always tell my Bertie, I say 'You go and enjoy yourself while you can.' I certainly did when I was a young woman." She chuckled. "Miss Bonningham should go with you, of course. I wouldn't wish to keep her tied to me all the time. Well, I might *wish* it for the pleasure of her company, but I'm not so selfish as to deprive you all of it."

What could Miss Bonningham do in the face of such praise? Of course, she reassured the older woman that she'd much rather take some rest as well.

Willingham, puffed up by his victory, raised his eyebrows at Ernest. "If you're busy, of course, Mr Thompson, I wouldn't dream of keeping you from your duties. We will look after Miss Walker."

Hare felt sick. With just Brandon and Anastacia there, sooner or later they would notice Willingham's constant hints and it would all come out. She didn't have the courage to look up at Ernest. He must judge her so.

"I was merely thinking of the comfort of Lady Winchfield,"

Ernest said, evidently faking good humour. Poorly. "However, I wouldn't forego the pleasure of all your company. And the lunch. While the landlord at my lodgings is a very pleasant and, by all standards, excellent woman, there's only so many times a week a man can stomach thin beef and swede broth."

With that settled, the group made their way out of the gallery and towards the street, where Ernest went to flag down a carriage for Lady Winchfield and Miss Bonningham.

As they waited on the pavement, Miss Bonningham positioned herself close to Hare. While she couldn't say much without being overheard by the rest of the party, she gave Hare's hand a quick squeeze. "You can do this," she whispered, all the while glaring at Willingham's back. As if he could feel the older woman's eyes on him, he turned his head, ever so slightly towards them. Just so much that both could see the mocking smile that stretched his lips.

They didn't have to wait long for a carriage and as Ernest was helping Lady Winchfield up, Brandon took the opportunity to come up closer. "You needn't force yourself, Thompson," he said lightly, though Hare noticed his strained expression. "I promise I will take excellent care of Miss Edwina."

"I know you would," Ernest said. "But my sister wouldn't forgive me if I didn't join you all. For propriety's sake." Over his head, Miss Bonningham gave Hare an alarmed look.

Hare swallowed. This was not good. Brandon was clearly not the jealous sort. Yet if even he had noticed something about Ernest's behaviour to concern him, then that meant she needed far more caution. "The more the merrier," she said weakly, as Brandon and Ernest were staring daggers at each other, while Willingham looked on with amusement.

"It's quite a space," Willingham said, looking around the Trocadero restaurant. The afternoon crowd had come in by now and, though the group managed to secure a table, the space felt as busy as a market day in a village. They were seated in a booth, Hare wedged between Brandon on her left and Ernest, with Willingham and Anastacia seated opposite.

"I expect it's nothing much compared to what you're used to in New York," Anastacia said.

Willingham laughed. "I won't contradict you there." He leaned towards Brandon. "It's true, that is where the money is these days and money likes grandeur. London has the respectability of age to it. We can but compete in size." He winked at Hare, who fought hard against nausea. Nobody else seemed to have noticed the double meaning. Perhaps it was too outlandish to suspect it here, in this place.

"I think it all hinges on the food, doesn't it?" Anastacia said. "What use is a gilded table, if you leave hungry."

"I agree with my sister." Brandon rubbed his hands together. "Now what shall we have? Just please tell me nobody is having pea soup. It's rather like watching someone drink pond water."

"As long as there's no pond-skaters, it's still preferable to watching someone eat oysters." Anastacia leaned towards her fiancé. "I don't believe we ever had the oyster discussion."

"I don't believe we have." He looked at her fondly. *He used to look at me like that.* Hare shuddered. For Anastacia's sake, she hoped there was something genuine behind the look now.

Willingham noticed her slight movement and rubbed his moustache with his middle finger, like he was considering a horse he was thinking of buying. He never used to have a moustache. It made him look ridiculous, like a vaudeville villain. Which, Hare supposed, he was in a way. "Are you not a fan either, Miss Walker?" he said. "You're suddenly looking somewhat green."

"Oh please, we're friends here, Sam." Anastacia gave him a playful smack on the shoulder. "Just call her Edwina. It's so stuffy, with 'Miss This' and 'Lady that'. She's my friend, so that makes us practically family, don't you think? And you've met before so there's no need for awkwardness."

Brandon's jaw hung open. "You can't just announce it, Stacia! It's not up to you." He turned to Hare, "I'm sorry."

"I certainly don't mind dropping the honourifics, if Miss Walker doesn't." Willingham said with a small bow of the head.

Hare understood the challenge. As she opened her mouth to respond, she felt someone squeeze her right hand under the table. She didn't need to look. Ernest understood. She squeezed back and heard Ernest exhale to her side. "I don't mind at all, *Sam*. After all, like Anastacia says, we're among friends."

"Anastacia is often right," Willingham said, poring over the menu. "I make it a policy never to disagree with her, in fact."

"It's made so much easier by the fact we're often of one mind where it matters." Anastacia practically beamed. Hare felt like her stomach turned into a small hard rock. She tried to smile placidly, as her friend extolled her fiancé's virtues. "You know, Edwina, Sam has been so supportive of our endeavours. I don't know if you know, but he studied art for a while, back in New York, before he went into business for his family."

"Oh?" Hare lifted a glass of champagne to her lips. She didn't enjoy it, but it was *de rigeur* at city luncheons, apparently. She genuinely wished it was at least thrice stronger.

"Come now, *Edwina.*" The sound of the name on his lips made her skin crawl. How things change. "You surely remember. We were even in a class together, you know."

"In a class?" Brandon turned to Hare with an impressed look on his face. "You attended the Art Students League classes as well? They allow women in?"

"Oh, yes," Hare said. "As long as they have the money to pay with." She kept her face blank. She couldn't show how she felt. Not in front of Brandon, not in front of Anastacia. But she felt Ernest's eyes on her and she felt the comfort of his presence. He moved his leg under the table cloth, so their knees touched. From anyone else it would have been an unforgivable affront. But from him, in this moment, it felt like the greatest show of solidarity she'd ever experienced.

"See, Ben, the Royal Academy would do well to observe." Anastacia smacked her hand on the table as Brandon tried to object. Softly, but still. "Did you know, Edwina, that the Royal Academy only started allowing women to attend the life drawing classes a few years ago? And even with that, they carefully limit our numbers on their courses. 'A female invasion' they call it. And over there in New York, the women work alongside men for the betterment of their craft and nobody bats an eyelid. And why should they?" She made a sweeping gesture towards Hare. "Edwina did the same work as everyone else, after all."

"Oh, not sure I'd say *the same*." Willingham's eyes twinkled. He was enjoying himself, the bastard. "But yes, she was the *model* student."

Anastacia, who was gratefully missing his allusions was looking down into the menu. "That is precisely the sort of discrimination that needs to be rooted out of the society if we want to move forward into this new century with a better system."

"Agreed," Willingham said.

"I didn't realise women's rights were of such concern to you, Willingham." Brandon said,

"Oh, Sam is so invested in the cause!" Anastacia, leaned forward, looking around, as if the room was full of spies.

Hare stared silently, not sure how to respond. "Indeed?" she said, finally. Her eyes briefly locked with Willingham's. He was taunting her. Daring her to contradict her friend. And she should have. She felt Ernest's presence next to her, like a red-hot iron, about to brand her as the coward she was. She looked down. She didn't have to look at Willingham to know he triumphed. She didn't need to look at Ernest to know his disappointment in her.

"Edwina knows well about all of my efforts to elevate the female sex." Willingham smirked.

"Shall we order?" she said in a small voice, though the prospect of food made bile rise up to her throat. But the menu in her hand offered a temporary refuge from the conversation.

"It's really quite a shame you didn't pursue painting further," Brandon said to Willingham. "My sister says you're quite accomplished."

"She flatters me." Willingham raised Anastacia's hand to his lips. "But the truth is, while I enjoyed the art scene, the real world came calling soon enough. You know how it is. Business responsibilities cannot be put off forever. And then I found I had the knack for making money. And multiplying it for my investors as well. And it's a different kind of satisfaction." Anastacia looked at her brother, who visibly tensed up. Hare had a feeling it wasn't the first time he'd heard it. "I could offer my investors ten percent within two years of setting up."

"'The future's Rockefeller,' one paper called you, I believe." Anastacia beamed at her fiancé, either ignoring, or not noticing, her brother's discomfort.

"Indeed," Ernest said, "very impressive," he added, more for something to say, Hare suspected.

"I have investors up to my ears, it's really somewhat tedious." Willingham leaned back in his seat, seemingly reading the other men's lack of enthusiasm as an invitation to elaborate. "I had to begin turning them down. But for you, Thompson, I'd make an exception, if you like. For friendship's sake."

"You're too kind." Ernest gave a curt bow. Hare thought Willingham was going to say more, but then the food arrived, saving them from having to continue with the subject.

"Are you looking forward to the masquerade, Edwina?" Anastacia asked as the waiter carried in the meat course.

"I am," Hare lied. "Masquerades are so… diverting?" She

searched for a positive way to describe a crowd of rich people prancing about in ridiculous masks.

Anastacia wasn't fooled. "See, Ben, I told mother that masquerades were ridiculous." She shook her head. "When actual *fauns* walk the streets of London, putting on a horned mask is less diverting than it might have been in her youth. Ludicrous."

"I don't believe I said that." Hare blanched at the thought of offending Brandon's and Anastacia's mother.

"But it's what you meant!"

Hare pretend-coughed into her napkin to cover up laughter. "Have you thought of a costume yet, Anastacia?"

"I have one or two ideas." Anastacia waved her hand in the air. "Anything comfortable will shock my mother and that counts as a double win for me."

"I believe I'm winning already, no matter what you choose to wear." Willingham kissed Anastacia's hand.

HARE COULDN'T RIGHTLY SAY whether the lunch was any good. It all tasted like wood chippings as far as she was concerned. But she smiled and talked to Brandon and commented on the exhibition and generally did what Miss Bonningham had tutored her so well in: being pleasant. Still, she was so grateful once the meal was finally over. She'd go back to the Winchfield house and talk to Miss Bonningham. Who probably would urge her to try and land Brandon as soon as she could. But could that still be the plan? Hare thought of being a sister-in-law to Willingham and she nearly returned the food she just ate. And the thought of just letting Anastacia be married to the man… But what else could Hare do? She was stuck. If only Anne hadn't taken that money. If only…

"Edwina?"

She realised with a start that Brandon had been trying to get her attention.

"I'm sorry, I was lost in thought." She looked up at him. There was nothing but concern in his eyes. She wondered for a moment what it would be like to be married to such a man. What it would be like to be married to him honestly, without scheming. Without pretence. There was a time where she couldn't have even imagined a human like that. One that was kind.

Yet now this potential marriage too seemed like prison. And she knew the dark-haired man sitting on the other side of her had something to do with that.

"You went a bit pale." Brandon furrowed his brow. "We best get you back to the Winchfield house so you can rest. It's been a taxing morning."

"I think that'd be best," she said. "Thank you."

"I'm going to enquire after my sister, so I'll be glad to accompany you." Ernest stepped forward.

"I have already offered to do so." Hare was surprised to hear Brandon say. There was a new edge to his voice. "In any case, didn't I hear you say your sister always feigns illness to avoid the need to go to such affairs?"

"That is my suspicion, but I'd be remiss in my brotherly duties if I didn't make certain she's alright."

"Why don't you both go," Anastacia piped in. Hare met her eyes. Interest and… was it irritation? She couldn't have known about her and Ernest, could she? *There was nothing to know about,* Hare corrected herself. Nothing happened. Nothing of importance. But if others started noticing…

"After all," Anastacia added, looking to her brother. "It wouldn't be quite appropriate for you to be left alone with Edwina without a chaperone."

"I seem to recall you didn't have such qualms when Thompson was accompanying her."

"That's different, Ben," Anastacia explained as if he was a child. "Ernest is the brother of Edwina's hostess and, besides, *he* is not courting her." Did Hare imagine it, or did Anastacia give Ernest a very pointed look at those words.

Hare could feel blood rushing to her cheeks. She wasn't an expert on such things, but even she knew it wasn't appropriate to say the word 'courtship' out loud, not until it was *official.* Anastacia caught her eye and the understanding of what she was trying to do hit Hare. Was Anastacia pressuring her brother right now? While it was a nice feeling to be wanted as a family member, Hare knew down to her bones that said feeling would go away very quickly, once Anastacia got a hint of Hare and Willingham's past relationship. Or of the way it made Hare feel to have Ernest close.

In the end, Hare returned to the Winchfield house wedged in the hack between the suddenly sullen Duke and Ernest. She tried making conversation a couple times, but both men responded with barely more than grunts, as each shot the other warning looks over her head. It was like travelling inside a thundercloud.

And when they both insisted on calling on Lady and Lord Winchfield on their arrival at the Winchfield house, each of the two men apparently unwilling to let her pass the threshold of the house with the other, she was perfectly happy to leave them both disappointed by excusing herself to lie down.

CHAPTER 23

The next morning after breakfast, Hare's head was still pounding, so she was very glad when Lady and Lord Winchfield left the house for the day.

Miss Bonningham, who was clearly horrified by what happened at the Royal Academy, kept looking for an excuse to speak to Hare alone, but the Dowager Lady Winchfield required the "dear Anne's" presence for most of the morning.

Hare picked up a sketchbook and pencil and set herself up alone in the library, which had a very pleasant cushioned window seat. It had the added benefit of having heavy drapes to the side of it, which Hare drew around herself. Thus cocooned, she processed her feelings the best she knew how. Her hand glided smoothly over the paper, the loose lines revealing images she wasn't even expecting. She liked working like that. A few lines crisscrossed and her mind pushed her towards an image revealed within. An oval turned into an eye, a straight line extended into a nose. A trick of the shadow on the paper's rough texture, cast by her own hair, revealed the shape of a hand, thrown over the head in a gesture of impatience, its sooty outline made clearer with the practiced movement of her own fingers.

In her focus, she hardly noticed the creaking of the library door, or the soft thud of it closing. So when the drapes covering her seat were suddenly pulled back, she practically jumped, a stifled scream escaping her lips.

"I thought I'd find you in a place like this."

"Willingham!" She practically hissed at him. "What are you doing here?" She glanced towards the door. "Why is the door closed?"

"For how I got in, I was let in by the butler, as is the proper way." He held out his hand in a silent offer of help. She pushed his hand away and got up from the seat. The window alcove suddenly turned from a refuge into a trap and she would face the man standing. His nose twitched in a small sign of irritation. "I closed the door, as I didn't think you'd like anyone overhearing what I have to say."

She got up and put a few paces between them. "You shouldn't be here." Her hands glided over her skirt, smoothing it. She wished she had a heavier shirt on. And a sweater. She wanted more layers between her body and his gaze.

He narrowed his eyes. "Oh, I think we both know which one of us doesn't belong here, Miss *Walker*." He grimaced at the fake name. "An interesting choice of name. Trying to walk away from your life, are you?"

"I don't see how that's any of your business."

Willingham watched her with a smug look on his face. Now she thought of it, that was pretty much the default look on him. He was smug when happy, smug when annoyed, smug when he woke up in the morning and he was definitely smug when he rolled off her in the night. How had she not seen it before. He picked up her sketchbook with a lazy movement and inspected it briefly. "Interesting."

"Not particularly."

He glanced at her. "Is Mr Thompson on your mind, Hare?" He dangled the sketchbook in front of her. "I'm almost jealous."

She snatched at the drawing, but he held it out of her reach. "What do you want, Sam?"

He skewed his head to the side. "I always liked how your lips looked when you said my name, you know."

"Just get out." She pointed to the door. He didn't move, of course, as she knew he wouldn't.

"How did you manage it?" He laughed softly. "That was the question that kept going round and round in my head last night. How did a mythic whore from New York suddenly appear in London, apparently on the verge of an engagement to the season's most eligible bachelor?"

Hare's hand shook. She clasped her hands behind her back to stop herself from lunging at him. "A whore, was I?" She forced herself to look him in the eyes. She wouldn't cower from him. She wouldn't give him the satisfaction. "If that's what I was, then who made me into one? I believed you when you said you'd marry me. If it's a sin to let myself be tricked, then what does that make you?"

"Please." He laughed then. She wanted to claw out his eyes. "No need to play the innocent. For all your protestations, you must have known I wouldn't have married you. Why, the very first time I laid eyes on you, you were naked for all to see, sprawled out over a draped fabric." He rubbed his chin, staring her down. "You were quite the prettiest thing I'd ever seen, I don't mind you knowing."

"I was never a *thing*." She straightened her back. "If you saw me as such, it's your shame, not mine."

"Oh it is?" He walked towards a wing-backed chair and sat in it, crossing his legs. She felt like a student called out in front of the school master. He steepled his fingers in front of his face and watched her for a while. "I wonder if your new friends would take quite the same view of the situation." He shrugged. "I'm not a monk. Many men in my position kept a mistress. The indiscretions of youth. And a purchase of a mythic bed-warmer, whilst not exactly genteel, would be seen as mere entertainment, such as would be expected of a wealthy man." He shook his head. "As for any promises you might be remembering. I needed none to get you and so nobody would credit your words. That I preferred a willing companion in bed, now who could begrudge me that. Nobody would ever think you could genuinely believe a man like me would marry you. That would have made you either an idiot or a schemer hoping to trap me."

"Why not both?" She laughed mirthlessly. "Only an idiot would seek to trap a man like you." It's what she thought of herself in any case, wasn't it? She was an idiot to believe him at the time.

"Careful, Hare." His face darkened. "Remember, I hold your fate in my hands. Now, there need be no bad blood between us. I understand we're to be family soon."

She said nothing, but she was sure the disgust she felt must have been plain on her face.

He sighed and stood up abruptly, closing the distance between them. "Perhaps I am somewhat to blame, it's true." He reached out and touched a lock of her hair. He gave it a small tug, forcing Hare to take a half step towards him. "I might have behaved pettily in the end. In fact…" He took a breath. "…in fact, I know I did. I thought you'd be humbled if I'd threatened to sell you on. Just so you'd finally understand your position. You were not as grateful for all you received as you should have been. You were growing demanding, forgetting the proper respect you owed me."

"Respect I owed you?" She repeated dumbly.

"Indeed, you understand." He nodded with approval. "And yet here I find you, trying to trick decent people into accepting you. Now," he leaned forward till his mouth was inches away from her ear, "that doesn't feel very *respectful*, does it?"

A wave of fury rose up in her and she swung her hand to slap him. He caught it with a smirk. She wiped it off his face, as her foot connected with his shin.

"You bitch!" He turned on her and Hare was sure in that moment that he'd have killed her if he only thought he could get away with it. But the one thing Samuel Willingham had always prided himself on was his self-control. And so he straightened up once more and gave Hare a measuring look. "Alright, I suppose you think I deserved that."

"I ask again, Sam, what is it you want?" She took a deep breath. She wouldn't cower before this man. "If you're planning on exposing me, just get it over with."

"Look at you," he said, crossing his arms on his chest. "As proud as a queen. I'm very curious, how did you manage it all? When I signed the papers over to that sour-faced headmistress and the summoner performed the binding switch, you had nothing and yet here you are, across the world, draped in finery." He smiled at her. He was in control and he knew it.

"If you're not going to tell me what you came here for, I think it's best you leave," she said.

A familiar angry glint in his eye made her square up her shoulders. She couldn't show him she was afraid.

"Are you trying to provoke me, Hare?" He took a step forward. "I assure you that'd be unwise. You were bound to me. You're mine still."

"You let me go," she said, looking him straight in the eyes. "You let me go and I'm nobody's now. I'm free."

He laughed, throwing his head back. "You're smarter than that, Hare. You're not free. You can never be free. This is not your world and even as you profess your independence to me, you're busy trying to find another master."

She didn't say a word, but continued watching him like he was a rabid dog.

"Very well." He turned on his heel and walked off to the drinks cabinet. "Do you want one?" he asked without turning around, then poured himself a glass of whiskey without waiting for her reply. He drank half of it before he spoke again. "I don't know how you managed this. You're pretty enough, of course, so no wonder that idiot Brandon was left drooling over you, especially with the—" He waved his hand around. "—with whatever this little magic thing you have performed on yourself. I didn't realise you even had this much ability left in you and to be honest I resent not having been informed of the fact. But, while it's interesting in a purely scientific sense, in more practical terms, I find it all somewhat inconvenient."

"Why do you want to marry Anastacia?" The words came out before she had the chance to stop them.

"I think you best call her 'Lady Anastacia', don't you?" He glanced at her over his shoulder. There was a heavy vase within Hare's reach on the coffee table and his head was *right there*. Hare wondered how difficult it would be to dispose of a body.

"Well?"

"Why wouldn't I marry her?" He turned around and leaned against the heavy wooden cabinet. "She's rich, she's pretty enough in her own way and she has the kind of connections a smart business man wouldn't scoff at."

"She's also got a brain in her head," Hare said. "It came as a surprise to me, by the by, what a dedicated champion you are of women's emancipation."

He laughed, nearly choking on the whiskey. He put the glass back down and wiped his mouth with a handkerchief. "Yes, that one came as a surprise to me too. Still, a bored rich girl is allowed her hobbies. Once we're married she'll naturally become too busy for that nonsense soon enough."

"Does she know that's how you feel about it?"

"I think that's enough about my fiancée, don't you think? I get the sense you're about to start pontificating and we both know how I feel about *that*." He waited for her response and after a moment he nodded, satisfied. "Good. Now, I had a good think about our situation last night. And I found that in a way, it all seems to have worked out perfectly. I won't stand in the way of your little scheme to marry Brandon. If he's fool enough to marry a penniless mythic for her pretty face, then who am I to stop him."

"...but?" Hare narrowed her eyes.

He laughed at her expression. "*But* if you so much as whisper a word of reservation in front of Anastacia, if you as much as breathe in the way I don't like in front of her, I'll make sure you're arrested."

"On what charges exactly?" *Dear God, please don't let him know...*

"Theft, of course." He watched the realisation wash over her.

"I never stole a cent from you."

"Perhaps not," he admitted. "But I bet you stole something from *someone*. Because unless you were a stow-away, then you must have scrounged up at least thirty dollars for the tickets to get here. So, in absolute terms, it wouldn't be a complete lie. And, let's face it, Hare—" Willingham scratched the skin behind his ear. "—we both know who people will believe. Do you understand me?"

She wanted to scream. To march right over to Anastacia and tell her everything about this horrid man. Everything he'd done. Then she thought of Ernest. She imagined the look of disgust on his face, when he'd find out who she really was.

"I understand." She hated herself for those two words.

"Clever girl." He nodded approvingly. "Now, you realise that my benevolence doesn't come free. I'm a businessman after all."

She stared at him in silence.

"Brandon is a decent sort of chap, but so far, an excessively tight-fisted one. You will address that fault of his."

For a moment she was too shocked for words. "What do you mean?"

He rolled his eyes as if she was being deliberately obtuse. "You will get him to invest in my business, of course. You can think of yourself as my silent partner." He let his eyes fall to take in her frame. "Maybe not too silent. I like the noises you make." He laughed at her expression. "Don't pretend to be a prude, Hare. After all, we both know better. I need you to convince Brandon to join my venture. Once he does, the rest of them will as well, you know how those things work."

"And if I refuse?" She straightened herself.

His eye twitched. "You are too smart for that, my dear. Refuse and I will make sure you land in jail, or worse. Do you grasp my meaning?"

She gave a curt nod.

"Excellent." His expression relaxed and he rubbed his hands together, like they'd just agreed on a game to play during a house party. "Now, don't make that face," he said, lifting her chin with two fingers. "This is a good thing, really. For both of us. You told me once that you just wanted to be near me. And now you've got your wish. Funny how things work out for the best, don't they?" His other hand snaked behind her and he pulled her closer. "Because now we get to spend a whole lot of time together. Aren't you glad?"

"You arrogant—"

"A-ah, careful..." The hand he still held by her face slid towards her hair. He suddenly grabbed a fistful and pulled her face up, ignoring her pained squeal. "You don't want to hurt my feelings, do you?" He brought his face closer and inhaled deep. "God, I missed you. I didn't think I would, you know, but now you're here, I'm so, so glad..."

"Let me go!" Hare reached her breaking point and pushed at him. Unfortunately, he was still holding onto her hair and he twisted his fist once to turn her head up, exposing her throat.

"You missed me too, I know you did," he murmured, as his free hand bunched up her skirt. "I'm in a mind to remind you just how much."

"Get your hands off her!"

Hare couldn't quite see what happened, except that the pressure on her hair suddenly stopped. She was pushed off balance and fell to the floor. As she looked up, she saw the enraged face of Miss Bonningham, who was still holding her shoe in her hand, which she'd presumably used to hit Willingham. She must have heard from the butler that he had arrived.

"Get out of here!" Miss Bonningham, red in the face, was breathing heavily, fury twisting her features. "Or I will call the servants. How would it look to your fiancée if she found out you tried to force yourself on her friend?"

Willingham blinked a couple of times, apparently too shocked for words. It didn't last. He threw his head back and laughed.

"Well, Miss Bonningham, that was unexpected, I admit."

"Men like you never expect to be refused what they want, so it doesn't surprise me." Miss Bonningham stood between Willingham and Hare. "I know all about you."

"That's interesting, because, you see, before I handed the binding document to you, I'd never heard a word about *you.*" *The arrogant prick.* He'd seemingly recovered his composure and he measured the two women with a cold, calculating look. "Hare will fill you in. But, as you might have anticipated, you don't really get a say in what happens next. I'm terribly sorry, Miss Bonningham, but you have bet on the wrong mare." He glanced at Hare. "We will continue this conversation soon enough, Hare. Don't forget what will happen if you upset me. I'm sure once you've had the chance to think about it, you'll soon realise that pleasing me is a far easier option. And, after all, you have managed it well enough in the past." He began to walk towards the door, pausing as his hand rested on the door handle. "You'd do well to remember. I *own* you." And with that he left.

As soon as Willingham was gone, Anne hurried up to Hare. "Are you alright? Did he hurt you?" She ran her hands over Hare's head, smoothing her hair.

Hare looked up into the other woman's eyes and burst out crying. Long sobs shook her body, as Miss Bonningham wrapped her arms around her and rocked her back and forth, making small, reassuring noises.

It took a good few minutes before Hare composed herself.

"I worried this might happen ever since I heard his name yesterday." Miss Bonningham shook her head, passing her handkerchief to Hare. "What a mess. But he can't do anything. What does he hold against you, except your mutual past? To expose you, he'd have to expose his own conduct and while it would harm us more, I'm sure he's not willing to jeopardise his marriage to Lady Anastacia."

"He said he'd accuse us of stealing." Hare stared at the pattern on the carpet, as her fingers raked through the soft pile of it.

Miss Bonningham went quiet. "What does he know?" She shook her head. "He can't possibly know, I'm sure of it. He'd never even met me before."

"No." Hare's voice was flat, like she'd cried out all the emotion out of it. "He would accuse me of stealing from *him*."

The older woman's arms dropped limp by her side. "He'd do that." It wasn't a question. They both understood the kind of man he was.

"Is there any money left at all?" Hare asked.

"Not enough." Miss Bonningham understood Hare's unspoken question. "Not enough to take us away from his grasp. I… I wish I'd taken more."

"Then we'd likely be in even more trouble now." Hare wiped her eyes. "I wish I'd never met him."

"Wishes don't change reality." The older woman shook her head. "We must face things as they are."

"We could tell the truth," Hare said.

"The truth…" Miss Bonningham laughed. "And which truth is that? Because the facts are not in our favour. Who here would care about what drove us to make the choices we made? We'd be out on the streets. We're trading on my reputation here and your beauty. Those are the only tools we have and they're both pretty useless if Willingham decides to expose us."

"I could get work," Hare said, quietly. "Mrs Brown said as much."

"Your scribbles won't stretch even as far as a solid roof, Hare." Anne held out a hand to help Hare get up. "We've come too far to swap penury in New York for an even grimier existence in London."

"I can't…" Hare closed her eyes. She could still smell him on her, feel his hand on her hair. She shuddered with revulsion. "I can't let him…"

"Dear God, child!"

Hare opened her eyes to see Miss Bonningham's aghast face.

"Who do you take me for, Hare? I'm not some madam at a brothel. You think I'd let that vermin use you like that?" Hare almost said that Anne had no compunction about marrying her off to Viscount Culross, but then she felt her heart soften as she saw how truly disturbed Anne was.

"But that leaves us with a problem, Anne," Hare said. "What are we to do? Like you said, it's only a matter of time before we're either exposed for the money you withdrew in New York, or before Sam decides to accuse us."

Miss Bonningham stood up and began pacing around the room, like she often did when thinking. "I've dealt with bullies my entire life. You can hardly run a school without coming across a few bad apples. We need to attack before he makes his move."

"I thought the agreed strategy was to lead the children onto the right path with kindness?" Hare's feeble attempt at humour only seemed to irritate Anne.

"Whoever has the time for that?" Miss Bonningham rolled her eyes. "What good can kindness do with someone like Willingham? But now, I don't know much about him, not compared to you." She tapped her chin. "Is there anything you know about him that can protect us? I've met a few rubber barons in my time. There were precious few among them who had nothing to hide, that's for sure. So in terms of what he's hiding... apart from your relationship, of course..."

Hare shook her head. "He never involved me in any of his business dealings. Or his life, for that matter, not really." She looked down at her hands and picked on a bit of skin around her nail. "I suppose you must think I was a simpleton, but I was so desperate to believe him. He told me it wasn't the right time to introduce me to his social circle, because he needed the investors to see him in a certain way. Marrying me could have brought on the wrath of the wives, you know better than me how the New York society works. He said once his business venture was secured, everyone would be too involved to cut him out. And so I waited. And waited. But the investment meetings never seemed to stop. And when I finally confronted him, well, you know what he did then. I was lucky you were the one to offer for me, truth be told."

"Yes." Miss Bonningham nodded. "But none of that quite explains why he's suddenly in London. If his business was running so smoothly in New York, I wonder if he would have made the journey. Everybody knows where the real money is these days. And for him to marry Lady Anastacia... I beg your pardon, I know she's your friend, but you must admit she is somewhat of an odd duck."

"Yes, she is." Hare laughed softly. "And she's quite magnificent for wild fowl. But you're right. She's an odd choice for Sam. Do you think he could be after her dowry?"

"Again, there are bigger dowries back home."

"That leaves one question." Hare locked eyes with Miss Bonningham. "What's the reason he had to leave America?"

CHAPTER 24

Ernest hadn't slept. Back at his office he found himself staring at the stack of briefings on his desk. The letters seemed to float before his eyes. He couldn't help but feel he'd handled things like an idiot. Of course Edwina thought Brandon a better option for a partner. Even aside from the man's wealth and title, he had been clear from the very beginning about his interest in her. There were no half-uttered sentences, no mixed signals.

And by contrast, what had Ernest done in all this time? He had to be objective here, though it pained him. Because what she was seeing was merely a man who had acted disloyally to his best friend. A man so scared of what people might say, that he only expressed his interest by skulking around in dark corners. Literally.

He put his forehead on his desk and laced his fingers over his head. All this didn't paint a pretty picture. And that was without her even knowing the whole truth of him. She had been surprised how young Ernest was when his family sent him away. But she never questioned it. And Ernest wanted to tell her so badly. But he couldn't. He couldn't bear to see the pity in her face. It was enough he couldn't erase the memory of his mother's eyes with that same expression. His mother's husband's eyes? He somehow didn't remember. Maybe it was because the older Mr Thompson never quite looked at him.

So here was the truth. Ernest was not the best option for Edwina. He knew it. But knowing didn't change his feelings. So what should he do now? Pretend he didn't feel what he did? Pretend he was better than he was? Or to just… give up. But how well had that worked for him so far? He tried to give her up, he tried to be happy for her and Brandon. But he couldn't.

And now Brandon knew. Ernest was certain of it. Their exchange at the Trocadero made it clear. So what were they now? Rivals? Ernest laughed. How melodramatic. He wished he could talk to his best friend about it. But he imagined Brandon wouldn't be inclined to offer much guidance on how to steal a girl away from him. So now Ernest was stuck in his own head, trying to convince himself that there was a chance Edwina might prefer him after all, in spite of all logic pointing towards him being the insane choice.

It was so pathetic. If he was being honest with himself, he just wanted to be picked. To be the one chosen for once. He needed it. So what was he going to do about it?

He gave the pile of untouched work on his desk one forlorn look and stood up. If he wanted Hare to see him as a legitimate choice, then he just had to grow a damn spine and make himself into one.

It was a bit of a walk to the Winchfield house, but that was a good thing. The weather was fine and the steady march helped calm him.

He walked in a sort of a haze, mostly staring at his feet. A hack driver shouted at him as he jumped out of the way at the last moment. He'd better pay more attention. He barely stood a chance with Edwina as it was. A corpse couldn't very well court a girl.

He finally arrived at the Winchfield house. He hesitated before knocking. What if she didn't want to see him? He did go off in somewhat of a huff after they talked back at the Royal Academy. He reddened remembering his reaction. He could finally admit to himself, he was jealous. But what right did he have to be jealous of her, when he never even declared his own intentions. He sighed and once more lifted his arm to knock. But before his knuckles had even brushed against the green door, it swung open, revealing the butler's somewhat unimpressed face. Ernest let out a surprised squeak, which earned him a pitying look from his sister's servant.

"I'm afraid, sir, you just missed Lady and Lord Winchfield.", The butler said, stepping aside to let Ernest in. As Posy's brother, Ernest had a privileged access to the house. "They're not expected for another two hours at least."

"That's quite alright," Ernest said quickly. "Is Miss Edwina home?"

"She is currently in the morning room with her aunt and the Baron's mother." The old servant had a way of expressing a great deal without moving one muscle. Ernest could feel the unspoken judgement lingering on every word. *Dammit.* He should have asked after the Dowager. "There is a planned tea with a number of Lady Winchfield's friends, but that is not until three this afternoon."

"Brilliant. I'll find my own way," he said, as the butler was about to lead him to the room.

Ernest took a deep breath before entering. Edwina sat on a green-upholstered chair, outlined against a tall window. She was evidently barely listening to the conversation between her aunt and Lady Dowager and was looking out into the garden, her back-lit profile looking like some wistful romantic painting. She heard him before the other two women did and they locked eyes for a moment. Her expression softened for just a heartbeat and a warm feeling in his chest swelled as he realised she was just as happy to see him as he was to see her.

But a moment like that couldn't last and Miss Bonningham finally noticed him. "Mr Thompson! What a surprise to see you here. I'm afraid your sister is out."

"Good morning, Miss Bonningham. Yes, the butler's already told me as much. I was hoping to speak to Miss Walker, if you don't mind."

Miss Bonningham narrowed her eyes, as she clearly *did* very much mind. She opened her mouth to object, but Edwina was already getting up.

"It's about an artist Lady Anastacia wanted me to meet," Edwina said. "She asked as a friend," she added and the words had a visible effect on her aunt, who seemed to relax slightly.

"Very well," Miss Bonningham said in curt tones. She gave Edwina a pointed look, the meaning of which Ernest couldn't quite decipher.

"Shall we go to the library?" he asked the moment they were out of the room.

They walked down the corridor in silence, each glancing quickly at the other. As they were about to enter the library, however, somebody knocked on the front door. Without thinking, Ernest walked up to the door and opened it himself. A middle-aged man in a somewhat dusty coat and a bowler hat stood outside. He hastily threw the rest of his cigarette onto the street when he saw Ernest.

"Can I help you?" Ernest said. The man annoyed him for no better reason than that he was delaying his conversation with Edwina. It already took up most of his courage to approach her in the first place and he worried he might lose his nerve entirely.

"Yes, sorry." The man sniffed. He was very short, barely reaching Ernest's shoulder and he had an emotive face with quick, intelligent eyes. "I'm Bronek Sputnek, at your service." He patted his pockets with an impatient gesture and pulled out a slightly moist-looking calling card, which he practically pushed in Ernest's face.

"A detective?" Ernest furrowed his brows.

"One of the best in the business, if I dare say so myself." Mr Sputnek clicked his heels and puffed out his chest.

Behind Ernest, he could hear Edwina shifting her weight. She walked up to the door and stood next to him, breathless.

"I'm looking for one Anne Bonningham, previously of the Bonningham School for Young Ladies in New York and I was informed she's in residence here?" Mr Sputnek said, casting a curious glance towards Edwina.

"Ye—"Ernest began to speak, but Edwina squeezed his hand hard.

"Miss Bonningham is not at home!" she pushed forward, her skirts pressing against Ernest's side.

"I see." The little man took out a handkerchief and dabbed his brow. "May I enquire when she's expected to be back?"

Ernest, too dumbfounded to speak, cast Edwina a questioning glance, but said nothing. He could see the blush creeping up her neck.

"Not till the weekend, at least," she said. She didn't look towards him, her whole body rigid. *She's a dreadful liar,* he thought, just as the detective evidently thought the same thing. Mr Sputnek looked at him quizzically, waiting to see him confirm or contradict her.

"Should we pass on your regards?" Ernest beamed a smile at the man.

"And you, sir, are?"

"Ernest Thompson." He held out a hand.

"Ernest Thompson *Esquire,*" Edwina added quickly. Ernest raised his eyebrows at her.

"My pleasure, my pleasure to be certain." Mr Sputnek shook

Ernest's hand with great vigour, his curious eyes fixed on Edwina. "Miss...?"

"Miss Edwina Walker, my fiancée," Ernest said, before she could utter a word. Her mouth twitched but she showed in no other way that she had even heard him.

"A lucky man..." Mr Sputnek mumbled and squeezed the tips of Edwina's fingers.

"I'm terribly sorry we cannot invite you in, Mr Sputnik—" Ernest said.

"Sputnek."

"Yes, of course. We have a prior engagement, but we will be sure to send a message if Miss Bonningham comes back earlier."

"If you could perhaps give me her current address, I might—"

"*Goodbye,* Mr Sputnek," Edwina said sweetly and closed the door in the man's face.

Edwina and Ernest stood quietly for a moment, both staring at the door.

"He knew you were lying, you understand." Ernest said conversationally. Edwina tried to pull her hand out of his, but he just held it tighter. "And now, so do *I*." He turned to her. "I think we best discuss it in private, don't you?"

"I think..." Her eyes were wide with panic. A part of him felt ashamed that she was scared of him. A small part.

He half-dragged her into the library and closed the door behind them.

"I think we should keep it open," she said, but trailed off at the expression on his face.

"You want to explain to the whole household why you're lying to detectives, Miss Walker?"

She walked up to the bookcase and stared at it, dragging the tips of her fingers across the spines. Ernest suspected it was mostly to keep her back to him.

A dangerous strategy. He moved towards her, so close that if she took a deeper breath she would touch him. He could see the tension in her shoulders. She was afraid. A part of him wanted to reassure her, but then a part of him wanted to throttle her also, so he didn't touch her.

"Tell me what's going on."

She looked stricken and glanced towards him over her shoulder, to then return to studying the spines of the books. It was likely the most attention the Winchfield library had had in a long time, he thought.

"Don't even think of lying to me, Edwina. You're a dreadful liar, you realise."

That made her turn around, clearly not eager to concede even that much to him. But as she opened her mouth, she must have realised how silly it would be to argue the point of her skills of deception.

"It's not your affair," she said finally.

He remained silent, watching her with what he hoped was a cool judgement. Though when she looked up at him like that, her chin jutted out, cool was the last thing he was. He had to stay on point though.

"You're a guest in my sister's house. You have become closely… involved… with my closest friends. With *me*." He felt he needed to add that last point even though the initial reason for his visit had to wait. Back to the question. "*And* I would like to point out, you have just involved me in your lie. So I ask again, why was Mr Sputnek looking for your aunt?"

Her eyes widened for a moment.

"Or should I just ask her?" He moved as if he was about to leave. Edwina's hand shot up and she grabbed his sleeve.

"Don't." She closed her eyes and then seemed to come to a decision. She looked back at him. "Miss Bonningh… My aunt… She's in trouble."

"What kind of trouble?"

"I understand her establishment was not very successful near the end." Her eyes glanced towards the door. "It would be very embarrassing for her to have it found out." Edwina's ears were bright red now.

"That's not the whole truth though, is it?" He cocked his head to the side. He was too close to her. The rose smell filled his nostrils and he couldn't think. He took a half step back. Her fingers still clutched his jacket sleeve. He glanced down and she must have realised she was holding onto it. She released his arm, but something made him grab onto her hand. She wasn't wearing gloves and instinctively he laced his fingers with hers. "Edwina..." he said, hating the pleading note in his voice. "I am not your enemy. You know that, don't you? Please, just... Just tell me. I will help you."

She looked aside, but he noticed she didn't try to pull her hand away. "You can't help me."

"Not if you don't tell me what's happening." He inched closer. "Is this why you told me... You told me my position is not enough?"

"Ernest..." She was going to push him away, to tell him she wouldn't let him in. And the thought of that was unbearable.

"If you have no feelings towards me... I want you to know, I will accept it. My feelings for you are not conditional. And neither is my offer of help." He could see her chest rise and fall and he just wanted to pull her closer. But he didn't move. It was her choice. It had to be.

"And would you be so set on helping me if I were not your sister's guest?" She swallowed hard.

"I'm rather certain you are." He allowed himself a small smile. *A big mistake*. Her eyes darkened.

"Very well," he said. He tightened his grip on her hand and gave it a tug, causing her to lean slightly towards him. "If you were not my sister's guest—and if we ignore the fact I would never have even met you if you weren't—I would probably be less invested in whatever scheme you have going. But I *do* know you. Or at least I *think* I know you." She chewed on her lip, focussed on his words. "And I have grown to… to care very much for you. If I can help you, I will."

"Why?" She was so close to him now, but made no attempt to move away. Her fingers were still laced with his and he let his thumb stroke her hand.

"Why what?" He was looking at her lips, which was probably a mistake. Lips could lie. He should have been more angry with her. She was hiding so much clearly. But he couldn't hold onto that anger.

"Why do you care for me?" She turned her large blue eyes towards him. He lifted his other hand and brushed his knuckles against her cheek. He knew his answer would be important. That she was giving him a chance and a chance like this one would not come again.

"You're beautiful…" he whispered. She frowned and he chuckled. "…but anyone can be beautiful. And anyone can see beauty."

"What else then?"

He barely noticed when it happened, or which one of them initiated it, but she was pressed to him now, the full length of her body flush against his. A breath caught in his throat and he fought hard to calm his breathing.

"It's the bits that others don't see, that you keep hidden. You don't seem to trust anyone," he said finally. "And I don't know why. But sometimes, sometimes, I feel like you believe you can trust me and then you let me get a glimpse at you, at the real you. When you talk about art and get excited about helping others achieve their goals. It's not like the witty dinner conversations, or how you flirt with all the men you've been brought here to impress. In those rare moments, when you look at me like this, I feel like you're *choosing* me and I just want you to choose me over and over again."

"But you see…" She lowered her head and rested her forehead on his chest, too embarrassed to let him see her face. "I think…

No, I *know*, you wouldn't choose *me*. Not if you knew everything about me."

"I'm sorry," he said. Her hair, piled high upon her head, tickled his face and he let himself inhale the smell of her, burying his face in the curls. "I'm sorry I didn't make it clear. That I let you think I would let anything keep me from choosing you. When I should have made it clear I already have."

She turned her face back up towards him and there were tears in her eyes. "Don't say that. Don't—"

"It's Willingham, isn't it?" He hated to bring up that name now. But he had to know. He had to be certain. And when she turned away and a tear started rolling down her cheek, he *knew*. "He hurt you."

She nodded, a barely perceptible movement of the head. *I'll kill him*. Anger pulled on his heart. He didn't think he'd ever been this angry. He didn't think he was capable of it.

"Did you.. Do you still care for him?"

Something changed in her expression and Ernest exhaled slowly. "He can't hurt you." He tucked a lock of her hair behind her ear. "I don't care what happened between you. Not as long as you don't care for him anymore."

"I hate him," she said it with so much suppressed fury, Ernest smiled. He was glad and he realised, he'd been worried. Worried she still held some feelings towards that man.

"We can hate him together, then." The light came in through the window, lighting up the back of her head. He wondered if Willingham had ever seen her like this. Vulnerable in the morning light. Anger rose up in his chest. "I feel like I already got a head start on that."

She snorted, but then grew serious again.

"There's more." He wasn't asking. He just stated a fact and they both knew it. He was not a religious man. As a child he'd pretty much given up on any chance of divine intervention, but he felt he now understood the urge to appeal to a higher power.

Please... He wanted her to trust him. To see he would stand by her.

"I have no money." She sucked in a breath, as if shocked at her own admission.

"That's no secret. Nobody pretended you're an heiress."

"An heiress!" She laughed and brought her hand up to cover her eyes. Like a child, who thinks others can't see her when she can't see them. But now that Hare started, she seemed unable to stop. "I'm as close to an heiress as... as you are to the Queen!"

"But your parents were respectable people, there's no reason to—" A flick of her eyes, as her hand fell limp by her side. And suddenly he knew. "You weren't telling the truth about your parents." His own voice sounded flat to his ears.

She looked at him with a stricken expression. A small nod.

"So... your aunt also wasn't telling the truth about your parents..." Something Posy had said before came up again in his memory. "Is she even your aunt?"

She didn't reply, they both knew she didn't need to. He let go of her hand and took a step back, running his fingers through his hair. He looked around the room. Then, without word, he walked towards the library door.

"Ernest, please—"

He lifted his hand and with one smooth motion locked the door. And if he felt a small sense of satisfaction at her shocked gasp? Well, he was human, after all.

* * *

HARE'S HEART felt like it was going to leap out of her chest. He was going to leave her here. He was going to tell everyone she was a fraud.

Which she was.

She wasn't just a scam artist. She was a failure at it. She should have lied to him; after all, it wasn't just her secret. But she found she couldn't. Maybe he was right, maybe she was simply a bad liar after all. But she was so tired. And she was tired of lying to him. *Idiot.* Did she think he wouldn't mind? That he wouldn't care that she had been lying to him, to his sister? It was all ruined now.

And he would hate her.

She found it was that last thought that truly broke her. She felt the tears running down her face as he turned away. He wouldn't look at her. He must have felt disgusted. With her. Maybe with himself for caring about her.

And then he locked the door. The key turned with a loud *click*. He turned back towards her. And as he watched her from across the room, it occurred to her she ought to be scared. She was an impostor. She wasn't the well-born, well-connected woman he had thought she was. The thin veneer of respectability, which had been her equally thin armour, was peeled away.

But then he turned towards her and she knew she was safe. "I thought you wouldn't want someone to accidentally stumble upon us and hear whatever it is you have to say."

She could feel the weariness in his tone and she steeled herself.

"In such situations I think it's best to begin at the beginning," he said as the silence stretched.

She couldn't help but allow herself a small smile at that. "Do you often find yourself in *such situations* then?"

"No." He almost smiled. "Not often. But as the law and all the associated breaches of it are my profession, you'd be surprised at the number of dissemblers I've come across—"

Hare flinched. But then, that's what she was, wasn't she?

"So who are you, if you're not Miss Bonningham's niece?" He folded his arms and leaned against the door, watching her with his half-closed eyes. He looked so *relaxed*, dammit.

"My name is Hare," she said finally. And that simple confession seemed to open something up within her. She waited for the realisation to dawn on him.

"Hare?"

She exhaled slowly and allowed the glamour to fall off her like a heavy cloak. She stood in front of him as she was. She waited for him to react, but his expression was inscrutable.

"I see." His eyes were going over all the tiny changes in her appearance. The sheen of her hair, the large cat-like eyes, the angles of her cheekbones and chin. All subtle, of course. All damning.

She needed to fill the silence. "Anne's business was going badly. And my life, such as it was, was falling apart. So she freed me and we made the journey here, where we could have a fresh start."

"And by your life falling apart, you mean..." His posture barely changed, but she could see the tension building up within him.

"Willingham." Her legs felt like jelly and she sat down in a chair. She couldn't bear to look at Ernest now. She knew it was coming, but she wanted to delay the moment she had to face him. She spoke quickly now. "He met me when I worked at the Art Student League."

"Worked?"

She heard the unspoken question and bristled. "*Worked.* As in 'officially bound according to the municipal regulations concerning mythics in New York'."

He winced.

"It is cheaper to bind a mythic to a school as a professional model and muse than it is to pay a woman her wages." She didn't dare look at him. "More respectable too. That way the artists don't need to pollute their eyes and their canvas with the form of a fallen woman. A mythic is just a thing after all. Still nature really." She could feel the silence stretch between them as he considered her words. To his credit, he didn't show the contempt he must have felt for her.

"And Willingham? How did you meet him?"

"He..." She closed her eyes. She didn't want to bring up the memories of back then. Of how she saw things, when the world seemed so much brighter and so filled with promise. "He seemed... different. Rich men often feel entitled to mythic women. I could tell those from a mile away usually. But he behaved... respectfully. Like I imagined he would have if I was the daughter of his parents' friends. Bought my binding papers from the League, promised he would free me. He was kind."

"Until he wasn't, I imagine."

"I don't need you to explain to me how stupid I was. Believe me, I know." She locked eyes with Ernest. "But it happened so gradually. And then, when he was done with me, I was truly left with nothing. I was lucky he sold my papers to Anne. Who freed me."

"And you couldn't think of a better form of employment with your new-found freedom than to assume a false identity?" He raised an eyebrow. "Are there no jobs in New York?"

She laughed. "Not the kind behind the counter anyway." Her laughter died on her lips. "It's funny, isn't it, how the same men, who are all too happy to destroy you, will then see you as unfit to even serve them a drink." She fidgeted, picking on the skin around her finger.

"Don't do that." She didn't even realise as he approached and put his hand gently on hers.

"If I married well, then me and Anne would be safe. Taken care of." She chanced looking up at him. He looked stricken.

"I need a drink." He strode towards the drinks cabinet and poured two glasses of what might have been brandy.

"I don't..."

"Just drink it." He shoved the glass in her face, then sat in the chair opposite to her.

"Do you love Brandon?"

What was the point in lying anymore. At least now, in this room, she could be honest. "No. He's a decent man and I like him. But no, I don't love him."

His shoulders seemed to drop a couple inches and he drank from his glass.

"That isn't to say I would have been a bad wife to him." It felt important that he knew that all of a sudden. "He knows I have no money. He is interested in me because of my looks and because of our shared interests. Because of how I make him feel. How I make him feel, that's not a lie."

"You don't actually believe that, do you?"

She watched him for a moment. "I suppose not. Because who I am doesn't actually matter to you people, does it?"

"But none of us actually knew *what* you are," he pointed out. He emptied his glass. "Now I at least understand Willingham's not-so-thinly-veiled insults at Trocadero. I expect he didn't tell Anastacia about your relationship. If he knows her at all, then he knows she would break off the engagement if she found out about you two. Not that she's a prude, but I imagine a 'deboucher of impoverished mythic maidens' is not exactly the kind of man she imagined herself marrying."

"No, I suppose not." She rubbed her temple. "Anastacia is really quite special, isn't she?"

"She is."

She tightened her lips. She felt resentment build up in her chest. "Of course."

He smirked. "I was agreeing with you."

She knew she was being ridiculous. But hearing him praise Anastacia in the same moment as he was uncovering all of her own secrets felt like too much. She didn't want him to compare her to Anastacia. She couldn't bear it.

"And what about me?" He turned to her suddenly.

"What about you?" She knew what he meant, but she'd be damned if she made it easy on him.

He stood up and began pacing the room. He laughed. "I suppose I deserve that. You know I came here to ask you..." He coughed. "To ask you to consider... I thought you might..."

It was too much for Hare. She put the glass down and stood up next to him. "Tell me."

"It doesn't matter anymore, does it?" He wouldn't look her in the eye.

"I suppose it doesn't. Not in any real sense," she admitted. "I'm not the paragon of respectability you thought I was. I did warn you, your position couldn't survive my past."

"No, you didn't lie to me, on that score at least." He turned his face towards her, but was still looking down. His fists kept clenching and unclenching rhythmically.

"So now that we're all clear and we know nothing can come of it. Will you tell me what you came to tell me anyway?"

"Why?" He finally looked at her, but she felt no triumph.

She shrugged. "Because you wanted to." Her lip trembled, so she pressed her lips together until she thought she could keep her voice steady. "Because you never will get a chance to again. And because you know I can't hold you to anything. Now that everything is out, what is there to lose? I know—" Her voice broke. "I know you hate me now. I have lied to you all. I didn't set out to hurt any of you. But it doesn't matter what I intended." She raised her hand when Ernest opened his mouth to interrupt her. "I *know* it doesn't matter. You have all been nothing but kind to me and I was happy to just go along with it, knowing my past couldn't stay hidden forever. So please, just tell me what you wanted to tell me before. Before you found all this out. Consider it your revenge, if you like."

"My... revenge?" He cocked his head to the side, watching her like some curious bird.

"Because I know nothing can come of any of it now," she said. "Because once you leave this room, you're honour-bound to expose me. And, you know what? I want you to. It's exhausting." She was talking quickly now. It was such a relief, in a way, to speak truthfully. She and Miss Bonningham would have to figure something out. Because she wouldn't leave the old school mistress to the vultures. Funny how exposing her shame brought her pride back to her. She stood up. She was done being small. "It's exhausting to have to lie to people who're my friends. To be constantly fearful of being discovered. And have what discovered exactly? That I'm not human? That's my crime?" She looked him in the eyes and her own grew glassy with angry tears. "Your kind steals mine from their homes, brings them to this ugly world, which binds us, *diminishes* us. And worst of all, slowly takes away our very memories of who we were before." She pressed the palms of her hands to her temples. "You humans take and take and then look at us like we're nothing. So thank you. Thank you for forcing me to tell you the truth."

"Thank… me?"

"Yes." She nodded. "I can't make up for the lies I've told and no doubt your sister will feel embarrassed at having welcomed me into her home, but you know what I've realised?" A tear rolled down her face and she wiped it away with her sleeve.

"I don't, but I'm sure you will tell me."

"None of you will suffer for this. You will continue on with your pampered lives, as if nothing happened. You will forget about me. And I? I will be alright." More tears were rolling down her face and she swiped at them impatiently. She didn't want to cry now. She was being brave now, she would face it head-on. "I'll leave and I'll look for work and I will be alright. And if Willingham—" She paused as Ernest's face twitched at the name. "And even if he comes through on his threats here, I'll find a way…"

"Threats?" There was a dangerous edge to Ernest's voice. "What threats."

Hare's hand flew to her mouth. She hadn't meant to say that. She straightened herself. "No matter. As I was saying—"

"Oh, I think it matters very much," he said through gritted teeth.

"Ernest..." She looked down, her hands clasped together, so tightly, she could see her knuckles whiten. "It's *not* your concern."

"I decide what is my concern, Hare. And I assure you that I intend to make Willingham's behaviour my business."

Something like a small spark of joy lit up Hare's heart. She squashed it. It meant nothing. Ernest was simply looking out for his friend's sister. He likely thought Hare even worse than Willingham. "Of course, you will have to tell Anastacia about that man. I'd do so myself, but it would be my word against his and... well, we both know my word is no longer worth much here." She looked aside. "But Samuel knows it too. So don't underestimate him. I will write a letter if you like. Explaining things."

He watched her for a moment, his eyes darkening. "You'll just leave then?"

She nodded. "I think it best." She wouldn't tell him about Samuel's threat. He would just likely think she was fishing for sympathy. "After I tell your family, Anne and I will go. We've caused enough trouble." Her chin trembled, but she dug her nails into the palm of her hand and managed to keep her composure. She had no right to feel sorry for herself really. "And, you see, I told you already I'll be fine. But..." She paused. She had no right to ask. But she might never have another opportunity. "Before I go, I'd like to hear what you came here to tell me."

"Why?" He was watching her. She could feel his dark eyes on her. She couldn't meet his eyes, she daren't. "You just told me why you were planning to marry Brandon."

"I know."

His voice had a sharp edge to it now. "You told me, in detail, how you were going to trick him into marrying you so you could use his position and money as a shield."

"I know."

"So what do you want from me?"

"I suppose..." She laced and unlaced her fingers. "I suppose I'd like to know what might have happened, if things were different. Is it wrong of me to ask?"

"You know it is."

She closed her eyes and gave a sharp nod. She didn't want his pity and she was done with his judgement. She walked towards the door, but he blocked her way.

"Please let me through," she said. "I will go and tell your family everything. I will leave today and you never have to see me again."

"You think that's what I want?"

She laughed. "Isn't it? It should be."

He raked his fingers through his hair. "So what, you just wanted me to tell you... You wanted me to tell you I was in love with you and then you were just going to leave?" He raised his voice then. "What do you want from me, Hare? You want me to tell you how I love you, even in your silences and even in your fits of temper, that I love your ambition and the softness you're trying to hide so much? How I can see how you silently berate yourself for every impulsive word or gesture and I want to be the one to make you feel comfortable and safe and fill you with so much joy that it would erase the memory of the people who did this to you. You want me to say it all, expose myself, lower myself before you. All so you can just *leave*?" He took a half step towards her, then stepped aside and made a sweeping motion towards the door. "But by all means, go! You can leave knowing you were successful. You have tricked my friend into planning a future with you and you have tricked me into falling for you and betraying my friend's trust, just for a hope of you. A hope you never shared."

"You love me?" She felt as though somebody had reached into her chest and squeezed at her heart.

"That's not what I—"

"You can't take it back!" She smiled, she couldn't help it. "And thank you. I will always remember that."

"So that's it?" He seemed puzzled.

"That's it," she said. She walked towards the door and put her hand on the key. "Except one thing." She knew she shouldn't say it. She knew she'd regret it. "I love you too." She began to turn the key, but he was quicker. With one smooth motion, he turned her around to face him and, before she had the time to draw another breath, he kissed her.

CHAPTER 25

S*he was going to leave.* His mind was working furiously. He should let her. He should allow her to go and tell the old Lady Winchfield everything. And then tell Brandon and Anastacia.

Except she would leave then. Leave and never return.

But then she said it… He wasn't sure he heard her right. He felt the words more than heard them. And then he knew he could never let her go.

All thoughts left his head. He heard the gasped surprise as he pulled her towards him. He didn't mean to kiss her. And then suddenly when he did, it was all he wanted to do. Her hands went up his side as he pressed her close to his chest. He flicked his tongue across her lips, wanting to taste her, devour her. She let out a small moan and pressed her fingers into his back. Suddenly it was too hot, his cravat was suffocating him. He slipped his fingers under the knot and pulled at it. The damned thing only seemed to get tighter. Then he felt her fingers trace down his neck and she undid the knot. He broke the kiss and looked at her, his hands cradling her face. Her eyes were still glassy from the tears and the tip of her nose reddened. Her lips were kiss-bruised. He gently traced their outline with his thumb.

"What?" Her voice was uncertain.

"Committing you to memory." He brushed his knuckles along the line of her jaw, her impossibly high cheekbones. How the dark arch of her eyebrows lifted in surprise at his words. "I want to remember this. All of this."

He wasn't making sense. But she seemed to understand him. She nodded and pulled his head down, till their lips met again. He pressed into her and she winced, as the door handle dug into her back.

"Sorry," he said. He glanced around the room. An unfashionably large mahogany desk in the corner, too large and heavy to remove from the library without taking the door frame out, much to his sister's chagrin. He slid his hands under Hare's hips, lifted her up and carried her onto the desk. She was significantly heavier than he expected and she raised an eyebrow at the grunt as he struggled to lift her.

"Now finally I have something worth holding onto," he said, nipping at her neck.

She opened her legs to allow him to stand closer and he pressed against her, welcoming her warmth. He could feel her breasts press against him and he began to pull her blouse out of her skirt. His hand slid under the fabric and travelled across the rigid planes of her corset till he touched the soft cotton of her shift. Ernest growled as his fingers felt the swell of her breast. The corset ran up only half way up her chest and the rest of it would need only a small tug, to spill over the top and right into his hand. He shifted, his erection pressing uncomfortably against the fabric of his trousers. He pulled away, suddenly embarrassed. Hare deserved more than this. She'd regret this. He knew she would, when he had given her a chance to think.

She watched him with a glazed-over expression, her mouth

slightly opened, all pink and wet. He looked away. He couldn't say what needed to be said if he was looking at her. "We should stop." His voice came out scratchy.

She was silent for a heartbeat and he chanced looking at her again. She looked hurt. And… ashamed. It almost broke his heart. "You're right," she finally said. "I'm sorry, Ernest." She made small desperate movements to try and straighten up her skirts.

"*You're* sorry?"

"I want you to know, I didn't… I wasn't trying to manipulate you." She swallowed and her hand went up in a self-conscious gesture, as she tried to bring a semblance of order back to her hair. "I didn't plan this."

He watched her for a moment. Half her hair had tumbled down and now she was trying to tuck it back into the bun on top of her head. However, every time she managed to tuck one strand in, another escaped its confines. It was like watching someone try to drain an ocean with a bucket.

"Plan?" She had no idea how expressive her face was. For someone engaged in a scam, she was truly terrible at dissembling. A part of him, the less than kind part, if he was being honest with himself, somewhat enjoyed her discomfort. "You mean, how you kissed me just now? It did cross my mind." It didn't, but that would have made him look stupid.

"*You* kissed *me*!" She shot him an angry look. "You think I was trying to trick you into keeping all this secret?" She pushed at his chest, trying to extricate herself. "I know I probably deserve it at this point, but I won't be treated like some…" She pursed her lips. "Anyway, it was clearly a mistake. I certainly didn't plan to entrap you."

"But maybe I did." She froze. He moved closer to her, letting one hand rest on her thigh. You'd think with the volume of the skirts she was wearing she wouldn't have been able to feel him, but her eyes widened, as his hand slid up her leg, till his thumb rested on her hip bone. "Do you think you're the only one with secrets? Maybe I was the one trying to entrap *you*?"

"Trap me into what?" she said mechanically, seemingly hypnotised by his hand. It wouldn't do. He pinched her chin between his thumb and forefinger and lifted up her face, forcing her to look at him.

"Into taking what you want." He kissed her again, more gently this time, his lips barely brushing against hers. He leaned his forehead against hers. "Tell me, Miss Hare, what *do* you want."

She gasped and pulled him closer, wrapping her legs around him. Her skirts had ridden up to her knees and he let one hand trace the outline of her stockinged calves, moving up till his fingertips felt the bare skin of her thigh, slipping under the hem of her undergarments. "Can I…" He didn't finish the sentence, waiting for her. He felt like he'd go mad if she'd make him wait for her answer a second longer.

Then her fingers were on his, guiding his hand up. Her skirt was now draped around her middle. He resisted, even as it required all of his self-control to do so. "You have to tell me what you want, Hare…"

She squealed in outrage, which brought a smile to his lips.

"I need to hear it. Tell me what you want." He tried to keep the urgency out of his words.

She replied with a little indecipherable sound.

"What is it?" He bent his head and gently grazed the skin on her neck with his teeth, his tongue flicking out where he knew the skin was the most sensitive. She moaned and dug her nails into his back.

"I want…"

"What?" he whispered into her ear as he pulled her closer to the edge of the table. He needed her to say it, more than he had needed anything in his life. It had to be her choice.

"You. I want *you*."

He looked at her then, at her beautiful face with the eyes unfocussed and at the red blush spreading through her cheeks and neck and down underneath the thin fabric of her blouse where her chest rapidly rose and fell. He cradled her face in his hands and pulled her towards a kiss. "Then you shall have me."

CHAPTER 26

She'd gone mad. There was no other explanation for what was happening to her now. She should go. Leave. She knew it and he knew it and yet both of them stayed. And he asked her. He forced her to decide and a small part of her felt anger, at how he took away her ability to deny how much she wanted this. How much she wanted him. There would be no tomorrow for them, they both understood it. *And yet and yet...* She couldn't force herself to leave him. Not when his lips traced a line down her neck... He dug his fingers into her hair, before moving them down to the nape of her neck, where four little buttons pulled together the edges of her shirt's high collar. She let her hands do their own exploring, unbuttoning his waistcoat and letting her fingers move over where the crisp fabric of his shirt was. He groaned in frustration, a feeling she shared wholeheartedly. There was too much clothing between them.

She pushed at the fabric with both hands and both his jacket and waistcoat fell to the ground. He tugged on her blouse, pulling it entirely out from her skirt and over her head. He bent down and kissed the swell of her breasts, as his fingers tugged at the edge of her low-cut chemise. He swore softly as his fingers pulled at the corset.

"There has to be a better way to design it," he muttered.

She giggled at that. *Giggled! What was wrong with her!* She gently pushed his hand away and undid the busks on the front of her corset. He watched her with a hungry expression, as she unhooked the fastenings one by one. The moment the corset fell away, he tugged at her chemise. The thin fabric ripped at the shoulder, but she couldn't bring herself to care. He took a step back and she immediately felt cold. She reached out, but he kept his distance, just out of her reach, looking at her. He gave her a warning look as she attempted to cover her exposed breasts with her hands.

"Don't." He dragged his hand across his mouth. "I want to look at you. I've wanted to see you like this since I first met you."

She took in a sharp breath and pulled her hands away. He took a step towards her and slowly, reverently even, he ran a thumb over the puckered skin around her nipple. She shivered.

"Are you cold?" He locked eyes with her. And before she could reply, he shook his head and said, "Can't have that." And he brought his mouth close to her breast, taking her nipple between his lips. She reacted instinctively, pulling his head towards her. She ran her fingers through his hair. It felt so soft to the touch and his mouth felt so good on her. So warm.

"You like that." It wasn't a question. He looked up at her with smug satisfaction.

"Yes," she said. "But I think it's unfair…"

"What?"

"You still have your shirt on."

"So I do." He chuckled and pulled at his buttons. She helped him pull his shirt off his shoulders and she was surprised at her own eagerness. The thought made her pause.

He froze up, sensing her sudden hesitation. He stood there, motionless and just waited for her. She looked in his face. This man, this beautiful man looked so scared all of a sudden. His lips moved like he was about to ask a question. She placed her hand flat on his chest. He was holding his breath, waiting for her. She'd never felt that. Even back when Willingham feigned tenderness towards her, back when he was all kindness and solicitude, there was no doubt that their kisses, their lovemaking were about him. She didn't realise that it could be different.

Her gaze softened and she reached and held her hand to his cheek. He leaned his face against her palm, like a cat looking for attention.

Which is when the handle of the library door rattled.

Hare squealed and she scrambled about, looking for her corset. Ernest seemed less panicked, looking between her and the door.

"What are you doing?" she practically hissed at him. "Get dressed!"

And then the infuriating man had the gall to laugh, to actually laugh.

"Shh!" She put her finger to her lips. "Do you want us to get discovered?"

"I think that's pretty much done, don't you?" he began buttoning up his shirt though and cast a long look over her half-naked body. "We've been alone in "conversation" for a good while and even an aunt as amiss in her duties as yours—" He rolled his eyes. "— Sooner or later would have to search for you, if for nothing but propriety's sake. In any case…" He glanced to the door, which still remained shut for the moment. He put on his waistcoat and jacket with the sort of relaxed grace that seemed tailor-designed to irritate her. There was no urgency in his movement, which the situation very clearly demanded. "They'll be back with a spare key at any moment and no matter how quickly you manage to get dressed—" He glanced at her as she was furiously trying to pull the corset over her chemise. "Speaking of which, it's a great number of items you have on."

She cast him an irritated glance, as she was trying to arrange her torn shift under her corset. "No more than any other woman these days."

"I'm inclined to think it's too many."

"Well, it's your idiot kind that invented all this." She felt herself blushing, but would not let the man distract her. He clearly wasn't grasping the seriousness of the situation. She pulled on her shirt even as she darted towards the open window. She poked out her head and brightened. There was nobody in the alley by the house and the servants' exit, which led through the narrow staircase close to her bedroom was *right there*. "Tell them I went to my bedroom with a headache." She flung one leg over the parapet, when she suddenly felt Ernest's fingers wrap around her wrist in a vice-like grip.

"What in the name of the Almighty do you think you're doing?"

He looked angry. She instantly bristled. What business did he have being angry with *her* right now? She was the one coming up with a way out of their predicament.

"Is jumping out of windows your go-to solution to every problem?"

"It's a very good solution to this particular problem," she said.

The door handle rattled again. They both looked at it and at each other.

"It'll be fine. Look, I don't hold this against you," she said. She was fighting to stay calm. She was going to be reasonable, even if he wasn't. "Nothing happened really."

"You call this *nothing*?" Rage practically radiated off him and his grip on her wrist tightened.

"Ernest, it's done," she said. "I will tell your sister everything and leave. If they find me here then it could hurt you, as well. You'd be labelled the worst sort of libertine and even if nobody held it against you and even *if* the servants keep their mouths shut, your sister will be furious with you. My reputation might be non-existent, but your character is very much crucial to your career. So just let me *go!*" Something in his eyes changed. Instead of letting her go, he pulled her closer. They must have looked ridiculous, her sitting astride the window-sill.

"This is a matter of choice, Hare." There was a strange sort of heat in his voice, which sent a current down her spine. "And as I see it, we can choose each other here."

"What?"

"If we're married, there's no scandal, not really." He smiled and brought her palm to his lips. "And hedonism within marriage hardly carries the same sort of stigma."

She looked at him like he'd lost his mind, which he very much might have. But there was no humour in his words. On an impulse, she pulled on his collar and kissed him. For the first time in months, she felt free. She felt reckless and she held onto the feeling. *Because, by God, she'd miss it.* She broke away and pushed at his chest. "No." The word was out before she knew it and she knew immediately it was the right one.

He let go of her wrist. He looked crushed. And she almost told him then. That this was for his own good. That he'd see it in a while. That he'd understand that she was looking out for him.

But before she could speak, he turned away from her.

She threw her other leg over the parapet and slid down into the alley. And just in time, for the library door opened just as her feet touched the ground.

"Ernest?!" Lady Winchfield's voice carried over the parapet. "Why did you lock yourself up in the library?"

"I wasn't feeling well and wanted to take a quick nap." Hare winced. *At least that would explain his unkempt appearance.*

"You're an odd man, brother." The Baroness seemed to shrug it off, which was just as well. Hare began creeping towards the servant entrance, but something in Lady Winchfield's tone made her pause. "Where is Edwina? I was told you had asked to speak with her." There was a clear edge to the woman's tone and when Ernest said Hare had gone up to her bedroom with a headache, his sister sighed with relief. "Good. I will admit, Ernest, but that I was worried when I heard you'd been talking to Miss Walker for a long while. Since Bertie's mother is so entranced with Anne, she barely paid attention to it. But surely you must be aware of the impropriety of spending a length of time with a young woman in this manner. All things considered."

Hare bit her lower lip. They were well beyond impropriety at this stage.

"I suspect you have a point to make there, Posy." Ernest sounded cold. He had a cordial relationship with his sister and Hare had never heard him speak to her in in quite this tone.

"You must realise that Edwina is on the cusp of making a very advantageous match and I won't have you do anything to spoil it." Posy's voice grew closer and Hare hugged the wall, hoping it wouldn't occur to the Baroness to look out. "I don't know if you're aware, but Miss Bonningham's circumstances are... reduced."

"Did she tell you that?"

"Not in so many words," Posy admitted. "But it's clear as day to me. She's frugal beyond mere prudence. And her clothes show more wear than can be explained away easily. Bertie noticed it first and, as you can imagine, he was rather displeased at a guest in his house being less than well-turned out, though he wouldn't say so to her." She paused then, because she knew her husband. "I told him not to."

"Very well." Ernest sounded weary. Hare heard the creak of the window seat as he shifted his weight. "What does Miss Bonningham's money or lack thereof have to do with me?"

"Oh, don't be dense!" Posy was pacing the room, the click-clack of her small heels beating out a steady rhythm. "You know if Brandon marries Edwina, he'll be happy to provide for her aunt as well. Truth be told, he'd barely notice the expense. As

Miss Bonningham is a dear friend of mine, I feel I owe it to her to look to her future in this regard."

"And what about Edwina's future?"

Hare closed her eyes. She really should have left. But she wanted to hear what Ernest was going to say. If she was being selfish, so be it.

"So you *do* harbour some ill-conceived hopes in her direction. I was afraid of that." Posy sighed loud enough that even Hare could hear it. "Brandon is a decent man and will treat her well. Ernest, you know I want only the best for you, but you have to be sensible. I hope you do marry one day, but I feel it my responsibility to look after Miss Walker's and Anne's well-being and neither your position nor income can match what they can have with Brandon. And given your particular… situation, you must admit Miss Walker would be unlikely to consent to marrying you, were she to be made aware of all the facts."

"You can say what you really mean, Posy. Don't feel you need to spare my feelings."

Hare knew she should have left. That whatever came next would be private and she had no business knowing it. But she stayed, praying none of the servants would come around the alley.

"Ernest, you're my brother and I love you. To me, you're my family and always have been. But the world works on more than feelings."

"I have father's name." Ernest lowered his voice so that Hare could barely hear him. "I'm legally his."

"Only because his own parents threatened to cut him off, should he bring the shame of a divorce on them. Ernest, I don't want to be cruel. But it's not exactly a secret. You know father sent Bertie a letter before we were married. Telling him not to entertain his wife's bastard son." She cleared her throat.

Hare brought her hands to her mouth, scared she might betray herself. Not because of what the Baroness had just revealed. But because she heard it in his voice, the shame he tried to hide. That the source of the shame was so outside of his control was immaterial.

Posy continued, "Bertie might have his faults, but he has, to his credit, not been overly bothered by that. But others would not be so understanding. And if it came out that Miss Walker jilted a Duke over a bastard son of an American socialite? Well, she'd be shunned. All those admiring her now would turn away from her. And from you as well, I might add, if you lost Brandon's support. A situation you can ill afford in your profession."

"I know."

Hare could hear the weariness in Ernest's voice. It was so ridiculous, really. The things humans fretted over. But, she knew, no matter how *she* felt about it, no matter how her kind might have felt about it, this was his reality. Being a child born of an affair barely registered for Hare as a thing to fuss over. But for someone like Ernest, in a place such as this, surrounded by these people… A sadness squeezed her heart. That he should have this put on him, for him to believe this affected his worth… She wished she could comfort him. But she'd lived with the humans long enough to know Posy was right. This revelation would change his position. His position, which a relationship with a mythic would make untenable.

"I won't ask you if you have feelings for her. I think it best remain unsaid if that's indeed the case." Posy continued.

Hare closed her eyes. The words were true. It didn't make them any easier to hear.

"But for her sake, as well as yours, you must be sensible." Lady Winchfield's voice caught, like she was on the verge of tears. "I only wish to protect you."

"I know, Posy." There was deep affection in his voice. "But I think you need not worry. I don't think Miss Walker harbours any great feelings towards me."

Hare couldn't listen anymore. She snuck into the servants'

entrance and raced up the staircase towards her room, making sure not to be seen by the small army of servants the Winchfields kept. Only once she reached her room, did she feel like she could breathe again. She walked in and once the door slicked shut behind her, she leaned her back against it and slumped to the ground.

"Did you get lost, Hare?"

Hare's eyes snapped towards the sound. Miss Bonningham sat as rigid as a reed on Hare's bed, half her face obscured by the shadow.

CHAPTER 27

"It's not—" Hare started, but Anne raised her hand to stop her.

"I'm not prone to acts violence, Hare, but if you dare say that it's not what it looks like, I might very well lose my composure." The *domovoy,* who sat in his favourite spot on Hare's bed, hissed at the schoolmistress and made a warning swipe with his paw. Anne blinked a couple times, then stood up and walked towards the narrow window, looking out, as if to avoid looking at Hare. "What it very much *looks like, Hare,* is that you have compromised yourself. Not only that, but your glamour is down, meaning you have exposed us both. I am partially to blame, of course. I have clearly given you too much credit. So just tell me this. Is there a chance this thing—" she made a vague gesture towards Hare, without looking at her. "—this thing that is not what it appears, can result in a pregnancy?"

"No."

"Well, I suppose it's something to be grateful for at least."Anne exhaled slowly. "We're in enough trouble as it is."

"More than you know." Hare pressed her fingers to her temples. The *domovoy* jumped off her bed and rubbed himself against her leg. She bent down and patted his head. She would take what small comfort she could.

Anne snapped her head around and stared. "What did you do?"

"Ernest knows everything, Anne. It's over."

Anne didn't respond at first. She just collapsed to the floor, like all the energy went out of her.

"A detective came to the house. Looking for you." Hare closed her eyes. "Ernest saw me lie to him and confronted me about it. He knows everything. And..." She looked at the other woman. "A part of me is glad."

The older woman put her face in her hands and a sob shook her body. Hare went to sit next to her and put her arms around her. A strange sort of tenderness gripped her. "We'll be fine, Anne." She stroked the other woman's head, as if she were a child.

"How much time do we have?" Anne sniffed and wiped at her face with her hand.

"I told the detective you'll be gone till the end of the week."

"No." Anne stared at her. "How long did Mr Thompson give you to tell the truth to his family."

Hare hung her head. The words brought her back to reality. That she would have to come clean to Lady Winchfield. To Anastacia, to Brandon. That within a day, she'd be alone again. She went from being alone, unmoored in this world to being a niece, a valued guest, a friend. To Anastacia, she was a co-conspirator even. She loved the feeling of it. Only now, when she was on the verge of losing it all, did she realise how much she loved it. And by tomorrow she'd be alone again. "I promised to tell the truth immediately. I suppose we should pack first, but that's about it."

"How ridiculous." Anne harrumphed, then gave Hare an appraising look. "Judging by the state of you, I don't think Mr Thompson would be as unforgiving as all that."

"Anne!" Hare reddened. "He knows we've been lying to his family and to his friends." *What would he think of her if she delayed?*

"And you're forgetting Willingham's threat." Miss Bonningham shook her head. "That sort of man never discards a tool. And that's what you are to him now. An unexpected, yet a useful one. Do you think he'd just let us go?"

"No." Hare remembered Samuel's expression. His smug assurance that he could ruin her with a single word. "I know he wouldn't. But if we just left, if we disappeared—"

"He'd find us before the week was out." Anne shook her head. "And who'd believe us then? Two frauds and runaways. No." She grabbed Hare's hand. "But, Hare, I've been thinking about this. About how Willingham practically demanded you marry Brandon and convince him to invest in his business. Why would he ask that? Especially when he's already marrying Brandon's sister?"

"I don't know."

Anne huffed, clearly exasperated. "He was the golden boy of New York society, Hare. He had everyone who matters invest in him. I heard often enough of his genius. In my position it was considered imperative that I keep a watchful eye out on the men deemed worthy of attention. My job was, after all, to ensure my students' parents' investment in their future paid off. Willingham had his pick of the rubber barons' daughters. And yet now he suddenly comes to London, travels across the ocean, all to marry a mythic-sympathising blue stocking?"

Hare felt like she needed to protest. "Anastacia is a wonderful woman. Sam should consider himself lucky to have someone like her."

"Oh yes, because he seems just the sort of man to value her finer qualities." Anne rolled her eyes. "Think about it for a moment, girl. Everyone knows where the real money is these days. And it is not in London. Yet he travelled all this way. Rather abruptly too, by the sound of it. And now he needs *your* help of all people to secure extra funds for his investments?"

"That's…" Hare closed her mouth. "Do you think he's in some sort of trouble?"

"I would stake my life on it." Miss Bonningham nodded. "Which I might yet do. Because we have to obtain proof. And once we're cast out of Posy's home, we will not have the opportunity to get it. But he's staying with the Duke's family for the moment. Meaning all of his possessions are in the Brandon residence. "

"The masquerade ball." Hare looked at the other woman, understanding dawning. But her heart sank at the thought of having to break her promise.

CHAPTER 28

Ernest didn't go back to his lodgings after leaving his sister's house. His rooms were comfortable enough and cheap, which was their primary attraction. But they had not even the slightest semblance of a home. He knew he wouldn't be able to fall asleep anyway, so what was the point, really. So he went to the only other place he could go, his office. He threw himself into his work, which he'd been somewhat neglecting of late.

If he was reading through the contracts and the case files, then at least he wouldn't be thinking of the message he knew was coming. That Edwi— That Hare had told his sister everything.

And then she'd be out of his life forever. If he focussed on the legal briefs, then he wouldn't be thinking about that.

He waited for the news all through the evening. And then the morning came and went and still no messenger came. His sister would rightly be furious. She surely would call on him. He imagined Hare cast out, she and her aunt packed off into a carriage to drive them far away. His sister was occasionally prone to theatrics. She'd probably send the two women as far as she could to avoid the scandal. Posy liked to think herself nobody's fool and there was no question, but that her old teacher had made a thorough fool of them all.

And Hare…

But what could he do? He would be useless. Utterly useless.

She said 'no'.

No to a future with him. No to allowing him to protect her. Even with the truth about her out in the open now, she still didn't think he was good enough. He shook his head as if he could shake the thought out of it. Because once you looked at the truth? She *was* everything he'd thought she was. Beautiful, mysterious, clever. What was her home, her real home like? A place beautiful enough so she wouldn't seem so completely out of place there? Did she think of that, when she looked at him? She didn't even know the full truth about *him* and she still didn't want him. She had given her answer and it was his duty to accept it.

He wasn't good enough. And she knew it.

His eyes itched from poring over his papers all night. Certainly not because he was the closest to tears he'd felt since he was first packed off to England as an eight-year-old. At least then, once on board he was able to cry freely without garnering too much attention. The long journey over the Atlantic was the only time he'd ever been allowed to cry, he realised. Before and after, tears were scolded or beaten out of him.

And yet he felt like crying now. It wouldn't do to wet his papers though. And so he plodded on, cocooning himself in his task.

"Mr Thompson?" A young, nervous looking clerk peeked from behind the door. "There's a lady here to see you. She says it's urgent."

Hare! He stood up so quickly, he knocked his thigh on the edge of the table. A sharp pang of pain shot through his leg, but he didn't care. He beamed towards the door, but his face fell almost immediately, as the person standing there was not Hare but Miss Bonningham, looking even more pinched than usual.

"Oh... Miss Bonningham." They stared at each other for a moment. "To what do I owe the pleasure?"

A worry crept up. Was she going to ask him to stay silent? To plead their case? No, the woman wasn't an idiot. *Did Hare know?* The thought was unwelcome.

The woman waited for the door to close behind the clerk.

"I know I'm likely the last person you wish to see right now." She hesitated, her fingers fidgeting with the strap on her handbag.

"As long as we understand each other then." He leaned back in his chair and drummed his fingers on the table. He didn't care to put her at ease. If she spontaneously combusted right there and then in his office, he wouldn't even spit on her to put the fire out. "To what do I owe your visit? I understand my sister must have cast you out by now. If so, you're looking for help in the wrong place."

She looked up at him sharply. She didn't reply at first and, not waiting for an invitation, she sat herself in the chair opposite him, as straight and proud as if she was a queen and not a scam artist. Fine, if she wanted to play it that way.

"Your sister doesn't know yet." Miss Bonningham appeared unperturbed, but he could see the tight grip she kept on her purse. "That is what I've come to talk to you about."

Her words hit their mark. Hare hadn't kept her word. She hadn't yet told Posy of her deception. It shouldn't have surprised him. Isn't that what they said of mythics? Them being full of tricks and deceptions? And yet it did surprise him. Painfully.

"You must know your position is untenable," he said through clenched teeth. "I know decency might mean little to you. But I assure you, I will have no qualms about exposing your scheme."

"And yet, you're yet to do so." She raised one eyebrow. "Something tells me it's not for my sake."

He reddened. "I have given Edwi— Miss Hare a chance to do

so first. Which I believed she would do. If I was mistaken, trust me: I will not hesitate to remedy the situation."

"Even if it means sending Hare to prison?"

Ernest opened his mouth and closed it again. He repeated the exercise a couple of times, till he realised he must have looked like a sort of land-bound carp. Miss Bonningham stared at him and to her credit, there was no victory in her eyes. Funny that. He'd taken a dislike to her as soon as he met her, seeing as she had been so hell-bent on pushing Hare into a hastily arranged match. But now, when he actually had a proper reason to hate the old bat, he suddenly felt sorry for her. Her skin was sallow and her eyes were pink-rimmed. And though she had tried to appear composed, her hands were in constant motion.

"My sister wouldn't do that," he said, in a kinder tone. Good God, Posy wasn't that sort of a person. She was somewhat shallow and cared about appearances only a smidgeon less than her husband did, but she wasn't *vicious*. Unless… "She wouldn't do that, unless it's been found you have stolen from her." *God, please no.* He remembered what Hare told him. And this woman sitting in front of him, no matter how pitiful she looked now, was, in fact, a thief as well as a liar.

But the look Miss Bonningham shot him at those words was so full of outrage that it reassured him immediately. Still, she clearly needed to correct him. "Though it's true I have deceived Posy, I did so out of desperation. I would never steal from her. She was my student, you know. My favourite student, truth be told and I had many over the years. It creates a bond between women. Not that I would expect you to understand."

"Perhaps not." The woman had nerve, he could give her that much. "But since I know my sister, I know how preposterous it would be to accuse her of such viciousness that she'd be willing to accuse you on false charges."

"I never said it'd be your sister." She watched him for a moment.

"Who then?" He scoffed. "Brandon might like Miss Hare, but he's hardly the type to hurt her over this…" There was a look on the woman's face that made him trail off. He stared at her for a moment and then the realisation dawned.

"Willingham."

She nodded.

"But that's ridiculous." He stood up and started pacing back and forth in his office, knocking some papers off his desk in the process. "How would that benefit him? It would only expose his past relationship to her and Anastacia would never marry him then!" She wouldn't marry him even without it, not if he had anything to do with that, but he didn't say as much. It wasn't any of this woman's business.

"He intends for Hare to marry Brandon. He threatened to falsely accuse her if she refused."

"What?!" That was it. He was either going insane or the world was. One of the two for certain. Maybe both. He ran his fingers through his hair.

"Perhaps you should sit down." The woman nodded towards his seat. "And I will tell you what we intend."

CHAPTER 29

He agreed.

She should have been relieved. It was all very reasonable really. Anne had explained the situation to Ernest and he offered them a temporary reprieve. Just until after the masquerade ball. Just long enough for them to collect the evidence from Sam's room. *The evidence she wasn't convinced was even there*. She groaned.

Her eyes were focussed on the needle. Up and through the fabric. Pull till the thread was taut. Stab the fabric again.

The *domovoy* watched her through half closed eyes. The creature had barely left her side since she freed him.

"Maletki, don't you have somewhere to be? " She put the fabric down. "You're free now."

You gave me a crust. You gave me a saucer of milk. And you gave me myself back. I sit where I will.

The *domovoy* purred and stretched and walked by her leg lazily, letting the tip of his tail tickle her knee. She laughed, in spite of herself.

"I will be gone soon, Maletki. And I might not have a crust to spare when I do, you realise it?"

And where would I go, little fay? The cat jumped up onto the seat next to her. *The gate to my world is as closed as the one to yours. I will stick by the one who respects me.* Maletki looked over her work with distaste. *I thought you could sew. Do you need* domovoy *assistance? It will cost you a crust, but I could fix it for you.*

"No, little friend." She rubbed him behind the ears. He was more like a cat every day, she thought. "My mistakes are mine to fix."

She turned her eyes back to her work. She had known Ernest would have agreed to the plan, of course. He was that sort of a man. There was a part of Hare that wished he hadn't agreed. A part that hoped he would rage and march over to his sister's house to expose them all. It would have given her a reason to resent him.

Hare shook her head and stared at the fabric in her hands. She'd begged off a lunch with the Duke and his sister, feigning a headache. The truth was she couldn't face seeing any of them. And not just because Willingham would likely be there, watching her. With his disgusting little veiled comments and that smug look on his face. How could she ever have imagined him decent, or kind? She ought to have her head examined.

And now that she actually met a man who was all those things, she had managed to make him thoroughly despise her.

Why was it that she only allowed herself to appreciate Ernest when there was no hope for them? On her return from his office, Miss Bonningham related their conversation in painful detail. He had agreed to delay telling his sister till after the masquerade ball. But he made it clear he wanted his hands washed of them and their affairs as soon as possible. Hare couldn't sleep the whole night after. He did the decent thing, as she knew he would, but it was more than likely he thought she had manipulated him. He had visited his sister only once since then and, though his manners were perfectly cordial, he had made a point of avoiding her. She felt two inches tall every time his gaze glanced over her.

And why wouldn't he think ill of her? In spite of everything it could have cost him, he still wished to be with her. And she had rejected him. That she had rejected him for his own good was beside the point really. Why would her intentions matter to him? She lied to him and then she rejected him. Those were the only facts that mattered.

She held out the garment she was working on to inspect it at arm's length. Lady Winchfield had encouraged Hare to rummage through the attic, where Hare found this moth-infested gown, that she was now trying to fashion into some kind of a passable costume. Miss Bonningham suggested the maid might be asked to work on it, but, frankly, if Hare wasn't allowed to tell the truth to her hosts, then at the very least she would minimise any inconvenience she might cause them. A ridiculous stand to take this far into the game, but it made her feel better.

In any case, she was skilled enough with the needle for the quick alterations needed. The facemask was all dusted and ready. The masquerade was that night and she was betting her life on a long shot. She cast a critical look over the gown in her lap. It was, it had to be said, somewhat hideous. It was the kind of green that did nothing for her complexion and so entirely suffused in trimmings, she was going to look like a box of overpriced chocolates. Since humans had discovered the method for summoning the creatures of the other worlds, their style and fabrics became more refined, touched with the skilled hands and the remnants of magic stolen from elsewhere.

But such careful attentions never touched the ugly garment in Hare's hands.

She didn't mind that. She would only wear it for a few hours and then she'd shed it, just like her fake name, her fake face and her—very much real—friends.

They would all hate her after tonight.

Ernest hated her already. Not for the first time this morning, Hare felt her eyes fill with tears.

"Why are you sad?"

She almost jumped with the shock and ended up pushing the needle into her finger.

"Ouch! Stephen, you startled me!" She put the pad of her pricked finger in her mouth.

"Are you a bampire?" he asked, his pale eyes narrowing with suspicion.

"A bampire?" Her mouth hung open, as Posy's son climbed onto the sofa next to her.

"A bampire," he replied and rolled his eyes. "Open." He leaned forward and put his fingers on Hare's chin, to which she objected weakly.

The *domovoy* made a chortling sound from the edge of the sofa, then bolted before Stephen could turn his attentions to the very fluffy creature at Hare's side.

"Steffen"!" Francine Winchfield burst through the door and stood like a diminutive valkyrie, her hands on her waist, all outrage. All she needed to complete the picture was a little horned helmet. "Why you do?" She gestured towards him.

"I believe Stephen was enquiring whether I'm a..." Hare glanced at him.

"A bampire." He scoffed at his sister and went back to inspecting Hare's mouth.

"Stephen, I would really like to know what you're doing."

"So would I."

Hare's heart leaped at the familiar voice. She looked to the door. Ernest stood behind Francine, his hands folded behind his back. But the moment she saw his face, any hope she might have held out left her. He wasn't even looking at her, focusing his attention solely on Stephen.

"Steffen wants to check if Aunt Edwina is a bampire." Francine turned to Ernest and spoke in the tones of a school mistress when addressing a particularly dense student.

"Indeed." Ernest's eyelid twitched, like he *almost* wanted to glance at Hare. Instead, he chose to address his niece. "*Miss* Walker is not your aunt, Francie." There was tension in his voice.

Hare tightened her lips into a line. It's not like she *told* the girl to call her an aunt. What did he want, for her to be mean to a child?

"Oh." The disappointment made Francine's mouth droop for a moment. Ernest picked up the girl and walked up to the seat opposite Hare's.

"Stephen, why did you say Miss Edwina was the… the thing you said?" Ernest asked.

"She drank blood!" the boy pointed an accusatory finger at Hare.

"I beg your pardon?" Hare felt as if she was having an out-of-body experience.

Ernest looked equally puzzled.

"She *did*!" Stephen folded his arms. "She put a needle in her finger and then blood came out and then she put it in her *mouth*!" He grimaced and shook his head in disgust.

"Ah, I see." Ernest nodded seriously. "Excellent powers of deduction there, Stephen."

"Are *not*!" Francine stuck out her tongue at her brother.

"So what is the next step in your investigation?" Ernest placated Francine with a pat on the head and leaned forward. *He was enjoying this.*

"I will check her mouth." Stephen nodded sagely. He'd reddened with pleasure at his uncle's praise. "You always have to check the mouth of a bampire."

"But what if Miss Edwina really turned out to be a bampire?" Ernest rested his chin on his fist. "Surely, if she turned out to be a blood-thirsty monster—"

"Really?!" Hare couldn't help feeling somewhat outraged.

"Like I was saying, if she turned out to be a blood-thirsty monster, I think it would be safer if I investigated instead."

"Would it?"

Stephen looked at her for a moment, then nodded sagely. "Yes." He made space, while Ernest put Francine on the floor and crossed the room with alarming speed. He leaned over Hare, bringing his face so close to hers she felt she could barely speak. "Open." He said in clipped tones.

"You can't be serious!" Hare made a face.

"You were right, Stephen!" Ernest said, his face still inches away from Hare's. "A very serious case of bampirism."

Stephen squealed, while Francine was standing on her tippy-toes, looking somewhat doubtful.

"The only cure is garlic." He nodded towards Stephen. "Quickly! Take Francine and bring some from the kitchen!"

Stephen was already out of the door, while Francine stayed behind, one finger tapping her lower lip, as she stared at Ernest.

"Go on, Francie, you better bring some garlic," he tried again.

"And then Miss Edwina will stop being a bampire 'miss' and be *auntie* again?" The little terror folded her dimpled arms on her chest and stared at Ernest.

"No, what—?"

"You better help your brother," Hare said with a smile, very much aware of Ernest still hanging over her, one arm by the side of her head. "Make sure he doesn't do anything silly."

That seemed to work. Francine sighed and nodded sagely, accepting her responsibility for her older brother and trotted out of the room again, leaving Ernest and Hare alone.

The moment stretched.

Finally, Hare cleared her throat. "Are you going to hover over me like this for very much longer? Only I have a costume to finish." She smiled, hoping to relieve some of the tension in the air.

It didn't work. He straightened up, as though he'd forgotten that he was still leaning over her, but he didn't take his eyes off her.

"You spoke with Anne," she said. Which was an inane

comment, really. Funny how the act of talking was more important to her composure than the content of her words.

"Yes." He kept his hands in his pockets and rocked back and forth on the balls of his feet, as if he couldn't quite decide what to do. "I was surprised, of course."

She didn't miss his meaning. "I want you to know I'm not trying to delay the inevitable. I will tell your sister everything. But it's not just me. Willingham has threatened me and Anne both. And if you knew him like I do..." Her voice caught in her throat and she faked a cough, trying to cover up the emotion. "Believe me when I tell you, he'd follow through on it."

"Is there any truth to what he means to accuse you of?"

The question took her by surprise and she flashed Ernest and angry look, half rising from the sofa. "I am *not* a thief!"

He raised his eyebrows at her. "Forgive me for checking. After all, I have found out you're a liar, an imposter and a con artist, as well as an accomplice to—" He put his finger on his chin as if he was racking his memory for something. "—oh yes, an accomplice to an *actual* thief. It would not be such a great stretch."

Hare breathed deeply, her hands falling limp by her side. She bent down to pick up the costume she'd been working on. "Very well, I deserve that," she said, her eyes dangerously wet all of a sudden. "Anything else?"

"Don't forget "a bampire"."

She frowned. *Was he laughing at her?*

"Very amusing." She sat back down and picked up the needle again, even though, if she were being honest, she couldn't really see much. But holding a needle made her look composed, so that's what she would do. She jabbed at the fabric in her hands. It was nowhere close to where the stitch was supposed to go, but how would he know that.

"Did you *mean* to sew the sleeve to the bodice?"

Dammit.

"You might as well get it all off your chest." She put the needle down. She wasn't fooling anybody. "What else am I? A liar, a con artist, you might want to slide "a mythic whore" in there somewhere. Then you can feel *really* superior." She looked up. "I'm going to leave after the ball, with or without the evidence of Sam's wrongdoing. You will never see me again after that. Now can you please leave?"

"Very well," he said and started walking towards the door. *Please don't leave.* She had asked him to go, but to see him walk away knocked the air out of her. As if he could hear her thoughts, he stopped dead in his tracks. "No." He turned around and faced her again.

She couldn't be in the same room as him. It was too dangerous."Very well, then I will leave." She rolled up the gown in her arms and tried to escape with as much dignity as a person holding a huge pile of frilly fabric could muster. He stepped in front of her. "Please get out of my way, Ernest." She was vaguely impressed with herself. Her voice sounded very calm. Matter-of-fact even.

"I never called you… that thing you said. I *would* never."

She made the mistake of looking up. His jaw was tensed and he looked angry. Or ashamed. Somewhere between the two. Which wasn't that surprising, she thought. Nobody liked to feel ashamed. Anger was but a stone's throw away whenever shame or guilt reared their heads. She knew the feeling well.

"Did you hear me?"

It startled her to realise she'd been standing there for a good twenty seconds, just staring at him. "Yes, I heard you. You didn't call me that. The truth is, you didn't have to." She made sure to put as much emphasis into the next words as she could. "You thought it though, didn't you?"

His face reddened and he grabbed her arm. "That's not true!"

"No?" She turned her head to the side. "As you say, my mistake." Sarcasm was practically dripping from her words.

"Hare, I don't… I would never."

"It's alright." She tugged at her arm and he released it. "It doesn't matter anyway. I will be gone soon. And then you can just forget all about me."

"What if I don't want to forget about you?" There was a note of pleading in his voice. She stared at him. What did the ridiculous man want? He wanted her gone, then he didn't, but then resented her for asking two days' reprieve.

"I'm not sure you yourself know what it is you want, Ernest."

He looked as if she'd slapped him, standing there staring with his mouth hanging open.

Just at that moment, little Stephen burst into the room, followed closely by his sister. "We have garlic!" He shoved a clove into Ernest's palm.

"I will take it." Hare snatched it and gave Ernest a tense little smile. "We bampires like to heal in private." She looked down and, for the children's sake, she added. "Like cats." And then she left. And while she wasn't sure if she did a lot of healing the rest of the afternoon, she certainly did a lot of crying.

CHAPTER 30

Masquerades were ridiculous. It was a testament to how secure and bored the upper classes were, that they would purposefully introduce confusion and mystery into their lives, as an *amusement* of all things. The whole evening, the bemasked men and women would mingle, altering their voices to add to the effect, getting a thrill out of interacting with people who didn't know who they were.

Ernest saw no appeal in that, truth be told. He liked to know who he was dealing with and wanted to *be* known. Especially in the light of recent events, flirting with strangers felt like a particularly bad idea. Which was, everyone agreed, really the whole point of masquerades. But for once, he didn't put up a fight. That in itself was unusual enough for Posy to become somewhat suspicious. He had to, at different occasions, reassure her that he neither planned on escaping early under the cover of darkness, nor did he have any particularly shameful debauchery in mind for the evening. The latter he had to emphasise with more exasperation than he usually allowed himself with his sister. Who did she take him for? Prince Albert?

In any case, he had agreed to meet his sister and her party at the venue.

While he waited, he looked around the beautifully decorated hall. He had to admit, Brandon's mother was very good at what she did. The windows were open, which was thoughtful, really. He was already sweating under the owl mask his sister had forced him to wear. He had originally planned on coming disguised as a solicitor, but the plan was not met with Lady Winchfield's approval.

There were a few mythic servants, the only ones who required no costumes. He knew none of them were bound, Anastacia had seen to it. But it mattered little. Once summoned, they couldn't go back. And what else could they do but fulfill the Beau Monde's endless appetite for mythic domestics? It was strange to watch them now weave their way between the guests. The real thing next to a pale imitation and yet it was always the latter with all the power.

Brandon and Anastacia came out to greet him, both dressed as some nondescript Roman characters. Brandon claimed to be a different philosopher every time anyone asked him and Anastacia just rolled her eyes and said that togas were the most comfortable option. Ernest caught a quick glimpse of Willingham, who was already oiling his way around the crowd, speaking to the richer guests in hushed, urgent tones. He wore no mask. Ernest supposed the respectable persona Willingham put on was mask enough. He had barely paid Ernest any attention beyond a cursory greeting. And why would he? Ernest had no money to invest and no great sway in society.

Anastacia seemed to notice her fiancé's lack of courtesy towards Ernest and excused it with a nervous smile. "He's so focussed on his business at the moment," she whispered, leaning close to Ernest. "It's at a delicate stage and investment is all he needs to propel it further." She cast an admiring look at the man.

"He is proud, you see and doesn't want to rely on his family's money."

"An admirable conviction." Ernest sipped at his champagne. If the evening was a success, they would soon find out just how deep Willingham's convictions really were.

"You don't much like him, do you?"

Ernest was momentarily grateful for the owl mask, as his expression surely would have betrayed him. Anastacia was staring at him with narrowed eyes.

"What makes you say that?" Not a denial, but close enough to one. He was as bad at outright lies as Hare, he realised.

"I'm not blind, you know!" Anastacia rolled her eyes. "And while I appreciate the brotherly protectiveness, I wish you and Brandon would just trust my judgement in this."

"Brandon doesn't approve then?" Ernest glanced at his friend, who was greeting his guests. As if he felt Ernest's eyes on him, Brandon turned his head towards him. He'd been acting cold all evening. And, well, Ernest couldn't blame him exactly. But it did hurt. And what hurt even more was that he was the only one of the two of them who knew that in this contest, they were both destined to be losers.

Anastacia followed Ernest's gaze towards her brother and sighed, shaking her head. "You know how Brandon is. Everyone thinks him soft because of how easy-going he appears to be in public. But he doesn't mess about when it comes to family and business."

"Has Willingham given him cause to worry about either then?" Ernest tried to keep his voice casual, but Anastacia wasn't fooled for a moment.

"What did he tell you?" she demanded.

"Brandon didn't say anything to me." Ernest lifted both hands up. And, of course, it was true.

"Well then..." Anastacia brushed her blond hair off her face, seemingly placated. "I think my brother is just old fashioned. He dislikes speculation. Especially when he can't see the physical product from the investment. But the world is changing, you know." She shrugged. "And Sam explains it so well. I wish Brandon would listen."

"Indeed..." Ernest's attention was turned towards the party entering the hall now. His sister, dressed as a... *was it a tree?* And behind her Bertie, then...

Behind the Winchfields trailed Miss Bonningham, whose costume was a modest little mask. And behind them all... While Hare wore both a large mask and a wig, Ernest would know her anywhere. She was squeezed into the hideous green gown he'd seen her working on, but she made it work. He swallowed. She made it work *too well.* He became uncomfortably aware of it at the exact same time as seemingly every other man present. Hare's dress was dangerously low cut and, honestly, Ernest had to fight the urge to stomp over there and bodily shield her from the gaze of everyone in the room.

But she seemed to have no self-conscious bone in her body and she chattered pleasantly with everyone who approached her.

If the point was to be inconspicuous so that she could sneak off to ransack Willingham's room, then her outfit was a complete failure. There wasn't a man alive who could ignore her. And indeed, a host of men, including Brandon and Willingham, snaked their way towards the new arrivals.

"If you'll excuse me," Ernest said to Anastacia, but before he could take half a step, her hand shot out and grabbed his sleeve.

"Don't."

He looked at her in surprise.

"Ernest, I believe I told you no more than a minute ago that I'm not blind. Do you have cause to doubt me?"

"Errr..." He could think of no clever response.

"My brother isn't either, you realise." Anastacia took a deep breath and released it slowly. "You are free to pursue whoever you wish. But Brandon is serious about Edwina. And I admit, selfishly, I would love her for a sister. So I ask you, don't mess it up."

"I think it's rather up to the lady herself, don't you think?" He didn't know where the words had come from. A platitude. A false one, he realised. He glanced at Hare and a cold feeling squeezed his heart. Because when had it ever been up to Hare? She was trapped. And then judged for the cage others put her in.

He had judged her as well. And what was worse, she knew it.

And soon, very soon, she would be gone. Gone without knowing that he finally understood.

"I must..." He saw Willingham approach Hare, a smug smirk turning up the corners of his lips. Hare gave the man her hand, which he lifted up to his lips. She bent her neck and laughed and gave nothing away. Ernest's skin crawled. How could she have the strength to hide her disgust, her fear.

A blush had risen on her neck, the only sign of the emotion she felt.

Ernest walked towards her, like in a haze.

He practically elbowed his way through the throng of men surrounding her and when he finally reached to take her hand in a greeting, the only thing he knew was that he could not let her face this night alone.

CHAPTER 31

She instantly knew it was him behind the owl mask. He'd been looking at her ever since she arrived. He gave the tips of her fingers a light squeeze and it made her feel less alone, even as Willingham seemed to hover around her the whole time, circling the perimeter like a predator. *Which was as she'd planned it.* Anne shot Hare a look to show she'd noticed.

"May I ask for this dance." Ernest gave a curt bow and before she'd had the chance to respond, he led her onto the dance floor, just as the band began playing the first waltz. Hare caught a glimpse of Brandon in the crowd. Was he dressed in... *Good grief.* The man was in a toga, both his arms and calves showing. It seemed the point of masquerades, she supposed, that the normal rules went out the window. Every now and again he would glance towards the door.

"I wonder that you recognised me," she said to Ernest, absent-mindedly.

"You mean, between the dead squirrel on your head and the dusty mask?"

She gasped and pinched his shoulder. "The wig isn't that bad!"

"Ouch, alright then. Just a gently mauled squirrel then." This earned him another pinch. He pulled her closer, as they circled round the hall. "I've seen your gown already, remember? When you were working on it."

"Ah." She felt a little silly.

"And how did you guess it was me?"

She rolled her eyes, not that he could see with her mask on. A very *hot* mask. She felt like she had her face pressed against an oven. "I could have spotted you from a mile away."

"Could you really?" He seemed somewhat *too* pleased at her words.

"I've excellent powers of deduction."

"Yes." He twirled her around again and there she saw Willingham standing in the corner. He was staring right at her.

"Don't be scared," Ernest whispered in her ear. "He can't hurt you."

"Don't be ridiculous." She laughed mirthlessly. "Of course he can."

Ernest stumbled and recovered in half a step. Clearly he wasn't used to quite this much cynicism. But frankly, Hare didn't feel like sparing his feelings.

"He can hurt me in a dozen different ways. And he *will,* given half a chance." She raised her face and looked into Ernest's eyes. "But don't worry, I don't plan on giving him one." Which was, strictly speaking, not true. Her and Anne's plan was somewhat imperfect on that point. "I will be ok," she said, more for her own sake than his.

"What are you planning?"

"Well, the first question is, do you know which room is his?"

"Of course not."

Well, it was worth a shot.

"Then the first step is to find out where the Duke's family placed him. I can't go through his documents if I don't know where they are."

"And how do you intend to find out?" She could sense the growing tension in his voice. "Lady Brandon has easily two dozen rooms where she could have stashed him. It's not like you can ask anyone exactly."

"As a matter of fact I can," she said, with far more confidence than she felt. "Now, if you would please deposit me close to him."

"What are you talking about?"

She patted his shoulder twice. "Don't worry your pretty head about it."

He narrowed his eyes at her and squeezed her hand rather too hard. There were many couples on the dance floor and so nobody seemed to notice.

She threw her head back, nearly dislodging the huge wig she was wearing. He was right, dammit, it did look like a dead squirrel. Or a dozen. "Don't worry, I will make sure to be out of your hair soon."

He stayed quiet for a moment. "Tell me what you're planning."

"Absolutely not."

"Hare..." There was a warning in his voice, which only served to irritate her.

"It's none of your business," she said. "*I'm* none of your business really. Not after tonight."

"I'll be the judge of what is and isn't my business."

She tried to increase the space between them, but he held on tight to her waist.

"It's not enough that you're a solicitor, now you're trying to be a judge as well?" she said lightly. "I'm not your business, Ernest and after tonight I hope to not be your problem either."

"I don't see you as a problem."

Her temper flared up at that. "Honestly I don't care what you do and don't see anymore. So if you'll excuse me." She pulled on his hand and stepped to the side, bringing them closer to where Willingham stood.

"You're not supposed to be leading."

"You know, I'm heartily sick of men telling me that," she said, before grabbing the hand he kept on her waist and yanking it off her. He could do nothing but move her out of the dance floor, as anything less would have caused a scene. But she could feel the anger radiating off him.

"Please let me help you," he whispered.

She was aware of Willingham's eyes on her. She could see him in her peripheral vision, as he was edging closer, staying close to the wall.

"I'd rather not rely on your help," she said, meeting his gaze, so he couldn't miss her meaning. "Relying on your kind has never worked out for me in the past and I'm not that much of a gambler to keep trying. I'm thirsty, would you mind bringing me a drink?" She said the last part loud enough so that Willingham could hear. Ernest paused for a moment, waiting for… what? He'd made it clear what he thought of her. He couldn't blame her for believing him.

And then he walked off, leaving her alone.

"IT'S GOING to be a long night. You should pace yourself, *Miss Walker*." Willingham appeared by her side as soon as Ernest walked away.

"My disguise is less effective than I thought, clearly."

"Oh, don't be surprised, I'd know your body anywhere." He cast a glance at her chest. It took every last bit of her self-control to not punch him. "And you're displaying it so proudly for all to see tonight."

"I'm surprised you're not dancing with your fiancée." She fanned herself with a huge feathered thing Posy had pushed into her hand earlier. "She might not like you talking to strange women instead of paying attention to her." She had to be careful. Sam wasn't a complete idiot. He'd know something was up if she became too friendly too quickly.

"Anastacia is an accommodating woman." He smirked. "As are *you*, I hope."

She wasn't sure how to respond so she gave half a nod.

"Brandon's planning on proposing soon, you realise." It wasn't a question so she didn't reply. "You will gratefully accept, of course. I'm thinking a double wedding." He gave a small chuckle. "When you think about it, we're all going to be bedfellows of sorts." He guffawed. Sam was always very good at amusing himself, that much could be said with certainty. In contrast, Hare threw up a little in her mouth.

"You seem to have it all planned out."

"I like to plan ahead, yes." He stood shoulder to shoulder next to her, as they both faced the dance floor. "Some would call it a virtue."

"Glad to hear you have at least one of those."

"Thank you. From someone who has lost hers that is even more meaningful."

The mask felt oppressively hot. The fan wasn't doing an awful lot either, mostly because she was effectively fanning a sheet of papier-mâché.

"You have always blushed rather prettily," he said. She knew what she was doing wearing this gown, but it was one thing to plan around a lecher's preferences and another to carry the plan out. She felt horridly exposed, even if she knew he couldn't very well do anything to her when surrounded by Brandon's guests.

"Come now," he said, encouraged by her silence. "We were rather good friends before. No point in holding onto a grudge." He wiped his hand across his mouth while giving her an appraising look.

"I suppose not," she said through gritted teeth.

"I always knew you were a smart girl." He nodded. "No need to be so serious about it all. You're going to be a duchess of all things. Rather a surprising status ascension for a mythic from New York. We'll be friends yet, you'll see."

"And friends have each other's backs," she said.

"Or *fronts*, if the right opportunity arises." He looked pointedly at her bosom.

"You're being dangerously obvious, don't you think?"

"Come now, it's the new dawn! The old Queen Vicky is on her way out and the future king despises prudes. I'm just keeping up with the times."

"I think you will fit rather seamlessly with those 'new times' then."

"I'll take it as a compliment." He grinned. "The future is bright, Hare, if only you give it a chance."

Now was the time. She turned towards him and lifted her chin. "I suppose I might as well then."

He paused for a moment and searched her eyes for any sign of deception.

"I hope you mean it, Hare. You know I'd hate to have to remind you of the consequences, should you choose to back out."

"What do you expect from me?" *What if Miss Bonningham was wrong? What if the only dark secret here was hers? She would be really stuck then.* She fanned herself more vigorously.

"Oh, it's very simple. I only ask that you are a *very* good fiancée to him." Willingham said, looking around the dance floor. Hare followed his gaze towards where the Duke was conversing with his mother and sister. "After all, you should thank him appropriately for offering you a chance at the high life you want so badly." He turned back to her and looked her up and down slowly. "You will make Brandon so happy, he'll do anything you ask. And what you'll ask is his investment in my venture, of course."

Hare forced a small laugh. "You have great faith in my charms."

"Faith is for those without control. If you somehow fail to do what I ask, if you provoke me in any way whatsoever, I can get you arrested. And you know mythics found guilty of theft are sold for rebinding. Your kind can't be trusted after all. A thief that can alter their appearance?" He cocked his head to the side. "So you see, I need not worry about your cooperation. The consequences—should you betray me—assure your participation. *You,* however, need to rely on your *faith* in my goodwill. See how that works?"

"*Your* goodwill?" She couldn't keep the sarcasm from her voice.

"Speaking of my goodwill..." There was another note in his voice, a dangerous one. "Don't you think it's high time you made some effort to secure it?"

She froze up. This was what she expected. She and Anne had discussed it. But now, faced with this man, she wanted to lash out, or run, or both. But she didn't move a muscle.

"I've missed you, Hare," he said. "Well, maybe not *you* so much. But you were better than a mediocre fuck, truth be told and while Anastacia is likely to be very useful to me, I don't have very high hopes of her in that regard."

"I'm honoured."

"I thought you might be. And I know you ought to be *very* motivated to keep me on your good side. Also, this *is* a rather tedious ball..."

She stayed silent for a moment. Just enough to steady herself. "I will meet you in your room."

"No time like the present," he said, sliding closer to her.

"In two hours." Her heart beat so fast she felt like it was going to jump out of her chest. "We can't leave together. Tell me which one is your room and I will wait for you there. In two hours." She waited for what seemed like an eternity.

Something cold slipped into her hand.

"My key." He said. "The second door on the left down the corridor up there." He pointed with his chin. "Till then, Miss Hare," he said and then he walked off towards his fiancée.

She gripped the key tight in her fist. "Thank the gods for the predictability of arrogant men," she muttered to herself.

"Do you count me among them?"

CHAPTER 32

She stood as rigid as a statue for a moment before facing him. "I thought I told you to leave me be."

"Leave you to the tender ministrations of that lech and, by your reckoning, a criminal?" Ernest shrugged. "I think not."

"I have what I need," she said, turning away. "I must find Anne." Something glinted in her hand.

"Is that a *key*?"

He couldn't see her face, hidden as it was by her mask. But her eyes flitted to the side.

"You either tell me right now what's happening, or I will force it out of you, in front of all of Lady Brandon's guests."

She nodded sullenly and opened her hand for a moment, just long enough to let him see the room key inside.

"How did you obtain it, may I ask?" He knew already, but he would hear it from her.

"How do you think?" She jutted out her chin.

He didn't trust himself to speak. A wave of anger rolled across him. He would have to kill Willingham, there were no two ways about it.

"I have two hours before he goes up there," she said. "Plenty of time for me and Anne to find what we need and disappear if we fail."

"And if he notices you gone and decides to check up on his room?"

She scoffed. "He will not suspect me going against him. He doesn't think I have it in me."

"I will go." The decision surprised him as much as it did her. "It's not safe for you."

"It's not safe for you either," she said. "If you're caught rummaging through his room, you'd be risking your career as well as your friendship with Brandon."

"I think we both know my friendship with Brandon is strained by a far more serious matter than me getting caught in his guest's room." He wished she would look at him then. To see her acknowledge at least what had happened between them. It was driving him mad. This acting like nothing happened. He could half believe it hadn't happened, that it had all been a dream. But then he still remembered her smell and how she tasted on his tongue and he was so desperate for her to admit to it.

But she didn't look towards him, not then. It was as if he hadn't spoken at all.

"In any case, Anne has worked as a school mistress for decades. You'd be unlikely to find anyone better at snooping, even if you were to interview the best detectives from Scotland Yard."

"Miss Bonningham is full of surprising talents." He looked to the door and his mouth went dry in shock. His hand instinctively sought out hers. "I don't know about Scotland Yard, but there's a detective right there."

"*What?!*" She looked around the dance floor till her eyes found Mr Sputnek, casually chatting to the butler, who had the expression of someone who'd found something rather unpleasant stuck to the sole of his shoe. "What is he doing here?"

"No doubt hoping to find Miss Bonningham."

A curious look flashed in her eyes. "I think I have found a way for you to be useful. If, that is, your offer of help still stands."

He looked at her. She tried to keep herself up straight, but he could see that she didn't know if he would or wouldn't help her. It filled him with shame. He wanted her to have no doubts. But, he realised, it was a selfish thought. Because he hadn't yet earned her trust. He would now. "Whatever you need," he said. And he meant it. Whatever she needed. *Anything and everything.*

"I SEE you haven't a costume, Mr Sputnek?" He'd walked up to Mr Sputnek, who was dabbing his forehead with a handkerchief. The little man instantly turned towards him, a broad smile on his face.

"Mr Thompson! Or Esquire Thompson? Mr Esquire?" He sniffed. "I'm afraid you'll have to forgive me; I'm not well acquainted with the etiquette here."

"'Mr Thompson' is quite alright," Ernest said. "I'm impressed you can tell who I am behind this mask."

"Oh yes." Mr Sputnek seemed quite pleased at that. "You see, in my line of work, one has to pay attention. And your voice is quite, quite distinct."

"Is it? I didn't realise."

"Oh yes, your accent, you see..." The detective was talking, but it didn't stop him from scanning the ballroom with those sharp eyes of his. "I would be a poor sort of sleuth indeed, if I couldn't recognise my fellow countryman, no matter how polished his accent. I was wondering if you could direct me towards that charming fiancée of yours? I understand she was Miss Bonningham's companion on their passage from New York?"

Ernest froze up. Mr Sputnek watched him carefully, as if challenging him to contradict that point.

"Of course." Ernest gave a smart bow. "I believe she was just dancing over there." He pointed to the end of the hall, the farthest from where Hare stood, talking to Miss Bonningham in hushed tones. "Let me assist you."

"That would be most kind, yes."

"May I ask how you have come to be here, Mr Sputnek? I don't imagine you have an invitation to the ball?"

The detective flashed Ernest a wide grin. "You have your ways, Mr Thompson Esquire and I have mine."

"Quite." In the corner of his eye, Ernest could see Hare and Miss Bonningham making their way towards the side door, which would lead to another staircase to take them upstairs. *Clever girl.* If they took the main staircase, Willingham would be bound to notice them and get suspicious. "May I ask what it is you require of Miss Walker, Mr Sputnek?"

"I'm afraid that's strictly confidential." The American kept dabbing his forehead. The room was rather warm, but Ernest honestly felt it was excessive under the circumstances. "Are you certain she came here? I admit the masks do complicate matters somewhat. She was a bigger lady if memory serves and I do not see a woman who would match that description here."

"Oh yes," Ernest said smoothly, placing a hand on Mr Sputnek's shoulder and practically spinning him around. "I think I just caught a glimpse of her over there."

CHAPTER 33

"What are we even looking for?" Hare looked through the papers casually scattered across the small writing desk. Willingham had always been a bit of a slob.

She was glad she could take the mask off at least. It was really unbearably hot.

"Anything that might point to him swindling his investors, of course." Miss Bonningham moved swiftly and methodically, as she looked through the man's bags, of which he had many.

Hare made a small noise in her throat. She wondered how she would be able to tell such papers apart. It's wasn't like Willingham was likely to keep a diary that read 'Ha-ha, I have swindled Mr X of a thousand dollars today before breakfast.' One had to at least have a clue of what one was looking at. Hare had frankly little experience with how speculators operated. But she dutifully looked around the desk, pulling out everything from the drawers.

"Don't waste any time being neat," Anne said without looking up. "If we find what we need, then it won't matter. If we don't, then it won't matter either, as we'll be in prison in the worst-case scenario and on the run if we're lucky."

"Fair enough." Hare pulled on the second drawer of the desk. It was locked. She brightened somewhat. In stories, villains always kept incriminating evidence in locked drawers. It was bound to be a good sign, surely? She swiped her hand across the desk and picked up a small letter opener. It had a carved ivory handle decorated with pearl inlay. Willlingham always did try to have the best of everything. She jammed the knife between the lock and the wood of the drawer.

"What did you find?" Miss Bonningham looked up with interest.

"A locked drawer." Hare bit her lip as she wiggled the knife. "Since I don't have a key, I thought I'd try to break the whole thing."

"Or." Miss Bonningham patted the day trousers Willingham had discarded on the chair by the bed. She put her hand in the pocket and turned to Hare with a triumphant look. "We could use the key!"

"And what exactly are you two looking for?"

The voice made Hare's blood run cold. She turned around to see Willingham casually close the door behind him. He barely glanced at her, instead walking towards the commode. He opened the top drawer and, as casually as if he was offering them a cigarette, he pointed a gun straight at Hare's chest. "I did warn you not to disappoint me."

After about ten minutes of wandering around the ballroom, Mr Sputnek seemed to finally lose his patience. "Are you certain Miss Bonningham and your fiancée are even here?"

Ernest shrugged and gave the detective his most innocent smile. "I promise I don't mean to be wasting your time, Mr Sputnek. The masks do complicate the matters, as you have yourself so aptly said." He was enjoying himself, he noticed with a surprise. He was lying to a detective, was acting as an accessory to theft and he frankly didn't care. It would be disastrous if it was all discovered, of course, but he found himself questioning whether he even cared anymore.

"Ernest!"

Damn it. Ernest spun around to see Brandon and his sister come up towards them.

"You've been circling the room like a squirrel looking for last year's nuts, so we were rather concerned," Anastacia said with a raised eyebrow. "And who is your friend?"

"Bronek Sputnek at your service, Miss!" The detective pulled his hat off his head and stared at Anastacia with open-mouthed admiration.

"Mr Sputnek? I don't believe we've met." Brandon shot his sister an amused look. The detective was still gaping at Anastacia, to the point of not noticing Brandon's outstretched hand.

"I'm just helping Mr Sputnek with a small matter," Ernest said, hoping they wouldn't notice quite how vague he was being.

Anastacia narrowed her eyes at him. Oh, but of course she would notice.

"I hope the matter doesn't take too long," Brandon said. "My dearest mother seems determined to make each guest of female persuasion dance every dance and my legs are about to give out. It's only fair you do your share."

"Why not employ Willingham for the task?" Ernest rolled his eyes.

Mr Sputnek snapped his head towards Ernest. "Willingham, did you say?"

Anastacia shrugged. "Sam said he wasn't feeling well. He just went up to his room to rest up before dinner."

God no. "When?"

Mr Sputnek tried interjecting, "Is it Mr Samuel Willingham?" but he was ignored by everyone.

"A few minutes ago." Brandon looked at him in surprise. "Say, are you quite alright?"

"Where is his room?"

"What are you—?"

"WHERE?" he practically roared.

Brandon blinked a couple times. "Up the staircase, the second door on the left. But what—"

Ernest didn't hear the rest of the question. He was already running, pushing the dancers out of the way.

* * *

"DON'T DO ANYTHING STUPID, BOY." Miss Bonningham straightened herself up to her full height. "There's no need for such theatrics.

"I wouldn't move if I were you, old girl," Willingham said, his eyes fixed on Hare. "The headmistress act might work well on girls in pinafores, but it's not going to help you here, I promise." He nodded towards Hare. "I admit I'm disappointed. I was suspicious how agreeable you were making yourself. I hoped you were merely learning to be smart." He shook his head. "We could have worked well together, Hare. If you gave it a chance."

"If I wanted 'work' like that, then I could have stayed where you left me," Hare said through gritted teeth.

"Don't get missish with me." He laughed then, an ugly noise. "We're all adults here. If you didn't know how the world worked then, then you surely do so now. But in any case, you're out of chances, I'm afraid."

"What are you going to do?" Miss Bonningham edged towards Hare. Willingham swung the gun to point at her face.

"You move again, you die." He pointed the gun back at Hare. "I'm going to shout for help, you see. You will both be discovered just how I found you. Elbow-deep in my possessions. At which point I will have to come clean about all your crimes, of course." He put a hand on his heart. "I've been waiting to see what your true intentions were, till now, but I'm sad to see the leopard doesn't change its spots, after all."

"Clearly not," Hare said, contempt dripping from every word.

Willingham narrowed his eyes and Miss Bonningham whispered, "Don't antagonise him."

"Very good advice right there, Hare. Shame you didn't receive it earlier." He looked at the pile of papers at Hare's feet. "What were you looking for? Money, I suppose?" He laughed and shook his head. "If you were so desperate to get back on your feet, all you had to do is spend a little time on your back." He laughed at his own joke.

Hare couldn't think, she couldn't stop herself. She grabbed an ink stand off the desk and flung it in Willingham's face. The ink poured out in a wide arc and the bottle hit him harmlessly on the forearm, as he instinctively brought his right arm up. The moment the gun wasn't pointed at her chest, Hare grabbed the small chair by the desk and swung it around, trying to hit him. "Anne, run!" she screamed just as the door swung open.

* * *

ERNEST BURST through the door and for a moment he couldn't quite figure out what was happening. Willingham was on the floor, with Hare bashing him with the broken remains of a chair, as Miss Bonningham was struggling to pin down the man's right arm, which held... *Dear God.*

Ernest shot through the room and put his foot down on Willingham's wrist, forcing him to release the gun.

Willingham howled and lashed out, hitting Miss Bonningham in the face, before turning towards Hare. He grabbed a fistful of her hair and pulled with a sadistic smile. The grin died on his lips almost immediately though, as he stared uncomprehendingly at the wig in his hand.

"What in the devil is going on here?" Brandon's voice came

from the doorway. Ernest didn't bother looking around. He'd been struggling to pin Willingham down, which didn't prove to be easy.

"Willingham!" The horror in Anastacia's voice was enough to wake Willingham from his momentary stupor.

"Stacia, I've been attacked."

"With your own gun, held in your own hand?" Ernest said through gritted teeth. Willingham stared daggers at him. His face was half-covered by ink, which, combined with his furious expression made him look like he had the war paints on.

"I demand that you explain yourselves."

Ernest glanced around to see Brandon looking like a storm cloud, looming over them in a fury he'd never seen in his friend. "Ernest, for God's sake, get off him. Why are Miss Bonningham and Hare in here and what the devil has been happening?"

Ernest shot Willingham a warning look and removed his knee from the man's shoulder. He wasn't moving fast enough, for Willingham pushed at him and got up, his hands sliding over his clothes to straighten them up.

"I came up to my room to rest and those two—" He gestured to Hare and Miss Bonningham. "—were going through my things." He turned to Anastacia, his look suddenly somber. "They were no doubt trying to steal from me. Again."

"'Again?'" Anastacia looked between Willingham and Hare, the latter standing straight, her chin up, looking like some kind of an Amazon. "I don't understand."

"I have never stolen as much as a pin from you, you unbelievable—"

"I have warned the two of them." Willingham ran his finger across his forehead, smearing the ink further. He stared at his fingertips for a moment, before dropping his hand again. "Those two are nothing more but scam artists and thieves. I've come across Miss Walker, which is to say *Hare* in New York. A rather popular mythic courtesan, she had tried to worm her way into being my mistress and when I rejected her advances, she stole from me and ran. I can only assume they used the money to pay for their passage here."

"You liar!" Hare half jumped, her hands outstretched, as if she'd claw his eyes out. Ernest was faster, grabbing her by the shoulders.

"It won't make things better to attack him," he whispered.

"It would make *me* feel better." She glanced at him but didn't try to shake his hands off her.

Willingham sniggered at her attempt and turned bodily away, his full attention on his fiancée. Anastacia, for her part, seemed frozen in the spot and all blood seemed to have left her face as the man continued. "I told them they'd have to come clean or I'd tell you the truth myself. They no doubt wanted to steal from me as revenge before running off."

"I can't believe it." Brandon looked at Hare with a stricken expression, which told Ernest that he very much did believe it. Ernest felt unreasonably angry, that a man who was ready to marry Hare, would be so quick to believe the worst of her and on nothing more but on a word of a slimy bastard like Willingham.

"Ed—Hare, is that true?" Anastacia said with a stricken expression. "All this time?"

"I never stole anything from him!" Hare reddened as those gathered looked around the room, with the papers and clothes scattered all across the floor. It didn't look good for her and she knew it.

Ernest squeezed her shoulders lightly, so she'd look up at him. "Did you find it?"

"Find what?" Brandon and Anastacia asked at the same time.

"The proof that Willingham is the true scammer here." Hare looked at Anastacia, a pleading expression on her face. "Some of what he said is true. I'm not Miss Bonningham's niece." Her eyes grew glassy. She straightened up and let the glamour drop from her face, to the shocked gasps of Anastacia and Brandon both.

"I'm sorry for deceiving you all. But *he's* the villain." She pointed an accusatory finger at Willingham. "He is planning on marrying you for your money and connections, after having defrauded his American investors. Me and Anne were looking through his things to try and find the proof."

"And did you find it?" Brandon asked, his voice as taut as a piano string.

"Not yet," she admitted. Ernest swore under his breath. She glanced at him. "But it's here! You must believe it."

"You're asking us to believe you, after you have just admitted to lying to us. About *everything*." Brandon wasn't trying to be unkind, Ernest knew it. But the words must have hurt Hare anyway. He could feel her shoulders trembling. He squeezed them for a moment. To show he was still there. She wasn't alone. Brandon noticed and narrowed his eyes before continuing. "And you're asking that we believe you again, with no proof to support your words?"

Hare pointed at the desk. "This drawer, it's locked. We were about to look inside before he burst in on us with his gun!"

"Yes, the gun?" Brandon turned to Willlingham. "In *my* house?"

"I'm a businessman." Willingham tried to assume a dignified expression. "I keep one for protection."

"Open the drawer," Anastacia said, staring at Willingham.

"I hardly—"

"Open. The. Drawer."

"Very well." Willingham shrugged and pulled a key from the inside pocket of his jacket. He put it in the drawer's lock and opened it with a flourish.

They all leaned in, trying to peer inside.

At the bottom of the drawer sat travel papers, a leather wallet and a pair of cufflinks.

Willingham sniggered and made a dramatic gesture toward the writing desk. "Please inspect, everyone." He shook his head. "I would have hoped that my fiancée at least might have more trust in me, but I have nothing to hide."

"I wouldn't be so sure about that."

They all turned towards the door, where Mr Bronek Sputnek stood, his hands folded behind him.

"And *you* are?"

"Bronek Sputnek, a private detective, at your service." The small man beamed at Brandon.

Miss Bonningham made a small whimpering noise by Hare's side. Hare took her hand and gave her a reassuring, tight little smile. The older woman held onto Hare as if onto a life raft.

"Excellent." Willingham gave Hare a sickly smile, which made Ernest want to strangle him, "How fortuitous. Detective, if you will, arrest them please. I will be pressing charges."

Mr Sputnek cleared his throat. "I'm afraid you misunderstand, Mr Willingham. You see, I'm here for you."

The room went instantly quiet. Everyone stared at the man, as he swayed back and forth, clearly enjoying the moment.

"Mr Willingham, I have been employed to bring you to justice, on the charges of theft, forgery, extortion and a number of other, smaller offences." The little detective smiled. "I'm afraid your investors back in New York are rather determined. And so, while I have alerted the Scotland Yard, I would advise you to come with me peacefully."

"But..." Hare stammered. "You were asking after Miss Bonningham."

The detective glanced at Hare with interest. "Miss Walker, I take it?"

She nodded dumbly. "Hare. It's just 'Hare'."

"It had come to our attention that Miss Bonningham, who had been charged with the education of no fewer than ten of the victims' family members had absconded rather abruptly, leaving the country barely one month after Mr Willingham. It's also become apparent that she'd left the country in the company of none other but Miss Hare, Mr Willingham's mythic—" He glanced around the room and reddened. "—acquaintance... Yet by the time the ship arrived at the London dock, there was no mention of her. You must understand that Miss Hare was seen as a potentially important witness to the case and her strange disappearance piqued our interest." He nodded at Hare. "We were rather worried Mr Willingham might have disposed of you. I'm glad to see it was not the case."

Willingham stared at Mr Sputnek, then at Hare. His face grew red and, before anyone could react, he had launched himself at his gun, still on the floor. He swung the barrel towards Hare. "No!" Ernest screamed and lunged towards her. *Too slow. Much too slow.* Hare closed her eyes as the gun fired. At the same time, she found herself shoved out of the way and a splatter of something wet and sticky hit her face.

Miss Bonningham was now standing there, shielding Hare and swaying on her feet, staring defiantly at Willingham. The bullet had hit the older woman's shoulder, spraying Edwina's face and the wall behind them with blood.

Willingham aimed at Hare again, but this time Ernest was faster, grabbing him and pushing him to the ground.

Hare fell to her knees and pressed her skirt to Miss Bonningham's shoulder, trying to stem the bleeding. She cried, muttering thanks, while Anastacia ran to call for a doctor.

As Mr Sputnek attended to Willingham, Ernest ran towards Hare. "Are you hurt?" He put his hands on her face, checking for injuries, wiping at the blood with his sleeve. "Are you well?" Hare nodded, too numb for words.

"I'm so sorry..." he whispered. There were tears in his eyes. "I wasn't fast enough..."

"It's alright, young man," Miss Bonningham croaked. "I was." She patted his knee and passed out.

CHAPTER 34

Once the doctor had announced Miss Bonningham out of immediate danger, she and Hare were packed off into a carriage and taken to the Winchfield house, at Posy's insistence.

The small part of Ernest's brain that wasn't completely distraught was rather impressed with his sister's determination, once everything had been explained.

"I have brought them into our house and so they are my responsibility," she said coldly, when Lord Winchfield tried to oppose the plan.

Ernest went in the carriage with Hare and Miss Bonningham, of course, the latter doused with laudanum and barely responsive.

The entire ride Hare held onto Miss Bonningham's hand, as the old school mistress snored. Ernest wondered how the fake familial bond seemed so real all of a sudden. He wanted to say so much and yet he just continued sitting there, twiddling his thumbs. Hare had pushed away any offer of physical help. And why wouldn't she. She had to be saved by the elderly school mistress, because he had failed to protect her. He closed his eyes, squeezing them tight. He wanted more than anything to let her know she could rely on him now, that he was going to be there for her. But why would she believe him? He fell short, again and again. A breath caught in his throat.

"What?" Hare asked, half inclining her head towards him.

"I was just thinking how you two really seem to care for each other now," he said, not altogether untruthfully. He just wished he could tell her the rest of it. Tell and be believed… "I didn't much like Miss Bonningham when I first met her, I'll admit. But what she did in there was—" He searched for the right word. "—heroic."

Hare stayed silent for a while. "I suppose we only have each other now."

The words felt like a sharp needle in his chest. "Hare, I…"

"I'm very grateful, Ernest," she said quickly, as if she could hear the words he hadn't said and was determined not to let him continue. "You really did save us. If it hadn't been for you and for Mr Sputnek, of course, it would have ended very badly for us. But now…" She sighed. "Now that the truth is all out, Miss Bonningham and I will be alright. I just wish that we hadn't involved you and your family in this fiasco." She looked at him then, her blue eyes glassy, as she struggled to contain the emotion. "I'm truly sorry, Ernest."

He opened his mouth to tell her that he didn't want her to be sorry, because he himself wasn't. That she wouldn't be alone. That he was there and she didn't need to worry anymore. But before he managed to say any of that the carriage stopped and the moment was gone.

A FLURRY OF ACTIVITY FOLLOWED, which made any private conversation impossible.

The Dowager Lady Winchfield screeched with shock at Miss Bonningham's wound and wept into her handkerchief, while

Posy took charge with all the determination and authority of a navy general.

Once Miss Bonningham's wound was dressed and she was safely stashed in bed, Hare sat down with the Winchfields and Ernest and told them the whole story.

Ernest kept glancing at his sister, who sat there with a stony expression on her face. Lord Winchfield kept interrupting until his wife silenced him with a glare.

Once Hare had explained it all, they all stayed quiet for a moment.

"I am truly sorry, Lady Winchfield," Hare said after a while. She kept her head down. Ernest wanted to go over to her to offer comfort, but he knew his sister and it would not have been a smart move.

"Whether or not you're sorry Miss Walk— Miss Hare," Posy corrected herself, "is immaterial. The facts are, you have lied to us and used me to try and trick one of our oldest family friends into marriage. You have also made me an accomplice in your deception." Posy sighed. "And while I wish you to understand, I hold no prejudice against your kind, you have put me in a position where I have been introducing a newly freed mythic into the Beau Monde society, vouching for your reputation with mine."

"But you hold no prejudice, sister?" Ernest said. He met her eyes quite calmly.

She sniffed. "It's most unfortunate that Miss Bonningham has been wounded. I do, of course, feel a sense of obligation towards her. She was the most beloved teacher and I did consider her a friend. After she recovers, however, I will consider my obligations fulfilled and she will need to leave my house."

"Absolutely not."

Everyone turned in shock towards the Dowager Lady Winchfield, who, until that moment, had been quietly sobbing into a handkerchief.

Lord Winchfield scratched his head. "Mummy, I really think—"

"I will *not* allow you to turn dear Anne away in her hour of need." The old woman tightened her lips, while folding her damp handkerchief. "While she has made a mistake, grant you—"

"That was *not* a mistake!" Posy half rose, before her husband's hand on her shoulder calmed her enough to sit back down. "She has purposefully deceived us, taken advantage of our hospitality and has in effect severely damaged all of our reputations. I must think of my children!"

"Miss Bonningham can do no harm to us," the Dowager said. "Well, perhaps she did hurt our pride, but that might not be such a terrible thing, truth be told. And while I can't condone her actions, I am not so blind to the ways of the world that I can't recognise desperation when I see it." She stared at Posy. "I will not turn a friend away." She then turned towards Hare. "It *was* desperation, was it not, child?"

Hare nodded. "Anne's school was failing. She would have been destitute. And as for me… Willingham sold my binding to Anne without a second thought… She freed me." She swallowed. "I agreed to join her. New York was never home and I had nothing and no prospects there."

"No prospects indeed!" Posy huffed, slapping her knee. "Perhaps no prospects of a marriage to a Duke! But when one finds herself in a difficulty, surely gainful employment would be the preferred option to an honest soul, instead of—" She waved towards Hare, a disgusted look on her face. "—of this charade."

Anger boiled inside Ernest at his sister's words. "It's easy enough to judge, Posy." He looked at Hare. "Yet you know very well what threat it is to turn a servant away with no references."

Hare reddened. "I might have been free. But I was still a mythic and nobody trusts unbound mythics, not even for scullery work. Not even people I knew before. My choice was to allow myself to be bound again, or… or to sink further."

"It's the way of the world," the old Lady Winchfield said, shaking her head, as they all sat there, heads bent down. After a moment, the old lady straightened herself up and looked to her son and daughter-in-law. "As the question of gainful employment has been broached, I have decided I am in need of a private secretary."

"A what?" Bertie wiped his brow, as if the concept required a huge deal of mental exertion.

"A private secretary," his mother repeated, straightening up her sleeve. "Or a companion. Whichever you find more appropriate. Either way, Anne is staying with me."

"Mummy, I'm not sure her staying here…"

Lady Winchfield gave her son a withering stare, which silenced him immediately. "Bertie, you're my son and I love you, but if you insist on treating me like I'm senile, I will be forced to smack you." When she was certain there was to be no further opposition from her son, she turned to Posy. "I've grown very attached to Miss Bonningham. So attached, in fact, that should you send her away, I'm quite certain to die of a stroke."

"What?" Posy blinked a couple times.

"Mummy, please don't say such things!" Bertie had gone into full-blown hysterics at this point, as the old Lady Winchfield nodded grimly.

"Indeed. I am certain of it. In fact, I feel tension building up behind my eyes as it is." She pinched the bridge of her nose and shook her head.

Lord Winchfield turned to his wife. "Posy, by the love of God, *do* something."

His wife sighed and looked to the ceiling, as if it could offer assistance. "What will it take to relieve the dangerous tension, Mummy?"

The older woman straightened up and without missing a beat, said, 'I will have Anne stay with me and I will brook no further discussion on the subject."

Posy closed her mouth and Ernest knew she was defeated. But then she turned back towards Hare. "Very well. But what about *her*?"

Hare worried a bit of her dress's frill between her fingers. Ernest realised that there was still a stain of blood on her sleeve, from when she held onto Miss Bonningham. She seemed to notice it at the same moment and winced. "I will leave," she said. "Of course I will. If you will allow me to clean myself first."

"There's no such hurry," Posy said after a while. "We don't need to be heartless about it. The morning is soon enough." Ernest reddened and was about to say something, but his sister gave him a measuring look. "My brother reminded me that the references might be an issue. I will be happy to give you any references you should require. As long as you avoid the families to whom you've been introduced as Miss Walker, you should find no issue with securing employment. I suppose the changes in your face might further help obscure your identity."

Hare gasped.

"I will not have it said," Posy turned towards her mother-in-law, "that I don't understand the 'ways of the world'."

"Thank you." Hare nodded. "Thank you so much."

"Very well." Posy stood up. "Find Mrs Beats, the housekeeper, in the morning. I will give her the instructions to write whatever it is you require. Now, I believe we should all retire." She smiled at her husband. "It's been a rather eventful evening."

As she was leaving the room, she turned once more towards Hare and hesitated before speaking. "I wish you well, Miss Hare. I'm quite angry, you understand. One doesn't like to find oneself deceived. But I like you. And I wish you well."

CHAPTER 35

Hare knew she should try to sleep. To get as much rest as possible. She stared at the ceiling of her bedroom, her small travel bags all packed up. Things had worked out better than she could have imagined, really. In the morning, she would call on Anastacia and Ben. She owed them an explanation, if they wished for one. There was a good chance she wouldn't be allowed past the front door.

She groaned as she turned to her side. The only friends she had in the world and she had betrayed all of them. At least Miss Bonningham would be safe. Hare was hardly certain of her ability to earn enough to support herself, so it was a great relief that Anne at least would be well taken care of. Then Hare's mind drifted towards Ernest. She covered her face. She ought not think about him. He would be as relieved to see the back of her as the rest of them.

She wished she hadn't told him… How humiliating. To tell someone you loved them, when you knew all along that they wouldn't believe you. And why should he. The facts all spoke against her.

She would never see him after tonight. And yet to know he

was out there, thinking ill of her, resenting her. It was too much. She would exorcise this feeling. Eventually she'd succeed in forgetting him. But, she had to admit to herself as much, probably not tonight.

And if all that had been not enough to chase the sleep away from her, the infernal clock was ticking, ticking, tocking, tocking, so loud, she felt it ringing in her bones.

She sat up in the bed. It was hopeless. She couldn't expect to fall asleep with that noise echoing through the corridor. She swung her feet onto the floor. It felt pleasantly cool against her bare feet. She flexed her ankles. If she was quick, she could still get a couple hours of sleep.

The night was warm, so she didn't bother with a blanket. She'd be out and back in a couple minutes and the whole household was fast asleep. Though how they could sleep with this noise was beyond her, frankly.

It was unfortunate that the servants decided to restart the damned clock right when Hare's life was due to fall apart, but she supposed they couldn't have anticipated it.

She padded to the door and then turned into the corridor, trailing one hand along the wall.

When she got to the room with the clock she paused. Even in her sleepy state, she could tell something wasn't quite right. She narrowed her eyes.

An orange glow spilled out of the room's half-open door and into the corridor.

She took another cautious step.

"Hare?" A hopeful voice came from inside the room.

She gently pushed at the door. There, beside the grandfather clock's open belly, sat Ernest.

She didn't say anything for a moment, looking first at Ernest, then at the clock, then at him again.

"I was hoping—" he started, then pointed to the clock and gave her a sheepish smile. "I was hoping you'd come."

"You restarted the clock," she stated the obvious.

"I wanted to talk to you."

"There's not a lot left to say, Ernest." She hugged herself with one arm. "I'm leaving tomorrow."

"I don't want you to." He stood up then, his hands fisted by his sides.

She looked at him as if he'd gone insane. "What we do and don't want hardly matters now, don't you think?" She looked away. "I'll be glad to be gone, truth be told. I will make my own way now. I'll be fine, you don't need to worry about me."

"Are you really?" He walked up towards her and brushed his knuckles across her cheek. "Are you really glad?"

There was something in his voice, an edge she didn't recognise.

She pushed his hand away. If he touched her like that again she might cry. And she didn't want to cry in front of this man. "It's a good deal better than weeping about it, don't you think?"

"Are those our only two options then?" he asked, so low she could barely make out the words. "To be glad about being away from each other, or cry and still be separated?"

"I don't think…" She didn't know what she thought. What was the point of thinking of things that couldn't happen.

"What if there was a third option," he said.

She looked at him then. There was a strange sort of determination in his eyes, his dark eyebrows furrowed.

He leaned towards her, till she could feel his breath on her cheek. "What if you stayed with me?"

It was a stupid thing to do, she admitted to herself. But when she looked into his dark eyes, for a moment she believed it. She would let herself believe the possibility of it. She turned her face upwards and brushed her lips against his.

He kissed her lightly, barely a touch. Then he moved his face a few inches away from hers.

He didn't say anything, he didn't have to.

She slipped her left hand into his and led him out, down the dark corridor, to her room.

He followed her inside and closed the door behind.

She was suddenly embarrassed. She told herself she knew what she was doing, but when they were alone in her room, her courage wavered. She took a tentative step to her night table and rested against it. She stood like that for a moment, uncertain, not quite brave enough to turn towards him.

"Hare…"

She closed her eyes. She heard him take a step. He stood behind her, close enough that she could feel the warmth emanating from his body, close enough that she could smell him, but not close enough for his body to touch hers. He put his hand on her forearm and she felt the hesitation in him.

"I don't want to…" He paused. She wouldn't hurry him. She wanted to hear him say it. "I don't want to do anything you're uncomfortable with. I want you to know… I'm not Willingham."

She turned towards him. Of all the things she thought he might say, that was certainly not one. "I know that!"

He looked down, clearly shamed by the vehemence in her voice. "I need you to know, Hare. I mean to do things right by you. I won't do anything to hurt you. I could never—"

She kissed him then, pressing hard against the length of his body. He moaned as her tongue flicked across his lips. She trailed her fingers down his neck, towards the buttons of his shirt. His skin felt flushed and soft.

"Wait," he said, holding onto both her hands. "I need to tell you something first."

"Tell me?" Hare looked at him through glazed eyes. She didn't want to talk anymore. She was all talked-out. She wanted him to kiss her again and to keep kissing her. "Later," she said, moving forward. It was a lie, of course. She knew it was. There would be no later for the two of them. But there was the now. The lovely, delicious now. And she didn't want it interrupted anymore.

"No, wait." He moved back, a small smile on his lips. "I want to, *believe me* I want to." He swallowed hard and closed his eyes for a moment, as if he were trying to calm himself. "But there's something you need to know about me. Something you need to understand."

Hare looked at him, uncomprehending.

"I'm a bastard," he blurted out. "I and Posy share a mother, but my father… Well, my mother had an affair, you see."

"I know." She nodded.

"What?" It was his turn to look shocked. She almost laughed at his expression.

"I overheard you talking to Posy."

He raised an eyebrow.

"Very well, I was eavesdropping." She shrugged. "But what does it matter?"

"What…" He chuckled. "It matters a great deal, Hare. I need you to understand. My family had all cut me off, except for Posy, of course. A divorce would have been a terrible scandal, so my father suffered my existence under his roof, until the earliest possible time he could send me off.

"My mother was given a choice: to remain married to my father, or to keep me." He laughed mirthlessly. "And, I don't blame her. But if you stay with me, there is no family to fall back on, no money except what I can make. I need you to know that. I don't want you to be deceived."

"That's your terrible dark secret?" She shook her head in disbelief. She put both hands on either side of his face. "You think any of it makes you less in my eyes?" She laughed. "You humans, you always think the way you judge each other has some universal value to it. I might not remember as much as I'd wish from my world, but I certainly know being a bastard is not the indelible mark of shame you think it is."

He stared at her and then leaned forwards. "Just… Choose me, Hare. Please. Just choose me."

"I do," she said. *For tonight at least.*

He laid her down on her bed, slowly, reverently, like she was a porcelain doll about to break. It was like he was scared she might slip away, should he get too firm a grip on her. She laughed then. He looked at her, confused.

"I'm sorry, I..."

He brushed his fingertip across her lower lip. "What's so funny?"

"Nothing, I..." She searched for an explanation for this strange lightness she felt. "I suppose I have never felt... I feel secure and sure because... Because I can see *you* don't. Oh, that's a horrid thing to say, sorry!" She covered her eyes with her hands. What a thing to tell him.

But he pulled her hands away. "Look at me, Hare."

She peeked. He was standing there, shadow falling across half of his face. "I understand."

No, he didn't. He couldn't have, when she wasn't sure how to explain it herself. But she felt she had to. "It's just... You care if I care and that's... I've never had that."

"I understand."

She could see the corner of his lips go up. She didn't want him to laugh. She wanted him to know, to truly know what she meant.

"Since I've been summoned, men here have always felt entitled," she whispered. "To touch me, to kiss me, to... to rescue me even."

"You mean like when you nearly bit my head off for chasing the mob away from you and that bird creature when we first met?" He cocked his head to the side. "I can't apologise for that."

She huffed. "I *know!*" How could she make him see. "It's just that you don't–"

"I *understand.*"

And then, suddenly, she knew that he did.

He followed her onto the bed and kissed her again, before straightening up to pull off his shirt. His skin glistened in the lamp light filtering in through the window. She traced her fingers across his chest. He was beautiful. She wondered if he knew. But then a moment later she couldn't think of very much at all as he put his hands on her ankles and began pulling her nightshirt up, slowly. He didn't break off eye contact and she sensed his hesitation. All she had to do to stop him was say a word. Instead, she braced her feet against the bed and raised herself, allowing him to slide the fabric up over her hips and waist.

Once he took her nightshirt off, he knelt on his haunches and just watched her, his fingers grazing the skin of her thigh.

She saw herself reflected in his eyes and she'd never felt more beautiful, or more powerful.

He finally bent down, kissing down her neck, tracing the line of her collarbone with his tongue. His hand moved up her ribcage, till it reached her breast. She dug her fingers into his hair.

"You're spilling out of my hands." He chuckled and looked in her eyes. "Such bounty."

She arched her back as he put his lips on her, tracing the pink around her nipple.

She gasped.

"Is that alright?" He looked up.

"Just… surprised." She looked down at him. "Don't stop now!"

CHAPTER 36

She smelled of roses. And of something else too. A scent uniquely hers. He wanted to taste her, to bury himself in her. He nibbled on the peak of her breast, which caused her to make a small noise in the back of her throat. He groaned. He thought he couldn't possibly get any harder, but that small sound made him feel like he'd rip the fabric of his trousers. He began unbuttoning them, but her hand on his stopped him. He looked up at her.

"Let me do it," she said.

Without responding, he rolled onto his back and stretched his arms above his head. She sat up and trailed one finger down his stomach towards the waistband of his trousers. He enjoyed this view of her. Her heavy breasts and the lines forming on her belly as she leaned forward. He wanted to run his hands across all the folds and the beautiful swell of her stomach and her hips. He licked his lips. He wanted to taste her, every inch of her. But he let her lead. He sensed she needed this. This control. So much of her life had been beyond her control. But she'd lead here. He'd wait till she was comfortable. Even if it made him dastardly *un*comfortable. He wished she would work the buttons faster.

She pulled the fabric off him. He lay there, as exposed for her as she was for him and he felt like he might die if she didn't touch him. He waited as her eyes brushed across his body. She leaned forward and pressed her palm to his cheek.

"I love your eyes," she said.

He wasn't sure how to respond. "My eyes?"

Hare nodded. "They're the first thing I noticed about you. They're beautiful."

"My eyes were the first thing my father noticed too, I'm told," he said dryly. Mr Thompson and his wife were both pale, with light blue eyes. Even if his father hadn't already suspected his wife, Ernest's colouring would have instantly betrayed her secret. "I've always hated my eyes for that."

Hare shook her head. "I won't allow it."

"What?"

"I won't allow you to continue hating any part of you," she said and lay alongside him, pressing her body against his. She placed her palm against his face and looked at him. *Saw him.*

And, as if for the first time, he saw her. She glowed, his lover. Her eerily huge eyes lit up as she looked at him.

"What are you?" he asked and was instantly ashamed at how that light dimmed in her for a moment. "It doesn't matter to me," he added quickly. "Whatever you are is perfect to me. I just wondered..."

"I don't remember," she said. "Some of us remember more than others. But for me... All I remember is all I am now. There are things... Things I recall sometimes. Little sparks, no more."

"Is there a way... Is there a way you can show me?" He hesitated. Was he being rude? Hurtful? He just felt the need to know her, as she knew him.

She lifted a hand and looked at her fingers for a moment. "The magic is mostly gone. But I will try." She looked at him intently. "I will try for you."

She put her fingers on his temples and the world suddenly

exploded in colour. A lush green forest grew around them, sparkling like nothing in his world ever did. A structure of… was it glass? No, water, moving yet holding shape, grew out of the ground. And there, the greatest wonder of them all, was Hare. And in that moment he saw nothing else, wanted nothing else.

The vision around them was gone as quickly as it appeared. "I can't hold it any longer…" She was shy, as if embarrassed at her miracles being not enough.

He took her hand and pulled it to his lips. Her skin felt glorious. So soft and warm. He couldn't wait any longer and pulled her closer still. "Love me and I will learn to love myself also," he said. His right hand snaked towards her front. Her eyes widened for a moment, before she opened her thighs, granting him access. He cupped her there, the soft curls tickling the palm of his hand, as he moved one finger closer to her centre. He lay on his side and kissed her deep as he began drawing slow circles around the sensitive nub at her opening. He went slowly, letting her body language guide him in what brought the greatest pleasure. He drew one finger along her inner lips and she gasped.

"You like this," he said, a grin stretching his face.

"Don't stop."

He moved his fingers faster, as her breath quickened. She clutched at the bedsheets by her side. "Don't. Stop."

He leaned forward and kissed her again, as he continued to move his fingers, matching his speed to her breaths. She grabbed his shoulders, digging her nails in. She leaned her forehead against his and he stared as her mouth made an "o" shape and her whole body went rigid, her chest rising as he felt her pulsating around his fingers. She was so wet. He wondered what she would taste like and, on an impulse, he brought his hand up and licked the moisture off his finger.

Her eyes went wide before a lazy smile spread across her face. She placed her palms on his chest and gave him a push. Before he realised what she was doing she straddled him. She guided him to her entrance and lowered herself, inch by inch, agonisingly slow. Just when he thought he wouldn't be able to take anymore, she began moving. A moan escaped his lips. He didn't want it to end. He wondered absent-mindedly if anything had ever felt this good in his life before. He wondered if he could take up permanent residence inside her. It'd be hard to conduct business in this manner, but he didn't much care. He wanted to stay like this, with her beautiful breasts within his grasp and her hips moving like... *Oh God.* And then he couldn't think of anything much at all, when she threw her head back, her dark hair falling in waves over her bare shoulders.

She said his name and he couldn't hold it in. He dug his fingers into her hips as he spilled inside her.

He felt her muscles tense around him and she collapsed on top of him.

They stayed like this for a while, as their breath returned to normal. She made as if to move off him, but he growled and held her in place. "Not yet," he managed. *Not ever if he could help it.* And she seemed to understand and nuzzled her face in the crook of his neck.

"I love you, Hare," he said. She was quiet for a moment, for just long enough that his heart sank.

"I love you too."

And all was right in the world.

CHAPTER 37

She woke before he did.

The daybreak just began to colour the sky above Mayfair's many chimneys. For some the day had already begun and she could hear the clatter of many heels on the paving beyond her window. She glanced towards Ernest. He was sleeping on his side, nestled against her, one arm thrown across her belly. A lock of hair fell across his eyes and moved with the breeze coming in from the partially open window.

A wave of tenderness washed over her. He loved her, this beautiful man. He wanted her as she was, knowing who she was. He hadn't said so, but she didn't doubt he'd marry her if she allowed it. Which is precisely why she couldn't allow it.

It would have been different with a man who wanted her simply because he thought her beautiful. Or from a good family. She had felt shame at the trickery Anne and she were playing on the Beau Monde. But none of those people truly cared about her. She was a pretty body with a respectable name. But Ernest knew who she truly was and all she'd done. And he still loved her, wanted her. In spite of what it would do to his career, his relationships. It would be the greatest betrayal, for her to let him keep her.

SHE INCHED her way out of the bed, stopping any time she thought she felt a change in his breathing. Once she was out of the covers, she put on her clothes quickly. She'd laid them out the night before, knowing she'd be expected to leave as soon as possible. She picked up her packed bags and walked to the door, where she hesitated. She wanted to look at him again, to commit his face to memory. But she didn't quite deserve that, she decided. Not as she was about to break his heart. She didn't deserve any comfort at all. And so she left, softly closing the door behind her.

Where do you think you're going? Maletki padded beside her as she made her way down the stairs.

"You stay, cat," she said. "I don't even know where I'm going, I can't take you with me."

The *domovoy* looked her over lazily. *Will it have a bed, the place?*

"I certainly hope so. Likely not much besides."

A bed is good. I like sleeping on a bed.

"You're not invited Maletki." She was getting exasperated.

I am free, young fay. And I go where I will. He rubbed against her leg and it made her smile. It was more of a comfort than she liked to admit.

THE HOUSEKEEPER, Mrs Bee, a matronly brownie, was already waiting for her, with ready-made references. Plural. The woman had written out no fewer than five separate references, praising Hare for her work in five different roles at the house, some more plausible than others.

"A stable hand?" Hare smiled as she looked through them.

"Yes, well..." Mrs Bee looked embarrassed. "I wasn't sure what position you will be looking for, you see, so I wanted to give you options. So few of us have any, you know."

Hare's eyes began to prickle and she wiped them with the back of her hand. *Options*. It's been so long since she had any.

"Thank you," she said and then she embraced the older mythic, who stiffened and then awkwardly patted Hare on the shoulder.

"There, there," she said. "It's quite alright. We all try our best in this world, don't we?"

Hare nodded and left.

She walked quickly, not quite sure where she should go first. That is, she knew where she *ought* to go, but wasn't entirely certain she had enough courage to do so. She stopped in the middle of the pavement, clutching her carpet bag in one hand and a small suitcase in the other. Her shoulders hurt, but she was frankly a little scared of putting the bags down, even for a moment. If someone should snatch them then she'd really have nothing.

She wondered if Ernest had woken up already. She imagined how he'd feel once he found her gone. She imagined he'd be relieved. As much as he cared for her and she didn't doubt he did, he would in time realise just how catastrophic it'd be to marry her. Willingham would be gone—hopefully in chains—on a ship back to the States by the end of the week, if there was any justice. But it didn't mean the news wouldn't get out. And then Ernest would be judged for marrying her. She didn't want that.

He'd be hurt if she left and hurt if she stayed. If she had to choose, she'd pick the option that didn't ruin his whole future.

It took a while, but she finally arrived at the Brandon house. It seemed even more intimidating in daylight, the white columns towering over her. Now the question was, which door should she knock on? She glimpsed to the left, as a maid hurried inside with a basket. The family, now knowing her station, might insist on her taking the servant entrance. She had humiliated them, after all.

She hesitated. How strange it was to think she might have become the mistress of this house. If she didn't mind also being Willingham's slave. A shiver ran down her spine. She straightened her back. She was Hare once more, she reminded herself. And Hare never cowered.

She scaled the steps towards the portico over the door, but before she had the chance to knock, the door swung open, revealing not the butler, but the somewhat dishevelled-looking Anastacia.

"Were you going to knock? I've been watching you for going on five minutes now." Anastacia folded her long arms and watched Hare with a great deal of irritation.

"Ana— Lady Anastacia," Hare corrected herself.

Anastacia cocked her head to the side. "'Lady', is it now?"

"You did say you reserved the title for those you didn't like," Hare said, with a small, shy smile. "I expect I fit that description now."

"I didn't know you had a flair for the dramatic," Anastacia said. "All things considered, I think you might as well come in." She walked inside, with Hare trailing behind.

"I rather expected you to come," Anastacia said. "You know, Ben did not, but I told him he was always prone to underestimating people." She paused, as a thought occurred to her. "I think I rather *over*estimate people as it transpires. I never used to think so." She shrugged. "I will have to think on that."

"I suppose." Hare wasn't sure what the expected response was and decided it was safer to just agree.

"Ben, you owe me a shilling," Anastacia announced triumphantly, as she pushed open the breakfast room door.

Brandon looked up from his eggs. He placed his fork down and wiped his mouth before replying. "You know very well, I did not agree to the wager." He tried to take on a casual tone, but there was a new tension around his eyes and he looked like he had no sleep.

"I'm sorry to disturb you," Hare said. "I expect you're all quite tired after yesterday."

"No use pretending otherwise." Brandon said, standing up. He gestured to the seat next to him. "My mother asked for a tray this morning, so we won't be disturbed."

Hare inclined her head and instinctively looked to Anastacia who nodded an encouragement, before raising her eyebrows in surprise. "Your bags?"

"Oh, yes, sorry." Oh great, now she was all flustered. Hare wondered how many people have ever entered this room carrying a carpet bag. She expected not many.

"Jim, if you'd please take Miss..." Anastacia glanced at Hare. "Miss Walker's bags for now."

"It's Miss Hare," Hare said. Ben and Anastacia both looked at her curiously.

Anastacia recovered rather quickly and nodded to the footman who quickly took Hare's luggage, clearly sensing the trio wanted to be left alone.

Hare sat in the chair. She wished she had her bag still. Something to hold onto. As it was, she was having the hardest time trying not to fidget. "Thank you for allowing me the chance to explain."

"Oh please." Anastacia waved her hand dismissively. "You know very well we are both positively *dying* to hear the full story. It was rather... chaotic yesterday." She sounded flippant, but Hare noticed her red-rimmed eyes and the dark half-moons below them.

"I'm very sorry," Hare said.

"A fine start." Brandon nodded. He had returned to his eggs. "Now, which part are you sorry for exactly?"

Hare burst out in a nervous laughter. "All of it?" She tried. "No, that's a lie. I'm sorry I was unlucky enough to have been summoned. I'm sorry I ever met Willingham. I'm sorry that led me to the kind of desperation that made me board that ship with Miss Bonningham. I'm finally very, very sorry that I hurt you both." She looked to the ceiling and waited till the burning sensation in her eyes went away.

The silence stretched between them.

"I find it hard to believe Sam could be such a villain," Anastacia said finally. "No, of course I can *believe* it. After all, I was here at his arrest. And even if Mr Sputnek hadn't presented sufficient evidence, Sam's reaction would have shown his guilt all on his own."

"You must despise me," Hare said quietly.

"Despise you?" Anastacia reached out and squeezed Hare's hand. "I *thank* you."

"What?" Hare had nothing clever to say for once. She sat there with her mouth hanging open.

Anastacia laughed when she looked at her. "Hare, do you know how absolute is the power an English husband holds over his wife? And without you, I wouldn't have known what that man is capable of, when offered power over another." She shook her head. "I owe you a debt for what you showed to me, before it was too late."

"That is..." Hare felt a tear run down her cheek. She wiped it away. "You're very kind."

"I know." Anastacia leaned back in her chair, looking smug. "I keep telling Ben." She glanced at her brother. "Of course, there *is* the question of your attempts to trick my brother into a marriage, which I take to less kindly."

"Of course.' Hare turned to Brandon. He wasn't quite looking at her, staring instead at his cup of rapidly cooling tea. "Be—Duke, I am very sorry. I wish I could take it back. I'm... You were both really excellent friends to me. Anastacia has shown me that there are options, possibilities for me…" She smiled. "Even if she wasn't aware of it at the time."

Ben put his fork and knife down and pushed himself away from the table. He took a deep breath, as if trying to give himself courage and turned his whole body towards Hare. He reached over the table and took her hand. "I understand," he said, simply. "At least, I *think* I can understand. I have never, nor will I likely ever, be in a position where I'd be forced to experience the sort of desperation which has propelled you and Miss Bonningham to take the risks you did."

"That's…" A sob shook Hare. She covered her mouth. "This is too much. You're… Thank you."

"Isn't that a lovely scene." She turned around. In the door to the room stood Ernest, looking decidedly worse for wear. His hair fell in a wild wave over his eyes and his clothes were crumpled.

"Thompson!" Ben half-rose from his seat. "What are you doing here this time of day."

Ernest glowered and—too late—Hare realised Ben was still holding onto her hand. Before she knew what was happening, Ernest crossed the floor and lunged at his friend, hitting him on the jaw.

Anastacia screamed and ran around the table to get to them. Brandon recovered surprisingly quickly, elbowing his opponent in the ribs. As Ernest struggled to catch a breath, Ben socked him straight in the jaw. Ernest kicked out with his foot, missing the Duke by a good half yard.

Hare stood up, frozen to the ground, watching the somewhat ungainly spectacle, as the two men rolled around on the floor, swearing and aiming punches which missed much more often than they found their mark. Anastacia, presumably in an attempt to separate them, kept hurling at them all the small objects she could collect from the table. She managed to hit her brother as often as she did Ernest, but as none of her makeshift missiles were able to cause any real damage, Hare wasn't sure either of them noticed, until finally Anastacia grabbed the carafe and splashed them both with water.

"What, what?" Ben spluttered as he got up. He paused, momentarily confused and brushed a cucumber slice off his head. It fell with a sad little *plop* to the floor.

Ernest stood up and for a moment Hare wasn't sure if he wasn't going to attack Ben again. But then his eyes met hers and she felt as if she'd been plunged into ice water.

"I was hoping I wouldn't find you here," he ground out. "But I see I was an idiot after all." He looked at Ben. "I hope you two are very happy," he said in a tone dripping with sarcasm, before he turned around on his heel and marched out of the room.

Ben looked a little unsteady on his feet. He leaned heavily on the table and pulled himself into his seat. He looked from Anastacia to Hare, then to Anastacia again. "Should we?" He coughed. "I think I need some wine, or possibly something stronger. So." He looked at Hare. "You and Thompson, huh?"

Hare looked down, blushing.

"Oh, I see." Brandon rubbed his jaw where a bruise was already forming. "Well, it appears I was really quite naive, wasn't I? Should we go after him to explain then?"

"Certainly not!" Anastacia said. Hare and Ben both looked at her. She coloured. "He was very quick to jump to conclusions, wasn't he?" She nodded to Hare. "You should at least make him sweat a bit longer."

"I believe he sweated more than enough while pummelling me." Brandon took the wine carafe Anastacia brought to him. "So, you want to go after him?"

"I will do no such thing," Hare said. "I'm afraid there's no future for me and Mr Thompson." It hurt, but she needed to say it out loud, for herself as much as them really.

"Why not?" Brandon looked at her. "Beyond his lack of boxing skills that is?" He sighed. "I'm honestly rather angry at him, right now. But then it was a lesson for me as well. I will be honest, it had never once appeared plausible to me that you might not be entirely and completely enamoured with me."

Hare smiled and shrugged. "I've always had a rotten taste in men."

Ben laughed. "That's an answer that pleases me well enough." He poured himself a glass of wine and downed it. "So, why not him then? You could do worse, I'll tell you straight out."

"Oh, I know." Hare tensed her shoulders and sniffed. "But he couldn't."

Anastacia came up to her and put her hand on Hare's shoulder. "Are you sure that's what you want?"

Hare snorted. "What I want!" She shook her head and patted Anastacia's hand. "I want him to be happy. And he will be, in a short while, once I'm gone."

"I wouldn't be so sure," Brandon muttered.

"What will you do now?" Anastacia asked.

"Don't worry about me." Hare smiled weakly, for the first time since she'd arrived. "I have a plan of sorts."

CHAPTER 38

Whichever Hungarian had first invented a tie ought to have been hung from one. Ernest tugged at his collar, as he scaled the steps towards his office. The damned thing was as itchy as a dozen Scottish jumpers, an extra irritant he could well do without.

He supposed he ought to have eaten something, but he didn't want to go to the club, he feared coming across Brandon at his favourite restaurants and the corner pie shop reminded him too much of his afternoon with Hare. Everything, in fact, reminded him of Hare. When it was sunny he thought of her. When it rained, he thought about their first walk from Mrs Brown's. Food and lack thereof all seemed to conspire against him. He supposed hail might be free of reminders. It rarely hailed in September though, which was just his damned luck. It had been months since he'd seen her and yet no matter how much he worked, he couldn't quite erase her from his mind.

For the first few weeks he'd find a way to not-so-casually glance through the papers' social pages, but there were no announcements. An engagement of the Duke of Brandon ought to have been the news of the season, but then, he supposed Hare's particular situation meant they might have preferred to keep things a bit low key.

She told me she loved me.

He shook his head. It was what he desperately wanted to hear her say. And she simply sensed it. She was good at that, being who you needed her to be. *A professional muse,* he thought with enough bitterness to drown a martini. He pushed the door to his office open and beelined for the desk, staring down a pile of papers he was meant to get through that afternoon.

"You look terrible, Thompson. A hard day?" The question made him jump.

Brandon sat in the corner of his office, the legs casually crossed.

Anger rose up in Ernest. It wouldn't do to attack a man inside the office, he supposed. He turned his back on him and pretended to rearrange his papers. "What are you doing here?"

"You do hold a grudge, don't you?" Brandon still went for the conversational tone, though his voice became strained. "I did think you would have come to visit in the last couple of months. To apologise if nothing else."

Ernest laughed. "I'd rather not be a witness to your premarital bliss, if that's all the same to you." He flexed his hands and leaned on his desk, squeezing his eyes shut. "You won, Brandon. I lost. I always lose." He winced. He hated how whiny he sounded, even to his own ears.

Brandon clearly agreed, for Ernest didn't even need to see him to know his old friend was rolling his eyes. "How maudlin."

"So what if I am?" Ernest spun around. "Perhaps I have a reason to be!"

Brandon tapped his knee thoughtfully. "Only of your own making."

"Oh yes, if only I'd had the foresight to be born a rich Duke!"

"I wasn't born as rich as I am and you know it." Brandon turned his head to the side. Ernest knew the man took great pride in having increased his family fortunes threefold since he took over the running of the estate. And under normal circumstances he would have been the first to agree.

But now he just shrugged. "Oh yes, fates have been *so* cruel to you."

"You act as if I'd wronged you." Brandon stood up. "As if it wasn't you who'd stolen my fiancée from under me!"

"She wasn't your fiancée yet!" Ernest cleared his throat and lowered his voice as he saw the clerk's head pause with curiosity through the glassed-through panel on the door. "And in any case, you won. What else do you want?"

"Won?" Brandon stared at him blankly.

"I suppose congratulations are in order." Ernest folded his arms. "I'll be sure to send a note. I'm afraid I'll be feeling rather poorly on the date of the happy event."

"You thought..." Brandon blinked a few times, then burst out laughing.

Ernest shifted uncomfortably.

"You think..." Brandon wiped away a tear and sat back down in the corner chair. "You actually thought I'd be marrying the woman who'd admitted to a plan to trick me into matrimony and then fell in love with my best friend?"

Ernest's mouth went dry. "What do you mean?"

"I mean the only thing keeping you from her is you, you absolute ninny!"

CHAPTER 39

Hare stood behind a small door. She glanced at the piece of paper Mrs Brown had given her. This was the address. She shifted her weight. The art materials were heavy, but she didn't exactly have a lot of money to waste on a hack, so she'd walked all the way from her lodgings on foot. She smiled. It'd be worth the long walk. A portrait commission! Mrs Brown acted somewhat cagey about it, but she did say it could be "future defining". That could only be good.

After she'd left Brandon's house, she went straight to Mrs Brown's. The gallery owner was shockingly unshocked by Hare's appearance. Hare more than suspected Mrs Addison might have been involved. Mrs Brown already had a few small commissions for magazine illustrations, as well as invitation and menu designs lined up, which she said she thought Hare might be good for. Once Hare had proven herself a diligent and competent worker, the number of commissions gradually increased. Hare's pay was very poor indeed, but it paid for a bed at Mrs Smythe's Boarding House for Respectable Young Women and the occasional meat pie. Hare might or might not have formed an alarming pie habit.

From Anastacia, who kept in touch, Hare learnt the news that

Willingham's extradition had been expedited, due to the sheer volume of the money he'd defrauded. She'd never see him again. Few things brought her as great a pleasure as this. Miss Bonningham had also sent Hare a letter. Her close relationship to Posy's mother-in-law had grown closer still and reportedly even Posy began to thaw a little. After all, it turned out that a hint of a scandal was not quite the destructive force these days as it used to be. Hare smiled at the thought. If the world was really to come to an end on the stroke of midnight the 30th of December 1899, as some predicted, then at least it looked like it was going to go on a high note.

So, all in all, Hare was simply too busy to think about Ernest. Much. She hardly ever thought of his eyes anymore, at least when she wasn't drawing with ink. And she practically never thought of how warm his skin was, unless she was in her bed.

He was in the past now. And, she thought as she pulled up the brass knocker on the door and let it fall with a loud bang, her immediate future consisted of a rather profitable portrait commission.

An older, energetic-looking woman opened the door before Hare could have even considered knocking again.

"You must be Miss Hare," the woman said with a smile. "I'm Mrs Dulwick, the housekeeper. Please come in, we've all been waiting for you!"

"That's… nice?" Hare found herself practically spun around, her jacket all but yanked off her back and her hair pins and hat pulled off her head so fast she wondered if some of her hair didn't go with them. She needed to revise her initial impression of Mrs Dulwick. The woman was energetic in the way that a monsoon was moist.

Mrs Dulwick shepherded her into a small, but pleasant sitting room. It was very bright, with a window coming out into a little garden. There were two large chairs and a side table.

"Please wait here for a moment," the housekeeper said and turned to the door.

"Mrs Dulwick," Hare said, clutching her bag of supplies.

"Yes, Miss Hare?"

"Whose house is this?" Really, she felt rather foolish asking such a question. How many guests might one have who were not at all sure who they were visiting?

Mrs Dulwick just nodded. "I'll bring the tea in."

Hare put her bag down and took a couple steps around the room. The walls were wallpapered, but otherwise quite bare. In fact, the rest of the room had very little in it. Perhaps the owners had moved recently. Hare looked through the window. A robin sat on the fence and stared at her with no fear. It was either clever enough to understand there was a window between them, or so used to humans it didn't care either way. Hare tapped the window pane with one finger. She wished she had the time to paint the bird since it posed so nicely.

The sound of a tea tray being laid on the table made her jump. She turned around, only to see Mrs Dulwick swiftly make her way out of the room, leaving behind the tea, along with a gaunt-looking Ernest.

Once the door closed behind the housekeeper, Ernest opened his mouth to speak, but Hare raised her hand and he remained silent.

They stared at each other for a while, while Hare looked for the right words. *'How dare you?' Slightly too Voudeville. 'Are you insane?' Too combative. 'I love you. I've missed you.' As if.*

So she settled for the comfort of formality. "Good morning, Mr Thompson." She inclined her head. She didn't quite trust herself to shake his hand, not yet.

She opened her bag and began pulling out her supplies. "It's my understanding you wish for a watercolour portrait of yourself. I think it's best we get started right away, so as to not take up too much of your valuable time."

He looked surprised, but then recovered with admirable aplomb. "I have cleared my schedule this morning, Miss Hare." He swept out the back of his coat and sat down opposite her. "Tea?" He gestured to the tea set.

Hare looked at it suspiciously. It was rather close to him. But she *did* want some tea. If only because she felt like her mouth went so dry her throat might close up otherwise.

"Would you like me to pour it?" He raised an eyebrow at her. How did he manage to look so composed?

"No, tha—" He was already pouring it, damn him. Now he held out the cup and saucer. The moment stretched.

"I'm reasonably healthy, Hare, but my hand will start shaking eventually." He smiled. *It's not 'Miss Hare' anymore,* she noticed and glared at him.

She practically snatched the cup from his hand, spilling some tea into the saucer. She took a sip, looking anywhere else but at him. Which somehow made it worse. She could feel his eyes on her. It was unnerving.

"It's a lovely home," she said, finally.

"You like it?" She felt the smile in his voice.

She nodded. "Very much so. Although," she paused, looking on the walls, "It's still quite bare. Which is why you are after a portrait, I take it."

"Hare..."

"It's quite the thing, portraits," she prattled on. "Photography is likely here to stay, but it's so much nicer to have a piece of art on the walls, something that's been made with a brush, if you catch my meaning."

"I'm so sorry," he said. She paused, looking towards the window, waiting for him to finish. "When I saw you were gone that morning, I was so scared. That in the end..."

"I think we'd best get started." She turned around to face him, cutting him off.

She had her sketchbook with her and she pulled it out now, as well as a small box of pencils. "I will do a few sketches today and then complete the watercolour at my lodgings. I should be able to deliver the final piece by the end of the week."

"Hare, you don't mean to say you're actually going to be drawing now."

This riled her up and she gave him a measuring look. "That *is* what you have hired me for, Mr Thompson. For a rather handsome sum. I would hate to be wasting your money or your time, but if you have changed your mind about the commission, then I will leave now." She made as if to stand up, but he reached out.

"No, please!" He raked his fingers through his hair. "Just... please, talk to me."

"You didn't hire me to talk," she said, testing the tip of her pencil. "Now please, try to make yourself comfortable." She put the pencil to the sketchbook, enjoying the way the graphite glided over the paper's texture. The tactile nature of it calmed her.

"Alright, then you can listen." He leaned back in the seat.

Just a sum of parts, she told herself, as she sketched out the sharp line of his jaw and the shape of his neck.

"It was wrong of me, very wrong, to assume you went back to Brandon."

"You won't find me disagreeing on that point," she muttered. He clearly took it for an encouragement.

"I was so scared you would choose someone else, someone—" He swallowed. "—someone better, that I had no room left in me for trust."

"You were right."

"What?"

"Well, not in thinking I was going to marry Ben, that was rather stupid of you." She sketched the straight line of his nose, the hooded eyes. "But I *wasn't* going to come back." She paused. "It's better this way."

"Better for whom?" His fingers kept picking at the fabric of his trousers. If he didn't stop, he'd soon wear out a hole in them.

"Us both," she said, finally. "You would never trust me, not really. What you did at the Brandon house, well that just proved it."

"I'm trying to apologise here!"

"Apologies mean little, Ernest." She shrugged. "They're just words. Your actions should have proven to you that, if nothing else, then the way we met and my earlier deceptions would have always left you doubting. Doubting both me and my commitment."

"But, you see, I understand it now." He half got up, but she snapped her head towards him.

"Please stay still, if you would; I can't do my work otherwise."

He sat back down.

"I trust you now."

"That's very magnanimous of you," she said. She put her finger to the paper and smudged the line of his hair. She smiled to herself, a small, private smile, at the unruly wave of it. "But the other issue remains."

"What issue?"

"If you married me, it would destroy you," she said. She hoped the words would be light. She almost managed to keep the quiver out of it. "No." She raised her hand, seeing he was about to contradict her. "Even if not everyone knows the details of my past, how would you explain that the woman once introduced to everyone as 'Miss Walker', suddenly became 'Miss Hare'? A mythic. A nobody. The fine folk of Beau Monde would never forgive you, or me for that matter."

"I don't care about that!"

She rolled her eyes. "I think you'll find you care *very much*. Since I've met you, I've seen all you do to try to fit in here. Your very livelihood depends on it, in fact. You've built your practice around the society that would reject you entirely for marrying me." She shrugged. "It's the truth, Ernest, you know it is. It's not merely that I am a nobody. I have tricked them. I walked among them as one of their own. Went to cafes with their young sisters and daughters, danced with their sons. Ate at their tables and sat in their velvet chairs. I broke their rules and made them treat me as one of their own. Think about it for a moment." She made an expansive gesture. "This whole country runs on the invisible lines nobody dares cross. And I did the unthinkable: showed them how imaginary those lines really are: nothing a fine frock and an introduction at a ball can't blur." She shook her head. "Miss Hare might find employment in their sculleries, but certainly wouldn't be welcome in their drawing rooms."

"But here's the thing," he said, more softly. "You wouldn't be 'Miss Hare' anymore."

"What then," she looked up. "Would you have me pretend again? Pose as a New York socialite? Keep up a glamour day and night? I won't do it, Ernest, I *can't*."

"No." She heard a rustling and glanced up. He was standing over her. As she opened her mouth to ask him to move away, he kneeled next to her. "You wouldn't be a 'Miss Hare'…" He took her hand. "…if you became a 'Mrs Thompson.'"

"Ernest…" She pulled her hand away. "I told you, I…" She stood up. "It's too much."

He stood up next to her and gently wiped at her cheek. She hadn't even realised she was crying.

"It would ruin you," she said.

"That depends entirely on one's perspective," he said. "I would consider myself entirely ruined, if I was forced to spend my life without you, for instance."

"But your work…"

"I still have friends," he said with a smile. He stood so close to her now. He smelled like soap and wood smoke. She breathed in and let herself lean closer. "I think Brandon has *almost* forgiven me, though he told me he intends to spend the rest of his natural life holding it over my head. Anastacia feels you have rescued her from marrying the worst sort of man and so she will be on our side. And you know nobody messes with Anastacia."

"No," she snorted. "I don't think anyone would dare."

"And also, you see, there's the problem..."

"What?" She looked up into his eyes.

"This house." He gestured around. "For one man living alone... It's far too large."

"Ridiculously so," she agreed.

"And there is an art studio set up in the attic, which I frankly have no use for."

"How impractical."

"And the bed is far too wide." His lowered his head, till his lips hovered just above hers.

"Sounds cold," she murmured.

"And, of course, there's the other matter." His lips brushed against hers, gently.

"What is it?"

"I love you."

CHAPTER 40

The New Year's Party, December 31st, 1899

"Now that is what I consider the pinnacle of art." Anastacia squinted, turning her head to the side.

"I think it's too flattering," Brandon said, sipping from his glass. "Though the pink bow does suit you, Thompson."

"My thoughts exactly," Ernest said, patting his friend on the back. He looked around the room. Hare had excused herself for a moment. He felt the lack of her in the air, the most unsettling feeling.

"If you keep turning your head so much, it's liable to fall off," Ben said. "It's not enough you married the woman? What else do you want, have her glued to your side?"

"One day you'll know what that's like, Brandon and I will make sure to laugh at you as well."

"I might have known already, if it wasn't for you," Brandon muttered into his drink as Ernest glared at him.

"Are you all ready?" Hare sashayed into the room. His breath caught in his throat. She'd changed into a black velvet dress, with masses of red flowers at the sides and across the front of the bodice. The low cut revealed a great deal of her shoulders and upper back. Ernest felt a moment's annoyance that his friends had already arrived and he wondered how quickly after midnight he'd be able to disappear into one of Winchfield's rooms with Hare.

His wife, as if hearing his thoughts, blushed and gave him a look. Then she walked up to Anastacia. "Here's the materials we've spoken about, Stacia." She gave her friend a discreet stack of envelopes.

"Do I want to know?" Brandon raised his eyebrows.

"What you don't know, can't hurt you," Anastacia said, putting the papers into her bag. "In any case, we best be going. Posy hates tardiness. You can't begin to imagine how much work she puts into those things. And a New Year's party has a lot of expectations attached, which you know well enough."

"Don't I just." Ernest rolled his eyes. "Though I suppose it's worth it, going through an evening of my sister's grousing, just to see my wife in this gown of hers." He put his arm around Hare.

"It's the end of the century," Anastacia said, as they walked towards a carriage. "Makes you think."

"I hope you're not in fear of the world ending tonight?" Ben said.

"Oh no, such careful timing would be rather too elegant for this messy place, don't you think?"

"I have no regrets either way," Ernest said. Though that wasn't, strictly speaking, true. He cast a long glance at his wife. He would deeply regret not getting to see how this gown of hers looked as it slid off her shoulders.

"Nor I," Hare said with a broad grin. "Though I do rather look forward to the future too."

"Don't worry, love." He leaned his forehead against hers. "I have a feeling that the best is yet to come."

EMAIL SIGNUP

If you'd like to hear when my next book is out, sign up to my mailing list through my website:

GabrielaHouston.com

We won't share your email address, and you can unsubscribe at any time.

SCAN ME

ALSO BY GABRIELA HOUSTON

The Second Bell

To the world you are an abomination; a monster with unholy abilities. You're shunned and left to fend for yourself. Your only chance of survival is to tap into that dark potential - would you do it?

In an isolated mountain community, sometimes a child is born with two hearts. Such a child - a striga - is considered a dangerous demon, which must be abandoned on the edge of the forest to protect the community. The only choice the child's mother can make is whether to leave her home with her infant, or stay behind and try to forget.

Miriat made her choice. She and her nineteen-year-old striga daughter, Salka, now live a life of deprivation and hardship in a remote village, where to follow the impulses of the other heart is forbidden.

But Salka is headstrong and young, and when threatened with losing everything, she is forced to explore the depths of her true nature, testing the bonds between mother and child.

SCAN ME

The Bone Roots

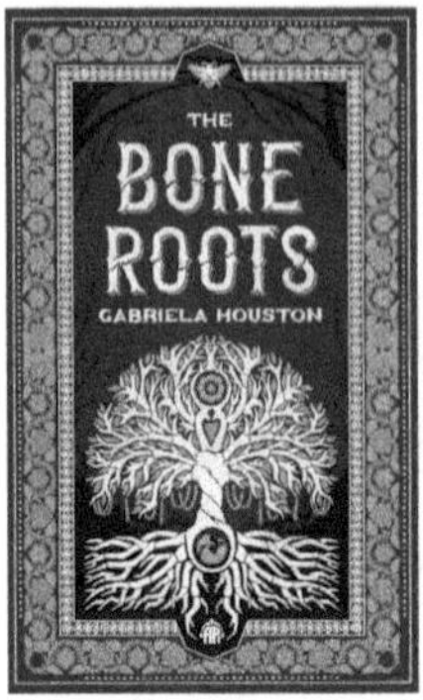

A tale of two mothers, each desperate to protect her child. But only one of them can succeed. And only one of them knows why.

The Bone Roots is a slavic-folklore inspired fantasy that explores how far a mother will go to protect her child...

It's been 40 years since the Fox took Kada's brother. Though she ran and kept herself hidden, she fears it may be stalking her again, this time to steal her daughter.

Every year, Vedma Kada gives thanks to the bone roots – those that belong to the child-bearing tree who gave Kada her desperately-wanted baby, Secha. Kada lives her life in service of the bone roots and the goddess Zemya, but they cannot keep her daughter safe. Not when Secha's emerging powers, both mysterious and brutish, threaten to out her for who she truly is...

Meanwhile Sladyana, a rich noblewoman, has spent the last fifteen years searching for her missing daughter, Luba. She was snatched from their home by the Fox thief and Sladyana has heard nothing from her since. But the one who gave Sladyana her daughter has come within her grasp once again, and so has the secret of her daughter's fate.

SCAN ME

www.ingramcontent.com/pod-product-compliance
Ingram Content Group UK Ltd.
Pitfield, Milton Keynes, MK11 3LW, UK
UKHW021857061025
8260UKWH00005B/519

9 781068 186608